THE
Marriage Game

· SARA DESAI ·

JOVE
NEW YORK

A JOVE BOOK
Published by Berkley
An imprint of Penguin Random House LLC
penguinrandomhouse.com

Library of Congress Cataloging-in-Publication Data

Names: Desai, Sara, author.
Title: The marriage game / Sara Desai.
Description: First edition. | New York: Jove, 2020.
Identifiers: LCCN 2019046001 (print) | LCCN 2019046002 (ebook) |
ISBN 9780593100561 (paperback) | ISBN 9780593100578 (ebook)
Subjects: GSAFD: Love stories.
Classification: LCC PR9199.4.D486 M37 2020 (print) |
LCC PR9199.4.D486 (ebook) | DDC 813/.6—dc23
LC record available at https://lccn.loc.gov/2019046001
LC ebook record available at https://lccn.loc.gov/2019046002

First Edition: June 2020

Printed in the United States of America
1   3   5   7   9   10   8   6   4   2

Cover art by Marina Muun
Cover design by Katie Anderson
Book design by Kristin del Rosario

the
Marriage Game

To Dad,
for everything

Acknowledgments

Without the support of so many kind and generous people, this book would not exist. Thank you to my fantastic editor, Kristine Swartz, for your enthusiasm and support and for including me in your amazing list of diverse authors. You have made a dream come true.

To my lovely literary agent, Laura Bradford, who has been on this journey with me from the start through its many forms and iterations. Without your encouragement, I would never have taken that step out of the shadows.

I am very grateful to the entire Berkley team. Thank you for the beautiful cover, your hard work and energy, and your attention to detail, and for sending my story into the world the very best it could be.

Mindy Kaling, Jameela Jamil, and Lilly Singh: thank you for paving the way. And thank you to Sahrish Nadim.

To Christa Desir, who once upon a time took a chance on me, and who has worked tirelessly to promote inclusivity in the publishing industry. You continue to inspire me every day.

Thank you to my family for laughing at me. I would never have found my comedy voice without your smiles.

And finally, to John and my girls. For your love and support, your patience and understanding, your hugs and kisses. You are my everything.

Dear Sir:

Please find attached to this e-mail the marriage résumé of my beloved daughter, Layla Patel, age twenty-six, who is in immediate need of a husband.

She is beautiful, intelligent, and well educated with a delightful streak of independence and a quick wit. She is a healthy girl who greatly enjoys her food. My daughter also loves music like the famous Nickelback band. She is a good girl—obedient, polite, and demure—with a deep sense of responsibility to her family and respect for her elders. She is devoted to her cultural traditions, but she won't wear a sari.

Her ideal match would be a successful and dependable professional who believes in duty and tradition. He will be fit, healthy, and well-groomed with good educational qualifications and a successful career. Above all, he will make my daughter happy and treat her with kindness and respect. He must also tolerate the company of a very large, loud, and loving family.

If you think you would be a match, please respond by e-mail or send your résumé to Nasir Patel c/o The Spice Mill Restaurant, San Francisco, California.

P.S. Discretion is essential. My daughter is not aware I have posted her profile online.

WHEN Layla walked into The Spice Mill Restaurant after yet another disastrous relationship, she expected hugs and kisses, maybe a murmur of sympathy, or even a cheerful *Welcome home*.

Instead, she got a plate of samosas and a pitcher of water for table twelve.

"There are fresh poppadums in the kitchen," her mother said. "Don't forget to offer them to all the guests." Not even a glimmer of emotion showed on her mother's gently lined face. Layla could have been any one of the half-dozen servers who worked at her parents' restaurant instead of the prodigal daughter who had returned to San Francisco, albeit with a broken heart.

She should have known better than to show up during opening hours expecting to pour out her heart. The middle child in a strict, academic, reserved family, her mother wasn't given to outward displays of affection. But after the emotional devastation of walking in on her social media star boyfriend, Jonas Jameson, as he snorted the last of her savings off of two naked models, Layla had hoped for something more than being put to work.

It was her childhood all over again.

"Yes, Mom." She dutifully carried the plate and pitcher to the table and chatted briefly with the guests about the restaurant's unique decor. Decorated in exotic tones of saffron, gold, ruby, and cinnamon with accent walls representing the natural movement of wind and fire, and a cascading waterfall layered with beautiful landscaped artificial rocks and tiny plastic animals, the restaurant was the embodiment of her late brother's dream to re-create "India" in the heart of San Francisco.

The familiar scents—cinnamon, pungent turmeric, and smoky cumin—brought back memories of evenings spent stirring dal, chopping onions, and rolling roti in the bustling kitchen of her parents' first restaurant in Sunnyvale under the watchful army of chefs who followed the recipes developed by her parents. What had seemed fun as a child, and an imposition as a teenager, now filled her with a warm sense of nostalgia, although she would have liked just one moment of her mother's time.

On her way to the kitchen for the poppadums, she spotted her nieces coloring in a booth and went over to greet them. Her parents looked after them in the evenings when their mom, Rhea, was busy at work.

"Layla Auntie!" Five-year-old Anika and six-year-old Zaina, their long dark hair in pigtails, ran to give her a hug.

"Did you bring us anything from New York?" Zaina asked.

Layla dropped to her knees and put her arms around her nieces. "I might have brought a few presents with me, but I left them at the house. I didn't think I'd see you here."

"Can we go with you and get them?" They planted sticky kisses on her cheeks, making her laugh.

"I'll bring them tomorrow. What have you been eating?"

"*Jalebis.*" Anika held up a bright orange, pretzel-shaped sweet similar to a funnel cake.

"Yesterday we helped Dadi make chocolate *peda*," Zaina informed her, using the Urdu term for "paternal grandmother."

"And the day before that we made *burfi*, and before that we made—"

"Peanut brittle." Anika grinned.

Layla bit back a laugh. Her mother had a sweet tooth, so it wasn't surprising that she'd made treats with her granddaughters in the kitchen.

Zaina's smile faded. "She said peanut brittle was Pappa's favorite."

Layla's heart squeezed in her chest. Her brother, Dev, had died in a car accident five years ago and the pain of losing him had never faded. He'd been seven years older, and the symbol of the family's social and economic strength; expectations had weighed heavy on Dev's shoulders and he didn't disappoint. With a degree in engineering, a successful arranged marriage, and a real estate portfolio that he managed with a group of friends, he was every Indian parent's dream.

Layla . . . not so much.

"It's my favorite, too," she said. "I hope you left some for me."

"You can have Anika's," Zaina offered. "I'll get it for you."

"No! You can't take mine!" Anika chased Zaina into the kitchen, shouting over the *Slumdog Millionaire* DJ mix playing in the background.

"They remind me of you and Dev." Her mother joined her beside the booth and lifted a lock of Layla's hair, studying the bright streaks. "What is this blue?"

Of course her mother was surprised. She had given up trying to turn her daughter into a femme fatale years ago. Layla had never been interested in trendy hairstyles, and the only time she painted her nails or wore makeup was when her friends dragged her out. Dressing up was reserved for work or evenings out. Jeans, ponytails, and sneakers were more her style.

"This is courtesy of Jonas's special hair dye. His stylist left it behind for touch-ups. Blue hair is his signature look. Apparently, it shows up well on screen. I didn't want it to go to waste after we broke up, so I used it all on my hair. I had the true Jonas look."

Unlike most of her friends, who dated behind their parents' backs, Layla had always been honest about her desire to find true love. She'd introduced her boyfriends to her parents and told them about her breakups and relationship woes. Of course, there were limits to what she could share. Her parents didn't know she'd been living with Jonas, and they most certainly would never find out that she'd lost her job, her apartment, and her pride after the "Blue Fury" YouTube video of her tossing Jonas's stuff over their balcony in a fit of rage had gone viral.

"You are so much like your father—passionate and impulsive." Her mother smiled. "When we got our first bad review, he tore up the magazine, cooked it in a pot of dal, and delivered it to the reviewer in person. I had to stop him from flying to New York when you called to tell us you and Jonas split up. After he heard the pain in your voice, he wanted to go there and teach that boy a lesson."

If the sanitized, parent-friendly version of her breakup had distressed her father, she couldn't imagine how he would react if she told him the full story. "I'm glad you stopped him. Jonas is a big social media star. People would start asking questions if he posted videos with his face covered in bruises."

"Social media star." Her mother waved a dismissive hand. "What job is that? Talking shows on the Internet? How could he support a family?"

Aside from her family's disdain for careers in the arts, it was a good question. Jonas hadn't even been able to support himself. When the bill collectors came calling, he'd moved into the prewar walk-up Layla shared with three college students in the East Village and lived off their generosity as he pursued fame and fortune as a social media lifestyle influencer.

"That boy was no good," her mother said firmly. "He wasn't brought up right. You're better off without him."

It was the closest to sympathy Layla was going to get. Sometimes it was easier to discuss painful issues with her mother because Layla had to keep her emotions in check. "I always seem to pick the bad ones. I think I must have some kind of dud dude radar." Emotion welled up in her throat, and she turned away. Her mother gave the lectures. Her father handled the tears.

"That's why in our tradition marriage is not about love." Her mother never passed up an opportunity to extol the benefits of an arranged marriage, especially when Layla had suffered yet another heartbreak. "It's about devotion to another person; caring, duty, and sacrifice. An arranged marriage is based on permanence. It is a contract between two like-minded people who share the same values and desire for companionship and family. There is no heartache, no betrayal, no boys pretending they care, or using you and throwing you away, no promises unkept—"

"No love."

Her mother's face softened. "If you're lucky, like your dad and me, love shows up along the way."

"Where is Dad?" Layla wasn't interested in hearing about marriage, arranged or otherwise, when it was clear she didn't have what it took to sustain a relationship. No wonder guys always thought of her as a pal. She was everybody's wingwoman and nobody's prize.

She looked around for her father. He was her rock, her shoulder to cry on when everything went wrong. Usually he was at the front door greeting guests or winding his way through the linen-covered tables and plush saffron-colored chairs, chatting with customers about the artwork and statues displayed in the mirrored alcoves along the walls, talking up the menu, or sharing stories with foodies about his latest culinary finds. He was a born entertainer, and there was nothing she loved more than watching him work a room.

"Your father has been locked in his office every free minute since you called about that boy. He doesn't eat; he hardly sleeps . . . I don't know if it's work or something else. He never rests." Layla's mother fisted her red apron, her trademark sign of anxiety. Pari Auntie had given the apron to her to celebrate the opening of the Spice Mill Restaurant, and she still wore it every day although the embroidered elephants around the bottom were now all faded and frayed.

"That's not unusual." Layla's father never rested. From the moment his feet hit the floor in the morning, he embraced the day with an enthusiasm and joyful energy Layla simply couldn't muster before nine A.M. and two cups of coffee. Her father accomplished more in a day than most people did in a week. He lived large and loud and was unashamed to let his emotions spill over, whether it was happiness or grief or even sympathy for his only daughter's many heartbreaks.

"He'll be so happy that you are home to visit." Her mother gave her a hug, the warm gesture equally as unexpected as their brief talk. Usually she was full on when the restaurant was open, focused and intense. "We both are."

Layla swallowed past the lump in her throat. It was moments like these, the love in two sticky kisses from her nieces and a few powerful words from her mom, that assured her she was making the right decision to move home. She had hit rock bottom in New York. If there was any chance of getting her life back on track, it would be with the support of her family.

"*Beta!*" Her father's loud voice boomed through the restaurant, turning the heads of the customers.

"Dad!" She turned and flung herself into his arms, heedless of the spectacle. Except for his traditional views about women (he didn't have the same academic or professional expectations of her as he'd had for Dev), her father was the best man she knew—reliable, solid, dependable, kind, and funny. An engineer before he immigrated to America, he was practical enough to handle most electrical or mechanical issues at the restaurant, and smart enough to know how to run a business, talk politics, and spark a conversation with anyone. His love was limitless. His kindness boundless. When he hired a member of staff, he never let them go.

All the emotion Layla had been holding in since witnessing Jonas's betrayal came pouring out in her father's arms as he murmured all the things he wanted to do to Jonas if he ever met him.

"I just bought a set of Kamikoto Senshi knives. They go through meat like butter. The bastard hippie wouldn't even know he'd been stabbed until he was dead. Or even better, I'd invite him for a meal and seat him at table seventeen near the back entrance where no one could see him. I'd serve him a mushroom masala made with death cap mushrooms. He would suffer first. Nausea, stomach cramps, vomiting, and diarrhea. Then liver failure and death."

Laughter bubbled up in her chest. No one could cheer her up like her father. "Mom has made you watch too many crime shows. How about just shaking your fist or saying a few angry words?"

He pressed a kiss to her forehead. "If I have to defend your honor, I want to do it in a way that will be talked about for years, something worthy of the criminal version of a Michelin star. Do you think there is such a thing?"

"Don't be ridiculous, Nasir." Layla's mother sighed. "There will be no murdering of itinerant Internet celebrities when we have a restaurant to run. Things are hard enough with the downturn in the market. I can't do this on my own."

Frowning, Layla pulled away from her father. "Is that why the restaurant is almost empty? Is everything okay?"

Her father's gaze flicked to her mother and then back to Layla. "Everything is fine, beta."

Layla's heart squeezed at the term of endearment. She would always be his sweetheart, even when she was fifty years old.

"Not that fine." Her mother gestured to the brigade of aunties filing through the door, some wearing saris, a few in business attire, and others in *salwar kameez*, their brightly colored tunics and long pants elegantly embroidered. Uncles and cousins took up the rear. "It seems you bumped into Lakshmi Auntie's nephew at Newark Airport and told him you'd broken up with your boyfriend."

Within moments, Layla was enveloped in warm arms, soft bosoms, and the thick scent of jasmine perfume. News spread faster than wildfire in the auntie underground or, in this case, faster than a Boeing 767.

"Look who is home!"

While Layla was being smothered with hugs and kisses, her father ushered everyone to the bar and quickly relocated the nearest customers before roping off the area with a PRIVATE PARTY sign. The only thing her family loved better than a homecoming was a wedding.

"Who was that boy? No respect in his bones. No shame in his body. Who does he think he is?" Pari Auntie squeezed Layla so hard she couldn't breathe.

"Let her go, Pari. She's turning blue." Charu Auntie edged her big sister out of the way and gave Layla a hug. Her mother's socially awkward younger sister had a Ph.D. in neuroscience and always tried to contribute to conversations by dispensing unsolicited psychological advice.

"How did you come here? Where are you staying? Are you going back to school? Do you have a job?" Deepa Auntie, her mother's cousin and a failed interior designer, tossed the end of her *dupatta* over her shoulder, the long, sheer, hot pink scarf embellished with small crystal beads inadvertently slapping her father's youngest sister, Lakshmi, on the cheek.

"Something bad is going to happen," superstitious Lakshmi Auntie moaned. "I can feel it in my face."

Mehar Auntie snorted as she adjusted her sari, the long folds of bright green material draping over her generous hips. "You thought something bad was going to happen when the milk boiled over last week."

"Don't make fun, Mehar," Lakshmi Auntie said with a scowl. "I told you Layla's relationship wasn't going to work when I found out she left on a full-moon night."

"No one thought it would work out," Mehar Auntie scoffed. "The boy didn't even go to university. Layla needs a professional, someone easy on the eyes like Salman Khan. Remember the scene in *Dabangg*? I went wild in the theater when he ripped off his shirt."

Layla's aunties groaned. Mehar Auntie knew the moves to every Bollywood dance and the words to every song. She was Layla's favorite aunt, not just because she wasn't shy to bust out her moves at every wedding, but also because she shared Layla's love of movies from Hollywood to Bollywood to indie.

"Mehar Auntie!" Layla gasped mockingly. "What about Hrithik Roshan? He's the number one actor in Bollywood. No one can dance like him. He's so perfect he hardly seems human."

"Too skinny." Mehar Auntie waved a dismissive hand. "He

looks like he was shrink-wrapped. I like a man with meat on his bones."

"Mehar. Really." Nira Auntie shook a finger in disapproval, the glass bindi bracelets on her arm jingling softly. She owned a successful clothing store in Sunnyvale and her exquisitely embroidered mustard yellow and olive green salwar kameez had a fashion-forward open back. "My children are here."

"Your children are men in their twenties. They're hardly going to be shocked by my appreciation of a well-muscled man."

"If you spent less time dreaming and dancing, you could have had one for yourself."

Layla winced at the burn. Mehar Auntie was well past what was considered marriageable age, but seemed content with her single life and her work as a dance teacher in Cupertino.

"Layla needs stability in her life, not some singing, dancing actor with no brains in his head." Salena Auntie pinched Layla's cheeks. She'd been trying to get Layla married off since her third birthday. "What will you do now? What are your intentions?"

"I'm done with men, Auntie-ji," she said affectionately.

"Don't call me Auntie." She tucked her gray hair under her embroidered headscarf. "I am not so old."

"You are old." Taara Auntie pushed her aside and handed Layla a Tupperware container. "And you're too thin. Eat. I made it just for you."

"What's this?"

Taara Auntie smiled and patted Layla's hand. "I've been taking cooking classes at the YMCA. I'm learning to make Western food, but I've added an Indian twist. This is Indian American fusion lasagna. I used roti instead of pasta, added a little halloumi cheese, and flavored the tomato sauce with mango chutney and a bit of cayenne. Try it." She watched eagerly as Layla lifted the lid.

"It looks . . . delicious." Her stomach lurched as she stared at the congealed mass of soggy bread, melted cheese, and bright orange chutney.

"You're going to put me out of business." Layla's father snatched the container out of her hand and studied the contents. "What an interesting combination of flavors. We'll enjoy it together this evening when we have time to appreciate the nuance of your creation."

Layla shot him a look of gratitude, and he put an arm around her shoulders.

"Don't eat it," he whispered. "Your sister-in-law tried her chicken nugget vindaloo surprise last week and she was sick for two days. If you're planning to travel in the next week—"

"I'm not. I'm staying here. I'm moving back home. My stuff is arriving in the next few days."

"Jana, did you hear that?" His face lit up with delight. "She's not going back to New York."

"What about your job?" her mother asked, her dark eyes narrowing.

"I thought it was time for a change, and I wanted to be here so I could help you . . ." Her voice trailed off when her mother frowned.

"She wants to be with us, Jana," her father said. "Why are you looking at her like that?"

"We aren't old. We don't need help. She had a good job. Every week I time her on the Face and she doesn't say anything is bad at work."

"It's called FaceTime, Mom, and it's not as good as being with the people you love."

"She loves her family. Such a good girl." Layla's father wrapped her in a hug even as her mother waggled a warning finger in her direction. Emotional manipulation didn't work on her mother. Neither did lies.

"Tell me the truth," her mother warned. "When I die, you will feel the guilt and realize . . ."

"Mom . . ."

"No. I will die."

"Fine." Layla pulled away from the warmth of her father's arms. It was almost impossible to lie to her mother when she started talking about her own death. "I was fired."

Silence.

Layla braced herself for the storm. Even though her mother was emotionally reserved, there were times when she let loose, and from the set of her jaw, it was clear this was going to be one of those times.

"Because of the boy?"

"Indirectly, yes."

"Oh, beta." Her father held out his arms, his voice warm with sympathy, but when Layla moved toward him, her mother blocked her with a hand.

"No hugs for her." She glared at Layla. "I told you so. I told you not to leave. New York is a bad place. Too big. Too many people. No sense of family. No values. You had boyfriend after boyfriend and all of them were bad, all of them hurt you. And this one makes you lose your job . . ." She continued her rant, mercifully keeping her voice low so the aunties wouldn't hear.

All her life, Layla had wanted to make her parents as proud as they had been of Dev, but the traditional roads of success weren't open to her. With only average marks and no interest in the "acceptable" careers—doctor, engineer, accountant, and *lawyer is okay*—she'd forged her own path. Yes, they'd supported her through business school, although they hadn't really understood her decision to specialize in human resource management. Her father had even wept with pride at her graduation. But underneath it all she could feel their disappointment. And now she'd disgraced herself and the family. No wonder her mother was so upset.

"Go back to New York." Her mother waved her toward the door. "Say you're sorry. Tell them it was a mistake."

"I can't." Her mother couldn't grasp Facebook. There was no way she would be able to explain YouTube or the concept of something going viral. And the temper tantrum that had started it all— the utter disappointment at having another relationship fail again? Her mother would never forgive her for being so rash. "I've really messed up this time."

Wasn't that the understatement of the year. Although the police had let her go with just a warning, she had spent a few humiliating hours in the police station in handcuffs and her landlord had kicked her out of her apartment. But those were things her parents didn't need to know.

Her father shook his head. "Beta, what did you do that was so bad?"

Layla shrugged. "It doesn't matter. I wasn't happy at my job and they knew it. I didn't like how they treated the people looking for work like they were inventory. They didn't care about their needs or their wants. It was all about keeping the corporate clients happy. I even told my boss I thought we could be just as successful if we paid as much attention to the people we placed as the companies that hired us, but she didn't agree. Things started going downhill after that. I have a feeling I was on my way out anyway, and what happened just gave them an excuse."

"So you have no job, no marriage prospects, no place to live . . ." Her mother shook her head. "What did we do wrong?"

"Don't worry, beta. I will fix everything." Her father smiled.

"Your old dad is on the case. As long as I am alive, you never have to worry."

"She's a grown woman, Nasir. She isn't a little girl who broke a toy. She needs to fix this herself." Layla's mother crossed her arms. "So? What is your plan?"

Layla grimaced. "Well, I thought I'd live at home and help out at the restaurant for a bit, and I can look after the girls when Rhea is busy . . ."

"You need a job," her mother stated. "Or will you go back to school and get a different degree? Maybe doctor or engineer or even dentist? Your father has a sore tooth."

"This one." Her father pointed to one of his molars. "It hurts when I chew."

Scrambling to come up with a plan to appease her mother, she mentally ran through the last twenty-four hours searching for inspiration, until she remembered toying with an idea on the way home. "I saw one of my favorite movies, *Jerry Maguire*, on the plane. The hero is a sports agent who gets fired for having a conscience. He starts his own company and he only has Dorothy to help him."

"Who is this Dorothy?" her mother asked.

"She's his romantic love interest, but that's not the point. I'm Jerry." She gestured to herself, her enthusiasm growing as the idea formed in her mind. "I could start my own recruitment agency, but it would be different from other agencies because the focus would be on the people looking for work and not the employers. You've always told me how in the history of our family, the Patels have always been their own boss. Well, I want to be my own boss, too. I have a business degree. I have four years of recruitment experience. How hard can it be?"

"Very hard." Her mother sighed. "Do you think you can just show up one day and have a successful business? Your father and I started from nothing. We cooked meals on a two-burner hot plate in a tiny apartment. We sold them to friends in plastic containers. It took years to save the money to buy our first restaurant and more years and many hardships before it was a success."

"But we can help her, Jana," her father said. "What's the use of learning all the tricks of running your own business if you can't share them with your own daughter? We even have the empty office suite upstairs. She can work from there so I can be around—"

"Nasir, you sublet the office to a young man a few weeks ago. He's moving in next week."

Layla's heart sank, and she swallowed her disappointment. Of course. It had been too perfect. How had she even thought for a minute that it would be this easy to turn her life around?

"It's okay, Dad." She forced a smile. "Mom's right. You always fix my problems. I should do this myself."

"No." Her father's voice was uncharacteristically firm. "It's not okay. I'll call the tenant and tell him circumstances have changed. He hasn't even moved in so I am sure it won't be a problem." He smiled. "Everything is settled. You're home. You'll have a new business and work upstairs. Now, you just need a husband and I can die in peace."

"Don't you start talking about dying, too."

But he wasn't listening. Instead, he was clapping his hands to quiet the chatter. "I have an announcement. Our Layla is moving back home. She'll be running her own recruitment business from our office suite upstairs so if you know of employers looking for workers or people needing a job, send them to her."

Everyone cheered. Aunties pushed forward, shouting out the names of cousins, friends, and family they knew were looking for work. Layla's heart warmed. This is what she'd missed most in New York. Family. They were all the support she needed.

Her father thudded his fist against his chest. "Our family is together again. My heart is full—" He choked and doubled over, his arm sliding off Layla's shoulder.

"Dad? Are you okay?" She put out a hand to steady him, and he swayed.

"My heart . . ."

She grabbed his arm. "Dad? What's wrong?"

With a groan, he crumpled to the floor.

"I knew it," Lakshmi Auntie cried out as Layla dropped to her knees beside her father. "I felt it in my face."

· 2 ·

"TYLER, the reason we've called you in here today is because we've decided to let you go. Today will be your last day."

Direct. Short and to the point. Sam didn't believe in beating around the bush when it came to mass corporate redundancies. There was no nice way to fire someone. No magic words, metaphors, or platitudes that would soften the blow. He told them outright and gave them a moment to absorb the news. It was the greatest kindness he could offer.

I'm sorry, the company is downsizing, and we have to let you go.

I'm sorry, but your division has been eliminated in the restructuring.

I'm sorry . . .

But not that sorry. His clients didn't hire him to be nice. They hired him to be the bad guy, and bad guys flew around the country firing hundreds of people and making the lives of the lucky survivors a living hell by cutting their benefits and salaries to a bare minimum.

Streamlined operations made for more efficient companies, and more efficient companies produced bonuses for shareholders. Corporate downsizing wasn't a job for the faint of heart. He had to lock away his emotions and become what they paid him to be: a bastard who raked in the dough.

He glanced over at Karen Davies, head of Kimsell Medical's

HR department, the edges of her severe blond bob curling under her chin. After the board of directors had approved Sam's recommendation for a deep 15 percent layoff to save the company from imminent bankruptcy, she had solicited recommendations from line managers about who should stay and who should go. Ultimately, the CEO was responsible for the terminations, but Karen was the public face, and it was Sam's job to assist her.

Forty years old, and with nearly twenty years of HR experience behind her, Karen didn't miss a beat. She smiled wide, blinding poor Tyler with her newly whitened teeth. "Thank you for the work you've done here. I'll go through the logistics and then answer any questions you may have."

"You have the right to consult an attorney." Sam slid the legal documents across the table. So far, so good. Tyler was in shock. If he recovered too quickly, vital minutes would be lost while they listened to stories about medical bills and mortgages, car payments and student loans.

Karen held up an envelope like she was on a game show, tempting poor bewildered Tyler with a secret prize. She was enjoying this far too much. Sam suspected she had a sadistic streak that had only now come out to play.

"If you sign today, we can give you your severance check now, or you can take up to five days to review the legal agreement with an attorney and wait." Her cold smile broadened to reveal the canines she had filed down to sharp points.

Very few waited. Stunned and terrified, most of them went for the easy money. Tyler didn't disappoint. He grabbed the pen that Karen had placed in front of him and signed on the dotted line.

After Karen had gone through the termination logistics, Sam walked Tyler out the door. "I know this is all a shock, but it could be the best thing that has ever happened to you. Now you are free to do anything, be anyone, start a new chapter of your life. Once you put the past behind you, the sky is the limit."

"I like that speech," Karen said when Sam returned.

"It doesn't mean anything." He'd felt compelled to do more than just give the redundant employees a farewell nod after his first week on the job when the guilt had almost overwhelmed him. Although he couldn't stop the process, he could, at least, give people hope.

"I love the whole termination process." Karen fiddled with the knot in his tie, pressing her free hand against his chest. "It gives me tingles. You must be jacked at the end of each day."

Sam bit back a sigh. Something about these termination situations made every Karen, Julie, Claire, Alison, Sue, and the occasional Paul or Andrew want to drag him into bed. Human resource managers were a horny bunch.

"Maybe after we're done, we could get a drink." She licked her lips like a predator about to feast. Karens were the worst. He rarely walked away from a Karen encounter with all the buttons on his shirt.

"I thought you got custody of the kids in your divorce." He tried not to sound too hopeful. "Don't they need you at home?"

She ran a finger over the buckle on his belt, her voice dropping to what he assumed was meant to be a suggestive purr. "They have sleepovers."

Single and thirty-two, Sam didn't find the word *sleepovers* as arousing as Karen clearly did.

"I heard you used to be a doctor." She leaned up to nuzzle his jaw. "James got a doctor kit for his tenth birthday. I could be your naughty nurse. What's your specialty?"

Sam thanked God he hadn't started a residency in obstetrics and gynecology but, given the situation, heart surgery was not much better. He also couldn't help but feel sorry for poor James, who clearly hadn't been asked if he minded sharing his toys with his mom. "I didn't finish my residency. I was planning to be a cardiothoracic surgeon when I decided to make a career switch."

She grabbed his hand and put it on her breast. "My heart's hurting now. Maybe you can fix it."

"Karen . . ." His voice caught when her long red nails grazed over his fly.

"The boardroom is free and I have the only key." Her talons locked on to his belt and she tried to yank him forward, but at six feet tall and 180 pounds of gym-honed muscle, he wasn't that easy to push—or pull—around.

"Tempting as it is, I have plans for the evening." He disengaged her hand, claw by manicured claw. Usually he had no qualms about slaking the thirst of a frisky HR manager with a casual hookup. With a sister to care for and a downsizing business to run, he didn't need the complications of a relationship in his carefully ordered life.

Tonight, however, he had to pick up his sister, Nisha, from rehab and then take possession of his new office. His business partner, Royce Bentley, had incited a mini riot at a company he had helped downsize with his callous handling of the redundancy process. The disgruntled employees had retaliated by vandalizing the Bentley Mehta World Corporation head office to the extent that the landlord terminated their lease to do a full renovation.

"Tomorrow, then. I'll bring the doctor kit and you can . . ." She grabbed his tie and pulled him close. ". . . Give me a physical." A statement, not a question.

Sam made a mental note to bring an extra shirt. He didn't have the heart to tell her that she wouldn't be banging strangers on the boardroom table for long. As soon she finished with the mass layoffs, Karen would be meeting with the CEO for a personal version of *Thank you and get out*. Sam's recommendation for a 15 percent cut across the board included HR.

"Remember that speech," he said to her on his way out.

"Why?"

"You might need it one day."

SAM parked his black BMW M2 outside the Sunnyvale Rehab Clinic. With its tinted windows and aftermarket black rims, his vehicle was more suited to a drug dealer than a corporate downsizer, but since they were both considered disreputable professions, he figured it was a good fit. Although he didn't need the power of the TwinPower Turbo six-cylinder engine to flee from the police, it had saved his ass more than once when the employees he had fired came looking for someone to blame.

He checked for traffic updates on his phone after opening the trunk for his sister's wheelchair. Nisha was usually exhausted after her rehab visit and would want to get home as quickly as possible. He had picked up the keys to his new office from Nasir two weeks ago, and they had agreed he would move in today. If the traffic was good, he should be able to accomplish both tasks and make it to the gym for a late-night workout.

"Hi, *bhaiya*." Nisha smiled, using the affectionate form of address for an older brother. She rolled her chair toward him, struggling over a gap in the pavement. Even with the exercises she did to strengthen her arms, she often had difficulty with uneven terrain.

Giving himself a mental kick for not greeting her at the door, he ran over to help. "Do you need a push?" Before she could answer, he grabbed the handles and eased her over the bump.

"I'm supposed to be learning to do things for myself." She brushed her long, dark hair away from a face that was a softer, rounder version of his own.

"Why strain yourself when your big brother is standing around with nothing to do?" He opened the door to the vehicle and helped her with the transfer, waiting until she'd buckled her seat belt before stowing the wheelchair away.

"You have a lot to do," she said when he joined her in the vehicle. "You should spend your evenings relaxing with your friends or going out on dates with hot women instead of driving me around. Ma and Dad are still waiting for some grandkids."

"Not going to happen." Nisha used a wheelchair because of him, because he had failed in his duty as a son. Relationships were for men who could protect the people they loved. Not one so focused on his career that he hadn't seen the danger until it was too late.

"How was rehab?" he asked to distract her.

"Hard." She fiddled with her seat belt. "How was firing people?"

"It's a job, Nisha. It pays the bills." He didn't love the work, but after he'd given up his dream of becoming a cardiothoracic surgeon and returned to school to complete a one-year intensive MBA, the opportunity to partner with Royce had fallen in his lap and he couldn't turn it down. Nisha's medical bills were beyond anything his parents could handle and, as the only son, it was his duty to ensure she got the care she needed. Not that he would ever let her know. As far as Nisha was concerned, the insurance payments from the accident were still coming in.

"Sorry." She gave him a contrite smile. "You always look so miserable when you come from work. I think the last time you smiled was when the Oakland A's qualified for the playoffs."

"I've been smiling inside through their four-year win streak."

He'd been a green and gold A's fan since he played T-ball, even though no one in his family shared his love of baseball. "If you come with me to the Bay Bridge Series this year, I might even laugh when they hit five."

"Maybe . . ." She looked away and his moment of pleasure faded. Nisha never went out. Except for her rehab and medical appointments or the obligatory family functions, she rarely left the family home after having had bad experiences with accessibility issues and awkward outings with her old friends. At twenty-seven years old, she should have been out socializing and pursuing her dreams, not spending all her time at home taking online courses and helping her mother prepare teaching materials for her third-grade class.

And it was all Sam's fault.

Nisha had agreed to a traditional arranged marriage when she finished her college degree. Thrilled at the prospect of having grandchildren to bounce on his knee, Sam's father posted her marriage résumé online. Over drinks one evening, Sam casually mentioned his sister's search for a husband to Dr. Ranjeet Bedi, a highly respected cardiothoracic surgeon at the hospital where Sam was a resident. After reviewing Nisha's online profile, Ranjeet requested an introduction. Despite their fifteen-year age difference, Ranjeet and Nisha connected. The families did their due diligence and approved the union. Six months later Nisha married a monster.

"Can you stay for dinner?"

"Not tonight. I'm taking possession of my new office after I drop you off." He stared straight ahead so he couldn't see the disappointment in her face.

Nisha always asked and Sam always refused. He spent as little time with his family as he could. Unable to deal with the fact that Ranjeet had never been held to account for his crime, Sam had turned his back on everyone and everything that could possibly be blamed—from the culture that embraced arranged marriages to the hospital that had refused to conduct an investigation into the "accident" that had happened on their property, and from the food he loved to the family that should have uncovered the true nature of the man who had married Nisha.

"You do get the irony of renting an office above a Michelin-starred Indian restaurant? It will be a real test of your will power not to eat the food."

"It's near St. Vincent's Hospital."

"Sam . . ." She gave him a pained look. "Please. I told you to let it go."

Nisha had only partial memories of the accident. She remembered going to the hospital to meet Ranjeet for lunch, an argument in the stairwell, and then waking up in the emergency room. Ranjeet offered a different version of events. Indeed, they had met for lunch. They argued in the cafeteria over his long hours. She was upset that he had to cancel their dinner plans and ran away. He returned to his office. Half an hour later he was called down to the ER.

The hospital saw no cause for an investigation. There was no reason to doubt the word of a highly respected surgeon who wielded significant power in the hospital, especially since his colleague from psychiatry said it wasn't uncommon for victims of trauma to piece together stories from fractured memories. They handed the matter to the insurers. As far as the hospital was concerned, the case was closed.

But Nisha continued to insist her story was true. After her marriage, she had discovered Ranjeet had a drinking problem and a vicious temper. Although he had never been physically abusive, his anger and verbal assaults scared her. It was not beyond imagining that he had lost control.

Of course, Sam believed her. He had never known his sister to be so certain about anything. He helped her divorce Ranjeet and then he started his own investigation, spurred on by rumors of a cover-up. But at every turn, the hospital shut him down. Disenchanted by a system that would protect someone whose actions were anathema to the fundamental principles of medicine, he walked away.

Still, he hadn't given up the hope of one day bringing Ranjeet to justice, and that meant keeping tabs on the surgeon by staying in touch with hospital staff and the friends he'd made during his residency. One day Ranjeet was going to reveal his true nature and Sam would be there to catch him.

"I think the new office is going to work out well for you." Nisha pointed to a hearse that had just pulled into the street in front of them. "It's a good omen to meet a corpse when you start out on a journey."

"You're spending too much time with Ma." Sam pulled up in front of the family home, a yellow four-bedroom, single-story rancher that they had remodeled to accommodate Nisha's wheelchair.

"And you don't spend enough."

"Don't worry about me, Nisha."

"I do worry." She leaned over and kissed his cheek. "You can't go through life alone."

· 3 ·

SAM walked quickly up the stairs to his new office suite, a box of office supplies under one arm. The scents of curry, coriander, and mild incense permeated the air, making his stomach rumble. An accident on the I-280 meant the one-hour journey had taken an extra forty-five minutes, and he would have to hustle if he wanted to get in a workout before the gym closed.

He reached the second floor and walked down the hallway, his footsteps muffled by the mint green carpet that matched the patterned wallpaper on the walls. The frosted glass door to the office was slightly ajar.

Puzzled, Sam pushed it open and walked into the small reception area. Twilight streamed through the large windows on the far side of the modern, open-plan office, spreading lazy orange fingers over the polished wood floor. A stack of boxes tottered inelegantly on the maple reception desk, and a ghastly purple couch had been placed against the wall beside a glass table with a sequined ceramic elephant base. Sam had little interest in interior decor, but the combination offended even his unschooled aesthetic sensibilities.

Crossing the floor past the reception desk, he entered the office proper. Recently renovated and boasting floor-to-ceiling windows, polished wood floors, and exposed brick walls, the spacious office also had a private boardroom and small kitchenette. Nasir had furnished the office with a large cherry boardroom table and two desks, one multicolored and made of metal rods and glass by an obscure interior designer named Eagerson, and the other a traditional two-pillar desk made of rosewood and nickel-plated brass. Sam had mentally claimed the traditional desk; the Eagerson was more Royce's style.

And then he saw her, shuffling through a massive pile of papers on his rosewood desk.

She was in her mid to late twenties, her long dark hair streaked electric blue and tied up in a ponytail that brushed the graceful curve of her slender neck. Long, thick lashes brushed over soft bronze cheeks, and her plump lips glistened.

He coughed.

She screamed.

He retreated a few steps, but not quickly enough to evade the barrage of office supplies flung in his direction. Small erasers bounced off his chest, and a sharpened pencil almost took out his eye. When she lifted a stapler, he held up his free hand, palm forward in a gesture of surrender. "Do you really want to compound your crimes by adding assault, or even murder, to the break-and-enter charge?" he asked, unable to hold back his irritation.

"Who are you? What are you doing here?" She grabbed her cell phone off the desk, brandishing it like a weapon. "Answer, or I'm calling the police."

"Please do. Then you can explain to them what you're doing in my office."

"This is my office." She thumped the stapler on the desk. "My father leases this space as well as the restaurant downstairs."

"And you are . . . ?" Beautiful. Stacked. Frightened. Furious. A number of adjectives came to mind, not the least of which described her generous breasts and lush curves. Too bad she had such terrible taste in music. Had she picked up that unfortunate Nickelback T-shirt at a thrift store? Or was she really a fan?

"Layla Patel. Nasir Patel is my father."

"I'll need to see some ID." He held out his hand, gesturing impatiently.

"Seriously?" Her eyes widened and her nostrils flared. "Is this the new way of breaking and entering? You ask for ID so you can make sure you're robbing the right place? How about you give me *your* ID so I can tell the police who to arrest?"

Sam added a few more adjectives to his list: snarky, sarcastic, sassy. He almost couldn't believe this was the daughter of the famous Indian restaurateur who had turned his ethnicity into a brand.

"Well . . . ?"

He tried to think of something intelligent to say. Anything. He was used to being in control of every situation and handling dilemmas quickly and decisively, but the longer he looked at her, the less able he was to command his power of speech. Everything about her was so vivid, so vibrant, from the shine of her knee-high boots to the fire blazing in her eyes.

"Sam." For a second, he forgot his last name. "Sam . . ."

Her lips quirked at the corners. "Samsam? That's your name?"

"Sam Mehta." He pulled himself together and took a step toward her, hand extended, as if he were meeting a business colleague and not a beautiful interloper with the most sensual mouth he had ever seen. "CEO of Bentley Mehta World Corporation, corporate consultants. I'm subleasing this office from Mr. Patel."

Her eyes sparkled, amused. "That's quite the title."

"I'm quite the guy." A little flirting never failed to soothe an angry woman. He needed to bring down the tension in the room so he could figure out the best way to convince her to leave without risking another office-supply attack. This was his office. He'd signed a lease and paid a hefty deposit. Maybe her father hadn't shared that information with her, but she knew now, and it was time for her to collect her things and leave.

"Well, *guy*." Her sharp tone suggested his flirtatious behavior hadn't had the desired effect. "I'm sorry but you'll have to find somewhere else to run your *world corporation*."

Sam didn't know why his company name would be the subject of such derision. Many of their clients were high-profile international companies, with offices in dozens of countries.

"I have a hard copy of the lease." He put his box down on the glass desk and pulled out the agreement. "Do you promise not to attack me if I bring it to you? Murder is an indictable offense and twenty-to-life is a heavy price to pay for a place to store the ugliest couch on the planet."

"It's not a couch." She sniffed. "It's a chaise longue. And it was a gift from my aunt."

"How unfortunate."

"Not for the people who sit there. It's extremely comfortable." She held out her hand. "Let me see the lease."

He approached with the document, keeping one eye on her free hand should she suddenly procure a pair of scissors. "Mr. Patel—"

"My father."

"The landlord." He wasn't going to let her get one up on him. "Gave me the keys two weeks ago. He told me everything was in order."

She flicked through the lease. "He briefly mentioned he'd rented out this space. He said he was going to call you and let you know that it was no longer available."

"He didn't call."

"Obviously. He had a heart attack and now he's in the hospital recovering."

Sam bristled at her sarcasm. He was used to women melting at his feet. Karen had just sexted him with pictures of herself in the boardroom in provocative poses, a plastic medical kit in her hand. How did he tame this wildcat? Did he turn up the charm? Soothe her with his deep voice? Dazzle her with his megawatt smile?

"I understand it's a difficult time," he murmured in the sympathetic tone he reserved for employees slated for redundancy who were not as accommodating as Tyler and felt the need to share with him the details of illnesses, accidents, mortgages, sick children, ailing parents, planned holidays, car payments, and rent obligations. Life was an expensive tragedy. But he had a job to do. Nothing ever swayed him, not even the women who offered their bodies for a chance to keep their jobs.

"Then you know why you'll just have to take my word that my father intended to terminate the lease."

"I'm afraid I can't do that," he said firmly. "I've already made moving arrangements. Signs and stationery are on their way, and I have a client coming to see me first thing in the morning. When your father recovers, I'm sure he can sort the matter out, but in the meantime, I have a business to run."

She tipped her head to the side. "What kind of business?"

Cute and sexy. Too bad about her prickly personality.

"Corporate downsizing." He crossed the room and pulled a stack of files from the box, thumping them down on the tragically modern Eagerson desk. "Companies call us in when they need to restructure or downsize, when they are in financial difficulty, or if there is a merger and acquisition that involves the reevaluation of staffing needs. We review their financial position, make recommendations for cuts and restructuring, and assist in the termination of unnecessary employees. My partner handles the international clients. I deal with domestic companies with a particular focus on health care. We also have a staff of six who work remotely."

She gave a disdainful sniff. "How ironic. I'm setting up a recruitment consultancy. I find jobs for people and you take them away. Figures."

"Companies can be more efficient when they get rid of the deadweight." He removed the pencils from his box one by one, lining them up neatly on the right side of his desk. "That means faster production, and better products and services for customers. It's a win-win for everyone." He willed her to move from the desk so he could see if she had an ass to go with those curves. If he was going to waste time indulging himself in this pointless conversation, he might as well enjoy the view.

"Except for the people who lose their jobs."

Ah, a bleeding heart. He should have guessed. "That's why there are people like you. I cut them loose, and you turn them into someone else's problem."

She sucked in a sharp breath and glared. He'd definitely hit a nerve with that one.

"They aren't a 'problem.' They are people who are out of work because cold, callous, corporate vultures like you only care about the bottom line."

He flinched inwardly. Not because he was ashamed of his choice of career—he was proud of what he'd accomplished in the last two and a half years—but because she'd hit too close to the heart. He had never been able to shake the guilt of working with Ranjeet day after day and not seeing who he truly was. He had pandered to the man who had made his sister suffer instead of protecting her like a brother was supposed to do.

"That's incredibly naive. No business can retain their staff indefinitely. Technology changes, jobs can be automated, and people lose the incentive to innovate or excel when their position is secure."

Her hands found her very generous hips. If it was a ploy to draw attention to her soft, lush curves, it worked because he couldn't tear his eyes away.

"My father has never fired an employee and they are just as hardworking and efficient as they were when he hired them." She rounded the desk, and he suffered a moment of brain freeze. Damn, she was the whole package. Beautiful face. Sexy body. Long legs. And those boots . . .

"Don't bother unpacking the rest," she said, tearing the lease in half. "I'm kicking you out now."

She was almost as strong willed and stubborn as he was. But he had much better taste in furniture.

He snorted a laugh. "I'd like to see you try."

"I'm sure you would," she snapped. "It's probably the only way you can get a woman near you with that giant ego in the way."

"I am hardly lacking for female companionship."

Layla rolled her eyes in an overly dramatic fashion. "I'm not interested in hearing about your visits to the nail bar. I just want you gone."

"It's not going to happen, sweetheart. I have the document in digital form, and the law on my side."

"Family trumps the law." She folded her arms under her generous breasts. Sweat trickled down his back. Karen had nothing on this woman, even with her creative use of a toy blood pressure cuff.

"Not in the real world. My attorney works upstairs. If you need further proof, I can ask him to join us and confirm that the lease is valid." Sam's attorney and close friend, John Lee, had connected Sam with Nasir Patel when he found out Nasir was looking for a tenant.

Her gaze flicked to the partially open door, a smug expression spreading across her face when a woman walked in carrying a multi-colored tote bag containing a fluffy white dog, its neck adorned with an enormous blue bow. Everything about the visitor screamed trouble, from her torn Slayer T-shirt to her deconstructed jean skirt, and from her strategically torn purple tights to the thick black shoes that looked like they had been nibbled by mice. Her shoulder-length dark hair had been dyed pink on the bottom, and she had a small silver ring in her nose.

"Daisy!" Layla rounded the desk to greet her guest. "And you brought Max! Let me give him a cuddle."

Sam's pulse kicked up a notch, and he readjusted his line of pencils, ensuring they were perfectly even.

"Hey, babe. How's the new digs?" Daisy released the animal to Layla, who gave it a quick hug before putting it down to wander unfettered around Sam's office.

"Unexpectedly occupied." Layla gestured to Sam, and Daisy turned to face him as if noticing him for the first time.

In that moment, as her gaze roamed shamelessly up and down his body, Sam realized three things: first, they would never get along; second, his path to quiet possession of the office had just become exponentially more difficult; and third, neither his charm nor his good looks were going to soothe this savage beast.

"Who's this?" Daisy narrowed her gaze as the dog sniffed his Italian leather shoes.

"Sam Mehta." Layla answered for him. "He says my dad leased the office to him before he had his heart attack, and he refuses to leave." Layla gestured to her curious friend. "Sam, this is my cousin Daisy Patel. She's a software engineer, but currently between gigs."

Sam had never met a woman more ill-suited to the name of a flower normally associated with happiness and joy. He gave her a curt nod and received a snort in return.

"He's got a stick up his ass. No wonder he's having trouble getting out the door."

Sam gave an affronted sniff. "I beg your pardon?"

"Out." Daisy pointed to the door. "Away with your handsome face and perfect hair and expensive suit and mouthwatering body. Her father just had a heart attack. Have you no sense of human decency?"

"Absolutely not." He pulled another file from his box and thumped it on the desk, the force more for effect than necessity.

"Is that *Absolutely not, I won't get out* or *Absolutely not, I have no human decency*?"

Sam didn't deign to answer her ridiculous question. "I have work to do."

"Should I call someone to rough him up?" Daisy asked, turning to Layla. "What about the Singh twins? They're home on leave from the National Guard. Or how about Bobby Prakash? He's head bouncer at that new bar in Chinatown. He said to call if I ever needed anything."

Sam tried to tune them out as they launched into a conversation about criminal-turned-bouncer Bobby Prakash, his childhood, brushes with the law, gangster friends, girlfriends, family, and pet boa constrictor. This was exactly what he'd been trying to avoid when he signed the lease. He wasn't interested in a busy office full of chatter, chaos, and noise. He wanted to work in a calm, peaceful environment where there would be nobody wandering the halls, banging doors, talking beside the water fountain, or flushing toilets when he was trying to work.

"Sam has a lease," Layla said, drawing Sam's attention with the use of his name. "Bobby can't throw him out if it's legal."

"The name is Mr. Mehta," Sam interrupted. "Sam is for friends."

"Do you have friends?" Daisy inquired. "You don't look the type."

"Of course I have friends." He'd lost touch with many of them after Nisha's accident, but he still saw John regularly at the gym, along with his sparring partner Evan.

"Are they imaginary or real?" Daisy gave him a condescending smile. "I'm guessing imaginary because no one wants to be friends with a jerk."

Sam scowled. "This is a place of business. If you wish to socialize, I suggest you go elsewhere."

"He's cute when he's annoyed," Daisy said. "Maybe you should keep him around for eye-candy purposes."

Layla gave him a sideways glance through the thicket of her lashes. "Don't compliment him. His ego is already so big, his top shirt button is about to pop."

The women chuckled and Sam's jaw tightened. Women adored him. Men admired him. Employees detested him. But no one ever, ever dismissed him. "*He* is, in fact, sitting right here."

"We're very aware of your presence." Daisy flashed him a sultry smile. "It's hard to miss the steam coming out of your ears."

Layla sighed. "What am I going to do with him?"

"Maybe if you ignore him, he'll go away. I think he's just desperate for attention. Max was the same when he was a puppy. Always whining, thumping his little tail, peeing in the corners . . ." She grimaced and looked around the room. "How long has Sam been here? Maybe you'd better do a sniff test."

Layla's gaze lifted to Sam and then away, but not before he caught the barest hint of a smile. Despite the poor taste in clothes, relatives, and furniture, she seemed somewhat stable. If he could just get her alone, he'd have no difficulty convincing her to move her business. Daisy, on the other hand, was clearly going to be a problem. He knew her type. Too shrewd. Too worldly. And too damn talkative.

He emptied his box while the women continued to talk about personal matters not meant for a man's ears. Daisy, it seemed, had undiscriminating taste when it came to hookups and an endless supply of anecdotes of encounters gone wrong. Layla spoke disparagingly about someone named Jonas and an unfortunate event she called "Blue Fury." He leaned a little closer, although he didn't know why.

"Do you know what Jonas did when I was on my period?" Layla asked, making no effort to lower her voice for what clearly was going to be a discussion about intimate feminine matters.

Sam stood abruptly, shoving his chair back from the desk so hard it hit the wall.

Daisy smirked. "Something wrong?"

"I have a prior engagement, but rest assured I will be back in the morning to sort this out." He returned his pencils to the box one by one before grabbing his gym bag.

"If you must come back, bring coffee," Layla called out.

"Two creams and two sugars for me," Daisy shouted. "Layla takes hers brown."

"Brown?" He looked back over his shoulder.

"Like her men." Daisy laughed so hard she fell off the desk, spilling Layla's papers and pens all over the floor. The dog barked in alarm and knocked over a wastepaper basket as it ran to Daisy, jumping on her and licking her face.

Sam stared at the scene behind him—his perfect office now chaos in its purest form.

He couldn't imagine a greater hell.

· 4 ·

USUALLY, the simple routine calmed her.

Knead the dough—squeeze, roll, press, and massage—until her hands ached and her fingers stiffened. If the kitchen was too warm or the dough was too soft, she would have to knead for up to twenty minutes to get the right firmness. Stopping to rest wasn't an option. Roti, a thin round bread similar to a tortilla, was an unforgiving beast. Slack off and it wouldn't puff up in the skillet. Then she would have to start the routine over again.

Today, however, she wanted to punch the dough. Not just because she'd celebrated a little too hard with Daisy last night, but because her perfect plan for reinvention was being thwarted by her father's failing heart and a good-looking ass.

The smell of *tadka*, as the spices hit the smoking oil in Pari Auntie's pan, distracted her from thoughts of her unwanted office guest. There was no scent so inherently Indian, and it brought back comforting memories of playing games with Dev in the kitchen after a long day at school.

"How's your dad doing?" Daisy sliced into an onion on the counter beside Layla. Despite being hungover, she had come to help out that morning, along with some aunties, while Layla and her mom were at the hospital.

Layla shrugged. "He's in a medically induced coma to help him heal from the heart surgery. The doctor said it's routine, but it's hard to see him lying so still."

"It's weird to be in the kitchen with only your mom shouting," Daisy said. "It seems almost quiet."

Longtime assistant chef Arun Shah handed Daisy another bag of onions. "Our new assistant chef calls her Mrs. Gordon Ramsay behind her back."

Layla laughed at the reference to the British chef known for verbally abusing his staff. Although she came across as quiet and soft-spoken in public, her mother had a big voice in the kitchen and was abrupt and unforgiving when she was stressed. She expected a lot of her staff, but no more than she expected of herself. And although she could be harsh, she was always fair and unfailingly kind. As a result, staff turnover was low and many, like Arun, had been with the family since The Spice Mill first opened its doors.

"Where's the prawn?" Layla's mother shouted out, adjusting the Giants' cap that she always wore when she was cooking, her long braid tucked underneath. She was a longtime Giants fan and had passed on her love of the team to Layla.

"One minute, Chef."

"Arun, I've seen snails move faster than you. Pick it up."

"Prawn in the window." Arun put a plate on the counter, ready to be served.

Layla's mother tested it with a fork. "Overcooked. What's wrong with your eyes? Are you getting too old for the kitchen?"

"No, Chef." Arun raced over to the gas stove. "Sorry, Chef. Three minutes and I'll have another plate ready."

"And you." Layla's mother poked the dough as she walked past. "More massaging. Less squeezing."

"That's what I said last weekend in bed," Daisy whispered.

Layla laughed as her fingers sank into the soft, warm dough. "Who were you with?"

"My Bollywood dance instructor. I couldn't help myself after he taught us 'Dard-e-Disco.' He looks just like Shah Rukh Khan, who is the only old Bollywood actor I legit have a crush on."

Daisy wiped a tear away with the back of her hand. There were tricks to cutting onions and she'd forgotten to use them. "You have to come to the next class. You're an amazing dancer. I always thought you'd be the next Mehar Auntie when you were old enough to be an auntie."

"Is that supposed to be a compliment?" Layla had always loved Bollywood-style dancing. She'd learned her first dance from Mehar Auntie and had taken lessons for years, culminating in a performance of "Nagada Nagada" at her high school talent show with Daisy and a handful of friends. "Anyway, I haven't danced in ages."

"It's like riding a bicycle," Daisy said. "Remember this?" She put the knife down and danced a few steps, hands swinging from side to side as she hummed the chorus of the familiar song. Layla stopped kneading to sing, and for a moment there was no Jonas or "Blue Fury," no sexy-but-irritating man in her office, and her father was about to walk through the door and hug her troubles away.

"Is this Bollywood or a restaurant?" Layla's mother shook her head. "Now you'll need to start again. Do I need to separate you two like I did when you were small? Alone, you are good girls. Together, you are rascals."

Daisy hung her head in mock shame. "Sorry, Jana Auntie."

"Hey, baby girl." Danny Kapoor, her mother's new assistant chef, joined them at the counter. With his big, brown, puppy dog eyes, sensuous lips, thick dark hair, and high cheekbones, Danny was more suited to walking down a runway than standing behind a stove—and he knew it. Even in the middle of meal prep, his shirt was open one button too many, and his hips moved in ways that were respectable only in a Bollywood film. Layla had met him a few times when she'd come home to visit, but they'd never had a real conversation.

"I heard you're going through a rough spot," his soft voice flowed over her like sickly sweet liquid caramel as he edged between Layla and Daisy. "Just wanted to let you know I've been there, and if you need to talk—"

"She has me," Daisy snapped.

"Of course she does," he said smoothly. "I just meant if she wanted the guy perspective or needed extra support, I'm always here." He flashed his charming smile at Daisy, who was now busy spelling *fuckboy* in onion slices on the cutting board.

Layla had met more than one fuckboy in her quest to numb the pain of Dev's death. Attractive, charming, yet notoriously selfish and careless with their overall actions, they didn't care how they affected other people as long they got what they wanted and had fun while doing it—and it was very clear where Danny's interests lay.

"That's very nice, Danny. I appreciate it, but I'm not—"

"You're still hurting, babe. I get it. Tomorrow, when you're ready, I'll be here for you."

"How's your girlfriend?" Daisy asked loudly.

"She's good." He leaned against the counter, seemingly unconcerned about being called out. "She travels a lot for her job. I think she's in Paris right now, so there is an empty space in my bed waiting to be filled."

"Danny!" Layla's mother shouted across the kitchen. "I'm not paying you to socialize. The potatoes aren't going to peel themselves."

"Later, babe." He blew Layla a kiss.

Daisy pretended to gag.

"He's harmless," Layla said. "Maybe he's what I need to get over Jonas. Sex with utterly no emotional connection."

"I thought that's what you've had for the last five years."

"What are you girls whispering about?" Pari Auntie called out, her arms elbow-deep in spinach. "Not men, I hope. These young people today . . ."

Charu Auntie walked past with a basket of okra. "Don't listen to her. An unexpected breakup can cause considerable psychological distress. The social pain has been associated with a twentyfold higher risk of developing depression in the coming year. It's important to lean on family and friends for support. You'll find that brain activity in the craving centers will have decreased significantly after about ten weeks."

"Actually, it's been almost two weeks and I don't think of him at all," Layla offered.

"Then you weren't truly emotionally invested in that relationship," Charu Auntie said. "Or you're a psychopath."

"Definitely a psychopath." Daisy sliced furiously, decimating the onion as tears poured down her cheeks. "She didn't feel anything when she stole the *pakoras* from my lunch kit in sixth grade."

Charu Auntie balanced the basket on one hip and adjusted her glasses. "Distraction and self-care are important to prevent a craving response in the ventral tegmental area, the nucleus accumbens, and orbitofrontal/prefrontal cortex."

"I think she's saying, in her oddly complicated way, that she thinks you should hook up with fuckboy Danny," Daisy said. "Too bad the sexy beast upstairs is such a piece of—"

"Shhh." She hadn't told her mother about Sam, for the simple reason that she knew her mother would tell her to let Sam have the office. But it wasn't right. Her father had intended to call him. And it was just common decency to step aside when someone's dad was in the hospital and his last wish had been for his daughter to work upstairs.

Layla squeezed the soft dough, imaging it was Sam's head. Squeeze. Pound. Thump. Poke. Anything to wipe that smug expression off his face. She should have just kicked him out and dealt with the consequences later. She was the queen of rash decisions, after all.

"You do what it takes to make yourself happy." Charu Auntie patted her hand.

"But no more boyfriends until after you're married," Selena Auntie called out.

"She's not going to get married if she rolls roti like that." Layla's mother poked the dough and sighed. "Remember to roll clockwise. Perfect circles. Not too thin."

"Listen to your mother," Taara Auntie said. "Learn all you can otherwise your mother-in-law will curse your mother if you feed her burned chapattis."

"You must be cursed every day," Salena Auntie muttered.

Taara Auntie huffed. "My boys love my fusion food. Last night I combined roti and pizza. My youngest called it rotzza. Or was it rotten? So many English words sound the same."

"They're teenage boys," Salena Auntie said. "They'll eat anything you put in front of them as long as it's not moving. And maybe even then."

Layla looked over her shoulder. Her mother was mixing batter for the ginger chai tea cake she brought to the local seniors' center every day. It was just one of her parents' many acts of charity, giving back to the community that had helped two poor immigrants become Michelin-starred chefs. "Mom, would you be disappointed if I didn't get married?"

Her mother stopped stirring and lowered her voice so only

Layla could hear, although with the sound of aunties chattering and pakoras frying and the general clang of pots around them, there was little chance of anyone eavesdropping. "I want you to be happy, but it's nice to have someone to share your life with. If you can't find a good man, your father and I can help you like we helped Dev."

"I don't want an arranged marriage."

"It's not like how it was in my day," her mother said. "I didn't have a choice. I thought my world had ended when my parents arranged my marriage to a man in America who I'd never met, but now I can't imagine life without him." Her voice caught. "Now things are different. It is an arranged introduction. We make a marriage résumé and let people know you are interested in finding a husband. If we find someone who would be a good match for you, we introduce you and you can talk on the phone or Internet and make a decision if you want to meet him. No time wasted on men who aren't interested in commitment. No breaking of hearts. We can be the Tinderbox everyone talks about, and if you don't like him you swipe him away."

Layla laughed. "It's Tinder, Mom. And right now I'm trying to figure out how to get my life back together. The last thing I need is a man to mess things up."

SOMETIMES Sam wondered why he had gone into business with Royce.

After two hours of listening to his business partner rave over Skype about the merits of group termination over individual meetings, the exciting prospect of firing workers online, and the wonders of replacing human workers with automation, Sam had had enough of his partner's high-handed disregard for anything but the corporate bottom line. Instead of creating jobs, Royce destroyed them. Instead of building firms, he raided them. Royce loved nothing more than walking into a business, firing all the staff, and flipping it to the highest bidder. It took a hard, ruthless man to do the job, and no one was as good at it as Royce.

Sam forced a smile for the face on the screen. Although it was three A.M. in Hong Kong, Royce was still in his shirt and tie, his brown hair gelled into its usual two-inch pouf with sideburns that curled around his ears. "Anything else? I've got a meeting."

It wasn't a lie. Any moment Layla was going to walk through that door, and he couldn't deny a curious sense of anticipation. He'd already moved her few possessions to the Eagerson desk and had been working for the last five hours in anticipation of the showdown that she was going to lose.

"I'll be leaving for Beijing tomorrow," Royce said. "If I'd known Gilder Steel wanted me to visit every location, I would have asked for more money."

"You love traveling," Sam reminded him. "You were going crazy stuck behind a desk. That's why you needed me."

"There are benefits to being trapped for twelve hours on a plane." Royce leaned forward until his face took up the entire screen. "I sat beside Peter Richards, the CEO of Alpha Health Care on the trip to Hong Kong. They've just taken over five Bay Area hospitals in the failing Sons of Hope Health System and are looking to restructure. One of them is St. Vincent's Hospital. When I told him you did your residency there, and that we've just relocated to a building only a few blocks from their head office, he asked us to pitch for the work."

Sam's heart skipped a beat. This was the opportunity he had been waiting for—a real chance for justice. If they won the contract, he would have full access to Ranjeet's employment file. It was slightly unethical—he had a clear conflict of interest—but if a criminal was walking free, if he could save even one other woman from his sister's fate and right the injustice done to her, then it was worth the risk. And maybe then he would find his own redemption.

"I assume you want me to prepare the pitch."

"It involves sitting behind a desk, so yes. I've e-mailed you the details."

Sam tried to rub the tension out of his forehead after Royce ended the call. Despite the personal opportunity, the restructuring meant that many of the people he had worked with at the hospital were going to lose their jobs. This was not the life he had imagined for himself. He had only ever wanted to be a healer, not the man responsible for destroying lives.

"You're back."

His headache disappeared at the sound of Layla's voice, and a thrill of anticipation shot down his spine. "Of course I'm back. This is my office. I've been here since seven A.M. working, as serious businesspeople do, not swanning into work at noon with a box of donuts in one hand and a cook pot in the other."

Layla pulled herself up with a derisory sniff. "This pot contains my mother's dal, which is the most delicious and comforting food in the universe. I was planning to share it, but now I'll just eat it all myself. The donuts are for dessert, which you are not welcome to have. And not that it's any of your business, but I was at the hospital at seven A.M. visiting my father, and then I was downstairs in the kitchen helping my mother. She's trying to keep the restaurant going on her own with the help of some inexperienced but well-meaning aunties, and it's not easy to do."

Sam opened his mouth and closed it again. She was being kind, caring, and helpful to her family. How irritating. There was no way he could push that line of argument and keep his self-respect.

"You're sitting at my desk." She put the pot on the reception desk and folded her arms.

Sam shuffled his papers, spreading them across the polished wood surface for no reason other than to keep his gaze off her distractingly perfect breasts. "I didn't see your name on it."

"Just look at your lease. You'll see it written across the top, or can't you read big words like *Patel*?"

"I don't recall seeing any identification," he countered. "For all I know, you could have just walked in off the street. You're certainly not dressed like you're running a business."

Eyes blazing, she glared. "What's wrong with how I'm dressed?"

"An apron and a pink tracksuit with *Juicy* written across the ass are hardly serious business attire and they certainly don't scream *swipe right* on desi Tinder."

Sam didn't know if there was such a thing as Tinder for people of South Asian descent living abroad, but if it did exist, he and Layla would definitely not have been a match.

Layla gave a growl of frustration. "You may be surprised to hear that I don't live my life seeking male approval. I'm just getting over a breakup so I'm a little bit fragile. Last night, I went out with Daisy and drank too much, smoked something I thought was a cigarette, danced on a speaker, and fell onto some loser named Jimbo, whose girlfriend just happened to be an MMA fighter and didn't like to see me sprawled on top of her man. We had a minor physical altercation and I was kicked out of the bar. Then I got dumped on the street by my Uber driver because I threw up in his cab. So today, I just couldn't manage office wear. It's called self-care, and we all need it sometimes. Danny certainly didn't mind."

"Who's Danny?" The question came out before he could stop it.

"Someone who appreciates all I've got going here"—she ran a hand around her generous curves—"and isn't hung up on trivial things like clothes." She tugged off the apron and dropped it on the reception desk.

"I'm not hung up on clothes, either," Sam teased. "When I'm with a woman I prefer her to have no clothes at all."

Her nose wrinkled. "You're disgusting."

"Go home, sweetheart." Sam waved a dismissive hand. "Put your feet up. Watch some rom-coms. Eat a few tubs of ice cream. Have a good cry. Some of us have real work to do."

Layla grabbed her pot and the box of donuts and marched into the small kitchen at the back of the office. Sam heard cupboards bang. Cutlery clatter. Angry mutters and a huff. A few minutes later Layla marched back out with a bowl of dal in one hand and two donuts circling her finger like rings.

Only when she sat down and proceeded to eat one of the donuts off her finger did he realize he hadn't done any work since she walked in.

"Donuts and dal are not two foods that naturally go together," he pointed out.

Layla took a giant bite and licked her lips. "Do you not have work to do? Or are you just going to sit there and look pretty?"

He was saved from laughing out loud when he noticed a man standing beside the empty reception desk, a bundle of papers clutched in his hand.

"Can I help you?" Sam glared at the intruder who had dared interrupt when he was about to defang the little viper in front of him with a few well-chosen words.

The visitor was shorter than Sam by a good few inches, his bronzed baby face clean-shaven, straight dark hair in need of a trim. He wore a ridiculously large sports jacket over a blue collared shirt and a pair of polyester pants two inches too short and cinched tight beneath his large belly with a worn leather belt.

"I'm looking for Layla Patel."

"That's me." Layla removed her donut rings and shot Sam a smug look. "I have a client!"

She couldn't have been more excited if this were the first client she'd ever had. Sam couldn't imagine keeping up that level of enthusiasm over the course of a day. Certainly, it would be an asset in her field. Maybe he'd misjudged her, and she was more successful than she appeared.

"Please come in." She motioned him forward. "What can I do for you?"

"Hassan Khan." His lips pulled back in a smile, all gums and little teeth. "I will be your new husband."

· 5 ·

"I beg your pardon?"

Hassan walked past Layla and held out his hand to Sam. "I spoke with Mr. Nasir Patel last week. He said his daughter needed a husband right away and we had arranged a meeting for today. When I arrived at the restaurant, one of the kitchen workers told me that Mr. Nasir was in the hospital, but that Layla was upstairs and looking forward to meeting me."

"I'm going to kill Danny," Layla muttered under her breath.

"She definitely needs someone to get her under control," Sam mused, stroking his upper lip. "She got into a bar fight last night, if you can believe it." Leaning forward, he shook Hassan's hand. He had no idea what was going on, but from the way Layla was glaring at her visitor, it was worth playing along if only to see her riled.

"My parents have given their approval subject to meeting the girl," Hassan continued. "They're excited to have a daughter-in-law who has had such excellent culinary training."

"Why are you talking to him?" Layla snapped.

"He's the man."

Sam couldn't help but smirk when Layla pressed her lips together, her brow creasing in a furious frown. This day was just getting better and better.

"Anything to do with me, you discuss with me," she said firmly.

Puzzled, Hassan asked Sam, "Would Mr. Nasir approve?"

"From what I know of her, I suspect Mr. Nasir wouldn't get much say in the matter." He let out a heavy sigh. "She is strong willed, unconventional, and definitely not what I'd call a traditional woman."

"This has nothing to do with you, Sam. Stay out of it." Layla's voice rose in pitch. "Clearly, I didn't know my father was trying to find me a husband. It's a bit of a shock."

"But it's utterly delightful," Sam said. "All our problems can be solved at once. You run off and marry Hassan. I stay in the office and get down to business." He was pushing it, he knew, but he couldn't help himself. Her passionate response to his teasing set his blood on fire.

Layla grabbed one of her donuts and hurled it at Sam with the kind of speed and accuracy he had only ever seen from the Big Three pitchers who had helped his favorite baseball team, the Oakland Athletics, win three AL West Division titles during their five years together.

Sam caught the donut in midair, catcher style. What an exhilarating day! Maybe he should consider another career change. He'd look good in the Oakland A's green and gold.

"Let's go to the boardroom so we can talk in privacy." Layla waved a slightly puzzled Hassan forward.

"Have a lovely chat." Sam bit into the donut although he usually didn't indulge in baked treats. Sugary sweetness burst across his tongue. Delicious. He'd been missing out. Maybe tomorrow he'd buy a box of donuts, too. "I'll get working on the wedding invitations," he called out. "Do you prefer pink or orange?"

"We'll be alone?" Hassan asked.

"Yes, we'll be alone," Layla said. "We need to talk about what's going on without any interruptions." She led Hassan into the boardroom and slammed the door.

Sam stared, unseeing, at his screen. Hassan seemed to be a very traditional guy with certain expectations and preconceived notions about how a woman should behave. He might even get the wrong idea about Layla's invitation to meet with him behind closed doors. But so what if he did? Layla clearly knew how to handle herself—as the marks on his shirt from the flying office supplies could attest. And, he was right outside.

Of course he'd also been outside when Nisha had been suffering Ranjeet's drunken abuse. Outside and far away. Unlike now.

Damn.

Sam grabbed the extra donut off the reception desk and opened the boardroom door. Steam hissed from the kettle on the credenza that had been set up for refreshments. Layla bent down to retrieve a carton of milk from the small fridge. Hassan's gaze locked on her ass.

Sam's protective instincts kicked into gear. He moved in front of Hassan, blocking his view.

"Why are you here?" Layla closed the fridge with a soft bang.

"I thought you might need a snack for your guest."

"The boardroom is fully equipped with . . ." Her words faded away when her gaze fell on the donut in his hand, and for the briefest of seconds, her face softened. "You brought the donut?"

"Yes." He was perversely pleased that she understood his gesture. "I believe it can be weaponized in the event of an emergency."

Layla turned away and poured the milk into a cup, but not before he saw a smile ghost her lips. "How do you go from ruthless capitalist matchmaking pimp one moment to considerate gentleman the next?"

"I'm a complicated man." He joined her at the credenza. "I thought I'd stay in case you needed more snacks."

"I'll allow it," she said magnanimously. "But I'll do the talking.

You can just scowl and look frightening and intense. It shouldn't be hard since it seems to be your normal state of being."

Sam snorted. "And here I thought I was doing you a favor . . ."

"Would you like some tea?"

"If it's not chai."

"No one hates chai. What kind of desi are you?" She filled a cup with boiling water and motioned for him to select a tea bag.

"The bad kind." His lips quirked at the corners. He'd smiled more since meeting Layla than he had in the last two years.

"I should have guessed." She raised an admonishing eyebrow. "You have *bad boy* written all over you."

"What are you going to do with Hassan?" He selected the Black Dragon tea simply because the name appealed to his senses. Anything that had to do with highly intelligent, powerful, fire-breathing creatures couldn't be bad.

"Send him away, of course. I'm not looking for a husband."

"Then why are you making him tea?" He added milk and three sugars to his cup while she delivered Hassan's tea and returned for her own.

"I feel bad for him." She kept her voice low. "My dad was just trying to help, and he clearly got Hassan's hopes up. I thought it would be polite to spend a few minutes getting to know him so he doesn't feel that I dismissed him out of hand."

"But you intend to dismiss him out of hand in any event, so why prolong the agony?"

"Because . . ." She sipped her tea, leaving the barest hint of pink lipstick on the rim of her cup. "I can't help but wonder. What if he's the one? Sometimes I think my dad knows me better than I know myself. What if he found the perfect guy for me and I kicked him out the door?"

Sam snorted a laugh. "You think Hassan Khan is your perfect guy?"

As if on cue, Hassan slurped his tea so loudly the sound echoed through the room.

"I think it's unlikely, but I need to make sure."

They joined Hassan at the table with their tea and a plate of cookies. Layla discreetly placed the donut on a napkin by her side.

"Tell me a little about yourself, Hassan," she said.

"My details are here." Hassan handed Sam a copy of his marriage résumé. With a loud huff of annoyance, Layla snatched the document from Sam's hand before he had even had an opportunity to peruse the first page.

"Why don't you just talk us through it?" She placed the document on the table in front of her but didn't spare it a glance.

"I'm . . . uh . . . thirty-five years old." Hassan frowned as if he wasn't sure about his age. "I came to America from Andhra Pradesh to further my education. I have an engineering degree and will be studying for my MBA. Full disclosure: I am GUC."

Now it was Sam's turn to frown. "GUC?"

"Good used condition." Layla dipped her head to hide her smile. "You obviously don't spend much time on Craigslist."

"How is it that you are 'used'?" Sam asked, his curiosity piqued.

"I've been in several relationships that didn't work out." Hassan shook his head. "They only wanted me for my body."

"I hear you." Sam nodded in sympathy. "I have the same problem."

Layla let out a snort. Droplets of tea sprayed across the table, hitting Hassan in the eye. Unfazed, he wiped his face with his sleeve and smiled like nothing had happened.

"Anything else we should know?" Sam was intrigued both by

Hassan's misadventures as a boy toy and Layla's unladylike response.

"My hobbies include extreme pogo."

"Watch your language," Sam barked. "There is a sort-of lady present."

"Sort-of lady?" Layla narrowed her gaze. "What's that supposed to mean?"

"It's a sport," Hassan interjected. "It involves riding and performing tricks on a special extreme pogo stick that can jump over ten feet in height."

Sam felt a curious sensation bubble up in his chest. "You bounce around on a giant pogo stick that goes ten feet in the air."

"Yes, sir." Hassan pulled out his phone and navigated to a video. "Here I am."

Something inside Sam threatened to burst as he watched ungainly Hassan bouncing through the air in the middle of a field. Sweat beaded on his forehead as he fought to master the unfamiliar emotion. What the hell was wrong with him?

"Don't laugh," Layla whispered under her breath.

Laughter. He remembered it now. How long had it been since he'd had a good laugh?

Layla dropped her hand under the table and dug her nails into Sam's thigh. Almost instantly, the uncontrollable sensation was replaced by another—this one familiar and likely to become problematic if he didn't get her hand off his lap.

"That's . . ." Layla cleared her throat. "Amazing, Hassan. Is there anything else we should know about you?"

"I am veg."

Sam waited for Hassan to elaborate, but the prospective bridegroom just smiled.

"I'm actually not a vegetarian." Layla's words tumbled over one another like she'd forgotten how to use her tongue. "I like meat. Love it, in fact. I have meat every day. I pretty much grew up in my parents' restaurant and they serve meat. Which I like eating. Lamb, chicken, beef . . ."

"I think she's trying to say she's carnivorous," Sam said, biting back his laughter. "Don't make any sudden moves or she might think you're prey."

Hassan opened his tablet and handed it to Layla. "If the interview portion is completed, my parents have prepared a test for you. You'll have five minutes to complete each section. Incorrect or missing answers will be penalized one mark, so it is possible to have a negative score, although that won't help your situation."

"What situation?"

"Your father said you were in urgent need of a man."

"She's desperate." Sam shook his head in mock sorrow. "If I wasn't here your very life would be in danger. It's an effort to keep her on this side of the table."

Layla squeezed his thigh again, her hand precariously close to his fly, nails digging in so deep his eyes watered. "You want danger, Sam? Keep talking."

"We don't want to have intellectually inferior progeny in the family," Hassan continued. "My parents have Ph.D.'s. My two brothers are doctors and married to doctors. I'll have two professional degrees when I'm finished my MBA. We don't want a spouse with a lesser intelligence."

"That rules you out," Layla muttered to Sam under her breath. Sam bit back a laugh. "He's not really my type."

"The academic section is first." Hassan pushed the tablet toward her. "For the fitness test we can go outside and I'll mark fifty yards in the parking lot for the sprint—"

"Fitness?" Layla's nose wrinkled in disgust.

"Just put a box of donuts on the finish line and she'll run the equivalent of a three-minute mile," Sam offered.

Layla turned the full force of her fury on him. "You're an ass."

Sam leaned back in his chair and folded his arms. "You say that like it's a surprise."

Hassan took back the tablet and tapped several boxes, filling them with black X's.

"What are you doing?" Layla studied the screen.

"Even temperament. Accommodating. Sweet disposition. Submissive. Compliant. You have five failing marks in the personality section."

"Seriously?" Layla spluttered her indignation. "No one can fail a personality test."

"You just did," Sam pointed out. "And to be fair, I saw that one coming."

"You're very different than your profile on desilovematch.com." Hassan held up one of the crumpled papers.

"Let me see that." Sam snatched the document and pushed to his feet, holding it out of Layla's reach. "Hmmm. 'Layla Patel. Age twenty-six. Height five feet, five inches. Weight—'"

"Give me that." Layla jumped up and lunged for the paper. Sam held it higher and she collided with him, losing her balance. He circled an arm around her waist to keep her steady, securing her soft body against his chest. Electricity arced between them, warming his blood as he felt the pounding of her unaccommodating heart.

"Bastard." She broke the spell, jumping to get the paper. Her body rubbed up and down against his. Too late, he realized the danger.

"Is this a sales technique?" he whispered in her ear. "A little demonstration for Hassan about what he can expect in bed? Or is it just for me? Because, sweetheart, if he doesn't marry you after this, I will."

Her nostrils flared, and she pulled away. "I wouldn't marry you even if you got down on your knees and begged."

"When I'm with a woman, it's not me doing the begging." Holding her at arm's length, Sam studied the picture of Layla in a bright pink salwar kameez, her hair tucked away in a matching pink headscarf, hands hennaed, face painted, her neck and wrists dripping with jewelry.

"It's hard to believe this is you," he said. "You look very feminine in shocking pink and quite unlike the kind of woman who would curse and throw herself at an innocent stranger in a frenzy of lust."

"I wasn't feeling any innocence below your belt," she said dryly.

With a chuckle, Sam continued to read the marriage résumé in his hand. He was enjoying her predicament far too much. "'Religious, healthy, cultured, obedient, polite, dutiful, demure, deep sense of responsibility to family, respectful of elders . . .'" Sam shook his head. "Not entirely accurate, I'm afraid. I am six years older than her and she was very disrespectful to me. Strong willed? Definitely. Healthy?" He looked down at a fuming Layla. "Show me your teeth. My grandfather owned horses and he always assessed their health by examining their teeth."

Layla cursed in Urdu using words he'd never heard from a woman before.

"Well, that was neither polite nor demure, and you aren't very obedient because the only teeth I see are bared, like you want to attack me and eat me for dinner." He turned over the page. "It also says here that you're a good girl." His voice dropped to a sensual purr and he leaned toward her. "Are you a good girl, Layla? You seem very bad to me. If you need a husband who can keep you in line, you'll have to up your game." Sam could almost feel Layla's furious gaze boring through his skull. He couldn't remember the last time he'd had so much fun.

"Is this your man?" a bewildered Hassan asked, looking from Sam to Layla.

"Hardly." She glared at Sam. "He's nobody. It's sad, really. He seems totally unable to comprehend that he has to leave."

Sam's body shook with repressed laughter. "I am all man, sweetheart, which I'm sure you know after you rubbed yourself all over me like a cat in heat."

"So she is available?" Hassan asked Sam. "We can finish the test?"

"I'm not doing any test." Layla gave Hassan a tight smile. "I'm terribly sorry for the misunderstanding. My father arranged this meeting without discussing it with me. I'm not looking for a husband."

"But you're old," Hassan said. "And in urgent need. Who's going to marry you if not me?"

"Someone with whom I can share interests and who supports my independence and my career. Friendship is key, as well as good communication so we have a lasting, maybe even loving, partnership."

"But you don't understand," Hassan persisted. "I need your family to cosign a loan as dowry so I can stay in the country."

Ah. The truth came out. Sam had been warned about the scam when his family was looking for a husband for Nisha. "So you weren't really looking for a suitable match or a lifelong companion, you just needed a way to get a visa." He stood so quickly his chair toppled over. "Get the hell out of the office before I toss you out in VBC."

"What's VBC?" Layla whispered as Hassan gathered up his papers.

"Very bad condition." Sam growled, sending Hassan scurrying out the door.

"Thank you for threatening to harm someone on my behalf." Layla made her way to her desk after Hassan had gone. "You'll have to forgive me if I don't look at you. I'm afraid I might die of mortification. I had no idea this was going to happen."

"You might want to take down your online profile," Sam suggested. "Hassan might be the first of many, and I don't want to have to deal with men beating down the door to get into your pants when I have a business to run."

"How considerate." She pulled up the desilovematch.com website. Sam blinked as his eyes were assaulted with flashing images of happy couples in traditional wedding attire superimposed on bright pink and orange screens.

"I can't believe people still have arranged marriages." His lips thinned in disapproval.

"My parents and my brother all had successful arranged marriages." Layla scrolled through the website. "My parents adore each other, and they found my brother the perfect wife."

"How perfectly wonderful." He couldn't keep the sarcasm out of his voice. What the hell was he doing? He had a business to run. One of his clients was waiting for a financial analysis. An HR manager wanted to set dates for layoff meetings. Karen had texted to ask if he had a stethoscope and a pair of rubber gloves, and Royce wanted to talk about a new contract. He was letting himself get distracted by a woman who shouldn't even be here, and drawn into a world he'd rejected years ago.

This had to end now.

He would ask John for a legal opinion on the contract.

And then Layla would be gone.

COULD this day get any worse?

Layla dropped her head into her hands and sighed. First, the visit to the hospital where her dad lay so unnaturally quiet and still, then rolling roti in the kitchen until her fingers ached. And now she had to deal with a cocky, arrogant bastard with no moral compass, strange men with marriage proposals, the knowledge that her father had secretly been trying to find a husband for her, and a website that wasn't going to let her in without a password.

"What's the matter?" Sam had returned to his desk and was banging on his keyboard like it had done something wrong.

"I can't find myself."

"That's very profound. I didn't expect that from you."

Layla groaned. "I can't access my profile. I suppose I could set up an account as a man and try to find it but I'm just not in a creative mood." She hesitated. "Do you have an account?"

He gave an affronted sniff. "Do I look like a man who has trouble getting women?"

She bit back the retort on the tip of her tongue. He was beautiful; if that was a word she could use to describe a man. His hair was thick, dark, and neatly cut, and his tanned skin made his light brown eyes seem almost caramel. With that strong jaw and full lips, he was the most breathtakingly handsome man she had ever met.

Sam smirked into the silence. "I'll take that as a no. But since I'm not going to get anything done with all that sighing, I'll set one up so you can find your profile." He crossed the floor to her desk.

"Who knows? Maybe I'll hit the jackpot and women will be beating down the door to get into *my* pants. Oh, wait. They already are."

She shifted her chair to give him better access to the keyboard, her body tingling when his arm brushed against her shoulder. "I appreciate the help, but don't think this means I'm letting you have the office."

"You can owe me a favor instead." He grinned, and her heart did a curious flip. Why did he have to be so gorgeous? All that tall, dark handsomeness, the mouthwatering body, the deep voice that caressed her skin like velvet . . . wasted on an arrogant, egotistical jerk.

"It's not a game."

"Everything is a game."

"You have a very cynical view of life."

"For good reason," he said quietly as he filled in the form on the screen.

She wondered what had happened in his life to make him so pessimistic. Outwardly, he had it all—looks, charm, a successful company, and the kind of confidence that she admired. There were hidden depths to Sam Mehta. Too bad he wouldn't be around long enough for her to explore them. She could learn a little something about him, however, by reading his online form.

Sam Mehta

Age: 32

Education: BSc, MD, MBA

She stared at him, incredulous. "You're a doctor?"

"I didn't finish my surgical residency. I thought it would be more fun to fire people for a living instead, so I left medicine, completed a one-year intensive MBA, and formed a partnership with Royce."

There was a lot to unpack in that statement, not the least of which was the pain in his eyes that he tried to hide by looking away.

"Brace yourself for the stampede." He clicked the DONE button and leaned back in his chair. "I'm about to unleash my formidable self on the women of desilovematch.com." Leaning closer, he read the words off the screen. "I'm looking forward to 'finding the happiness with someone new.'"

"Don't get distracted. You're supposed to be finding the happiness with me."

"That seems unlikely," he said with a bitter laugh. "I like demure, respectful, obedient women who don't throw stationery, call me names, and try to kick me out of my own office. And since I have yet to see you smile, I haven't even been able to assess the health of your teeth."

"Maybe you should say something funny; I might smile then."

"We matched." He pointed to the screen. "Given your violent antipathy to me, there is nothing funnier than that."

Layla quickly skimmed through her online profile. There wasn't much more to it than Hassan had printed out, save for the introductory paragraph that made her heart squeeze in her chest:

Beloved daughter
My Layla
Make her happy
Treat her with kindness and respect

"He loves you very much," Sam said.

"Yes, he does." Her voice trembled. "He wanted to fix my whole life but I was only with him for ten minutes before he had a heart attack. And it was my fault. I should have told him before I arrived that I was coming home for good. The shock was too much."

Sam squeezed her hand, his palm warm against her skin. "I'm sure that's not the case. If you check his medical chart, I'll bet they haven't written down 'Cause of heart attack: daughter shows up with blue hair and threatens to stay.' Although, if you're planning to meet more suitors you might want to rethink your next hair color choice."

"What if there are more?"

"You'll need to access your father's e-mail account to find out."

"I know his password." She leaned over him and opened a new window to access her father's e-mail. "He's been using the same one for years."

A few moments later she was in her father's e-mail account and scrolling through the unread e-mails in his personal folder, many wishing him a speedy recovery and some reminding him about unpaid bills. She made a mental note to deal with them later and clicked on a folder titled "Desilovematch." Her father had separated the file into subfolders: "Yes," "No," "Maybe." She opened them all and gasped as hundreds of e-mails filled the screen.

Sam let out a long, low breath. "You're a popular girl."

"My mother said he'd been locked in his office since I called to tell him about my last breakup. She didn't know what he was doing. I guess this was it." She opened her father's online calendar and checked it against the folders. "He made appointments to see the ten men in the 'Yes' file. Hassan was the first."

"Ten blind dates. You are a lucky girl."

Feeling nauseous, she sipped her water. Her father must have sifted through hundreds of marriage résumés to narrow the field down to these ten names. Ten men he thought would make her happy and treat her with kindness and respect, unlike Jonas and all the men she'd dated before him.

Layla had always considered herself a modern desi woman. She was as comfortable in a sari as she was in jeans and enjoyed hamburgers and potato chips as much as dal and curry. Her life revolved around Western friends and a large and extended family of immigrants from Northern India and Pakistan who had brought their culture and beliefs with them—one of which was the benefit of arranged marriage over the Western concept of love.

Despite Dev's wonderful relationship with Rhea and the success of her parents' union, Layla had never been interested in having an arranged marriage. Even after a string of failed relationships and heartbreak, she had always believed in true love. Her soul mate was out there waiting for her. All she had to do was open her eyes.

"Are you okay?" Sam's gentle tone pulled her out of her thoughts.

"I was just thinking."

"Don't try too hard. I thought I saw steam coming out of your ears." Sam stood, carefully adjusting his jacket as he made his way back to his desk. From the fit and the cut of the material, it was clearly high-end and likely very expensive. For the first time she noticed the fancy watch on his left wrist, the gold cuff links, and the crisply pressed shirt. His business wasn't a fly-by-night operation if he could afford to dress like that.

"Funny. You're a funny guy, Sam."

"I can honestly say no one has ever described me that way." He cleared off his desk, carefully putting his pencils and pens away. "I felt more comfortable when you were cursing like a sailor and calling me filthy names."

"Are you conceding defeat?" She tried to keep the hopeful tone from her voice when he tucked his laptop into his leather briefcase.

"Of course not." His dark eyes flashed with mirth. "I have a business meeting in half an hour which I had hoped to conduct here, but I'm too much of a gentleman to intrude on your privacy while you crush the hearts of ten sad and lonely men. I look forward to battling with you tomorrow, Miss Patel. May the best man win."

After the door closed behind him, she sat back in her chair surrounded by his warmth and the intoxicating scent of his cologne. She knew his type. Hated it. Arrogant. Cocky. Egotistical. Ultracompetitive. Fully aware of how devastatingly handsome he was. A total player. She would have swiped left if his profile had popped up on desi Tinder.

So why couldn't she stop smiling?

· 6 ·

CRAMMED between a dollar store and a run-down pawn shop, Joe Puglisi's Boxing Club was spit-and-sawdust at its finest. Sam had been training at Joe's with his friends Evan and John three times a week since he left medical school, addicted to the brutality of the early-morning training sessions as much as the actual fights.

"You warmed up yet?" Evan Archer called out from the free weights. Shorter than Sam by a good two inches, stockier and more muscular, Evan had the kind of messy blond hair women always seemed to want to touch. His eyes were hazel, shifting to dark brown when he was riled or pounding on Sam in the ring. A marketing consultant and amateur MMA fighter with ambitions of going pro, Evan embraced the idea that exercise was both a form of punishment and physically redemptive. Despite the bruises and brutally draining sessions, Sam never felt redeemed, but the physical pain that lingered after each session overrode the pain he carried in his heart.

"Joe came up with a series of unpleasant sit-up variations I need to get through. Give me five minutes, and I can meet you in the ring." Sam pulled himself up, breathing in the familiar scents of vinyl and sawdust mixed with sweat. The gym was his retreat, the only place he could put aside his emotional pain and pay in blood and sweat for what he'd done to Nisha and his family and the hundreds of poor souls he fired each month.

"He's weak," John shouted, his skipping rope whistling through the air, making his straight dark hair stand on end. A marathon runner, attorney John Lee didn't even break a sweat on Joe's cardio exercises, but he couldn't match Sam and Evan when it came to skill in the ring. "I think it's his age."

"We're the same damn age." And in the same situation with the ladies. Sam didn't want to commit and John couldn't commit. After being abandoned by his father, John had raised his younger brother singlehandedly while his mother worked three jobs to support them. He had put himself through law school and started his own firm, Lee, Lee, Lee & Hershkowitz, with three friends, but had been unable to move past his abandonment issues to maintain a relationship for more than a few months.

John transferred the handles of the ropes to one hand and jumped back and forth. "I've got that legal opinion you asked for in my bag. You can give Nasir's daughter the printed copy. There's no question you have the legal right of occupancy. But are you sure you want to do this? Nasir's a good guy, and there's no reason to think his daughter is lying. Legally, the office is yours, but is it right or fair to go against his wishes?"

Sam felt a strange tightening in his chest. He lay back, trying to breathe the curious sensation away. He was doing this for Nisha. For justice. The office location was a key element of the Alpha Health Care pitch, and he couldn't afford to lose it. "I know what I'm doing. I can handle her."

"Can you handle me standing over you with a victory grin?" Evan dropped his weights and joined Sam on the mat. Vastly more experienced, he had never lost a fight to either Sam or John over the years.

"Two shots. My fist in your face. Your face on the mat," Sam countered with a confidence he didn't feel in the least.

Evan clapped him on the back. "Someone's feeling lucky today."

Not lucky, but he'd woken this morning with a curious sense of anticipation. He didn't remember the last time he'd started his day with anything other than a feeling of dread, so this peculiar lightness in his chest had to mean this was the day Evan was finally going to kiss the canvas.

"You do seem unusually upbeat." John helped him to his feet. "You're not your usual sullen, morose, and uncommunicative self. Is it the new office? Change of scenery good for the soul?"

Sam's mind flashed to an image of Layla walking across the office, her jeans clinging to her curves, the dreadful Nickelback T-shirt pulled tight across her ample breasts. Then he remembered the office supplies flying at his face, the stubborn set of her jaw, her *Juicy* ass, and the hideous purple couch. Such an aggravating woman. And yet, when he thought of the way she'd rubbed up against him when she'd jumped to get the résumé, his lips quivered at the corners.

"Or is it the girl?"

Sometimes it sucked having a friend who was a lawyer. John was far too astute, and when he started with the questions, there was no escaping the truth.

"What girl?" Evan pulled two sets of gloves from the equipment box and handed one pair to Sam.

"The one he's planning to throw out on the street even though her father is ill."

Evan's face lit with interest. "Do tell."

Sam brought Evan up to speed on the office situation, the contract, and Nasir's secret plans to find Layla a husband.

"What does Royce think about the whole situation?" Evan and Royce had been friends since college. After Sam had left medicine and completed his MBA, Evan had hooked him up with Royce, who was looking for a partner to join his new consulting business.

"He doesn't know."

Evan chuckled. "Find her a husband and she'll be too busy planning her wedding to worry about setting up a new business."

Sam shook his head as he pulled on a glove. "She's stubborn as hell, irritating, strong willed, and far too competitive to give up the office because someone wants to put a ring on her finger." She was also the sexiest goddamn woman he'd ever seen, but that wasn't information he was willing to share. "She's disorganized, unprofessional, and her taste in furniture is even worse than her taste in friends."

"Sounds like my kind of girl."

Sam's stomach tightened at the thought of Evan with Layla. With his good looks and easy charm, Evan was the king of hookups. Sam couldn't remember a night when they'd left a bar together.

"She's not your type."

"I don't discriminate," Evan said, misunderstanding. "I like all women. Last week I hooked up with a girl who'd had plastic surgery to give herself elf ears. Her elf name was Buttorwyr. She kicked me out when I called her *Butt* for short."

"What a surprise." John made no effort to disguise the sarcasm in his voice.

"She won't be around long enough for you to work your magic." Sam climbed through the ropes to join Evan in the ring. "John says the law is on my side. I'm going to tell her to clear out her stuff by the end of the day." No second thoughts. It didn't matter that she was beautiful and smart and snarky enough to keep him on his toes. He couldn't afford to get distracted.

Evan smashed his fist into Sam's face, sending him staggering back into the ropes. The world began to spin, and he dropped to his knees, the side of his face throbbing from the powerful blow.

"What the hell was that?" he shouted, more angry with himself than with the friend who had caught him off guard.

Evan held out a hand to pull him up. "Wake-up call. You weren't paying attention."

"WHAT the hell happened in here?" Sam pushed his way into the office, shoving aside half-empty boxes of dishes, baskets of shoes, fuzzy blankets, bags filled with clothes, picture frames, stuffed animals, shampoo bottles, and bolts of colorful fabric.

"You're a late starter, I see." Layla looked up from the rosewood desk. She had removed all his belongings and scattered them across the Eagerson in a heap. "I've been up since five A.M. I spent two hours in the kitchen with my mom, visited my dad in the hospital, and made it here just as the movers arrived with my stuff from New York."

Sam stared at the mess aghast. There was no way he could work in this chaos. How would his clients even make it through the door? "Why would you have your personal belongings delivered to your office instead of your apartment?"

"First of all, I'm living with my parents while I figure my life out. Second, these aren't my personal belongings. This is what I had in my office." She leaned back in her chair, folding her arms under her chest, drawing his attention to the filmy white blouse that was unbuttoned low enough to reveal the crescents of her breasts.

He forced his gaze up only to notice that her hair was down and fell over her shoulders in thick, dark, glossy waves. How the hell was he supposed to focus when he had to look at her all day? Why couldn't she have worn something loose and hideous? Maybe a One Direction T-shirt or a woolly hat . . .

Sam lifted a bolt of fabric. "How was this used in the recruitment business?"

"I found it on sale in a small fabric store one lunch hour and put it under my desk and totally forgot about it until I was leaving. Isn't it pretty? I'm going to ask Nira Auntie to make it into a salwar kameez for me. She owns a clothing store on East El Camino Real."

"This is a place of business." Sam tossed the bolt into the nearest box. "Not a storage warehouse." He dropped his briefcase on the messy desk, cringing at the disarray.

"Chill, Sam. You are entirely too uptight. I'll get everything organized and you'll never even know it's all here." Layla grabbed a coffee cup from her desk and treated him to a view of her perfect ass molded by a tight black skirt as she walked to the office kitchen, her black heels clicking softly on the wooden floor.

He growled under his breath. This was warfare of the most insidious kind. He slid into his seat, cursing his new slim-fitting suit. Clearly the designer didn't have to deal with sexy women in tight skirts and high heels or he would have left a little extra "comfort" room for the unexpected expression of desire.

"If I were uptight, I would have tossed you and your couch out the first day I walked in here." He reached into his bag and pulled out the legal opinion.

"I heard that," Layla called from the kitchen. "And if you're done hating on my furniture, you can come and help yourself to some coffee and breakfast. I bought donuts and my mom made some dal parathas from yesterday's leftovers."

"Donuts and dal again? You're the epitome of culturally confused."

Layla shrugged as she emerged from the kitchen, coffee and treats in hand. "Dal is my comfort food. I'm still depressed about my breakup. The donuts are just part of my plan to work my way through all the bakeries in the city now that I'm back. You can join me, or you can just watch my hips expand."

Her hips were delightful just the way they were. Not that he was going to share his thoughts. He was already having enough trouble dealing with the situation down below.

He breathed in the rich scent of coffee and cursed himself inwardly for deciding to forgo his morning espresso in favor of trying to beat her to the office. He didn't function well without his caffeine kick, but damned if he was going to accept it now after she'd rubbed in her early start. "No coffee."

"I have chai if you prefer." Her lips curved in a teasing smile, but Sam didn't take the bait.

"I told you, I don't touch the stuff." Of all the traditional foods he'd given up, he missed chai the most. His mother had made the flavored tea by brewing black tea with her own special mixture of aromatic Indian spices and herbs. It was his comfort drink. But he didn't allow himself those comforts anymore.

"How about water? I watch a lot of science TED Talks. Your body is sixty-five percent water, so you must have had a glass or two in your life."

Too much talking. Too early in the morning. Given the hostile nature of his job, Sam preferred to start his workdays in peace. "Are you planning on poisoning me? Is that why you're pushing the beverages so hard?"

"I was trying to be polite. Obviously my efforts are wasted on you." Her breasts bounced gently beneath her filmy blouse as she walked back to her desk. Even if he'd wanted the coffee, there was no way he could stand up now and give her the legal opinion. It was going to take at least ten minutes of reading stock reports before he could even consider moving from his desk.

Sam pulled a sports drink from his bag. He'd already had his usual post-training breakfast: two egg whites, two slices of whole-meal toast with peanut butter, one glass of skim milk, and one banana, but the combined scents of coffee and dal parathas made his mouth water.

"Sugar water. I should have guessed." She gave him a cheeky smile as she settled in her chair. "Good thing you brought your own beverage. I considered adding a laxative or even a spoon of ipecac syrup to the coffee, but there's only one bathroom and I'll need to freshen up for my clients."

Coldhearted woman. She wasn't even ashamed to admit she'd planned to incapacitate him.

"Oh God," she blurted out, her gaze fixed on her screen. "Another desilovematch.com dude wants an appointment to see my father. What am I going to do?"

He was tempted to tell her to pick one and get married, leaving him in quiet possession of the office, but then he thought of Nisha. If he'd known how easy it was for a predator to hide behind degrees and awards and a charming smile, he would have torn up every résumé his parents received on her behalf when he had the chance.

"Tell him to take a hike."

She sipped her coffee, her brow creased in consternation. "I was going to contact them all last night, but then I started thinking about all the work my dad did to find them. He wrote that lovely profile, reviewed hundreds of résumés, talked to these guys on the phone, and arranged the meetings . . . And all the time he was thinking about me and what kind of person I was and who would make me happy."

"You couldn't figure this out for yourself?" He cringed inwardly at his harsh words. Who was he to criticize? He'd given up the pursuit of happiness long ago.

Far from being offended, Layla just shrugged. "I've gone from one disastrous relationship to the next. My last one ended when I found my boyfriend, Jonas, snorting coke off two naked models in our bed. The worst part was, he asked me to join them, like I was his pal instead of his girlfriend. And that wasn't the first time . . ."

Sam's eyes widened. This woman was full of surprises. "You've found other boyfriends in bed with models?"

"No." She sipped her coffee, her slender throat tightening as she swallowed. "But after my brother, Dev, died, I became very depressed and I made a lot of bad choices, especially with men. I missed him so much. He used to look after me when my parents were busy with the restaurant. He was a great big brother, always there to solve my problems . . ."

"I didn't know you lost your brother." He dropped the legal opinion on his desk. "If I said anything inappropriate . . ."

"No. It's fine." She lifted a dismissive hand. "It was five years ago. I'm over it."

Sam wasn't so sure. She was staring at her keyboard, coffee cup frozen in midair. Despite their antagonism, he had a curious urge to make her smile again. "Your old boyfriend sounds like an idiot," he offered. "You're hardly plain."

Her head jerked up, eyes flashing with annoyance. "I'll write that one down and stick it on my screen. When I'm having a bad day, I'll read 'You're hardly plain,' and it will make me feel so much better."

"Are you fishing for compliments?" He straightened the papers, arranging them in neat rows. "Doesn't seem to be your style."

"You're right." She placed her cup on her desk. "My style is jeans and T-shirts, and occasionally I'll go crazy with a kick-ass pair of boots."

"Those were good boots."

"Rein it in, tiger, we're talking husbands, not boots." She twirled back and forth in her chair.

"Right," he grumbled. "I forgot you were foolishly considering playing the marriage game."

"You don't approve?"

"Of arranged marriages? No. You can't possibly know everything you need to know about someone after reading their résumé and meeting them once or twice with your entire family present. It's a backward, antiquated tradition that needs to be legislated out of existence. A guy shows up with a bunch of degrees and a sizable bank account, wins the family over with false declarations and fake charm, and the next thing you know, your sister is in the hands of a monster." He didn't realize he had raised his voice until his words echoed around the room.

Silence.

"Are we talking about someone you know or people generally?" She studied him so intently he wondered if she could see into his soul.

"I've seen how it can go horribly wrong." There was no way he would let a woman as vibrant and vivacious as Layla suffer the same fate as Nisha.

"And I've seen how it can go right." She crossed the floor to his desk, stepping over boxes, hangers, and a curious stuffed sheep to reach him. "I'm not talking about forced marriages. I'm talking about an arranged introduction. That's how it was with my brother and his wife. Dev was busy with his career so he asked my parents to help him find a partner. They posted his profile. Rhea's family responded because she also had a busy career and no time to date. Our families met. Dev and Rhea clicked. They went out on a few dates. Three months later they were married. If it hadn't worked out, either of them could have walked away."

"So you want to be just like him? Is that it?" Sam asked bitterly. "Your parents found your brother a spouse and you want one, too?"

"Sam." She slammed her hands on her desk, her nostrils flaring. "Be serious, if that's even possible for you. I've never even thought about an arranged marriage until now. I always believed in true love, just like in *The Princess Bride*. I always thought my Westley was out there. I just had to find him."

Be serious? He couldn't remember a day since the accident when he'd been anything but serious. The burden of Nisha's pain weighed heavy on his soul, painting his world in shadows. How could Layla possibly mistake his caustic comments for humor?

"So, what's the problem? Just sit back and wait for this Westley person to show up at your door."

"This Westley person?" She gave him an incredulous look. "Have you not seen *The Princess Bride*? It's the greatest movie of all time. Westley was the perfect man. He was a poor farm boy who would do anything Princess Buttercup asked of him because he loved her."

"Sounds like an idiot to me," Sam said. "What kind of man lets a woman boss him around? Did he have no self-respect?"

"He had true love. And it never died, not when he had to leave her, nor when he came back years later and discovered an evil prince was trying to force her into a marriage she didn't want."

"So that's a no to the self-respect." Sam lined his pens up beside his pencils. "If he truly loved her, he wouldn't have left in the first place, especially if there were evil princes sniffing around his woman."

"He had nothing to give her so he went to seek his fortune. He wanted to be worthy."

Sam didn't watch many movies, especially not ones with princesses and true love, but the farm boy's quest for worthiness resonated with him. He had lost his sense of self-worth the day Nisha told him about Ranjeet's drinking and violent temper and her suspicion that he had been responsible for her accident. "Did this Westley person find what he was looking for?"

"He became a pirate, made his fortune, saved her from the marriage, and they lived happily ever after."

"There are no happily ever afters." Would that he had become a pirate and saved Nisha so she, too, could have had a happy life.

"I don't know, Sam." She sat on his desk, legs casually swinging over the edge like they'd crossed the stage in their relationship where the intrusion into his personal space was in any way acceptable.

Sam flipped over the legal opinion and held it on his lap because the alluring scent of her perfume and the soft curves only inches away were creating problems down below.

"What if my dad doesn't make it?" Her voice trembled. "What if this is the last thing he does for me? I'm tired of bad boyfriends. I want to come home every day and share my life with someone who's committed to the relationship in the same way as me. I came home to fix things, reinvent myself. New life. New job. New outlook. So why not extend that to relationships, too? Why not meet the men my father chose? They can't be worse than the guys I picked myself. They posted their profiles online because they want to get married. They aren't going to string me along and break my heart. Love is out of the equation."

"There are other options," he said brusquely. "You don't leave a decision that can affect the rest of your life to your parents. You're beautiful, smart, and ambitious. You don't need any help finding a date . . ." His voice trailed off when he registered the shock on her face. "What's wrong?"

"I thought you hated me."

"I hate that you won't get out of my office," he said quickly, trying to cover his mistake. "I don't know you well enough to hate you, although if you put a laxative in the coffee I can see things going downhill very quickly."

Her soft laugh warmed his heart. "I know you're against arranged marriages, but you've actually convinced me to give it a try. How different is it from Tinder except my dad did the picking and he clicked *yes* instead of swiping right? I won't have to deal with six-foot toned bodybuilders who turn out to be five-foot-five nerds who live in their mother's basement."

He found his indifference vanishing with disconcerting speed at the thought of Layla with toned bodybuilders and desilovematch .com strangers. "How are you going to run a business when you're constantly running out on dates?" he protested. "There are ten names on that list. It's crazy."

"I'll meet them in the boardroom," she said. "You won't even know we're here."

But he would know. He would look at them and wonder if there was a monster hiding beneath the mask just waiting to get her alone and away from her family so he could abuse her. And he would worry, just as he'd worried when she'd led Hassan into the boardroom and closed the door.

He glanced over at the purple brocade couch with its gold braiding and intricately carved rosewood frame, considering another tactic. "If they responded to the profile your father posted, they're likely to be very traditional. They'll get the wrong idea if you don't have a male relative present." He almost couldn't believe the words coming out of his mouth. Since when did he care about tradition or propriety? Or about this woman who was hell-bent on stealing his office?

"I don't need a man to find a man," she retorted. "Also, I can't let anyone in my family know. If they thought I was in the marriage market, they'd go crazy."

"Hassan was checking out your ass when I walked in. What would have happened if I wasn't there?"

"I would have kicked him between the legs and broken his nose if he'd tried anything." She punched the air, her fist whistling past his ear sending a rush of adrenaline through his veins. "I took Krav Maga in New York because my parents were convinced the city was full of criminals just waiting to pounce."

"So the office is going to become both a fight club and a brothel." His hand clenched beneath the desk in frustration. "I'll be sure to tell my clients to bring cash when they come for meetings."

"Fine. I'll meet them somewhere else." She tipped her head to the side, giving him a sultry, smoldering look that made him hold the papers in his lap an inch higher. "Unless . . ."

"Unless what?" The skin on the back of his neck prickled in warning.

"Unless you act as my chaperone."

"Don't be ridiculous," he spluttered. "I'm not a babysitter. And besides, you couldn't afford me."

"Maybe I could pay you another way . . ."

His heart skipped a beat, and for a moment he thought his fantasy of her in those boots on his desk just might come true. "I'm all ears, sweetheart. And a whole lot of something else."

"Not that." She groaned. "If you act as my token male relative for the interviews, I won't kick you out of the office. We can share."

"It's my office."

"That's up for debate."

Not anymore. He stared at the papers in his lap. Did he really want her gone? Especially now that he knew she was planning to meet prospective suitors on her own and throw herself into an arranged marriage with a virtual stranger? Images of Nisha flickered through his mind. Warning bells he hadn't heard. Signs he had missed. How could he let another woman suffer his sister's fate? What if one of the men on Layla's list turned out to be like Ranjeet?

Sam sniffed. "Are you asking me to be your pimp? How will I get my forty percent cut?"

"I'm asking you to use your formidable skills of selecting candidates for redundancy to weed out the duds on my dad's list while protecting my honor in return for peaceful cohabitation of the office." She grabbed a party horn from the nearest box and blew it loudly, making his ears ring.

"What the hell?"

"Christmas party, 2017. I have a whole box of them."

There was nothing peaceful about the office in its current state. Nor had there been any peace when Daisy and her dog had come to visit. Layla attracted chaos and he had spent the years since Nisha's accident trying to get everything in his life under control. The last thing he needed was the burden of helping a strange and obstreperous woman find a husband.

And yet he hadn't felt as alive in the last four years as he had in the last three days.

"I'll vet your johns," he said, thinking quickly. "But in return, when the blind dates are done, you walk away. The office will be mine, free and clear."

Silence.

Say yes. His heart thudded in his chest. For the first time in forever, he felt desire.

"You can't refer to them as johns," she said finally.

Sam breathed a sigh of relief. "They want sex. Safe, regular, readily available sex. That's why they signed up."

"You have a very cynical view of marriage."

"I prefer to think of it as realistic." He licked his lips in anticipation. "Do you agree to my terms?"

Layla nibbled on her thumbnail. "I have a condition of my own. If I don't find a husband, then you have to leave."

Sam's pulse kicked up a notch. He'd missed this. A fast-paced negotiation. A worthy opponent. A worthwhile prize. And the fact that his adversary was a beautiful woman he wanted to bed just made it more interesting.

"You have all the control. You could turn them all down just to win."

"I win either way." She picked up one of his pencils and twirled it over her fingers, a party trick he had never been able to master. "I get the office or I find a husband. But I'm willing to walk away if my father has found a suitable match. The office is your incentive, not mine."

Did he trust her? Yes, she was as genuine as they came, and her integrity made him even more aware of his failings in that regard. He'd been so blinded by the opportunities Ranjeet threw his way that he had missed all the clues that pointed to the fact his brother-in-law had a dark secret.

This was a chance to make up for past wrongs, to be the man he wanted to be while at the same time securing the office that would bring him one step closer to the truth.

"Agreed."

"And we hire Daisy as a receptionist slash office manager," Layla added. "We're going to have your clients, my clients, and ten suitors to deal with. She's a software engineer, but she's between jobs right now. She is incredible with numbers and getting things organized. I know she comes across as a little quirky, but—"

"Not Crazy Daisy. Pick someone else."

Layla twisted her lips to the side and looked around the office, considering. "You can have the rosewood desk."

"Let the marriage game begin!"

Her smile lit up her face. "And may the best woman win."

· 7 ·

"HIRED, fired, or desired?" Daisy's voice carried through the office, drawing Layla's attention to the man at the reception desk.

"I . . ." He ran his hand through his thick, dark hair. "I'm not sure."

Daisy sighed. "Are you looking for a job, planning to fire all your employees like a cold, ruthless capitalist bastard, or seeking a wife?"

"Daisy!" Layla hurried to the reception desk. She regretted telling Daisy about the game, especially since her cousin was less than supportive, but if Daisy was going to handle their visitors, she needed to know all the facts. "I told you before. No swearing."

The courier held out his tablet. "I have a package for Sam Mehta. I need a signature."

"How disappointing." Daisy scrawled her name on the electronic pad. "Are you sure you aren't looking for a wife? We have a single, slightly desperate twenty-six-year-old recruitment consultant available. She is smart, ambitious, pleasing to the eye, and she makes a mean *rogan josh*."

"Daisy!"

"Do you not make a mean rogan josh?" She feigned an innocent look as the courier hustled away. "Because the last time I visited you in New York, my taste buds exploded with pleasure."

"Where is Sam?" Layla checked her phone. "He's supposed to be here at twelve o'clock."

"He had client meetings this morning. Don't worry. He'll be here on time to meet Bachelor #2." Daisy fluffed her white cherry-print '50s-style skirt and settled in her chair.

Layla groaned. "You can't refer to them like that."

"Why not? They're all bachelors. He's number two on the list. You said you're playing a game. It's a perfect way to identify them. *Contestant* didn't seem right because that would suggest you're a prize, and although you are in a metaphorical sense, I wouldn't want to objectify you in any way."

Layla drummed her fingers on Daisy's desk. "What time is it now? We're meeting the guy for lunch and we have to leave enough time to get there."

"Relax." Daisy covered Layla's hand, holding it still. "In the week we've worked together, Sam has never been late for anything. It's unnatural. I think he might be an android. He certainly acts less than human."

"He's just a control freak." Layla took a deep breath to calm herself down. "I think it's kinda cute." Sam had been in and out of the office all week, but they'd had a few civil—and a few not-so-civil—conversations. Layla had also entertained herself by getting in early to mess up his papers and misalign his pens. One morning, she'd even turned his desk an extra five degrees to see if he'd notice—he did.

"You're siding with him?" Daisy's raised voice frightened poor Max, and he barked just as Sam walked in the door.

"Pardon me." Sam's voice dripped ice. "I thought this was a business, not an animal shelter."

"Max is an emotional support dog," Layla explained. "Daisy needs him."

"She didn't need any emotional support all week. Why now?"

"Have you looked in a mirror, dude?" Daisy picked up Max and gave him a hug. "One week with you and I need all the support I can get."

"She tried to work without him, but it was a struggle so I said she could bring him in. He's been very well behaved," Layla assured him. "He hasn't peed on anything—"

"That's a low bar."

"You're very cheery today," Daisy said in a voice that suggested she thought nothing of the sort. "Did you fire lots of people this morning? Feeling good? Rocking that *destroying lives* feeling? I guess you'll be going out to celebrate lining the shareholders' pockets after work. You can order a bottle of Cristal and some caviar and toast all the poor souls who are lined up at the food bank tonight."

Sam slid his gaze to Daisy. "I look forward to the day when your antipathy toward my business is so great that you feel you cannot in good conscience continue to work here."

"I look forward to the day you actually have a conscience and realize that you should honor Nasir Uncle's wishes and skedaddle," Daisy shot back.

"Kudos on the creative vocabulary." He sorted through his mail, strong hands deftly sorting the envelopes. Layla's skin tingled at the thought of being touched by those hands—held, caressed, stroked until she was breathless.

"You wouldn't believe how many languages I had to learn to get my software engineering degree." Daisy's voice pulled her out of the fantasy and her cheeks heated. What was wrong with her? This was Sam—Daisy's least favorite person in the world.

Sam's gaze drifted over Daisy's Riot Grrrl T-shirt. "I see English wasn't one of them."

Daisy's eyes hardened. "What degree did you get to crush human souls?"

"I'll tell you when I crush yours," Sam said, a half smile curving his lips.

"You're sexy when you threaten me," Daisy called out as he made his way to his desk. "Actually, you're sexy when you're not threatening me, but I like that little extra hint of menace."

"Why do you keep teasing him?" Layla asked.

"I can't help myself." Daisy stroked Max, who had finished chewing the arm of the chair and was now looking for something tasty to eat. "There's something about him . . . Who doesn't take advantage of the fact that we've got food from The Spice Mill in the kitchen every day? Who drinks English tea when we have a pot of your mother's homemade chai? Who doesn't want to hear 'Badtameez Dil' to get pumped for the morning? Or 'Mundian To Bach Ke' at the end of the day? He told me that if I wanted to listen to that kind of music, I should just put on 'Despacito.'"

"Not everyone likes curry and Bollywood." She offered Max a pakora from the bag she'd grabbed from the restaurant, and he gave it a curious sniff.

"He's brown. It's in the blood." Daisy pulled out her phone and took a picture of Max with the pakora between his paws.

Layla's gaze flicked to Sam. He was definitely an enigma. Careful observation over the last week had revealed that he worked out most mornings, ate healthy-albeit-boring food, had a coffee addiction, and was very focused and intense when he was working. "Maybe he has allergies."

"To Bollywood music?" Daisy held up her phone. "Let's put on *Mr. India* and see if he breaks out in hives."

"Do you like him? Is that what this is about?" Layla felt a curious pang of jealousy at the thought of Daisy and Sam together. It didn't make sense. She was done with dating and was now committed to a marriage of companionship with no risk of love and the pain that went with it.

"Are you kidding me?" Daisy snorted. "Me and him? Five minutes alone together and one of us would be on the floor with a steak knife through his heart. I am a free bird, my friend, still trying to figure out what I'm going to do with my life, and a man that uptight is the ultimate cage."

She wasn't wrong there. Sam cleared off his entire desk every night and wiped it down with disinfectant. Each morning he pulled out his pencils and pens and arranged them in a neat row beside the perfectly stacked files that sat squarely behind his laptop. He was always impeccably dressed, his tie perfectly knotted, and his hair smoothly combed. His attention to detail was disconcerting for someone who had never stacked anything neatly in her life.

"Did you send us copies of . . . ?" Layla hated to use Daisy's shorthand, but the numbers made sense. ". . . Bachelor #2's marriage résumé?"

Daisy nodded. "And the one for Bachelor #3. To be honest, I think you should consider giving Bachelor #2 a hard pass because Bachelor #3 is a firefighter and the picture he sent . . ." She fanned herself with one hand and held up his picture on her phone with the other. "I love a man in uniform. And he's got a big hose. I'm getting hot just looking at it."

"I can hear you," Sam called out. "This in an office. Please keep the discussion to a PG level."

"How about you keep your dirty R-rated thoughts to yourself," Daisy retorted. "We're looking at a picture of a firefighter holding a hose on the street to cool people off on a hot summer day. In my innocence, I can't even imagine what you were thinking."

"I thought you were using a metaphor," Sam said. "But clearly I shouldn't assume . . ."

Layla glanced down at the picture. The firefighter was bare chested save for the suspenders holding up his fireman pants, which were unzipped in a way that suggested he wasn't on his way to a fire. "That's . . . some hose."

"I can still hear you."

"He's jealous," Daisy whispered. "He wishes he could have a big hose that makes women wet."

Layla walked over to Sam's desk where he was already busy on his laptop. "Are you ready to go? I asked Dilip Sandhu where he wanted to meet and he suggested a new pop-up restaurant down the block. He said since the woman's family traditionally pays, he wanted to go somewhere he couldn't normally afford."

"How delightfully crass."

"It's called Space." She tried not to look at his hands as he finished typing, but with the fantasy still fresh in her mind, it was a losing battle. "It's very exclusive. The only reason I got a table was because the head chef knows my dad. They have twenty-four one-hour sittings every day with only one table per sitting."

Sam groaned as he closed his laptop. "I'd better grab some sandwiches on the way. It sounds like the kind of place you only get two peas and a sliver of asparagus on a piece of butter lettuce that was grown on the highest mountain peak of Nepal and watered with the tears of angels."

"Not a fan of haute cuisine?" She followed him down the stairs and out into the bright sunshine.

"I like food. Lots of it." He stopped at the nearest café and ordered three Reuben sandwiches, two Cobb salads, and three bottles of water.

"Would you like anything?" he asked after he placed his order.

Layla looked longingly as the server handed over his feast. "I don't want to ruin my appetite." She pointed to the baked-goods counter. "You forgot dessert."

"I don't eat sugar."

"Then the meal is wasted." She held open her handbag to reveal her secret stash. "I keep emergency desserts with me at all times—gummy bears, salted caramel chocolate, jelly beans, chocolate-glazed donuts—at least I think that's what they were, and this morning I managed to grab a small container of *besan laddu* and some *gulab jamun*."

"Are you expecting a famine?" Sam pulled out one of his sandwiches and ate as they walked.

"You never know when you'll need a little pick-me-up." She held up her phone and flipped to the marriage résumé of the man they were about to meet. "I'll brief you as we walk so you can stuff your face on our way to lunch."

"I do not 'stuff my face,'" he said with a haughty sniff. "But I do appreciate the offer."

"Dilip Sandhu. Age thirty-five. Five feet four and three-sevenths inches tall. No visible scars. One hundred and thirty pounds. Born in San Diego. Parents emigrated from Mumbai. Father is an accountant. Mother is a seamstress. No siblings. He works at a technology consulting firm as a weights and measures manager responsible for the delivery and implementation of services relating to the testing, calibrating, and certifying weighing and measuring devices. Enjoys dancing, cave diving, and musical theater."

Sam finished his sandwich and pulled out another. "This guy's perfect for you, albeit you'll need to wear flat shoes when you're with him. And maybe hunch a bit. You don't want to be too tall if you're spending your honeymoon in a cave."

"How would you know he's perfect? You don't know what I'm looking for in a partner."

"What are you looking for in a man? I'm curious." He bit into his sandwich, and Layla's stomach rumbled.

She'd never really thought about her ideal man, but she knew what she didn't want—anyone like Jonas or the string of men who preceded him. She pulled a donut from her purse and peeled off the paper napkins. "He needs to respect me and treat me as an equal. He has to support my desire to run my own business and not expect me to take on traditional roles."

Sam twisted his lips to the side as if deep in thought. "So, no missionary."

"Were you born like this or did you take courses on how to be a dick?"

A tiny grin hitched his mouth. "Missionary is the traditional position."

"If you're not going to take this seriously . . ."

His gaze fell to her mouth. "I'm taking it as seriously as you are licking that donut. I don't think there is even a speck of icing left. We should let Dilip know you are wicked talented with your tongue."

Such a waste of a breathtaking man.

"Don't you dare say anything about my tongue." She stopped in front of a bright blue door set into a concrete building on the street corner. "I have a sweet tooth and I am not ashamed. That's all there is to it. No need to mention donuts at all."

"How about buns?"

She looked back over her shoulder and caught him staring at her ass. She was wearing a tight black skirt for no other reason than she'd had a strange urge to feel sexy after Hassan shredded her the other day.

She gave a little wiggle before she walked into the restaurant and was rewarded with the sound of his sharp intake of breath.

"Layla?"

"Yes?" She turned in the doorway, caught a cheeky smile.

"I like sweet things, too."

"THIS isn't what I expected." Dilip carefully sliced his half-inch piece of deconstructed pommes dauphines served with a penny-size drip of fava bean foam reduction. His gaze flicked from Sam to Layla and back to Sam from the other side of the rough-hewn log table.

Space consisted of a giant concrete room with a naked bulb hanging overhead. With no windows, paintings, or decor of any kind, and even less food than Sam had predicted, it was the perfect venue for an interrogation, but a blind date with a potential spouse, not so much.

"I thought I'd be meeting with Mr. Patel and Miss Layla."

"It's just Layla." Sam interjected quickly to prevent the lunch from coming to a premature end. Five minutes into the interview, and he knew he was going to have to work hard to make this guy stick.

"Just Miss Layla." Dilip smiled. One of his oversize front teeth was chipped and crooked, and with his round face, overabundance of straight dark hair, and portly frame, he reminded Sam of a demented beaver.

"He means you can just call me Layla." With a sigh, Layla stared at her empty plate. She'd ordered the curated wild Alaskan sea cucumbers, sprinkled with artisanal milk thistle foraged at dusk from Springdale Farms and served in a sea of pureed stinging nettles. At least Sam thought that's what it was. She'd eaten the entire cucumber slice in one bite.

"Are you sure you wouldn't like something, sir?" The waiter, dressed in a grain sack with cutouts for his head and arms, hovered at Sam's shoulder.

"No, thank you." Sam rubbed his belly and let out a small burp. "I shouldn't have had that second Rueben on my way over. Or maybe it was the Cobb salad. I'm so full I couldn't even handle an amuse-bouche of fermented sardine foam or dihydrogen-monoxide consommé."

Layla kicked him under the table. Hard. But the bruise he'd get from the pointed toe of her shoe was so worth it.

"Mr. Patel would have liked to be here, but because he's ill, I'm taking his place," Sam explained.

Unfortunately, Dilip, manager of weights and measures, didn't think his answer measured up.

"You're her cousin?"

"No."

"Uncle?"

"No."

"Nephew?"

"No."

"Grandfather?"

"Are you kidding me?" Sam spluttered. "I don't have a single gray hair."

"Brother?"

"My brother passed away five years ago," Layla interjected.

"Sister?" Dilip wouldn't give it up.

Sam gave an affronted sniff. "Do I look like someone's sister?"

"These are modern times," Dilip said. "You could have gone through a change."

"I'm all man." Sam leaned back in his chair and spread his legs. "Every goddamned bit."

"I think he feels threatened," Layla gave Dilip an apologetic smile. "He usually only swears before ten A.M."

"I'll have you know, I am very secure in my masculinity." Sam puffed out his chest. "I have a yellow shirt in my wardrobe, and once I even wore it outside. Although to be fair it was two A.M. and I'd forgotten to take out the trash."

"Sam is a family friend," Layla offered.

"A married friend?"

"No," Sam said.

"Engaged?"

"No."

"In a serious relationship?"

"How about we give Layla a chance to ask *her* twenty questions?" Sam suggested. The dude was like a dog with a bone.

"How do you fantasize your relationship with your partner?" Layla asked.

Dilip choked on his fava bean foam reduction and fixed Sam with a panicked stare.

"I think she's wondering what you're looking for in a wife." Sam turned to Layla, making no effort to hide his smirk. "Or did I misunderstand?"

"No. You understood correctly."

"Too bad," he murmured under his breath. "I was hoping you had a secret kinky side. If you ever want to know what I fantasize about, I'll be more than happy to share."

Layla groaned. "I'm not interested in hearing about your aspirations to be a dancer in the Broadway production of *A Chorus Line*."

"I want someone to cook and clean, look after my parents, and manage the house," Dilip interjected. "She should also be willing to perform wifely duties and bear children."

"Wifely duties?" Layla hissed in a breath. "There is so much wrong with those words, I don't know where to start."

Sam sighed. This wasn't going well at all. If he was going to get her married and out of the office, he would have to move things along.

"He was kidding." He nodded at Dilip to play along. "It's a guy thing. We like euphemisms. He could just as easily have said doing the nasty, shagging, banging, screwing, humping, baking the potato, boning, boom-boom, four-legged foxtrot, glazing the donut, hitting a home run, launching the meat missile, makin' bacon, opening the gates of Mordor, pelvic pinochle, planting the parsnip, releasing the kraken, rolling in the hay, stuffin' the muffin, or two-ball in the middle pocket . . ." He trailed off when he noticed their shocked expressions. "Or sex," he added. "He could have just said that."

"No wonder you don't have a girlfriend." Layla gave him a withering look. "I can't imagine a woman who would stick around after you took her for a nice dinner and then said, *Hey babe, let's go launch the meat missile*, or my personal favorite, *release the kraken*."

"I didn't say *I* used them." Sam loosened his collar. Why was the restaurant so damn hot?

"You know them. That's bad enough."

Dilip tipped his head to the side. "What's a kraken?"

"That's what I'm going to do to Sam's head in about three seconds," Layla said.

Sam smirked. "A kraken is an *enormous* mythical sea monster."

"Are we in middle school?" Layla looked around the bare room in mock confusion. "Because I could swear you were just talking about the size of your—"

"How about sports?" Sam asked Dilip. Time to get things back on track before Layla made good on her threat. From the angry looks she was throwing his way, Sam didn't doubt she was fully capable of cracking his head. "I think everyone in this room has the same question. Where is the nearest cave, and can we have a demonstration?"

"Ignore him," Layla said. "He's just jealous because he doesn't do anything exciting. But my family is into sports. My mom and I love baseball. We're huge Giants fans. We never miss a home game."

"The San Francisco Giants?" Sam snorted a laugh. "They aren't a real team. That rich-kid pipeline has been running dry for years."

Layla dropped her head back and stared at the ceiling. "Don't tell me you support the poor A's from the wrong side of the tracks with the stadium that smells of sewage."

"It's about the game, sweetheart. It's about skill. We don't need a fancy ballpark on the cove to kick the Giants' collective ass. We've won sixty-three games in the Bay Bridge Series to your pitiful fifty-seven."

"Who cares about Bay Bridge?" she retorted. "The Giants won the World Series in 2010 against the Texas Rangers, 2012 against the Detroit Tigers, and 2014 against the Kansas City Royals. If you count their wins when they started out in New York, they have a total of eight World Series titles."

Impressive. She really knew her team. Clearly, this wasn't a fly-by-night fandom.

"Two thousand fourteen?" Sam scratched his head, unable to resist teasing her. "Was *that* their last big win? I know they lost ninety-eight games one season. I think that's some kind of record."

Layla growled so softly he wouldn't have heard if he hadn't been sitting on the bench beside her.

So cute. Too bad her team was trash.

"It was a bad year." She sat up and glared at him. "I'm not about to abandon my team for one bad year after decades of success. Everyone deserves a chance, whether it's finding a job or playing ball."

"You seem to have a soft spot for underdogs." He glanced over at Dilip "king of the underdogs" Sandhu, who was quizzing one of the waiters about dessert.

"And you lack faith in people." Layla unbuttoned the top button on her blouse and fanned her shirt as if she'd just participated in an activity that made her hot. Sam looked at Dilip to make sure there was no inappropriate staring, but the dude was fully engaged in his conversation.

"I'm realistic," Sam continued. "Appearances can be deceiving. Behind a mild-mannered man, there may lay a dark villain. I've made it my mission to root those people out of every company I visit so the businesses can thrive."

Layla's lips quivered at the corners. "Or so stockholders can get more money at the expense of average working people who are doing the best they can. No one is perfect, Sam. I've taken paper clips from my office and added a few extra minutes to my lunch break. Am I a bad person? If you came to my business, would you have fired me?"

Yes. But he had the good sense not to share his vision of the world that had lost its color and was now black and white.

"What are your ambitions in life, Dilip?" Sam asked after the waiter had taken Dilip's order.

"I want to become world manager of weights and measures." Dilip spoke carefully as if he'd rehearsed his words. "It will require a lot of travel, but with the wife at home looking after my parents and our kids, I think I have a good chance."

Silence.

Well, except for the sound of hope fizzling and dying.

"That's very . . . admirable," Sam said, scrambling for a way to save the interview. "He wants to rule the world. How much more ambitious can you get?"

Layla held out her hand. "Thank you for coming, Dilip. It was lovely to meet you, but I don't think it will work out."

"But I can dance." Dilip jumped up before Sam could stop him. "I've been learning 'Khaike Paan Banaraswala.'" He flailed in the empty space beside them, attempting to reprise Shah Rukh Khan's dance from the Bollywood movie *Don* with its famous spit-on-the-floor finish.

"Hugs, dude." The barefoot, bearded waiter in his grain sack uniform placed a blueberry on the table before wrapping his arms around the profusely sweating Dilip.

"He must think you were having an episode of some sort," Sam said when Dilip looked to him in confusion. "Just go with it. He probably doesn't get much love in the sack."

Layla kicked him again. Same place as last time. Still worth it.

After Dilip had finished his dessert—deconstructed artisanal blueberry pie with a dioxygen crust—and Sam had lost a fight with Layla over the astronomical bill, they bid Dilip a fond farewell and headed back to the office along the busy sidewalk.

"Take this." Sam handed Layla the paper bag from the café. "You must be hungry after our feast."

She reached for the bag. Hesitated. "Is it poisoned?"

"No."

"Squished?"

"No."

"Did you put a spider in the bag? If so, I'll have to burn it to the ground."

"No insects of any kind."

"Shards of glass? Hot chilies?"

"You don't get the full twenty questions, either." Sam led her to a bench in the shade. "I am giving it to you in good faith. Now eat it before you waste away."

"Thank you." Layla sat beside him and pulled out the Reuben. "Would you like some gummy bears?" She offered her handbag.

"I'd rather eat massaged bison balls with fermented kraut surprise."

Layla laughed, a real belly laugh that ended in a snort. It was the best sound in the world. Why did it have to come from the woman who irritated him the most?

"Poor Dilip. I felt sorry for him." She bit into the sandwich and groaned. "So good."

Sam felt that groan as a throb in his groin. Had they put something in the pureed Antarctic water? If anything, he should like her less after their lunch. She supported a rival team.

"It's not too late to call him back," Sam said. "You, Dilip, his parents, and your six kids could form your own Bollywood dance troupe."

"Give it up," she muttered under her breath.

"I never give up," Sam said. "It's my greatest strength."

"How do you know it's not your greatest weakness? Maybe there are times you should give up and you can't. I kept trying to be as good as Dev, but I never was. I kept trying to make my relationships work, but I couldn't. So finally I gave up on finding my Westley and now I'm going to marry someone I don't love so I don't have to deal with all the drama. Stubbornness isn't always a positive quality." She dabbed her mouth with a napkin, and Sam had a sudden urge to know just how soft her lips were and how they would taste with that little bit of mustard in the corner.

"It is if you call it tenacity." He'd tried every avenue to get justice for Nisha, and now that a door had opened, he was going to do everything in his power to get that contract. Nothing was going to stop him.

She tipped her head to the side. "That was very insightful."

"You sound surprised."

"It wasn't what I was expecting from a man who knows twenty different ways to say *sex*."

Sam preened. "That's nothing compared to the number of ways I know of having sex."

"Lucky thing you're not a Giants fan," she teased. "I wouldn't be able to control myself."

"Yes," he said as she licked the mustard off her lips. "Lucky."

· 8 ·

"BETA! We brought food."

Layla's heart skipped a beat when she heard Taara Auntie's voice in the hallway. She bolted out of her desk and ran over to Daisy. "Sam is going be back any minute. I can't let them know I'm working alone in an office with a handsome, single man."

"If you hadn't turned down Bachelor #3, it wouldn't be a problem," Daisy said. "You'd be engaged to Tarak the firefighter and writing wedding invitations to all his single firefighter friends so I could get laid."

"He showed up in sweatpants and a rugby jersey and he was obsessed with sports." Layla's pulse kicked up a notch as she contemplated how to avoid the auntie invasion. "He said he has a TV in every room of his house including the bathrooms so if he has to get off the couch he doesn't miss a second of his game. He wanted me to send draft menus of the food I planned to make for his sports championship parties: Super Bowl, Stanley Cup, World Cup . . . He boasted about all the famous players he knows. He offered to give me autographed balls."

"I'd like to receive autographed balls." Daisy snickered.

"Beta!" The sound of chappals thudding on wood grew louder. The Indian leather handcrafted slippers were useful both for walking and discipline, although it had been years since her parents had threatened her with a flying chappal.

Her heart pounded. There was nothing she could do. They knew she was here. She just had to get them out before Sam came back.

Max ran to the door, barking in excited anticipation. He knew when Taara Auntie was around, there would be human-size portions of food for him.

"There you are. And Daisy's here, too!" Taara Auntie walked in carrying a giant plastic container. "Good thing I made enough to share."

Salena Auntie came in next with Lakshmi Auntie behind her. Layla gave them each a hug. In their jewel-tone salwar suits, they brightened up the office. "It's so nice to see you. I'm afraid I don't have much time. I've got—"

"A bucket, I hope," Salena Auntie whispered in her ear. "That stuff is toxic. I had a spoon of it this morning and only now I was able to leave the restroom."

"I've never been up here before." Taara Auntie sidestepped them and walked into the office. "Nice and bright. Very modern. Which desk is yours?"

"That one." She pointed to the Eagerson.

"And who works at the other desk?"

"Uhhhh . . ."

"I do." A sly, wicked smile spread across Daisy's face. "I was sitting at the reception desk in case a client came in." She picked up Max and carried him to Sam's desk. "But here I am at my desk with its neat little rows of pencils and tidy little piles of paper and perfectly organized files."

Layla's skin prickled in warning. "Daisy . . . Maybe you shouldn't—"

"But what was I thinking?" Daisy brushed a hand over the pencils, scattering them across the desk. "It's much too tidy. I can't work like this." With another sweep, she spread the papers and files, spilling some on the floor. Max barked in excitement and she let him down to play in the mess.

"How is the business going?" Lakshmi Auntie placed a fishbowl on Layla's desk. Two little goldfish darted in and out of a pink castle and a few plastic plants.

"Not so great." Layla sighed. "I'm getting lots of calls from people looking for work, thanks to the family spreading the word, but no interest from the companies I need to hire them. I've been cold-calling every day, but the employers I've targeted are either using online services or they're working with other agencies. It's only been two weeks, but I thought things would be going better by now."

"Do you tell them who you are?" Taara Auntie asked. "Who wouldn't want to hire the daughter of two Michelin-starred chefs?"

"I do mention it sometimes, but it hasn't helped."

Lakshmi Auntie patted her arm. "Don't call on Tuesdays, Thursdays, or Saturdays. Those are bad-luck days. And wear a black thread around your wrist when you call."

"Superstitious nonsense." Salena Auntie shook her head. "How is she supposed to run a business when she can only make calls for half the week?"

Lakshmi Auntie shrugged. "I didn't make the rules, but I did bring her a pair of fish for good luck."

"Thank you, Auntie-ji." She leaned over to give her aunt a kiss.

"You have to try my new fusion dish," Taara Auntie called from the kitchen. "I call it ambrosia masala. Instead of chickpeas in a *channa masala*, I used marshmallows and added some mandarins and pineapple to the onions like in the American dessert."

Layla and her aunties made their way to the kitchen, where Taara Auntie was filling a bowl with her new dessert. Layla's stomach clenched when the scent hit her nose. "I would love to try it, but I've got a client—"

"What the hell is going on?" Sam's angry voice rang through the office.

"Oh. And here he is." She raced out to find Sam scowling at Daisy, who had her feet up on his desk.

He whirled around to face her. "Look what she's done to my—"

"Mr. Mehta. How nice to see you." Layla grabbed his hand and shook it hard. "Please play along," she whispered. "My aunts are in the kitchen. One of them is obsessed with matchmaking. If she sees you—"

"Who is here?" Salena Auntie called out.

"Just a client." Layla pushed Sam toward the boardroom, keeping his back to the kitchen so her aunties couldn't see his face. "I'm afraid I have to go into a meeting. Thank you so much for coming."

"Is he single?"

"He's in the arts," Daisy said. "Musical theater. Jobs are scarce so he's hoping Layla will find him a new gig. He was in *Annie* a few months ago. Maybe you saw him. He was the one wearing the curly wig and the cute red dress."

"Oh." Salena Auntie gave a disappointed sigh. "Arts."

Layla shoved Sam into the boardroom and closed the door. "Please, Sam." She stood with her back to the door and pressed her hands against his chest in case he tried to escape. "Just stay here until they leave. I know it's wrong, but you don't understand what they're like. They're desperate to get me married, and I don't want someone's husband's third cousin's son popping into the office with his mother because they were"—she made mock quotation marks with her fingers—"'Just in the neighborhood.' Or hearing how we're suited because we both like grapes and were born on a third Wednesday. I want to do this myself."

She looked up through her lashes to find Sam studying her intently. She suddenly became acutely conscious of how hard his chest was beneath his shirt, how his broad shoulders blocked out the room, how she could feel the rapid thud of his heart beneath her palms, and the warmth of his breath on her forehead. She drew in a deep breath and inhaled the sharp, rich scent of his cologne. He was so much bigger than her, so strong. If he wanted to get past her, it would be no trouble for him to move her aside. In fact, he could easily have resisted her pushing him into the boardroom in the first place . . .

"Pretty please with a cherry on top," she whispered.

His eyes darkened, smoldered. Electricity sparked between them. She had a curious urge to lean up and kiss him. It made no sense. This was Sam. The man she loved to hate.

"The dog goes." His deep voice rumbled in his chest, breaking the spell.

"What?"

"The dog goes or I walk out that door and tell them the truth."

Flames licked both her cheeks as his words finally sank in. Of course it had to be a negotiation. "You're talking about Max?"

"Are there any other dogs running around the office?" He drew in a ragged breath. "Yes, Max. This is a place of business. We can't have animals barking at me every time I walk by. It's unprofessional."

"Maybe if you didn't growl at him, you two could be friends." She shuddered, shaking off the inexplicable moment of desire.

Sam reached for the door and she pushed against his chest again. "Okay. Okay. I'll talk to Daisy. But he really is an emotional support dog. It's just been her and her dad and brother since her mom left them to pursue a career in New York. Max got her through a really rough time."

"Are you trying to get me to feel sorry for her?"

Layla shrugged. "She would hate that, but she hasn't gotten over her mom leaving the way she did. When my family found out her dad was struggling to cope alone, they stepped in to help—taking care of one another is what my family does—but it wasn't the same as having her mom around. I got Max from a shelter when she was really down. They've been together ever since."

"Most of my relatives are in India," he said. "And the few that are here I rarely see."

"Sounds lonely. I can't go anywhere without an uncle or aunt or cousin popping up. And they always have food. Daisy and I were in the movie theater the other afternoon and, this is no lie, Pari Auntie was there with her kids and an entire shopping bag filled with Magic Masala and Kurkure that she'd brought over from her last trip to India. And she was like 'Eat, eat' and I was like 'Okay, okay' because no one has to ask me twice to eat Magic Masala chips."

Sam frowned. "You see movies in the afternoon?"

"Don't judge me," she said. "I'm self-employed in a business that I can't seem to get off the ground, and I have a movie habit. And don't say *streaming services*, because some things just have to be seen on the big screen." She took a deep breath. Whenever she was around Sam she couldn't stop talking. One day she would run out of air. "How do you get your kicks?"

"Fight ring."

"I didn't mean literal kicks."

His lips quivered at the corners like he was fighting back a smile. "I train at an MMA gym five times a week. It's a good stress release."

"Sounds intense, but also kind of cool. Have you ever used your skills outside the gym?"

"No," he said after a long pause. "But once I was very, very tempted."

Disconcerted by the pain in his voice, she bit back her sharp reply. "For what it's worth, from what I know of you, the guy probably deserved it."

"Yeah, he did." His voice was hard and cold.

Heat engulfed her. The idea of Sam meting out justice *Fight Club* style made her body turn to mush. Seeing him vulnerable, even for a moment, made her wonder what hidden depths lay beneath that prickly shell.

"All clear!" Daisy shouted from outside.

Layla stumbled back when the door suddenly opened behind her. She lost her balance, hands flailing until she grabbed Sam's tie. Her foot hit something hard. Sam grunted, tipped forward. Unable to fight gravity, Layla went down, pulling Sam on top of her. They landed in a heap on the floor.

Daisy looked down from above. "Well, isn't this cozy?"

Max barked and licked Layla's face, his little tongue soothing the burning in her cheeks.

Layla turned her head and saw two pairs of shoes, one large, black, and shiny and the other pink Converse decorated with sparkles. Thankfully, no chappals.

"What the hell, Layla?" Sam spluttered. "That was a $200 tie!"

"Get off me. It's not my fault. Daisy should have warned us that she was going to open the door." She wiggled beneath Sam but his hard, heavy body was impossible to move, and the more she squirmed, the harder a certain part of it seemed to get.

"I thought you said no missionary," he whispered.

"Oh my God," she raged, keeping her voice low. "Are you getting off on this?"

"I'm a man. You're rubbing yourself all over me. What did you think was going to happen?"

"I thought you were all about self-control." Something she seemed to be lacking at the moment. Fire licked between her thighs. And the heat . . . She felt like molten lava was running through her veins.

"Not around you." He pushed himself up with seemingly little effort and held out a hand to assist her, as if he hadn't just thrown out a little three-word nugget that required further explanation. "Let me help you."

"No, thank you." She threw her forearm over her eyes, blocking out the world. "I would rather lie here and die of humiliation."

"No one has ever actually died of humiliation," Sam said, his voice amused.

"How would you know?" she spat out. "Have you read the death certificates of every person on the planet? I'm sure out of billions of people, there has been at least one death attributed to utter humiliation."

"You must be Nasir's daughter, Layla." The unfamiliar male visitor had a deep voice and a keen sense of observation.

Still lying on the floor, Layla moved her arm away. The visitor's black shoes were clean and polished, his dress pants smartly cuffed. He wore patterned argyle socks that reminded her of the ones Dev had worn for his high school graduation.

Sam crouched beside her and used two hands to pull her up to a sitting position. "Are you hurt?"

"How kind of you to ask about my well-being *after* worrying about your $200 tie." Still, she accepted his help because there was no way to get up gracefully in a skirt and heels.

"Layla Patel, meet my friend John Lee," Sam said. "He's an attorney in the law firm upstairs. He's the one who told me about the vacancy in the office."

"You have nice socks, John Lee." Layla shook his hand.

"Thank you." John was a good-looking guy, his face long and angular, a pair of wire-framed glasses perched on his nose. Slightly rumpled in rolled-up shirtsleeves, his pink-and-blue-striped tie askew, he looked more like a university professor than any lawyer she knew.

"Which Lee in Lee, Lee, Lee & Hershkowitz are you?" Daisy asked.

"The second." John bent down to pet Max, who soaked up the love, rubbing his head under John's broad palm.

"Cute dog. I'm sorry he has to go," John said. "I would have liked to get to know him better."

Daisy frowned. "Why does he have to go?"

Sam shot John a not-too-subtle warning look and drew a line across his throat.

"Sam doesn't want him in the office," Layla offered. "He thinks it's unprofessional."

"I told you not to tell him Max peed on his chair." Daisy picked Max up and hugged him to her chest. "I'll get it cleaned next week."

John gave Sam a puzzled look. "I thought they were le—"

"They aren't."

"Didn't you give her the—"

"No."

"We aren't what? Give me what?" Layla didn't have a good feeling about this hatchet job of a conversation. There was something going on that Sam didn't want her to know.

Sam clapped John on the shoulder and led him toward the door. "Everything's good. The office is working out well. I'm working on a big pitch, and Layla's getting her business up and running. She's having a hard time finding corporate clients but I think she just needs to figure out a marketing strategy."

"I do?"

"You should give her Evan's card," John said. "He's great at this kind of thing. And if I have any clients looking for staff, I'll send him her way."

"Who's Evan?" Her curiosity piqued, Layla followed behind them.

"And Daisy's doing a fantastic job at reception," Sam continued. "So I think we're all set here."

"Fantastic?" Daisy's eyes narrowed. "What were you guys smoking in there?"

"Bye, John," Layla called out as he pushed open the door. "Stop by anytime. We always have extra food from the restaurant. Just come and help yourself."

"That's a good idea," Daisy said. "Lure him back with treats. I've always wanted to get into a lawyer's briefs."

Layla followed Sam back to his desk. "Did you hit your head when we fell? Why did you chase your friend out of the office? And what did you mean about figuring out my marketing strategy?"

"I didn't realize you were struggling." Sam pulled out his phone and texted as he talked. "You don't seem to have a problem finding employees, but they don't pay the bills; the corporates do. And they don't know you exist."

"Thank you for mansplaining my job to me." Too bad Sam's clients were all about letting people go. With his corporate connections and her growing stable of workers, they could have made a good team. "The problem isn't that I am unaware of who pays the bills, but that I'm not good at selling myself to them. I didn't have to hunt for clients in New York. Glenlyon Morrell is one of the East Coast's biggest recruitment agencies. The clients just came to us."

"That's why you need a brand." His phone buzzed and he checked the message.

"They have my name," she protested. "My old boyfriend Jonas is a social media star and he uses his own name, Jonas Jameson."

"Social media is different." Sam sniffed his chair, wafting the air toward his nose. "He isn't trying to attract corporate clients. A company name gives the impression of stability and creates trust when you're dealing with other companies. It makes you appear polished and legitimate. Everyone who comes in here mentions 'Nasir Patel's daughter' or 'the daughter of the owners of The Spice Mill.' You're trading off your parents' brand. You need to figure out who you are and what core values you are going to bring to your company that will make you stand out in a crowded market. It was one of the first things Royce and I did when we went into business together and it made all the difference."

Although she didn't like to be told how to run her company—she had a business degree, after all—everything he said made sense. She vaguely remembered learning about branding in one of her courses, but she hadn't paid much attention because she was more focused on the human resource side of business operations. But why was he helping her? Where was the sarcasm? The cutting remarks? What was his angle on this?

Sam bent to pick his papers off the floor. Layla crouched down to help him. Maybe they didn't always get along, but Daisy had crossed a line messing with his personal space, and she felt bad that he had to clean up after her.

"What if I don't know who I am or what I really want?"

"Then I won't have to chaperone ten blind dates because you won't need an office."

Layla blinked and realized he was being serious. "That kind of sucks as a motivational speech."

"I have a better one, but I only use it when someone loses their job." He moved to stand at the same time as Layla and their heads collided, knocking her off-balance and onto her ass.

"Jesus Christ. I'll be lucky to make it out of the office alive today." Sam rubbed his head. "You're the most dangerous woman I've ever met."

"It wasn't entirely my fault." Dazed, she shook her head, trying to clear away the stars dancing in front of her eyes and stop the ringing in her ears.

He sighed. "I'll help you up."

"I am up."

"No, you're on the floor. Again." He kneeled in front of her, framing her face with gentle hands. "I'm checking for a concussion. Look into my eyes."

She stared into his warm brown eyes, floated on a chocolate sea. "Are you trying to hypnotize me? I have to tell you I'm very susceptible to suggestion. Daisy and I went to see the Amazing Sinbad at the Beacon Theatre in New York. He convinced me I was naked on the stage, and I screamed and tried to cover myself with a program before running out onto the street. Daisy had to bring me back so he could unhypnotize me, but I still wear two sets of clothes when I go to live theater."

"You really are something."

"Is that good or bad?"

"I haven't decided yet." His long lashes swept down when he blinked. She'd never seen a man with such long eyelashes, but then she'd never stared into a man's eyes for so long.

"You have nice eyelashes," she said. "Sexy."

His corded throat tightened when he swallowed. "I can honestly say no one has ever complimented my eyelashes before." His hands were warm on her cheeks as he carefully tilted her head from side to side. "I think you'll be okay. Any blurred vision? Nausea? Dizziness?"

Maybe she did have a head injury. She couldn't be seeing clearly if the man who was fussing over her was the same Sam who had been so worried about his tie. "No."

He released her face to run gentle fingers over her forehead. "I can already feel a bump here. We need to get some ice on it."

"You have a hard head."

"My dad used to say I had a thick skull, but that was when I was being stubborn."

She couldn't imagine Sam as a kid. There was nothing innocent or carefree about him. But she liked the little peek into his past.

"I think I'm okay to get up." She accepted his help and he pulled over his chair.

"Actually, I'll sit on mine. Daisy wasn't lying about Max's accident." She made her way across the office and sat behind her desk. "He was marking his territory. You're the only two males in the office, and he wanted to let you know who's boss."

"That's it. He's definitely gone. There can only be one alpha here."

Layla smiled with amusement. Sam was delightful when he was annoyed. "Lakshmi Auntie says the number three is unlucky. If Max leaves, we'll have bad luck, and neither of our businesses will succeed."

Sam sighed. "Don't tell me you're superstitious."

"I'm keeping the good-luck fish my aunt just gave me, and I won't be making any more calls on Tuesdays and Thursdays, if that's what you mean."

"Make sure you mention that to my friend Evan when you call him." He rounded his desk and handed her a card. "He's a PR and marketing consultant. He'll be able to give you tips about branding." He hesitated. "I'm meeting him for a drink tomorrow night. You can join us if you want and pick his brain for free."

Nausea rose in her throat, and it wasn't from her head injury. She had been unkind and now he was just trying to help. "Now I feel terrible. I would love to meet him. I really am sorry about the knock on the head and not telling you about Max."

"I'm not." Sam grinned and settled into his seat. "I switched our chairs."

· 9 ·

Sam threw a few dollars in the tip jar for the bartender of Red Rock, an upscale sports bar in San Francisco's Design District. What the hell had he been thinking inviting Layla out tonight? Evan was currently between girlfriends and desperate to get laid.

"Describe yourself in three words." Evan brushed back his perpetually mussed surfer dude hair and flashed Layla a sensual smile.

"Passionate. Caring. Impulsive."

Sam would have added *sexy* and *smart* to the list, but he wasn't about to share his opinions with Evan, who had been laying it on thick ever since they arrived. His gaze flicked to the clock above the polished wood bar, barely visible among the jumble of sports pictures and paraphernalia that covered the walls. How long should he wait before making an excuse to take her away? Evan was giving her some helpful tips, but he was also ready to make his move.

"Anything else?" Evan sipped his beer, watching her like a predator on the hunt. Sam had to bite back his irritation. He knew his friend was a player. Why had he expected Evan to act any other way after Sam had introduced him to the most beautiful woman in the bar?

"Competitive." Her gaze slid to Sam. "I grew up with a perfect big brother—straight A's, star athlete, scholarships, engineer—oh,

and he was a son. I banged my head against that wall all my life."
She shrugged. "Sam understands. It's a desi thing."

Sam looked away, his gut twisting at the reminder of his failure
as both a brother and a son. There was no game on tonight to distract him, but the bartender was taking requests for YouTube videos and playing them on the five screens positioned around the bar.
Too bad about all the cat videos. Sam wasn't a cat person. If he were
to get a pet, it would be a dog—big, strong, protective, and willing
to chase away intruders like Evan, who was all over Layla.

"I don't like the thought of this lovely head being hurt." Evan
brushed a gentle finger over her forehead, pulling Sam's attention
away from cats and cucumbers.

Sam's beer went down the wrong way and he choked. What the
hell was wrong with him tonight? His motives for inviting Layla
were entirely self-serving. Even without the game, she would be
more inclined to leave the office if her business was going well and
she could afford her own space. So why did he feel the urge to
punch Evan in the face?

"If you'll excuse me, I have to make a quick call and check in
with my mom." Layla slid off her chair and away from Evan's rov-
ing hands. "She's short-staffed at the restaurant tonight and I just
want to make sure she's doing okay."

After she'd gone, Sam glared at his friend. "I brought her to you
as a potential client, not a hookup."

"She's sweet, hot, and she's got a perfect ass. I'll do the client
thing tomorrow." Evan hesitated. "Unless you two—"

"No." Sam shook his head dismissively. "She's chaos in its purest form. The office is a disaster. It's like she's never heard of a
paper-free workspace. We've got a snarky manic pixie dream girl
receptionist who looks like she ran through a thrift shop on her

way to work, a purple velvet couch with lion's feet, hordes of aunties tromping through the office, and now John and his partners are going to be coming down every day for free snacks."

"I like them a bit crazy," Evan said, watching her talking on the phone across the bar. "More fun in bed."

Sam clenched his fist by his side. He didn't want that image in his head. After years in the downsizing business, he'd learned how to keep his emotions in check. What was it about Layla that turned him inside out? They had nothing in common. If she was interested in Evan, there was no reason for him to stand in the way. And yet, that was exactly what he was about to do. Evan didn't just love 'em and leave 'em. He screwed them and ran away. For the first time Sam wondered why he even called the guy a friend.

"Do me a favor and just help her with the branding," Sam said. "Keep it professional."

"Fine." Evan sighed. "For a start, she'll need to lose the blue streaks in her hair if she's looking for corporate clients. What's that all about?"

"Maybe it's a New York thing. She worked at a big recruitment agency there, Glenlyon Morell."

"I've heard of them," Evan said. "They're very conservative. No way would they be down with blue hair."

A hipster dude in Doc Martens, torn skinny jeans, and a pre-faded fake vintage T-shirt was eyeing Layla from across the room. He nudged his bearded friend, and the two of them sipped from their mason jars while checking her out.

"Maybe she dyed it after she had the bust-up with her boyfriend and moved back to the West Coast," Sam said absently, his hand tightening around his glass as he watched the two men watching Layla. "He's a social media star. Jonas James . . . Or something like that."

"Jonas Jameson." Evan tapped on his screen. "I've heard of him. He's got a lifestyle channel."

One of the dudes tossed the end of his plaid scarf over his shoulder and drained his jar. Sam tensed as he walked in Layla's direction.

"Jameson is a real piece of work." Evan scrolled through Jonas's channel. "He's got the same blue streaks in his hair as Layla. Was she in any of his videos? If she's trying to make a play for corporate clients, she might want to think about asking him to take them down."

"I dunno. I never really talked to her about it." The dude made a sudden turn and put his mason jar on an empty table. Sam let out a relieved breath.

"I think this might be her." Evan studied a video on his phone. "I can't really tell because my phone is busted. Third time I've cracked the screen. I'll send it to the bartender and we can watch it on the TV. Maybe she's giving makeup or hair-dye tips. We could learn something."

"Let me check it out first." Sam reached for the phone.

Too late. The video flashed on the screen.

By the time Sam was able to wrap his mind around the fact that the woman in the "Blue Fury" video, hair and face streaked blue, screaming and tossing clothes off a third-story balcony and into the grassy courtyard below was Layla, it was already over.

"I can't believe that was her," Evan said after "Blue Fury" was replaced with yet another cat video. "That was fucking awesome."

"She was hurting. She wasn't trying to put on a show." Layla had told him about catching her boyfriend cheating on her. She was a passionate woman, fiercely loyal to the people she cared about. No doubt she had expected her romantic partner to be the same. "I just hope she didn't see it."

"It's got over five million YouTube views, dude. Everyone has seen it."

Everyone including Layla.

Her stricken expression as she approached the table told him everything he needed to know. "What did you do?" she demanded, her furious gaze on Sam.

"Nothing. It wasn't—"

"You didn't tell me you were famous, babe." Evan gave her a nudge. "'Blue Fury.' I gotta say, a woman letting it go like that is pretty hot."

"I'm leaving." Layla grabbed her coat, her face an expressionless mask.

"Layla. Wait." Sam moved to join her and she held up her hand, warning him away.

"How could you do this?" She hitched her breath. "I thought you were doing something nice. But this really is a game to you." She pressed her palm to her lips. "Did you and Evan set this up? Do you think I'm going to walk away from the office because you humiliated me?"

"No. Of course not. I didn't know about the video. I mentioned you'd been with Jonas. Evan was checking out his channel when he saw the video—"

"Well, guess what?" She cut him off as if he hadn't spoken. "I've already hit rock bottom, and there's nowhere for me to go but up. I don't need any help. Not from you and not from Evan. I'm going to have the best damn recruitment business in the city and I'll do it on my own."

"Jesus Christ, Evan," Sam shouted when she walked out the door. "What were you thinking?"

"Come on. It was hilarious." Evan ran a hand through his shaggy hair. "Who doesn't like to see themselves on the big screen? Five million views and she's worried about fifty people in a bar?"

"You're an ass." Sam threw a punch and caught Evan in the jaw, knocking him off his seat.

"What the fuck was that?"

"You weren't paying attention."

Evan jumped up, tipped his neck from side to side, making it crack. This fight clearly wasn't going to end with one punch. "Well, I'm fucking paying attention now."

"LAYLA!" Sam ran through the SoMa district, blood dripping from his nose. He'd managed to get in a good first punch, but Evan had proven himself the better fighter yet again by drawing first blood before they both got kicked out of the bar.

Why did he keep making the same mistake over and over again? Why couldn't he protect the people he cared about? He knew what Evan was like. Once he had a couple of drinks, he started thinking with his dick.

Sam pulled out his phone and typed out text after text. If he could just get everything back under control . . .

But it was damn hard to focus when he didn't know if Layla was safe. Had he really introduced her to Evan to further his own cause or because he genuinely wanted to give her a hand?

Where are you?
SoMa isn't safe at night.
Stay away from 6th to 11th.
Are you driving?
Don't answer that. It's not safe to text and drive.
Let me know you're safe.

He stopped in front of an all-night '50s-style diner to staunch the blood coming from his nose with the bottom of his shirt. His nose wasn't broken, but it was going to be badly bruised.

His phone buzzed and he checked the screen.

I hate you.
You're a dick.
P.S. I'm safe.
P.P.S. What happened to your face?

Sam's head jerked up and he looked around. She could see him. A tap on the window drew his attention. Layla was inside sitting at a counter in the window, eating french fries and sipping a milkshake from a giant parfait glass.

Breathing a sigh of relief, Sam made his way through the bustling restaurant. The decor was classic '50s with a red and white checkerboard motif. Silver stools lined a curved counter where servers roller-skated back and forth to the partially open kitchen. Vintage movie posters, and photos signed by the era's greatest stars hung on the white-tiled walls above the red vinyl booths and small tables. Someone had put a few coins in the jukebox and Elvis's "Jailhouse Rock" cut through the noise.

"I already ordered." She barely glanced at him when he sat on the empty stool beside her. "I eat when I'm stressed."

"I'm just glad you're safe."

"Do you?" She looked up from her drink, meeting his gaze.

"Do I what?"

"Eat when you're stressed?"

Sam didn't know why they were having a conversation about food, but he was grateful she was speaking to him at all. "I usually just eat when I'm hungry."

"Yet another thing that we don't have in common." She sucked hard on the straw, her cheeks narrowing, lips pursed into a tight bow. All his blood rushed to his groin and he tried to push away the sensual visual image. But when she released the straw to lick the creamy drink off her lips, he let out a groan.

"You're really hurt." She handed him a napkin, and he used it to wipe the sweat off his forehead.

"It's nothing."

"You're dripping blood on my fries. It kind of looks like ketchup." She pulled the plate closer to her. "What happened?"

"I hit Evan. He hit me back." The two simple sentences didn't even begin to describe the fight they'd had in the bar. Real-life fighting was nothing like the controlled sparring they'd done in the ring. It had been no holds barred, no piece of furniture unturned, no thoughts about any bystanders, just a desperate struggle to survive.

She tipped her head to the side. "Because of me?"

"I was angry at myself for not stopping him in time."

Her face softened the tiniest bit. "Does he look as bad as you?"

Sam shrugged. "Not even close. He's semipro. He's been fighting for over fifteen years. I've never even won a sparring match against him. I got in my first punch because he wasn't expecting it. After that it was pretty much a humiliating beatdown."

"You should probably clean up in the restroom. I'll get some ice. Try not to look at any kids on your way. They might not have seen the *Creature from the Black Lagoon*."

Sam hesitated, still unsettled by her seeming nonchalance. Hadn't she just run from the bar distraught? Didn't she just text that she hated him? Maybe this was a ploy to get him out of the way so she could disappear again. "Will you be here when I get back?"

"Are you kidding? My burger is on its way."

By the time he returned, her meal had arrived along with a bag of ice. Sam tended to his face while Layla tucked into her hamburger. He liked that she enjoyed her food. He'd always wanted a girlfriend who didn't steal his dessert.

Except she wasn't his girlfriend, and she never would be. "I'm sorry about tonight." He closed his eyes as the cold pack soothed his skin. "I should have just set up a proper business meeting, but to be honest I didn't trust him around you."

She paused midbite. "Why? Is he some kind of violent criminal?"

"He can't resist a beautiful woman."

Layla's brow creased in a frown. "Is this part of the game you're playing? Showing up here, pretending like you defended my honor, saying nice things . . ."

He opened his mouth to answer, unsure what to say. "I'm not playing a game. You are beautiful, Layla."

Layla gave a tiny shake of her head. "I didn't feel beautiful when I saw the women Jonas had brought to our bed. Don't get me wrong. I have no desire to be that thin. I like my curves. But it was like he was saying there was something wrong with me, and it made me even angrier because he was right." She attacked the burger like it was a Scooby Snack. Did she really not see her own beauty? Evan had been falling all over himself to get her into bed, and the dudes with the mason jars weren't the only ones who'd been checking her out in the bar.

"What exactly do you think is wrong with you?"

"Do you want a list?" She took another bite of her burger. "Ever since Dev died, I can't hold it together. I was so depressed I slept with pretty much every guy in my college class, and then when I moved to New York to start over, I couldn't make my relationships work. Jonas was just the last straw. I didn't love him, but I wanted to love him, just like I wanted to love all the other losers I hooked up with. I think that's why I lost it when I walked in on him."

"I can't even imagine the pain of losing your brother."

She stared out the window for a long moment and then sighed. "You can see why an arranged marriage is my best option. I don't have to deal with love or emotional commitment. It's a contract. Two people with a shared interest in companionship and family with none of the heartache that goes along with it."

Sam flinched inside. "There's no guarantee you'll wind up in a better situation."

"That's true, but my dad knows me better than anyone. He wouldn't hook me up with a creep."

Sam hoped that was the case. His parents had done their best to screen out inappropriate suitors, and yet somehow Ranjeet had slipped through. Maybe things would be different for Layla. She deserved to be happy. Despite all that had happened to her, she remained upbeat and without any of the regret or bitterness that tainted his life.

"What if your dad doesn't know you as well as you think?"

"Who knows you, Sam?" She ran her finger gently along his swollen jaw. Far from pain, electricity zinged through his body, warming his heart.

"I'm a lone wolf."

"You are looking pretty feral right now." She pressed a soft kiss to his injured cheek. "I saw a documentary on wolves. They're pack animals. Their chances of survival go down when they have no family."

"I have a family." His hand went to his cheek where she'd kissed him. He could still feel the press of her lips against his skin. "I just don't spend much time with them. Work keeps me busy."

"That must be so incredibly hard for them. My parents called or texted me every day when I was in New York and once a week Daisy would set up a video chat for them. They just wanted to stay in touch."

Sam felt a thickness in his throat, a heaviness in his chest. He had never thought about the effect his actions would have on his parents or how they would feel when their son cut them out of his life. All he knew was a guilt that ran so deep he had to push away anything and everything that could possibly be blamed. Why would they want him around? He had failed them. He wasn't worthy of being their son.

"Are you okay?"

"Yes." He shook off the bad feeling. "Aside from the bruises, I'm perfectly fine."

They talked about baseball, the changes in the city since she'd gone to New York, and their shared love of the '50s music that was playing on the jukebox. There were no snarky comments or sarcastic remarks. She was thoughtful, intelligent, and knowledgeable about everything from Indian politics to global warming. He couldn't remember the last time he'd had such a lively and interesting discussion.

After she finished her meal and threatened to break his bruised nose when he offered to pay the bill, he walked her to her car, keeping a watchful eye on the street. He loved the area but it wasn't always safe at night.

"Thanks for coming to explain," she said when they reached her Jeep. "I was planning all sorts of nasty things to do to you tomorrow."

"Why am I not surprised?"

She gave him a quick hug. "Go home and look after those bruises."

Unable to stop himself, he wrapped his arms around her, and they held each other in silence in the still of the night.

"Sam?" She looked up at him, dark eyes glittering under the streetlights.

His gaze dropped to her mouth, those soft, lush lips silently calling his name.

"Yes?" His head dropped lower, heart pounding in time to her rapid breaths.

"I texted Daisy before you found me." She pulled away and gave him a rueful smile. "If I were you, I wouldn't drink the coffee for the next few weeks."

10

"FAROZ Jalal. Age thirty-eight—"

"He's too old for you." Sam held open the door to the busy coffee shop on the Embarcadero and gestured Layla inside.

Bemused by his gallant behavior, Layla waltzed through the door, imagining herself as a desi version of Scarlett O'Hara with an extra dose of tan.

"Did you hit your head on the way over?" she asked over her shoulder. "You're batting for the wrong team. You're supposed to tell me age doesn't make a difference. I like the idea of being with someone mature and worldly. It means I can be fun and silly. I can dance and sing and he'll look at me with fond amusement before sweeping me off my feet and ravishing me in bed with all the erotic skills he's learned in the extra years he's been alive."

Sam snorted. "It will make a difference when he's popping the Viagra and you're still at your sexual peak."

"That's a very pessimistic and utterly depressing way to view marriage." She looked around for a table in the big, open, industrial-chic coffee shop where Faroz had suggested they meet. "Very you. Are you being so down today because of your face full of bruises? They look worse now than they did on Saturday night."

She still couldn't believe Sam had fought with his friend over the "Blue Fury" video four nights ago. Never in her life had she imagined herself as a femme fatale, nor could she wrap her head around the concept of Sam as the good guy in any scenario. With the cuts and bruises on his face, he looked badass today, and she hated to admit how much it turned her on.

"I'm a realist," Sam said. "I suffer under no illusions as to the physical or emotional effects of aging."

"Now who sounds like he's old enough for some performance-enhancing drugs?"

Sam gave an affronted sniff. "I have never—"

"I'm just teasing, Sam." She wiggled her fingers. "You're always so serious, it makes you an easy target."

His jaw tightened and he cleared his throat. "Tell me more about Faroz."

Layla checked the résumé on her phone again. "He lives at home—"

"Christ. Not another one. Doesn't anyone have their own place?"

"Please don't swear," she said over her shoulder. "And if you do, use Urdu so people don't understand. Not everyone has the money to live on their own."

"He's thirty-eight, can't find a woman on his own, and lives at home. That equals loser," Sam said. "Why are you wasting your time? I want to get you married off and out of the office, but there's no way this guy is a real candidate. Why did you even agree to meet him?"

"Because he has an interesting job. He's in the CIA."

Sam swore in Urdu using a few words Layla hadn't heard before. "CIA agents don't tell people they're in the CIA. It defeats the entire purpose of being a secret agent."

"There's nothing I love better than a mysterious man." She put her purse on an empty table. "Maybe he did it for exactly that reason. You think he can't be in the CIA because he said he's in the CIA. It's the perfect cover. Just think, Sam. I could be married to a secret agent."

"I can't think. My head hurts trying to follow your logic."

"We can't all be smart." She grabbed his arm when he pulled out a chair to sit beside her. "Don't sit down. You'll need to find a different table."

"Why?"

"I don't want to hurt your feelings, but you kind of put a damper on the last date. You have a bit of an intimidating, unfriendly vibe going, especially when you scowl and glare at people, like you're doing now, and it doesn't help that you look like you were in a bar fight."

"I was in a bar fight." His forehead creased. "And I'm not scowling."

"Well, then, you're smiling upside down." She pointed to a table nearby. "You can sit there. Close enough to keep things respectable, but far enough that you won't scare him away."

"I don't like it." He removed his jacket and hung it carefully over the back of the nearest chair.

Layla had a sudden burst of envy for the long-sleeved fine cotton shirt that hugged his broad shoulders and muscular chest. When he adjusted his tie, his shirt tightened around well-defined biceps, and she let out a soft sigh. Four days ago, her lips had been only inches away from that chest and her body had been pressed against his. She'd felt something. And so had he. In more ways than one.

"Something wrong?" His lips tugged at the corners in a knowing smirk.

"No." She dropped her gaze, forced herself to study the slightly worn patina of the dark circular table. "I was letting out some air so I could take a deep breath to calm my nerves."

"I'm Faroz." A tall dude in a dark suit, sunglasses, and a crisp white shirt put two mugs of coffee on the table. "You were expecting me."

"This is Sam. He was just leaving."

"No, I'm not." Sam sat down beside her.

"I've taken the liberty of getting your coffee to save time." Faroz sat across from her. "A venti triple shot, almond milk mocha with extra whip and extra sauce. The warmed chocolate croissant is on its way."

"How did you . . . ?" She sucked in a sharp breath and looked at Sam in alarm. He responded by raising an open hand in a *told you so* gesture that did nothing to alleviate her concerns, and everything to ratchet her stress level up to ten.

"Classified."

Layla laughed. "Is it one of those *if I tell you, I'll have to kill you* kind of things?"

Faroz didn't smile. "Yes."

Sam edged his chair so close to Layla they were almost touching.

"I thought you were going to get a coffee," Layla said. "And we had agreed you would sit elsewhere."

His jaw set. "We didn't agree."

"Don't mind him," she said to Faroz. "He's harmless."

"I'm not harmless. I was in a fight." Sam gestured to his face. "I didn't like the way the last guy was looking at her." He growled under his breath, like he was a guard dog instead of a companion. Or maybe he was playing *Twilight*'s overly protective vampire, Edward, to her Bella. Did that make Faroz Jacob? She'd never liked the dark-haired werewolf. She'd been Team Edward all the way.

"Stop it." She glared at Sam. "You're being irritating, which is why I told you to sit somewhere else."

"Then I wouldn't have a chance to really get to know Faroz."

Sam pulled out his phone, his gaze locked on the man across the table. "Daisy sent me a copy of your résumé. You didn't provide many personal details, although it's good to know you have . . ." He read off his screen. "'. . . excellent analytical abilities, the ability to think creatively, foreign language skills, knowledge of foreign countries, culture, and affairs, the ability to write clear and concise text, strong interpersonal skills, and the ability to work under strict deadlines.'"

"It's all a cover," Faroz said.

Layla cocked an eyebrow. "You don't have the ability to write clear and concise text, strong interpersonal skills, and the ability to work under strict deadlines?"

"I'm not who you think I am." Faroz whipped off his sunglasses, and she stared into pupils so large his eyes were almost black.

Sam leaned forward, his face twisted in a scowl. "I'll tell you exactly who I think you are."

"Sam. No. Be nice." Layla gave Faroz an apologetic smile. "He's got protectiveness issues."

"There's no need to worry," Faroz said. "You're safe with me. I would never put you at risk. I am armed and trained in seventeen forms of combat." He moved his jacket to the side to reveal a weapon holstered across his chest.

Layla's pulse kicked up a notch and she reached for Sam's hand under the table. "He has a concealed weapon," she whispered to Sam, although Faroz could easily hear them.

"I see that." Sam threaded his fingers through hers and squeezed her hand. His skin was warm, his touch firm but gentle. It was difficult to focus on Faroz when currents of electricity were tingling over her skin. For all Faroz's assurances, it was Sam who made her feel safe.

Layla swallowed hard. "Are you expecting trouble in the coffee shop?"

Faroz looked from side to side. "I have many enemies. I can't be too careful, especially when civilians are involved."

"Jesus Christ." Sam's hand tightened around hers. "He's a nutjob."

"Sam!"

Sam cursed again in Urdu, this time making references to Faroz's mother, his questionable parentage, his likeness to things requiring sanitary disposal, and various animals.

"That's better," she said, "but it's still not nice to swear or call people names."

Faroz leaned back and sipped his coffee. "When I was held captive and tortured by foreign enemy insurgents, the names they called me would make your ears bleed."

"I would imagine being called names would be the least of your concerns if you were being tortured by enemy soldiers," Sam said, his voice thick with sarcasm. "Unless you have very thin skin."

Layla leaned forward, dropping her voice to a conspiratorial tone. "I think you should know that I'm a huge coward. I won't do well if people shoot at me or kidnap me to get to you. And if torture is involved, I'm a total baby. I'll tell them other people's secrets as well as my own. My friend Jenny, for example, has a tattoo of a llama on her left butt cheek, and Sam—"

"So about the whole secret agent thing . . ." Sam lifted Layla's cup and took a sip of her cooling coffee, his nose wrinkling as he swallowed.

"Classified."

Sam checked his phone again. "How classified can it be when you wrote on the marriage résumé that you posted online: 'Occupation: CIA'?"

"Also classified."

Layla shook her head. "I think the whole 'classified' thing might be a problem for me. Communication is the key to a successful marriage. What if I asked you how your day was, or whether you wanted samosas in your lunch, or if you wanted a quickie in the shower, and you answered *Classified*? It just wouldn't work."

Sam made a sound that was part choke, part cough.

"Are you okay?"

"I'm good." Sam cleared his throat. "I just wasn't prepared for your last comment and the coffee went down the wrong way." He gestured to a stony-faced Faroz across the table. "Not everyone will share your liberal views, so you might want to keep comments of a sexual nature to a minimum."

Layla laughed. "If you think doing it in the shower is liberal, I'll definitely never tell you what I got up to when I found a three-foot-high can of whipped cream at Costco and asked the New York Dolphins men's water polo team to help me carry it home."

"I didn't want to know that." Sam's jaw tightened. "And I suspect Faroz didn't, either."

"I'm joking, Sam. Lighten up. My apartment wasn't big enough to hold all of them at once."

Faroz put his sunglasses back on, as if that brief unfiltered glimpse of her had been enough. "I've seen things that would make you puke up a lung."

"Whipped cream and a water polo team do it for me," Sam muttered under his breath.

Still amused by Sam's reaction, Layla turned her attention back to Faroz. "What kind of things did you see that would make me puke up a lung? I'm asking for my mom. She loves gore."

"He won't tell you," Sam said. "It's classified. Although that raises an interesting issue. I thought CIA agents weren't allowed to operate on American soil."

Faroz nodded. "I'm undercover."

"As what?"

"A secret agent, obviously," Layla said.

Sam snorted a laugh. "If he's a secret agent, how can he be undercover as a secret agent?"

"Haven't you seen *Quantico*?" She sipped her coffee, now cold and sickly sweet. "Priyanka Chopra played a CIA agent who went undercover in the FBI and then she was undercover undercover and then undercover undercover in a secret organization. Or maybe I have one of the double-undercover parts wrong. Anyway, it's a thing."

Faroz's lips moved a hair width from their perpetually straight line in what Layla assumed was a smile. "You are very perceptive."

"She's a movie and TV addict," Sam said. "I'm amazed she has time to work."

"I don't watch horror. I'm easily scared."

Sam stared at her, incredulous. "You haven't seen *The Shining*?"

"No."

"*Psycho*?"

"No."

"*The Exorcist*? *Nightmare on Elm Street*? *The Texas Chain Saw Massacre*?—"

"What part of 'I don't watch horror' did you not understand?"

"But those are classics," Sam protested. "How can you call yourself a movie buff when you haven't seen some of the best movies ever made?"

"Are you seriously comparing *The Texas Chain Saw Massacre* with *Legally Blonde*?"

"I saw horrors overseas that would make you scream like a girl," Faroz said.

Sam tipped his head back and groaned. "Oh, for—"

"I am a girl." Layla pointed out. "Actually, I'm a woman. And this woman doesn't want to scream. She doesn't want to puke up her lung or have to witness the worst humanity has to offer. I'm cheerful, optimistic, and upbeat, and I want to keep it that way."

"The characters in horror films aren't always human." Sam mused as he stroked his bottom lip. "You've got your demons, evil spirits, zombies, malevolent ghosts . . . *Raat* was the best horror film ever made in Bollywood. If you want to feel fear, real fear, the kind that leaves you drenched in sweat—"

"I don't sweat," Layla snapped. "I glow. What I do want to find out is what Faroz is looking for in a wife." She smiled at her date, trying to see through his dark-tinted glasses. "It sounds like you're very busy leading your exciting and dangerous undercover life. Wouldn't you be better off checking Spy Tinder to find someone who really understands your line of work and can support you in the way a spy needs to be supported? It sounds like you need a *Mr. & Mrs. Smith* type of relationship, where you're both spies pretending to live an average life."

"I need a cover," Faroz said. "A nice normal family. Average-looking wife. Two kids. House in the suburbs. Dog. Minivan."

"Average-looking?" Layla huffed. "Except for a few inches and a couple of pounds, the only difference between me and Angelina Jolie, who starred in that film along with Brad Pitt, is the color of my skin. In fact, the other day someone came up to me and said, 'Hey, Ange. Did you get a tan?'"

"You're perfect," Faroz said. "The CIA can stage a wedding wherever you want. If you need guests, we can hire some—"

"Can we have elephants?"

"Okay. That's it. We're out of here." Sam stood abruptly, pulling Layla to her feet. "No elephants. No fake wedding. No fake CIA agent. He's probably some IT geek from Silicon Valley who only leaves his cubicle once a year."

"It's okay. I understand." Faroz held up a placatory hand. "It's a lot to take in. I know. Few people understand the sacrifices that have to be made to protect this great country of ours."

"Let's go." Sam pulled Layla behind him. "This isn't the guy you're looking for."

Layla giggled. "If you're doing the Jedi thing, you're supposed to wave your hand in front of his face and drop your voice a little before you say that."

Sam looked back over his shoulder. "Is there a non-horror movie you haven't seen?"

"I can't think of one right now, but you have to admit movies are very helpful for navigating unusual circumstances in life, like when you meet a CIA agent who is undercover as a CIA agent and wants to marry you as a cover for his spy activities. If I hadn't seen all the James Bond movies, all the *Mission: Impossible*s, and all the Jason Bourne movies, I would have freaked out and caused a scene and drawn the kind of attention he is trying to avoid. Maybe they would have kidnapped me because of course a hot guy like him would have a sexy girlfriend like me and they would know he'd come to rescue me even if it meant he had to risk his life and give up state secrets to get me back."

Sam froze. "What do you mean by 'hot guy'?"

"I have an arsenic pellet in my tooth," Faroz said. "I would die before I would betray my country."

"And . . . we are out of here."

"Wait." Layla peered around Sam. "I'm interested to know how Faroz got into the business. I can't imagine there are a lot of desi spies."

"Affirmative action," Faroz said. "I was recruited when I was nine."

"He's a Spy Kid," Layla said with delight. "Those were my favorite movies growing up. Have you come across Mr. Lisp?"

"No."

"Sebastian the Toymaker? The Timekeeper?"

"Are these fictitious characters?"

"They're as real as you." Sam's tone dripped sarcasm.

Faroz stood and straightened his tie. "As real as a game to find Layla a husband so you can have her office?"

Layla froze, her breath catching in her throat. "How do you know about that?"

"Classified."

Sam's face hardened, his entire body going still. "I'm gonna classify your ass."

"It was nice to finally meet you in person." Faroz kissed Layla's cheek. "If you change your mind, I'll know."

"Did you tell him about the game?" Body tense, jaw tight, Sam watched Faroz walk out the door. He was still holding her hand, and she was afraid to move in case he let go.

"No, of course not. The only person who knows is Daisy, and she wouldn't tell anyone, especially not a stranger. What about you? Who did you tell?"

"Evan. But he's probably forgotten by now. He's not really interested in other people's lives. And John, but he's a lawyer. That vault is always locked."

"No one else was in the office." Her voice dropped to a low whisper. "Do you think he bugged the phones? That would explain how he knew my drink order."

"If I did, it would mean I believe he really is a CIA agent, and I don't."

"I think we should get out of here," Layla said. "We've been standing here for so long, people are starting to stare, and maybe some of them are his spy friends, or worse, spy enemies. They're thinking maybe he and I hit it off, and I'm going to marry him, and they'll grab me at the wedding, and drive off, and my *lehenga* will be trailing out of the car, and I'll be screaming *Sam! Sam! Save me!* It will all be very dramatic, and when it's over, they'll make a movie about it with Priyanka Chopra starring as me. She'll have to gain twenty or thirty pounds, but she'll do it because she's a great actress and she'll want to really get into the role."

Sam stared at her for so long, she started to feel queasy. "Everything okay?"

"Why would you call for *me* to save you?" He led her out of the coffee shop. "Saving you would be Faroz's job."

"I don't know." She looked out over the bay, taking in the soft glow of the golden hour, that magical, romantic, fleeting moment between daylight and dusk when the sun began to dip below the horizon, enveloping everything in shimmering gold.

"I think it's maybe because you made me feel safe when Faroz was flashing his gun and telling us stories about being tortured. My subconscious must have figured you were my best bet for a happy Bollywood ending."

"You think I could protect you?"

He looked so bewildered that Layla had to laugh. "Of course I do. It's who you are. You might be trying to kick me out of the office, but you've been protecting me since the day we met."

11

"So what do people do after they've escaped from the CIA?" Layla asked as they stepped out onto the street.

"I don't think many people do escape." Certainly, Sam didn't want to escape now. Unsettled by Faroz's knowledge of something that they had shared only with their closest friends, he was almost overwhelmed with the urge to protect her and keep her close.

"The pier looks beautiful at night." Layla looked over the bay toward the city, the lights twinkling in the darkness. "Very romantic."

"I thought you'd given up on love and romance." He stood beside her, acutely aware of her body so close to his.

"I still believe in them. They just aren't for me."

Sam's stomach tightened. It felt wrong that someone as funny and warm and vibrant as Layla would resign herself to a life without love. "Maybe love will come later. My parents had an arranged marriage and it happened for them, in a fashion." His parents weren't soul mates in any sense of the word, but there was nothing they wouldn't do for each other.

"Mine, too. And for Dev and Rhea." She sighed. "It's almost like Dev took that away from me when he died. I can't even contemplate being close to someone because I just can't lose someone

I love again. I almost didn't make it the first time. If I hadn't moved to New York, I might have sexed myself to death."

Who were the losers who had taken advantage of a grieving woman? Sam's protective instinct flared, and he had to bite back the demand for their names. Confused by his feelings, he stepped away. "Where did you park? I'll walk you to your car."

"I'm on the other side of Justin Herman Plaza. I was at a marketing and branding workshop at the Women's Business Center this afternoon. They gave me some great ideas." She talked about the seminar as they walked down the sidewalk, dodging tourists and dog walkers, joggers and couples out for an evening stroll.

"Which way?" He stopped at the intersection.

"Let's walk past the Vaillancourt Fountain. Maybe they've turned it on and I can dance in it like Anita Ekberg did in *La Dolce Vita*, in one of the most romantic moments in film history."

Sam had no interest in old films, but the idea of Layla splashing in the fountain held considerable appeal. "There's nothing romantic about dancing around a rusted pile of steel and concrete," he said as they veered in the direction of the square.

"Is that all you see when you look at the sculpture?" she asked. "I used to imagine it was a waterslide and I could ride down the chutes. Even with the water turned off, I still feel the magic."

"I look at that pile of rusty pipes and harsh angles and see it as a metaphor for life." A crowd of tourists lumbered toward them, and he placed a hand on her lower back to guide her away. Her skin was warm beneath her shirt, her back a graceful curve beneath his palm.

They walked in easy silence across the square, stopping at the edge of the dry fountain.

"Time to open your eyes, Sam. There's beauty in the most hidden places."

Sam stared at the massive forty-foot concrete tangle of square pipes illuminated by a few perimeter lights. "It looks even worse than I remember."

"Stay right there." Layla dodged a late-night skateboarder and jumped down into the dry concrete basin.

"What are you doing?"

"I'm going to dance."

He glanced quickly from side to side. There were a few people taking pictures, a couple seated along the edge, and the skateboarders were practicing their jumps in the square.

"There's no water."

"I'll imagine it." She twirled around in front of the gaping maw of a concrete tube. "Do you know the song 'Dard-e-Disco' from *Om Shanti Om*?"

"Am I brown?" *Om Shanti Om* was one of the classic Bollywood films. He'd been forced to watch it countless times. His mother never cooked without a Bollywood film playing on the TV in her kitchen, and the songs from each one were burned into his brain.

"Look it up and play it for me. I'm going to teach you the dance." She posed for him as he joined her in the fountain, searching his phone for the music.

"I'll watch."

"You need to experience it, Sam. You can't live your life at a distance." She rolled her hips and danced a few steps, her hands stretching in the air. "Put your first two fingers together and place them on your thumb so your hands look like little wolves, then turn them up and twist into flowers. It's easy." She made the gesture. "Come on, lone wolf. I'm putting it in manly wolf terms for you. If the Khans can dance, so can you."

Sam seriously doubted his skills were on par with the Khans, two of Bollywood's most famous leading men. And how could he dance when Nisha could never dance again? How could he find joy in a fountain that represented a freedom she could never have? "Flowers aren't manly," he protested.

"Fine. You just stand there and wallow in your masculine pride. Cue the music so I can dance." Her hands flowed from hips to waist and then up to her shoulders as she practiced her moves. She was breathtakingly lovely, but it was the light in her face that drew him in—a joy he desperately wanted but could never possess.

"Imagine the water flowing through the pipes." She circled one arm and pointed with the other at the nearest open tube. "Imagine being young and riding the waves through the darkness and then exploding into the light."

Sam was imagining a lot of things as she undulated in front of him, and none of them involved being a kid.

"Do you see the beauty?"

"Yeah." Mesmerized, he watched her dance. "I see you."

"Come on. Dance with me." She held out her arms and he took a step forward, yearning for the freedom she offered, the beauty and joy she could find in a moment.

"Sam! Look out." Layla ran at him, hitting his body with such force, he stumbled back. His arms wrapped around her to keep them both from falling, just as a skateboarder shot out of the darkness. Momentum carried them into one of the angled legs of the fountain, the force of their landing reverberating through the structure with a low hum.

"Idiot!" Sam shouted at the skateboarder. "Watch where you're going." His pulse pounded in his ears so loud he could barely hear.

Layla drew in a shuddering breath. "Are you okay?"

He adjusted his grip, pulling her closer, enjoying the warm, soft comfort of having her in his arms. "Yes. You?"

"I'm fine." A slow smile spread across her face. "I saved you. Like Katniss saved Peeta in *The Hunger Games*."

"So now I owe you my life? Is that it?" he teased. Layla made him feel things he wasn't ready to feel. She made him think about things he'd buried years ago. She was redemption made real. But was he worthy of being redeemed?

"You owe me something." Her arms wound around his neck, soft breasts pressing against his chest. Her eyes softened, lips parted, head tilted back . . .

There was no resisting that plea. He crushed her to his chest, head dipping down. Their lips touched . . .

"Sam!" A woman's voice rang through the shadows. "I'd recognize that sexy butt anywhere. Why didn't you call? I missed you."

The hair on the back of Sam's neck stood on end. *No. It couldn't be* . . .

"I can't do this." Layla pulled away. "Not again." Before Sam could stop her, she climbed out of the fountain and ran into the night.

Sam moved to follow, but a taloned hand gripped his arm, holding him fast. He caught a whiff of Eau de Musk and his stomach clenched.

Karen.

"I'm so glad I bumped into you," Karen said. "I need your help. I got fired."

· 12 ·

IT was standing room only in the function space at Redwood Hospital. Layla's father was awake, but with visitors strictly limited to two at a time, the Patels had rented the room so everyone could have a snack while waiting their turn to visit.

"This is chaos." Pari Auntie shook her head. "So much shouting. So little respect. Nasir's sisters should see him next, but I saw Nira and Vij sneaking down the hall."

"I think they were going to get more plates." Layla looked around at the tables heaving with food, kids running around, cousins pranking each other, aunties arguing, and uncles trying to figure out how to get more power to the hot plates. It was no different from any other family gathering, except that her father wasn't around to take control.

Pari Auntie's head jerked to the side, and she shouted at Lakshmi Auntie, who was holding a lighter to a small bundle of incense. "Lakshmi! I told you. No fires. I don't care if flames will give him twenty years of good luck. If the sprinklers go off, we'll have to leave and no one will get to see Nasir."

"Pari! Your boys are fighting," Charu Auntie called out. "They just knocked over a bowl of gulab jamun. Someone find a mop. We need an extra table for food. Turn down the music. There are sick people down the hall."

Layla's heart sank when she saw the boys rolling on the floor. Nadal Uncle and Hari Uncle were trying to pull them apart. This would never have happened if her father had been here. Someone needed to take control. Wrangling rowdy relatives was far outside her comfort zone, but then so was running a business, and if she wanted to make it work, she needed to practice taking some risks.

"Quiet, please!"

Unbelievably, the noise stopped. "I've just come from my father's room," Layla said. "He's doing better, although he tires easily and can't speak yet. Visits will be limited to five minutes with everyone going in pairs. I'll hand out numbers. Charu Auntie will be in charge of letting people out."

"Numbers one and two," Charu Auntie called out. "Taara, he can't eat, so put that container away, and don't even think about putting it in his IV. We want him to live."

"I'm going to play his favorite Bollywood songs on my phone," Mehar Auntie said. "Zaina put them on for me. She's such a smart girl."

"My boys are top of their classes," Pari Auntie boasted. "Their teachers say they have never seen such clever, well-behaved children."

Nira Auntie lifted an eyebrow. "I thought they were suspended for setting fires in the restroom."

"They were innocent." Pari Auntie waved a dismissive hand. "But they hang out with such rascals . . ."

Layla knew all about rascals. Sam had barely been in the office in the five days following their moment in the park and the untimely arrival of his girlfriend. Or maybe she was an ex. Not that Layla cared. She'd been having so much fun with Sam that she'd almost forgotten why she'd decided to give up dating in the first place.

But the brutal reminder, along with his absence and the resurgence of the distressing feelings that had led her to toss Jonas's stuff off the balcony had just reaffirmed her decision to continue with the blind dates. Surely at least one man out of the ten would make a suitable spouse.

"Good job. Your dad couldn't have done better." Layla's mother joined her at the dessert table. Nothing was better in a stressful situation than a plate of Indian treats.

Layla bit into a soft coconut *laddu*, a round sweet made of coconut cooked with *khoya* and condensed milk, shaped into round balls and stuffed with almonds and cashews. "Did you talk to the doctor?"

"He said the pacemaker surgery went well, but we have to make sure not to cause him any stress. I told your father everything is fine. The restaurant is fine. Layla is doing well in her new business. Everything is good."

Layla opened her mouth to tell her mother about her blind dates, and closed it again. She had enough on her plate, and Layla was handling it well enough on her own.

"Yes, that's right." She forced a smile. "Everything is good."

"And soon your father will be home, shouting that someone burned the dal." She kissed the gold band on her ring finger, a wish for luck.

The tender gesture made Layla's heart squeeze in her chest. Her parents' marriage had been arranged, and it was one of the happiest marriages she knew. Her father had once told her the day he met her mother was the best day of his life.

"When did you know you loved Dad?" she asked.

"It was hard at first because we didn't know each other," her mother said. "Then we became friends. We started the restaurant together, and shortly after we opened, Dev was born. When he was only two years old, I walked into the kitchen one day and saw your father teaching him how to grind spices. Dev could barely hold the pestle. Your father was so patient and kind. It was such a small thing. But when he looked up and smiled at me, I felt a different feeling. One that I knew would last a lifetime. Love doesn't always hit like a thunderbolt. Sometimes it can grow quietly in the background until one day you realize it is there."

"Zaina! Come back with those jalebis!"

Layla caught movement out of the corner of her eye. Zaina raced past, a handful of jalebis clutched in her little fist. Anika was in full pursuit. Layla grabbed for her and lost her balance. She stumbled forward, hit a table, spilling a bowl of *kheer* as she fell. The rice pudding splashed over her clothes before landing in a puddle on the floor. Undeterred, she jumped to her feet and sprinted after her niece, leaving a trail of rice and pudding behind her.

So much for getting things under control. If this was the best she could do, what chance did she have with her business?

"What's the matter, bhaiya? You've been very preoccupied today."

Sam pulled himself out of his thoughts and forced a smile for his sister. He'd brought her to the hospital for a consultation with the surgeon who had handled her spinal surgery. Although the surgeon had been happy with her progress, he hadn't been able to tell them if Nisha would ever walk again.

"It's nothing."

"You didn't have to come if you had work to do. I could have managed on my own."

"The point is, you don't have to." His parents were away at a wedding, and he didn't like the idea of Nisha using the disabled transport service and dealing with the doctor alone. It also gave him an excuse to stay away from the office. Layla deserved an explanation. He just had no idea what he was going to say.

His body knew what his brain was only starting to admit. There was something between them that went beyond a friendly office rivalry or even a game—something real and raw that made him see every one of her blind dates as competition. Something dangerous for a man who couldn't be trusted to protect the people he loved.

"It sounds like someone's having a good time." Nisha smiled as they rounded the corner. "Oh, Sam! They're playing 'Choli Ke Peeche' from *Khalnayak*! Who would be having a Bollywood party in a hospital?"

"Stop!" A woman yelled. "Zaina! Get back here."

Seconds later a young girl barreled into Sam, hitting him so hard he staggered back a step. Jalebis scattered over the floor in front of Nisha's chair. Sam put a hand on the girl's shoulder to steady her and looked up just as Layla came running down the hall toward them.

"Sam!" She pulled up short, eyes wide. Milky liquid and grains of rice dripped off her Smash Mouth T-shirt, and he threw out a silent plea that she had defaced the logo on purpose.

"Is this yours?" He gently pushed the little girl toward her. He'd managed to avoid Layla since their encounter in the fountain by scheduling back-to-back meetings out of the office, and yet here she was, standing in front of him, covered in rice.

"Yes." Layla took the little girl's hand and drew her close. "This is my niece Zaina."

"I lost my jalebis." Zaina's eyes filled with tears.

"You go back into the room and I'm sure Jana Auntie will find you some more." Layla sent her on her way before bending down to pick up the spilled sweets.

"What's going on?" Sam crouched down to help her.

"My dad's awake and we rented the function room so everyone could celebrate and go and see him." She shrugged. "It turned into the usual family chaos."

Sam gestured to her dripping clothes. "You look like you just took a bath in a bowl of kheer."

"That is surprisingly accurate." She brushed a few grains of rice off her shirt. "How's your girlfriend? Sorry I didn't stay for an introduction."

"She's not my girlfriend. We worked together on a downsizing."

Layla lifted an eyebrow. "What exactly did you downsize that involved the removal of your pants?"

"Ahem." Nisha coughed and he glanced up to see her watching them, her eyes wide with curiosity.

"This is my sister, Nisha." His stomach knotted with the uncomfortable feeling of having his personal life exposed. He rarely talked about his family with his colleagues and friends. John knew about Nisha, but had never met her, and Royce didn't know he had a family at all. "Layla shares the office with me above The Spice Mill."

Despite the fact that Layla clearly needed a new set of clothes, she sat down on a nearby bench to talk to Nisha, a small courtesy for a wheelchair user that Sam didn't often see.

"I've always wanted to eat at The Spice Mill," Nisha said.

"You can have the next-best thing right here." Layla gestured down the hallway. "We're having a party to celebrate my father's recovery. Most of the food is from my parents' restaurant, with a few little extras from well-meaning relatives, but I can point out which dishes to avoid." She gestured to her clothes. "And I'm afraid all the kheer is gone."

Nisha laughed, and they launched into a discussion about food that somehow turned into a discussion about clothes and how Nisha hadn't gone to the wedding with their parents that afternoon because she didn't have anything to wear—something she hadn't shared with Sam. Suddenly plans were being made to take his sister shopping at Layla's aunt's store in Sunnyvale, and before he knew it Layla was accompanying his sister down the hall to the party room to make an introduction.

What was going on? Nisha didn't socialize. She went to rehab and her doctor's appointments and then she went home. She'd retained a few of her old friendships, but most of her friends had stopped calling when she refused all their invitations.

"Wait." His head still spinning by the speed of events, he raced after them. "I'm sorry, Nisha. I have a business meeting. I need to take you home."

"I can take her," Layla said. "I'll borrow my mother's car because my Jeep will be a bit of a challenge for the transfer. It's no problem."

Sam frowned. "You know about transfers?"

"My grandmother was in a wheelchair most of her life. She got polio when she was young. We all learned how to help. Nisha will be safe. Trust me."

How could he not trust her? She had just seen the most private, cherished, and personal part of his life and had embraced it. Instead of just politely greeting Nisha and walking away, she had befriended his sister and welcomed her into her family.

"I'll be fine, bhaiya." Nisha smiled. "I want to stay with Layla."

And in that moment, so did he.

· 13 ·

"Bachelor #5 is Harman Babu . . ." Daisy read from her phone as they dashed up the stairs, late to the office after helping with the lunch crowd in the restaurant. "Age thirty. Manager of Sports World Fitness Club. Professional bodybuilder. I think he's got two extra soda cans packed into those abs. I just want to lick him all over. Can I have him since you're getting busy with Sam?"

Layla groaned inwardly, regretting her decision to tell Daisy about the almost-kiss. "It was a mistake. I saved him from a skateboarder, the adrenaline was pumping, things got out of hand, and then Karen showed up . . ."

Daisy snorted a laugh. "Karen. He so doesn't belong with a Karen."

"Well, she seemed to think he belonged with her, and he didn't come after me. I think that made things pretty clear."

So why couldn't she stop thinking about how safe she'd felt in his arms, or how warm his breath had been on her lips, or how caring and sweet he'd been with the sister he had never mentioned before? She was looking forward to their weekend shopping trip. Nisha had been great fun and Layla's family had loved her.

Sam was waiting in reception, all cool and casual like he hadn't avoided her for five days only to show up at the hospital with a se-cret sister and disappear again for the rest of the week. "Harman wants us to meet him at his gym. Apparently some recruiters showed up and he's afraid to leave in case they want to talk to him. He's okay with me—"

"It's fine. I don't need you," Layla blurted out, trying not to think about their almost-kiss and how stupid she'd been to think it was anything more than a mistake. He hadn't even tried to explain about Karen when she'd seen him in the hospital.

Sam snorted his disapproval. "I promised to meet all the suitors with you, and I don't go back on my word, especially when we're in the middle of a game that I intend to win."

Her heart sank. Of course. It was still about the game. The almost-kiss clearly meant nothing to him. She was just another Karen.

She glared at him, but it was hard not to notice how gorgeous he looked today. His crisp white shirt was open at the collar, reveal-ing a hint of richly toned skin, and he had rolled up his sleeves, baring tanned forearms lightly dusted with hair. Layla had never thought of a man's forearms as being particularly sensual, but she couldn't tear her gaze away when Sam pulled out his phone.

"Let's get going," she said. "My Jeep is parked out front."

"I'll drive." Sam held out his hand.

"It's my car. I'll drive."

Sam bristled. "I'm the man."

"So?"

"The man drives. That's a man's job. Just like fixing things, building things, taking out the trash, proposing marriage, mowing the lawn, barbecuing, carrying heavy furniture . . ."

Layla snorted. "Wake up. It's not the '50s anymore. No one

drives this woman's Jeep. I can build anything from IKEA without help, and if I ever do find someone I want to marry, I'll ask the dude myself. However, if you want to take out the trash or fix the leaky faucet in the restroom, knock yourself out."

"How about Layla takes her Jeep and Sam takes his car and I promise not to tell anyone that you two single-handedly destroyed the environment?" Daisy suggested.

"That's ridiculous," Sam snapped. "We're going to the same place for the same reason. We only need one vehicle."

"This is my gig," Layla said. "I'm driving my car. If you can't get over your traditional sexist patriarchal controlling self, then I'll meet you there."

"THE speed limit is thirty-five miles per hour." Sam pointed to the sign when Layla stepped on the accelerator to pass a car in their lane.

"Thank you. I'm well aware of residential speed limits in this part of the city." Layla watched the speedometer climb. It was childish but his supercilious attitude made her want to do the opposite of what he told her to do. A ticket would be well worth the satisfaction of watching the worst backseat driver in the history of the universe sweat.

"There's a stop sign up ahead," he barked. "Start slowing down."

Layla's hands tightened around the steering wheel. "Be quiet, or I swear I'll stop this car and make you walk."

His hand clenched around the door handle, knuckles turning white. "You drive at excessive speed. You weave in and out of traffic. You tailgate people who are driving below the speed limit. And you stop only at the last second. What am I supposed to do?"

"You're supposed to be impressed by the fact that I drive a Jeep and have a clean record, that you're in a car with a woman that likes to drive fast and can do so safely, and tell me why you almost kissed me the other night."

Silence.

She didn't know where that question about the kiss had come from, and it had clearly made him uncomfortable. But at least he wasn't backseat driving anymore.

Sam cleared his throat. "It was a mistake."

"I'm glad you agree." She didn't really agree. Something had changed between them. She'd felt some kind of spark that had nothing to do with friendship and everything to do with Sam being smart, funny, protective, and exceedingly kind in a way she had never thought he could be. Not that it mattered. She wasn't looking for another short-term hookup, and she'd wasted enough time thinking about what might have happened if Karen hadn't interrupted them. With a sigh, she took a mental machete to her fantasies of speeding through the city to Sam's apartment, tearing off each other's clothes in the elevator, and barely making it through his door before they were overcome with helpless desire.

"Also, I want you to cancel your shopping trip with Nisha," he said. "It was kind of you to invite her, but you don't have to pretend to be her friend because she uses a wheelchair. She's been hurt enough."

"Wow."

"Wow?"

Layla shot him a sideways glance. "You are way overprotective. I genuinely like your sister. She's sweet and funny and I enjoyed her company. It doesn't matter to me that she uses a wheelchair. I grew up with a huge family and my grandmother wasn't the only person who used a mobility device. Patels don't treat people differently when they have special needs. We just try harder to let them know they're loved."

Sam went rigid, his eyes fixed on the road, corded throat tightening when he swallowed.

"Are you okay? Did I hit a pedestrian or something?" She slowed to a stop at a traffic light.

He pulled out his phone. "I need to check my messages."

"It helps if you turn it on," she said gently when she noticed him staring blankly at the screen.

The light turned green and she stepped on the accelerator a little too hard, sending the car shooting forward and Sam's head snapping back.

He shook himself and cleared his throat. "Do you want children in your arranged marriage?"

Layla frowned, trying to wrap her head around the sudden change of conversation. "That's a very personal question. But, yes. I want to have kids. At least three, so if the first one is a boy and the second is a girl, she won't feel like she's in a competition she can never win because she doesn't have a penis."

Sam lowered his window and drew in a breath of air.

"Shocked you, didn't I? Was it the word *penis* or the revelation that I would want children with a man I don't love?"

"I'm beginning to realize there is no end to your ability to surprise me."

Layla tightened her grip on the steering wheel. "Why did you ask me about kids? Are you worried I might be pregnant after our almost-kiss? Like some kind of immaculate conception?"

A laugh escaped him, a short chuckle that disappeared almost as quickly as it had come. "Harman is a professional bodybuilder. That means steroids. Prolonged use of anabolic steroids can have significant effects including reduced sperm count, infertility, genital atrophy, erectile dysfunction, and shrunken testicles."

"So you saw my *penis* and raised me a pair of *shrunken testicles*? I fold. You win. I dub thee Master of the Game." She tapped his arm with two fingers, trying not to imagine how it would feel to have that strength wrapped around her.

His face smoothed to an expressionless mask. "It's not funny."

"Definitely not if he isn't fully functional. But it doesn't make him a bad person, and your job is to weed out the disreputable characters, not the impotent ones."

Layla pulled into the parking lot of the sports center, and they made their way into the warehouse-style training facility. Upbeat rock music pounded through the speakers, almost drowning out the buzz of grunts, groans, and clanking weights. Bodybuilders and powerlifters cranked it out in every corner. The air was thick with testosterone and the scents of sweat and disinfectant.

"Sam, my man." A god walked toward them, wearing a teeny-tiny pair of red gym shorts and nothing else. Six feet tall, lean and ripped, with short, thick, dark hair, a shredded six-pack, perfect teeth, and a killer smile, he was a study in the perfection of the masculine form. "Old-school chaperone. I like it."

Sam and Harman did a manly fist bump slash handshake followed by mutual shoulder pats like they'd known each other all their lives.

"This is Layla Patel." Sam pushed her forward.

Layla opened her mouth but no words came out. Close up, Harman was even more breathtaking than his picture. She could see every muscle ripple as he moved, pecs so hard and smooth she could have bounced a penny off his bronze skin. "Give it here, babe." Harman held up a hand.

"Stop drooling," Sam whispered in her ear. "You look ridiculous." He lifted her hand and smacked it against Harman's palm in a humiliating high five she should have been able to manage herself if she hadn't been drunk on Harman's beauty.

"She's quite traditional," Sam said. "She's not used to seeing bare-chested dudes."

"I've seen lots of shirtless men," she muttered under her breath. "Shortless ones, too. Tons."

Sam lifted an eyebrow. "Really? Do tell."

Harman laughed—at least she thought it was a laugh—although it sounded more like a girlish giggle. "Well, she'd better get used to it. Finding clothes to fit these pythons"—he held up an arm at a ninety-degree angle and flexed his biceps, making it swell to the size of a puffed naan—"is pretty damn hard."

"I hear you." Sam nodded as if he, too, were so pumped up on steroids he couldn't find a shirt to wear.

Layla snorted. "Oh, please."

Harman led them over to a small lounge with red leather seats and a big-screen TV showing highlights of yesterday's football game. Over chocolate protein shakes, they traded information about their work and interests. Harman's entire world was his sport. He traveled only for competitions, knew nothing about politics or world affairs, and hadn't eaten sugar in the last ten years.

"So what are you looking for in a wife?" Layla asked. "Companionship? Friendship? Homemaker? True love?"

"I need a brown girl," Harman said.

Layla choked on her shake. "You need a brown girl?"

He nodded. "I want to be the first desi Mr. Olympia, so I'm all about the brand. Brown skin. Brown hair. Accent. Some days I'll throw on a turban. Other days I'll wear a *thawb*. And when there's a ceremony happening, my PR guy, Steve, and I head down to the local cultural center for some photo ops. Diwali. Ramadan. Vaisakhi. I celebrate them all."

"Those are ceremonies from three different religions, and clothing from two," she pointed out. "Is there not one faith you follow?"

"I didn't want to leave anyone out."

Layla shook her head in disbelief. "So that's all you want out of a marriage?"

"I'm not going to lie to you," Harman said. "Bodybuilding is my life. I don't have time for relationships, but Steve says there's tons of guys who do what I do. I need to stand out. I need a brand. We did some brainstorming and came up with *brown*."

"Brown is your brand?"

"You got it, sista." He made a hand gesture that was a cross between a fist pump, a finger wave, and a snap. "There aren't many desi bodybuilders out there. I'm going to be number one."

"I'm not your sister," she muttered.

"But you could be my wife," he said earnestly. "I need someone for photo ops and interviews and to keep the fans at bay. I am constantly being propositioned and, to be honest, I'm getting tired of being objectified. I want people to see me for who I really am—a perfect specimen of the ultimate masculine form."

Layla frowned. "So you *do* want to be objectified."

"Only for my art," he admitted. "And for the fame and money that come with winning titles. But not in my soul."

"Jesus Christ," Sam muttered under his breath.

"At least he's honest about who he is," she snapped.

"We'll have to tone you up for the pictures," Harman said. "You can go on my diet. Lean proteins, healthy fats, fibrous vegetables, and high-quality carbohydrates. That means no sugar, fried foods, or white flour. Four to six weeks and you'll be slim and trim and filled with energy."

Her face heated, and she wrapped her arms around herself in a protective hug. "I beg your pardon?"

"Steve!" He waved over a slim blond man wearing a leather vest over a Twenty One Pilots T-shirt and a skintight pair of khaki pants. The dude had a large camera around his neck and a tripod in his hand.

"Snap a few shots," Harman told him. "See how we look together." He pulled Layla to stand in front of him. "You okay if I put an arm around you for the pictures?"

"Um . . . sure."

Harman positioned himself behind her, one arm across her body, the other flexed by her head, his hips pressed against her rear. "She's gonna lose that extra weight, Steve, so angle us with her middle in the shadows."

"Get your hands off her," Sam growled.

"Relax, dude. We're just doing a couple of test shots."

Steve snapped a few pictures. Layla made note of three things: first, Sam was right about the effect of steroids on reproductive organs; second, she felt absolutely nothing being pressed up against a perfect specimen of the ultimate masculine form; and third, the moment he let her go, she was going to smash her fist into his perfect nose.

Her gaze flicked to Sam. Every muscle in his body was tense, and he was eyeing Harman with visible disdain. Not once since she'd known him had Sam ever criticized her appearance. She'd felt comfortable enough with him to dance in a public fountain, and when he'd held her in his arms for their almost-kiss, she hadn't felt anything other than his equal.

"Smile," Harman said. "How are her teeth, Steve? Will she need caps or just whitening?"

Layla spun around, pulling her fist back, ready to strike. Only, Sam anticipated her move. He grabbed her hand, pushing it down as he wrapped his strong arm around her body.

"Don't do it," he warned, keeping his voice low. "His face is part of his aesthetic. If he loses his career, you might face a lawsuit that will bankrupt you. And you'll lose your chance to be Mrs. Harman Babu."

Her body warmed from the press of his hard chest against her, the strong arm holding her tight, his breath hot against her neck. Fire raced through her veins, searing her nerve endings and making her skin tingle. Why couldn't she feel this with Harman? Why did she have to feel it for the one man on earth who irritated her the most—the one man who made her feel alive?

Oh God. She didn't want Harman. She wanted Sam.

"ARE you crazy?" Sam walked quickly through the parking lot after saying good-bye to Harman. He caught up with Layla just as she reached her Jeep, his heart pounding in frustration. "Why did you agree to go out on a date with him? He said you needed to lose weight and had bad teeth. You were going to punch him in the face."

"He apologized. He said in his world anyone with more than five percent body fat is overweight, and everyone has veneers. And what's wrong with getting in shape? He's better than any of the others. Why not give him a second chance?"

Sam leaned against the door, blocking her way. "So that's what you want? A boy toy?" Harman had seemed like an easy strike until he had somehow maneuvered his way into a date.

"Oh, come on. You have to give me a pass. I've never seen a man with a body like that. It was like looking at a rare painting, a perfect flower, or a glorious sunset. You can't not appreciate that kind of beauty."

"You could have done it with your mouth closed," he snapped. "I can't imagine what you'd be like at the Louvre. They'd probably have to follow you around with a bucket and mop." His blood pumped hot and furious through his veins, a potent cocktail of frustration, disappointment, and desire.

"I don't understand you." Layla glared. "He's got his flaws, but he doesn't seem like a bad guy. If I wind up marrying him, you get the office. Why are you so annoyed?"

"I'm not annoyed," he bit out, although his pulse had kicked up a notch, and he felt like spending an hour in the gym punching a bag and imagining it was Harman's face. "If you really want to waste your life on a shallow, egotistical airhead, you should do things the proper way. The families should meet . . ." He almost couldn't believe the words coming out of his mouth. He was anti-tradition. If anything, he should be delighted she had found a match so quickly. Hell, he should be on the phone right now arranging movers to get rid of the purple couch.

"My dad is still in the hospital."

"Then what's your hurry? Meet the other men on the list. Don't rush such an important decision." He took a deep breath and then another. When had he ever let his emotions override his common sense? Every day he dealt with angry employees. They called him names, threw things at him, questioned the existence of his soul. Nothing affected him. The walls that he'd built to contain his remorse and regret allowed him to do his job without succumbing to their pain. Except when it came to Layla.

"Are you . . ." She tipped her head to the side and gave him a quizzical look. "Jealous?"

"Don't be ridiculous. Once he ages, all that stretched skin is going to sag, his face will prematurely age, and he'll deflate like a popped balloon. Not to mention the hair loss and functionality problems."

Her eyes widened. "You are jealous. I thought you'd be happy."

"And I thought you were serious about finding a suitable partner, and not someone who just wants you to be his brown girl brand." He shrugged. "Cleary I was wrong. The game is over. I win."

"You win?" She was shouting now. Sam glanced around quickly to make sure they weren't disturbing anyone, but they were very much alone at the far edge of the lot where he had insisted they park to minimize the risk of her vehicle being scratched.

"You don't win, you conceited, egotistical ass. I'm going on a date, not marrying him." She moved closer, standing less than a foot away, seemingly unconcerned that he was eight inches taller and outweighed her by a good fifty pounds. What was it about Layla that brought down his defenses so easily? He couldn't even think straight. Wasn't this what he wanted? The office, and Layla gone?

"You're just dragging it out because you don't want to lose the game," he retorted. "I know your type."

"And I know your type. You've spent so much time hiding how you feel, you wouldn't know an emotion if it hit you in the face."

His lips pressed tight together, and he tried to find the inner calm that sustained him when he had to deal with disgruntled employees. But he was too wound up, too involved, too aware of the woman standing in front of him—the heat of her body, the flush in her cheeks, the rise and fall of her chest as she drew in breath after ragged breath.

"I know cowardice when I see it," he retorted. "You've let Dev's death define you. You're afraid to let people in because you're afraid of losing them. That's why you agreed to the date with Harman.

There's no chance you'll ever fall in love with him because he'll never love anyone more than himself."

"You don't know anything." She heaved in a furious breath, looking up at him through the thicket of her lashes. Her breasts brushed against his chest. Her soft lips parted.

His walls crumbled. With nothing to contain his emotion, he succumbed to desire. "I know I made a mistake letting you go the other night."

And then he kissed her. The world around him faded to the singular sensation of her lips on his, as soft and gentle as her words had been cold and harsh. All that mattered was the warmth of her body, and her sweet sigh of surrender as she melted against him.

So it was all the more shocking when she slapped him across the face.

· 14 ·

"WHAT the—" Sam's stunned expression would have been comical if Layla hadn't been so fixated on his soft, lush mouth.

"You didn't ask." She seized his shirt in both hands and dragged him down for another kiss. "And I'm angry with you."

Their mouths crashed together. Tongues tangled. He kissed her as if he wanted to consume her, devour her alive. Fierce kisses, hard kisses, desperate, wanting kisses. He tasted like chocolate and smelled like sin.

"Sam . . ." She pulled away. "I can't breathe."

"Neither can I." He wrapped his arms around her and drew her in for another hungry kiss. Hot, hard, and wet, melting her to the side of the Jeep. His tongue worked past her lips to plunge into her mouth, every stroke tugging at things low and deep in her belly.

Her hands moved to his chest, sliding over his pecs and the ripple of abs beneath his shirt. Harman was perfect but Sam was real, his body hard from his fight training, muscles thick from use. He hissed out a breath when her fingers grazed the top of his belt, his infamous self-control giving way to her curious hands.

"What are we doing?" he murmured as he drew her earlobe into his mouth, his five-o'clock shadow rough against her sensitive skin.

"I don't know, but don't stop."

"No chance of that." He shifted against her, his arousal as evident from his ragged breaths as the growing hardness pressed against her hips.

When he thrust a thick thigh between her legs, she rocked against him, reckless and wanton in her need for release. She was dying, burning, her body on fire. She'd never felt anything like the toxic combination of anger and lust that pounded through her veins. It made her head spin, drove logic away.

"Get in the Jeep." He reached behind her, pulled open the passenger door.

"You want to do it here? Like in *Titanic*?"

"Are you kidding me?" His voice dropped husky and low. "I'm taking you home where I can have you all to myself."

"In that case . . ." She handed him the keys. "Since I don't know where you live, I'll let you drive."

Moments later, Sam peeled out of the parking lot like fire was licking at their heels. He drove with one hand on the steering wheel and the other in her lap, his fingers threaded through hers. She'd always thought of herself as an aggressive driver, but Sam tore up the streets. By the time they arrived outside a boutique building in the Mission, her heart was pounding so hard she thought she'd break a rib.

Sam grabbed her when they reached the lobby. She caught a glimpse of mint-and-cream-patterned wallpaper, freshly painted woodwork, and a pastel painting of an old-fashioned streetcar, before he pinned her against the wall beside the elevator and kissed her. She scraped her nails over his chest, tearing a button from his shirt just as the elevator door slid open. Sam palmed her curves, kissed her harder as he backed her into the elevator and slammed his hand over the button to close the door.

"You want to do it here? In the elevator?" Layla was game for anything so long as it meant she got to take off his clothes. "*Fatal Attraction* style or *Fifty Shades Darker*?"

"Upstairs." He angled her head to deepen the kiss. Layla moaned into his mouth, grinding her hips against the bulge in his jeans. Sam answered with a groan, his fingers sliding under her shirt to stroke the bare skin of her stomach, and then higher.

Desperate to move things along, Layla pulled her shirt over her head.

"What are you . . . ?"

She unhooked her bra, and he gave a strangled gasp.

"No . . ."

"It's okay. I'm not shy." She whipped off her bra and tossed it on the floor with her shirt. "Come and get them." She gave her girls a shake in case he didn't get the message.

Sam's eyes blazed, his gaze lingering on her breasts with an intensity that took her breath away. But there was something else in his eyes.

Fear.

He's afraid of my breasts.

The elevator dinged. The doors slid open. Layla turned. Her brain registered a woman standing in the doorway. Her body froze.

"Good evening, Mrs. Goldberg." Sam shoved Layla behind him. "How are you?"

"Good evening, Sam." Mrs. Goldberg's voice was shaky, hoarse, but tinged with amusement. "I'm fine, thank you."

Sam shuffled sideways, keeping Layla back with one arm as they sidestepped out the door, his tattered shirt fluttering around them. "Are you going for your walk?"

"Yes, it's a lovely evening."

Layla peered out from behind Sam's shoulder and met the gaze of an elderly woman in a fitted cream suit, soft peach blouse, and a string of pearls. "Um . . . hello."

"And hello to you, dear. No need to hide. I was a nurse for forty years. If you've got it, flaunt it, because by the time you're my age you need a crane to hold them up." She stepped into the elevator and bent to pick up Layla's clothing. "You might need these."

"Thank you." Layla extended a hand from behind Sam to retrieve her bra and shirt.

"Good night, Mrs. Goldberg," Sam called out as he reached backward for the nearest door, still keeping Layla hidden.

"Good night, Sam and friend. Enjoy your evening. Try to keep the noise down."

"She seems nice," Layla said as the elevator closed.

With a growl, Sam unlocked the door, and then they were whirling, spinning around. Before Layla could get her bearings, Sam closed the door by slamming her against it.

"What just happened?" She blinked, trying to clear her vision as she took in the modern open-concept space with its concrete floors and striking architecture. Sleek cabinetry and high-end silver appliances dominated a large kitchen with quartz countertops and a distressed picnic-style wooden table. Soft evening light flowed through floor-to-ceiling windows, and abstract prints dominated the white walls. Cold, urban, and austere, it was utterly devoid of the bright colors, rich sensual fabrics, and ornate wood carvings that she was used to seeing in the homes of her desi family and friends.

Sam thudded one hand on the door behind her, leaned in so close she could feel the press of his chest against her breasts. "What were you thinking? You almost gave ninety-year-old Mrs. Goldberg a heart attack."

"She looked pretty spry to me." Layla gave a little shrug. "This whole thing was a fantasy of mine—racing through the streets, tearing off our clothes in the elevator, stumbling naked into your apartment . . . I guess I got carried away."

He cupped her nape, pressed his thumb under her chin and tipped her head back, scalding her with his heated gaze. "Was I in this fantasy?"

"Yes," she whispered.

He rewarded her with a mind-blowing kiss that made her knees weak. Was she ready for the reality of hooking up with the kind of man who could very easily break her heart?

"What else happens in this fantasy?" His hand slid beneath her skirt and he stroked a warm finger along the edge of her panties. Her pulse throbbed between her thighs.

"After we're naked, we have wild sex against the door."

Sam yanked on her panties, almost amputating her leg when the sturdy cotton briefs held fast.

"Sorry." Her throat worked on a swallow. "I wasn't planning for my fantasy to come true, so I didn't wear shreddable underwear."

With a soft chuckle, Sam undid the button on her skirt and dropped to one knee to slide it down her legs. Layla grimaced as he studied her plain white panties.

"You are so sexy." Sam leaned forward and pressed a kiss to her stomach as he gently slid her underwear over her hips. He looked up at her in a way no other man had looked at her before—as if he truly thought she was sexy in gray, worn, pima cotton high-waisted briefs pilling on the front and fraying around the thighs.

"What happens after we have sex against the door?" he asked.

"You carry me to the kitchen counter and smash all the plates onto the floor with one sweep of your arm so we have space to have more sex."

His palms covered her breasts, and he teased her, squeezing

gently as he nuzzled her neck. "Sounds unhygienic. How am I supposed to feed you afterward with no dishes?"

"I won't be hungry."

"You're always hungry." He bent down to draw her left nipple
between his teeth. "I like that about you."

Lust flooded her brain. She took a deep breath and tried to give
herself over to the pleasure of his mouth, but visions of Karen
danced in her head. "My nipples are dark," she blurted out.

Sam laughed around her breast. "I see that."

"If Karen is your type, you're probably used to seeing women
with pink nipples. I used to think there was something wrong with
me, but then I realized I'd look odd with pink nipples. My breasts
would probably look like scoops of chocolate ice cream with cherries on top."

Sam switched his attention to her other breast, licking and
sucking her nipple until it peaked. "I don't like cherries."

"Me, neither." She hesitated, thinking about Karen and her pale
skin, golden hair, and perfect figure. "What about chocolate? My
mom has a special recipe for chocolate gulab jamun. She uses *khoya*,
maida, cocoa powder, and drinking chocolate. After she rolls the
balls, she fries them in a *karahi* and puts a chocolate chip on top."

"Layla?" He pulled his T-shirt over his head, putting all
thoughts of food out of her mind. His chest was spectacular, firm
and smooth. Layla let her hands wander, tracing every sculpted
curve of his sexy six-pack abs and the deep V-cuts of his obliques.
She wanted to lick him all over.

"Yes, Sam?"

"Let's not talk about your mom or how she enjoys frying balls."

Her gaze dropped to the bulge below his belt. "That's probably
a good idea."

She pressed a soft kiss to his cheek, licked the strong line of his jaw, the chin with a tiny cleft in the center. She liked his scratchy stubble, the erotic burning sensation it made on her skin as he licked and sucked the sensitive dip between her neck and her shoulder. She also liked the confident way he touched her body, the soft slide of his fingers over her curves, his slow, methodical seduction, his attention to her every sharp breath. There were far too many things to like about Sam Mehta, and they weighed the balance against the reasons to push him away.

"Would you ever have imagined we'd be here, doing this, the day you walked into the office?"

"Before or after you threw your office supplies at me?"

"I'm serious, Sam. One month ago I was sitting at my desk with only a dream about starting something new and no idea how to do it, and all I could think about was how to get you out of the office. And now my dream is happening. I'm starting to build something great, and I'm doing it on my own. Having you in the office, watching you run your business, is inspiring. And instead of wanting to chase you out . . ." Her cheeks heated. "I want to let you in."

"I want you to let me in, too." He growled softly, his lips sliding down her neck to kiss the hollow at the base of her throat.

"I like your dirty talking." Her voice was breathy, husky, like she was femme fatale Krishna Verma in *Ishqiya*, the object of every man's desire.

"I like how you respond to my touch." His hand slid down over her hip, fingertips grazing her thigh.

Lifting her gaze, she saw the heat of desire in his eyes. Sweat trickled down her temple, her body wound so tight she thought she'd crawl out of her skin. She leaned forward and pressed a kiss to his mouth.

He circled an arm around her, drawing her close. "This is the last place I thought we'd ever be when you walked into the office," he murmured, cupping her face in his big, warm palm. "And after you dropped Daisy and Max and all your stuff on me, I wasn't sure I'd survive. I was used to calm and quiet. I was used to being alone."

She pressed her lips to his chest. "Your heart is still beating."

With a gentle thrust, he pushed her legs apart with a hard, muscular thigh. "You want to hear it pound? Open for me."

More dirty talking. She parted her thighs, wondering if it was possible to come just from words alone.

He slid his hand between her legs, eased his fingers into her heat. She shuddered as he worked his magic, making her dizzy with want.

It had to be a dream. She wasn't actually standing naked in Sam Mehta's apartment, so crazed with lust she wanted to tear his clothing off with her teeth. Any moment now she was going to wake up in her bed and . . . "Oh God." She was burning under the skill of his strong fingers, his breath hot against her neck. "Sam, stop. No. Don't stop. Yes. Stop. Take off your clothes."

"With pleasure." A grin spread across his face and he released her to yank open his belt and shove his clothing over his hips. "I like to know my touch drives you wild."

"What does my touch do to you?"

"See for yourself." He wrapped her hand around his hard length, tightening her grip into a squeeze. Layla gave him a slow, admiring stroke, releasing him only to allow him to roll on the condom he had pulled from his back pocket.

"You want me."

"Desperately." The soft rumble of his voice turned her liquid inside. "But if you want to stop or slow down . . ."

"Are you kidding?"

Before she could reach out and touch him again, he had her up against the door, one hand beneath her, holding her up, the other braced beside her. His mouth found hers, and he kissed her slow and deep. Layla seized his shoulders and looped her legs around his waist, grinding against him as hot shivers rippled down her spine.

"Are you ready for me?" He dragged hot, wet kisses across her collarbone before blazing a trail down her throat with his tongue, stopping only to press his lips into the soft hollow where her pulse was pounding in anticipation.

"More than ready." She arched into him, feverish with hunger, her hands roaming the warm skin on his back, down over the firm muscles of his rear. She couldn't remember ever wanting a man more.

With one strong thrust he was inside her. She moaned, overwhelmed by the delicious fullness of him, the strength and power surrounding her.

Sam's shoulders tightened beneath her hands. "You feel so damn good."

Too good. When had it ever been like this? A connection that went beyond physical to something she could feel in her soul. She rocked her hips, drawing him deeper, holding him closer. As they lost themselves in a frantic rhythm, there was no office, no list of suitors, no game. Instead, there was Sam, raw and real, the need building up inside her, and the ache of longing in her pounding heart.

Sam slipped his hand between them, finding the spot that would drive her over, and taking her to the edge with a firm stroke of his fingers. Her head slammed against the door and she cried out as pleasure crashed over her in thunderous wave, his name a guttural moan on her lips.

"Say it again." He thrust hard and fast, chasing his peak. "Say my name."

"Sam," she whispered.

With a strangled groan, he buried his face in her neck, his hard body shuddering as he surrendered all control.

"How does the fantasy end?" he murmured as he fell forward, one hand still holding her up, his forearm braced against the door.

"I don't know." She ran her hands through his soft, thick hair. "I always wake up before it's over."

"THANKS for meeting me. I hope you weren't asleep."

Royce shook Sam's hand in the parking lot outside The Spice Mill. Despite the fact he'd only just stepped off a flight from Singapore, he was clean-shaven and dressed in a crisp navy-and-white-checked shirt, pressed navy dress pants, bright white running shoes, and a loud, red and navy, tartan-style tie.

"It's five thirty A.M. Of course I was asleep." Sam ran a hand through his damp hair. He'd managed to get showered, dressed, and out of the condo without waking Layla up after he got Royce's text to meet him at the office. A small blessing, considering he didn't know how to deal with their night together. He'd never let a woman stay overnight. Nor had he ever slept with a woman he expected to see again. He couldn't take the risk that they would want more from him than he could give. But with Layla, he wondered if he could take that chance.

"This won't take long." Royce patted his satchel. "I only have a six-hour layover before my flight to London. I thought I'd check out the new office while we catch up on business."

Sam led him to the entrance. He could hear someone shouting in the kitchen, doors slamming, pots banging on a stove. He felt a small stab of guilt for keeping Layla up late. She usually helped her mother in the mornings, although from the sound of chatter echoing up the stairs, it was clear her mother wasn't alone. He'd left

Layla a note about the early-morning meeting. As long as he got Royce out of the office before she arrived, everything would be fine.

"Sounds like the restaurant is open. Tell them to bring up a couple of espressos and whip up a brioche, light on the butter."

"It's an Indian restaurant," Sam bit out. "They don't do espresso or brioche. And they aren't open yet."

Royce gave a dismissive wave. "They're service people. They like to serve. And I thought you said the owner told you they were struggling financially, which was why they were subletting the office in the first place. They'll be glad of the extra business."

"We have a coffeemaker upstairs, and I think there are some leftover donuts. We'll be fine."

"Don't you have a receptionist to handle these things?" Royce followed Sam up the stairwell to the office.

"She doesn't start work this early." For the briefest of seconds, he considered calling Daisy and asking her to come in to serve breakfast to him and Royce for the sheer amusement of listening to her swear into the phone. And if she did come to the office, he would get a front-row seat for the fireworks when she went head-to-head with Royce. He couldn't imagine two people who would irritate each other more.

"Fire her. We don't need the deadweight."

"She's strangely competent at her job so I'll keep her for the time being." He headed to the kitchen to make coffee while Royce checked out the office. By the time he returned with the beverages and a plate of stale donuts, Royce was sitting at Layla's desk.

"Great desk." Royce ran a hand over the pipework frame. "Excellent choice. This one is mine, I assume."

Sam snorted a laugh. "I'm more than happy for you to have it."

"Who's sitting here now? Your secretary?" He shuffled through

Layla's papers, seemingly unconcerned about notions of privacy or confidentiality.

"The landlord's daughter. She needed a place to work for a few weeks, and I said she could stay." He sat at his desk and sipped the coffee, almost gagging at the taste. For all Daisy's quirks and eccentricities, she knew how to brew good java.

"Looks like she's doing some branding." Royce held up a colorful logo design for a company called Excellent Recruitment Solutions. "Recruitment agency?"

"Yes." Sam studied the drawings. They weren't as professional as the logos Evan designed, but they weren't all bad.

Royce leaned back so far, Layla's chair creaked in protest. "Make sure you get a kickback if she wants to use you to source clients."

Sam winced. "She didn't ask, and even if she did, it would be inappropriate to hand out her card to people I just fired and then have them walk into the office the next day and see me here."

"I don't worry about that kind of moral or ethical stuff." Royce gave a dismissive wave. "But that's why we work well together." He leaned across the desk and stared at the fishbowl. "What's with the fish?"

"They're supposed to be lucky."

"She's going to need more than luck if this is the best she can do." He plucked a black Sharpie off the desk and absently scrawled on one of Layla's designs. "Amateurish. I hope she didn't pay someone to come up with this."

"Royce, put the pen down."

Royce pulled another design from the pile and laughed as he wrote on it. "Looks like a roll of toilet paper. No sense of color or style."

"Royce . . ." Sam pushed away from his desk.

"Boring." Royce wrote on another page and flipped to the next.

"Unprofessional. Is this a business or a kindergarten?" Flip. "Awkward. This star looks crippled, like it's missing some limbs." Flip. "And what animal is this? Its eyes are huge. It looks like it's on drugs."

"Those are her personal papers." Sam shot out of his seat, covering the distance between them in a few quick strides. But by the time he had reached Layla's desk and wrested the pen from Royce's hand, his business partner had managed to scrawl cutting remarks on most of the designs.

"These are appalling." Royce sneered. "Even the name. Excellent Recruitment Solutions. Dull as ditchwater. It's got no ring to it. No alliteration. Nothing to make it stand out from the dozens of other recruitment firms in the city."

"She's the landlord's daughter," Sam snapped. "Do you want us to get kicked out right before Alpha Health Care is supposed to let us know about the pitch?"

Royce put his feet on the desk and bit into a stale donut. His leather shoes were handmade by a small family business in Naples and shipped to him four times a year by courier. By contrast, Sam bought his Italian leather shoes off the shelf at Nordstrom. Shoes were shoes. He didn't need them hand embossed. They just needed to function.

"We have a lease—or sublease, to be precise," Royce said. "I'm pretty sure giving free branding advice isn't a stated cause for termination. Lighten up, partner."

Sam replaced the pen and gathered all Layla's branding designs together. "Put your feet down. While she's in the office, we need to show her the same courtesy and respect we would give any other business colleague."

"Seriously? Are you fucking her? She's a freeloader. We're the ones paying the rent."

"Your comments were a little harsh."

"They were a small mercy. I should leave her a bill."

Sam bundled the papers together and dropped them in the recycling bin. Better for her to think they had been mistakenly tidied away by the cleaning staff than to read Royce's cutting remarks.

"I like it here." Royce walked over to the window. "It's bright and spacious. I can walk from my condo, and my favorite deli is right around the corner. The restaurant on the ground floor is the only downside. It doesn't fit in."

"They have a Michelin star." Sam studied the road, looking for any sign of Layla's Jeep. "They've been written up in food blogs and magazines all over the world."

"That's great if they're located somewhere quaint and quirky where foodies hang out. But this is an office building on a street of office buildings. Coffee shops and delis will do well here, but not the kind of cuisine that takes hours to eat. You said they were struggling financially. Location is probably a big part of the reason. I'll let them know on my way out."

Royce had no clue. Sometimes Sam wondered how he had become as successful as he was.

"They'll have made a significant investment renovating the bottom floor. They aren't going to move because a stranger walks in and tells them they've got a bad location."

"We may have to convince them if we get the contract and need more space."

Sam frowned. "Between the two of us and the remote staff, we can handle one hospital just fine."

Royce took another donut from the kitchen and turned, studying the office. "What about five hospitals?"

"What are you saying?"

"I heard a rumor that Alpha Health Care has decided to do a

mass restructure of their health care holdings starting with the Bay Area. If we get the contract, it won't just be for St. Vincent's—it will be for all five hospitals, with the possibility of handling all Alpha Health Care's work statewide, maybe even nationally. We would need to hire more staff. One floor won't be enough, and a half-empty ethnic restaurant doesn't project the kind of corporate image that will convince Alpha Health Care that we can compete on a national level."

"You're getting way ahead of yourself," Sam said. "If we need that much space, we can move."

"Or we stay in the building that has the unique advantage of being only one block from Alpha's HQ and equidistant from three Alpha Health Care hospitals." Royce finished the donut in two bites. "I'm golfing with their CEO at Royal St. George's after I hit London tomorrow. I'll feel him out about the rumors. If they are true, our location will become a critical factor in securing the contract."

"All I care about is St. Vincent's. Do what it takes to make it happen."

"I always do." Royce sniffed. Turned. Sniffed again.

"Something wrong?"

"Do you have an animal in here?"

"Of course not."

"Smells like dog piss. Or maybe it's the fish. I'll dump them on my way out."

"Maybe it's your jacket." Sam quickly moved to intercept when Royce headed for Layla's desk. "I think you might have spilled your cologne. You should probably get it cleaned before your flight."

"Christ." Royce pulled off his jacket. "I'll have to buy a new jacket. That cute Canadian flight attendant is working the direct to London and we're planning to notch up the 'mile high' scorecard on the way."

Sam walked him out the door. "When will you be coming through again?"

"Not for another month, unless we get the Alpha Health Care contract. If that happens, I'll be back to work out the details." He looked back over his shoulder as he walked down the hallway. "And you'll need to get rid of the girl. I'm not sharing my desk."

"YOU'RE late. Bachelor #6 will be arriving in ten minutes." Daisy handed Layla a marriage résumé as she rushed in the door.

Still flustered from waking up alone with nothing more than a text from Sam about an early-morning meeting and a bowl of cold oatmeal in the kitchen, Layla stared at the résumé in confusion. "What is—?"

"His name is Baboo Kapoor," Daisy said quickly. "Age thirty-two. His parents responded to the ad. That should ring the warning bells."

"I texted you this morning and asked you to cancel the interview."

"Max stole my phone last night and I can't find it." Daisy gave her a rueful smile. "I think he buried it. I knew I shouldn't have bought that new phone case covered in tiny bones."

"Does Sam know the interview is still on?"

"I haven't seen him."

Warning bells tinkled at the back of Layla's mind. "He left me a note this morning saying he was coming in to the office for a meeting."

Daisy sucked in a sharp breath. "What do you mean *He left you a note this morning*?"

Layla's face heated. She brushed past Daisy and made her way to her desk. "Nothing."

"I know that look. That's not *nothing*. That's *I slept with him and I regret it and I'm ashamed to tell my cousin*." Daisy followed her to her desk. "Were you drunk? Stoned? High? Did he force you? I'm going to call Bobby Prakash and the Singh twins. By the time they're done with him—"

"He didn't force me," she said. "It was totally consensual. Actually, I started it."

Daisy gasped. "What the hell were you thinking?"

"I don't know." She shrugged. "We met Harman. He was the most beautiful man I'd ever seen. He wanted a companion, but he was happy for us to lead our separate lives. It was perfect. He was perfect—except that I knew I'd never feel good about myself when I was with him. That's not his fault, but I realized I never feel that way when I'm with Sam. He's handsome and successful, and he can be funny and kind, and I never feel like anything other than an equal when I'm with him. Anyway, I agreed to go out on a date with Harman because, aside from my issues, he's a good candidate. Sam wasn't happy about it. We had a fight that wasn't really a fight. I slapped him. Then I kissed him. Then we wound up at his place having the best—"

Daisy covered her ears. "Don't tell me. I don't want to hear the details or I might throw up all over myself, and I stole this skirt from Mehar Auntie's closet." She drew in a ragged breath. "This is Sam we're talking about. Public enemy number one. He's trying to steal the office. We hate him. Max hates him." She lowered her hands. "Don't you, Max?"

Max barked from under the desk and then jumped out, wagging his tail.

Layla sighed. "He asked you not to bring Max to work."

"This is your office, too. You like Max. I like Max. The fish like Max. Max likes Max. That makes five in favor of Max and one against. So Max stays."

"I think he's right." Layla walked over to her desk. "We are running a business here. I think we need to make things more professional. That means no dogs, no fish, proper office wear, and a proper business image. I've been struggling to come up with an idea for a brand, but Harman actually made it seem simple. Everything he is and everything he wants to achieve can be summed up in the word *brown*."

"Brown?" Daisy stared at her aghast. "That's going to be your brand?"

"No. But I'm going to try and come up with something equally simple. I've been toying around with a few ideas. I'll show you what I've done so far."

"He got to you," Daisy grumbled. "He's tainted you with his uptight Sam-ness. Wake up. Smell the chai. You're just on a high because he scratched your itch. You know it didn't mean anything to him. Was he there to give you a cuddle in the morning?"

"No."

"Did he make a delicious breakfast for you in bed? Did he pack you a lunch like Harrison Ford in *Working Girl*? Do you see him here having a meeting?"

Layla swallowed hard. "No, but I want to give him the benefit of the doubt."

"Why?" Daisy demanded. "Are you going to do him again? I thought this was exactly the kind of thing you were trying to avoid by finding yourself a husband—meaningless hookups with emotionally unavailable men that will ultimately end in disaster."

"I know. It's just . . ." She bent down to study the fishbowl. "What's wrong with the fish? They're not as energetic as usual."

"Maybe they're full. I gave them a few extra food flakes this morning. The big fish ate like a champ, but the little fish was sulking at the bottom of the bowl. You should really give them proper names."

"I can't commit to names just yet. What if they die? I thought I'd wait a few months and make sure they're strong enough to survive before I decide who they are." Still looking for her designs, Layla walked over to the printer, where she'd lined up the recycle bins for tomorrow's collection. Her logo designs were on the top, but each one had been defaced with harsh words scrawled in black Sharpie.

Stunned, she covered her mouth and gasped.

"Something wrong?"

"I guess Sam didn't like my designs." She held up the papers for Daisy to see. "I didn't even ask for his comments, but he scribbled on them anyway and then he tossed them in the recycle bin like they were trash."

Daisy's nostrils flared, and she cracked her knuckles. "You want me to kick his ass when he gets in?"

"No. I'll deal with him." She swallowed hard. "I didn't think he was that cold or callous."

"Seriously?" Daisy's hands found her hips. "He wouldn't get out of your office even after he found out your dad was in the hospital. He's trying to take what's yours. You woke up alone in his bed. Did you really think he was a nice guy?"

"Yeah," she said softly. "I did."

Daisy held up Baboo's résumé. "Now, this is a nice guy. Tall, handsome, nonsmoker, caring, family-oriented, loves pets, professional psychologist, open-minded with strong moral values . . ." She trailed off. "If I wasn't currently channeling my inner Goth,

I'd fight you for him, but I think my sass and kick-ass style might scare him away."

Layla had a feeling she was right. Daisy was wearing a wool hat, a tight black T-shirt, studded black leather belt, and a black chiffon skirt over leggings and thick black boots. With a studded dog collar around her neck and matching bracelets on her wrists, dark red lipstick and smoky black eyes, she was definitely not what Baboo's ultraconservative parents were looking for.

She took the CV and skimmed over Baboo's details. "My parents would definitely approve. Dev would have liked him, too."

"Are you kidding? Dev wouldn't have let you settle for anyone other than the ruler of a small country or a multibillionaire. No one was good enough for his little sister."

"He was a tad overprotective, but in a good way." A smile tugged at Layla's lips. She couldn't believe they were actually having a conversation about Dev. It was something she'd avoided doing for the last five years. Although she felt the familiar pang of sadness, for the first time she didn't feel like she was going to burst into tears.

"Dev wouldn't have liked Sam," Daisy said.

"Why not?"

"Sam took advantage of you. Single woman. On the rebound. Emotionally fragile. Looking for love. He pretends to be helping you. Lures you into bed with his gorgeous face and rock-hard bod. You do the nasty. Fall asleep in his arms. Then boom. You wake up cold and alone. I'm surprised he didn't steal your purse."

"There were two of us in that bed," Layla retorted. "I chose to be there for sex and nothing more. I'm not looking for love." She tucked the defaced logos under the résumé. For a short while she'd actually thought things were looking up, but if her ideas for a name and a brand were so awful, what chance did she have of making it work with either the business . . . or the man?

"CALL me Bob."

Layla smiled at the quiet, mild-mannered man who looked nothing like a Bob and very much like Vij Uncle, an economics professor at Berkeley. He was an inch or two taller than her, slim, and elegantly dressed in a crisp striped shirt, open at the collar to reveal a gold medallion around his neck. His dark hair was short and neatly cut. His bland oval face had no blemishes, and there was only the hint of a wrinkle in his perfectly proportioned forehead. Relaxed and at ease, he sat back, legs crossed, hands resting on the arms of the chair, head tipped slightly to the side as if he were waiting for her to begin. Everything about him screamed *share your deepest secrets* and she could just see him nodding in sympathy as his patients unburdened their souls.

"What's wrong with Baboo?" Sam had been less than pleased to discover that the meeting with Bachelor #6 was going ahead, and his conversation, since arriving at the office, had been peppered with sarcastic remarks.

"People find it hard to say." Bob smiled back at Layla, flashing her a set of perfectly white and even teeth.

"What's hard to say about Baboo?"

Layla shot Sam a glare. Aside from cursing at him when he arrived, she hadn't spoken to him since he walked into the office. Being trapped in the boardroom with him, knowing that beneath that handsome exterior beat a cruel and callous heart, was almost more than she could bear. "Bob is a perfectly fine name. So is Baboo."

"And Layla is a lovely name," Bob said. "Did you know it means 'dark beauty' in Arabic? It suits you."

"Thank you." Her smile faded when Sam scowled.

"It's a tragic name," Sam said. "Very unlucky. I'm sure you know the Arabian legend of Qays and Layla, a young couple who fell so deeply in love they were unable to contain their passionate devotion."

"What exactly does that mean?" Layla asked, hoping to distract him in case Bob was superstitious like Lakshmi Auntie. India had a billion-dollar superstition-centric industry focused on astrology, black magic, and fake babas. An unlucky name had derailed more than one prospective marriage. "Is it anything like being unable to contain your opinion about things no one asked you about?"

"I'm sure we can all guess what it means." Sam didn't address her sarcastic quip. "Layla used poor Qays for his magnificent body and then went prowling around for a new man only hours after leaving his bed. It caused quite the scandal in their conservative community. Qays was denied her hand in marriage and prevented from seeing her ever again, although why he would want her after that, I don't know. Distraught, he fled into the wilderness while chanting love poems about his darling Layla until he descended into madness and death."

"What one man sees as a tragedy, another sees as a romance," Bob said. "I've always thought of *Romeo and Juliet* as a love story."

"Me, too." Layla mentally ticked off a box in the plus column for Bob. "So do you think love can grow in an arranged marriage? Or are you looking for just a friend or companion?"

"Definitely love." He put a hand to his chest. "I'm a romantic at heart."

"Nothing says romance like finding a woman online," Sam muttered.

"So you're a psychologist." Layla tried to ignore the glowering man beside her. Seriously? What right did Sam have to be angry that the interview was going ahead? He'd shown his true colors by defacing her drawings. At least she knew he'd been in the office and not with another woman.

Bob nodded. "Yes, I study human behavior through observation and interpretation to help people cope more effectively with life issues."

Sam leaned forward. "Be careful. He reads people's body language and tells them what they want to hear."

"At least he's brave enough to tell people uncomfortable truths to their face instead of slinking out at dawn and scrawling on their personal papers like a child," Layla snapped. "And I'm sure he doesn't give advice unless someone has asked for his opinion."

"That's true," Bob said. "I would never presume."

Sam folded his arms across his chest. "Would you jump to conclusions or point fingers without gathering all the facts?"

"I do take my time to consider the entire situation before—"

Layla slammed her pen on the table. "Don't talk about me as if I'm not sitting right here, Sam."

"You started it."

She waved a dismissive hand. "I was making a general statement."

"About me."

"If I could interrupt." Bob's gaze flicked from Layla to Sam and back to Layla. "You mentioned reading body language, and that is something I have learned to do over my years of practice. But I can't see inside a mind. Every individual is unique, and I am very privileged to be in a profession where people trust me enough to share their innermost thoughts. In fact, I specialize in couples counseling, helping people breach the barriers to intimacy that are keeping them apart. I am a grateful guide on their journey to self-fulfillment."

"My apologies." Layla gave him a warm smile. "Unlike some arrogant, insensitive people I know, you are refreshingly humble."

"You're too kind." Bob leaned forward, his dark eyes focused, intent. "May I ask a question?"

"Of course."

"Are you serious about getting married? If you have feelings for someone else . . ."

"Yes, I'm serious. And no. I have no feelings—"

"Isn't that the truth," Sam interrupted with a snort.

"I have no romantic feelings for anyone in particular," Layla continued, emphasizing each word. "Especially not for people who act one way to your face and another behind your back."

"I'm looking for a woman who respects our traditions, but not a traditional woman," Bob said. "At your age, I would expect you to have had a boyfriend or two, but if you've had intimate—"

"I'm not that old." Layla bristled, cutting him off.

"In this market you are." Sam smirked. "Most of the girls who have responded to my desilovematch.com profile are under twenty-one. You're practically an auntie. I'm surprised your profile got as much interest as it did."

Layla narrowed her eyes. "Oh. I'm sorry. Did I ask for your opinion? Um. No. I didn't. And yet here you are unable to hold it in again. Maybe you should go get your black Sharpie and scribble what you really think about Bob on his CV and hide it in the trash."

"Should I come back another time?" Bob asked.

"No. Of course not." She forced a smile through clenched teeth. "How do you feel about your wife working? Are you looking for a career-oriented spouse or someone to stay home, clean up your mess, and eat cold oatmeal while you run out in the early hours of the morning for a fictitious meeting?"

Bob chuckled. "I enjoy my work, and I'm looking for someone

who has a fulfilling career outside of the home, but also likes to travel. My family owns properties in Sydney, London, Madrid, and Delhi. I employ a cook and a maid, so those skills are not necessary."

"How perfectly lovely." She shot a smug look at Sam. Another tick in the plus box. Bob was definitely a contender. Her parents would like him, too. He was a nice, average, reliable guy, albeit a little boring and bland. But if she were to score him on the list of traits that her fantasy man possessed, he would get a zero. There was no mystery behind that smile. No fire or fury. Bob wouldn't slam her against a Jeep and kiss her. He wouldn't tear off her clothes or have sex with her against a door. What you saw was what you got. And what you got was a brown version of everyman Bob.

"I have one more question," Bob said.

"Of course."

"Are you a virgin, madam?"

"Excuse me?"

Sam pushed away from the table, his chair scraping against the tile floor.

"I want my wife and I to truly belong to each other." Bob handed her a card. "This doctor is a family friend. He can do the premarital exam. If it all checks out—"

"No." Sensing Sam's fury, Layla slammed her arm across his chest as he rose from his seat with all the power and menace of a tsunami. "I knew this might come up at some point. I'm sure he doesn't mean to be offensive."

Sam growled. "And I won't mean to cause him pain when I rip off his arms."

"There's no need for violence," she said, thinking quickly. "I'm sure Bob will understand that I require the same of my partner. You can take him to the restroom and do his premarital exam."

Bob's eyes widened. "I beg your pardon?"

"Sam is a doctor. He'll be able to confirm you are untouched so we can truly belong to each other. Isn't that what you're expecting to hear from your doctor friend about me?"

"That's ridiculous. I'm a man."

"And I shouldn't have the same requirement? How is that fair? Are you afraid of having your intimate area examined and judged by a stranger? Or are you saying you're . . ." She slapped a hand over her mouth in mock horror. "Not pure?"

Bob looked shocked, then affronted. "I'm a healthy thirty-two-year-old man and I needed experience for the marriage—"

"So you're not a virgin?" Layla stood abruptly. "I'm so sorry, Bob. I'm afraid that's a deal killer for me."

"Now can I punch him?" Sam asked, his body quivering with rage.

"No, but you can walk him out." She felt curiously calm as she smiled at Bob. Only a few weeks ago she would have reacted in a much different way. But she was running her own business now and making mature choices about her future. "Blue Fury" was behind her. Except for falling off the sex wagon last night with Sam, she was a changed woman. She could fight fire with fire—not fury—and she didn't need a man to save her. "Thank you for coming. It was nice to meet you."

Decent—albeit traditional—guy that he was, Bob shook her hand. "I should have known when I saw your receptionist and her dog that we weren't a match. Your passion and fire would be wasted on me, Layla. You need to find your Qays."

"You want me to find a man I can drive to madness and death?"

Bob laughed, his gaze flicking to Sam. "I don't think you'll need to look too hard."

· 16 ·

SAM took a deep breath and then another, steeling himself for his least favorite activity of all time. Even as a boy, he had dreaded the family trips to the shops on El Camino Real in Sunnyvale. Invariably he would be dragged into an Indian clothing store, and hours would go by before his mother remembered she had a son who needed food and water. It was a torture worse than death—bright colors, loud music, unorganized racks and tables heaped with clothes, women roaming the aisles in packs, pouncing on him because he was the same size as a nephew or cousin who had wisely refused to be fitted for wedding attire . . .

There was no escape.

So why was he voluntarily walking into one of the hellholes now? Was he here for Nisha or to put things right with Layla? He hadn't had a chance to talk to her after Baboo's visit because as soon as the psychologist had gone, she and Daisy had disappeared for the afternoon.

He found Layla's aunt's store, Krishna Fashions, tucked away in a suburban strip mall at the intersection of the Lawrence Expressway and East El Camino Real. Widely known as Little India, the area had sprung up to serve the needs of the South Bay's South Asian population during the Silicon Valley boom. Anchored by the

Bharat Bazaar market, the area boasted a plethora of clothing stores, buffets, restaurants, cafés, and food stalls.

Everywhere sounds and scents assailed him. Store windows filled with brightly colored saris and salwar kameez enticed groups of aunties out for a Saturday stroll, while girls in pretty pink party dresses pulled their grandparents toward the *chaat* stands along the road, begging for walk-away treats. Across the road, a line had formed outside the door to the Pink Palace, famous for their *masala dosas*, the lacy, crisp rice-flour crepes stuffed with turmeric-spiced potatoes and onions he'd loved as a boy.

Sam pushed open the door only to be greeted by the glare of lights, the blare of Bollywood music, and a vast array of colors, patterns, and clothes. He wandered through the men's section as he searched the sprawling store for Nisha and Layla. It had been years since he'd shopped for traditional clothes. He doubted his *kurta pajama* or *sherwani* would fit him now. Although the pants were loose fitting, the long tunic would no doubt be tight around his chest after two years of daily workouts at the gym.

His hand slid over the soft fabric of an embroidered jacket as he remembered all the weddings, *sangeet* ceremonies, and engagement parties he'd attended over the years. He missed the dancing, music, endless food, *rishta* aunties trying to marry off all the single men and women, the drunk uncles, and the hours he'd spent with his friends at the bar checking out all the girls in their beautiful clothes. Had Layla been at any of those weddings? If she had, why hadn't he noticed her before?

"Are you looking for a sherwani?" A woman dressed in a plain beige sari, her gray-streaked hair pulled back in a tight bun, peered over the rack. She was accompanied by a slightly younger woman wearing a name tag that read DEEPA on her bright orange and pink salwar kameez. There was a strong family resemblance between them, although the older woman was about the same age as his mother.

"Over here we have the new styles." The older woman gestured to a rack of wedding attire.

"I'm just looking for my sister. She's here with her friend Layla."

"Layla is Nira's niece," Deepa said, gesturing to her companion. "They're in the changing room trying on clothes. I'll let them know you're here."

"This one just came in." Nira pulled out a long cream-colored jacket with heavy maroon embroidery. "Modern but traditional. Classy and elegant. You aren't a man who likes too much fuss so you'll appreciate that the decoration on this sherwani is just down the front and over the chest."

Sam studied the outfit. It was exactly what he would have chosen if he were getting married. "It's very nice, Auntie-ji, but I'm not going to any weddings, least of all my own."

"You never know. A good boy like you who looks after your sister, handsome and tall . . ." She slid her measuring tape around his arm. "Strong, too." She reached up to wrap the measuring tape around Sam's chest. "Fit."

"I don't—"

"It's perfect for you. I'll need to make some adjustments, but it should be ready for you in a week or two."

Sam grimaced. "Thank you, but I really don't need a sherwani—"

"You don't like our clothes?" Her mouth turned down in a sad smile.

His gut clenched. He was no good at this game. Usually his mother did all the bargaining when it came to buying traditional outfits. "Yes, I do. They're beautiful but—"

"So no problem." She continued measuring him, writing down numbers on the small notepad she had pulled out of her apron.

"I'm not getting married."

"Not getting married?" She waved a dismissive hand. "Of course you're getting married. A man like you was made to settle down."

"I'm not getting married now," he explained. "When I do—if I do—I'll get my clothes at the time."

"At the time? There is no time at the time." She snapped the tape after the last measurement. "I'll give you a special price. One thousand dollars. It will be ready next week."

"What's going on here?" Layla came up beside him, a sticky orange jalebi in one hand and a silver shawl in the other. "Are you getting married?"

"No, but your aunt seems to think I am."

Layla laughed. "What price did Nira Auntie give you?"

Sam's mouth opened and closed again. "I don't care about the price. I don't need—"

"See." Nira smiled. "He doesn't care about the price. He knows $1,000 for this quality is a good deal."

"For last year's style?" Layla fingered the material. "This isn't worth more than $700."

Nira slapped a hand over her heart. "Seven hundred dollars? You want me to give it away? I'll go out of business. He can have it for $1,100 and that's a final price."

"What happened to $1,000?" Sam asked.

"That was the old price." Nira shook her head. "You should have taken it before it went up."

"Seven hundred fifty dollars," Layla said. "And you're lucky to get an offer like that since it's covered in dust from sitting so long."

Nira brushed off the sherwani. "That's not dust. That's pure gold powder that we sprinkle on it for luck. Just one ounce costs over $100."

"Look at this thread." Buoyed by Layla's presence, he jumped into the game. He negotiated with clients and employees every day. How hard could it be?

"No, Sam." Layla groaned softly and shook her head.

"That's high-quality thread," Nira's lips quivered at the corners. "What was I thinking offering it to you for $1,100 when a sherwani of that quality usually goes for $1,200?"

"At the store down the street they are charging $700 for sherwanis that don't have threads on them," Layla countered. "Maybe we should go there."

"One thousand dollars and I'll throw in the *juti*." Nira smiled. At least Sam thought it was a smile, or maybe she was baring her teeth. "Special price on shoes for friends of family."

Layla glanced over at the rows of formal wedding shoes. "Embroidered. Not plain."

Sam made one last attempt to save his masculine pride. "I'm buying my sister's clothes so I can't pay more than $800."

Nira threw up her hands. "Any less than $950 and I might as well close my doors."

"You won't go out of business for $50, Auntie-ji." Layla held out her hand. "Are we agreed on $900?"

"It hurts my heart that family would take advantage of an old lady like me." Nira shook her head. "Eight hundred seventy-five dollars."

"Including the pajama," Sam added, gesturing to the pants that went with the outfit.

"You two together . . . rascals." Nira shook Sam's hand. "Eight hundred eighty-five dollars. Pay up front."

"What just happened?" Sam watched Nira carry the sherwani away.

Layla laughed. "We tag-teamed and now you're all ready for your wedding. You just need to pick out your shoes."

"I didn't come here to buy an outfit, I came for . . ." He trailed off when he saw Nisha laughing with Deepa by the fitting rooms. She was wearing a royal blue short-sleeved *ghagra choli* heavily embroidered with silver thread, a matching orange skirt draped over her lap, and a silver shawl over her shoulders. She clearly didn't need him. She was handling it all herself, as he had always known in his heart she could.

"I came to see you."

Layla finished her jalebi and licked her lips. "Here I am."

"We need to talk."

"I need to wash my hands. I was on my way to the restroom when I saw you about to be swindled by Nira Auntie. I was tempted to leave you to her mercy, but she had that special glint in her eye that meant trouble."

"She doesn't look like a swindler." He followed Layla through the racks of clothes to the back of the store.

"You obviously haven't seen *Dirty Rotten Scoundrels*," Layla said. "No one thinks a sweet old lady is going to soak them for all their cash."

His pulse kicked up a notch when they reached the restroom. This wasn't going as planned. "I shouldn't have left you at my apartment the way I did," he blurted out. "Royce had a layover and asked to meet at the office at five thirty A.M. I didn't know how things stood between us, so I took the easy way out."

Layla pushed open the door. "I got the message when I woke up alone and came into the office to discover my designs in the trash covered with horrible comments. But that's just how things roll with me. I have an uncanny ability to pick the wrong guys."

Sam leaned against the doorframe while she washed her hands

in the sink. "That wasn't me; it was Royce. He's brilliant at what he does but he lacks empathy and basic social skills. After I saw what he'd done, I put the papers in the trash hoping they'd be cleared away before you saw them. I didn't want you to get hurt."

She studied him in silence as she dried her hands. "I don't know why, but I believe you."

He let out a sigh of relief. "I'm glad to hear it."

"I'm just used to bad hookups. Some of them would leave right after we had sex, or they'd call a cab to send me home before I even put on my clothes."

"Maybe you picked those guys because they were safe," he suggested. "There was no risk of getting emotionally involved with them. No chance of loving them and losing them the way you lost your brother."

"That makes sense. I never thought of it that way." She leaned against the sink. "Is Royce back for good? What about the office?"

"Don't worry about Royce," he promised, although he had no idea what he was going to do. With an airtight lease and the importance of the location to the Alpha Health Care pitch, there was no way Royce would give up the office. "I'll figure something out."

"Does that mean we're still playing the game?"

"I don't know," he said honestly. "Are you still planning on meeting the rest of the suitors on your father's list? I can't be objective anymore. I'll hate them all."

A pained expression crossed her face. "I need the office, Sam. I can't just walk away. I'm not making enough money to pay rent, and my dad was going to let me use it for free. Working above the restaurant also means I can help out my family when they need me. And my aunties have been giving that address to people looking for work."

Sam needed the office, too. For Nisha. For justice. For his own redemption. But he didn't want to think about it right now, didn't want to deal with the complication. He wasn't interested in playing the game if it meant either of them would have to leave. He couldn't imagine not seeing Layla every day. Something had changed for him last night. He'd had a glimpse into the life of a man who was worthy of a woman like Layla. He wanted a chance to explore it, and he didn't want to waste any time.

After a quick look around to make sure they were alone, he walked into the restroom and locked the door.

"What are you doing?"

Coming up behind Layla, Sam brushed her hair over one shoulder, baring the slender expanse of her neck. "I want you," he whispered.

"Here? In the restroom?" She turned to face him.

"Here." He wrapped one arm around her and pulled her close. "Now." He nibbled the shell of her ear, tracing the gentle curve with his tongue. "Tonight." Skimming his lips down her neck, he breathed in the light, floral scent of her perfume. "Tomorrow." He dropped little licks and nips along her bare skin. "And the next day. And the day after that."

Layla let out a breathy moan. "This isn't a good idea, Sam."

"What are you afraid of?" He cupped her cheek, tilted her head back so he could stare into the warmth of her eyes. "Falling for me?"

Her eyes slipped closed and she drew in a ragged breath. "Yes."

· 17 ·

LAYLA'S heart thudded in her chest. He was so handsome, so sexy. Their night together had been incredible. But when she'd woken up alone, she'd felt that same sick feeling she had every time she met someone new. She was done with men who couldn't commit. She wanted something more, a deeper connection; a real relationship—even if it didn't involve love. But she didn't know if she could find it with Sam.

Sam cupped her nape, his thumb stroking her cheek. He bent down until his lips were only a breath away. "You take care of everyone. Let me take care of you."

"How?"

He gently cradled her face between his broad palms. Her lips parted with a sharp inhale and he pressed his mouth tenderly against hers.

The softness of his kiss was unexpected. Hidden away in the restroom, with no chance of being discovered, she gave in to her desire.

His fingers wove through her hair, and he pulled her closer, deepening the kiss, his tongue sliding into her mouth with a promise of making all her sex-in-a-restroom fantasies come true.

"How was that?" he murmured against her lips.

"I don't want to fall for you and lose you the way I lost Dev."

He tilted her head back, thumbs framing her face. "Trust me,

Layla. I'm not going anywhere. But I won't be able to sit through any more interviews with men who aren't worthy of you. I won't be able to be as restrained as I was with Baboo."

"You threatened to break his arms."

"I wanted to break his face."

She laughed. "That's a little excessive, don't you think?"

"A little bit much was asking me to take him into the restroom for a premarital exam."

She liked this about Sam—his ability to understand her insecurities and use humor to ease her fears. Her hands slid over his shoulders and she leaned up to kiss him again.

"I want you." His tongue swept through her mouth, making her shiver. She'd enjoyed sex with the men she'd been with, but no one had wanted her with an intensity that took her breath away.

"You've got me until someone needs to pee."

He gave a satisfied rumble, running his hands up and down her body. "Spread your legs."

And now, as if she weren't already wet from being kissed and caressed until her nerve endings tingled, the dirty talking in that deep, dark rumble of a voice spiraled her body into overdrive.

There was only one little problem.

"Sam . . . I'm wearing—"

"Not for long." He yanked open her skirt and shoved it down her hips. But when his fingers slid between her thighs, searching for the edge of her panties, they just kept sliding.

"What is this?" He backed away, studying her waist-slimming, tummy-tucking, thigh-squeezing, ass-lifting elastic shapewear with confusion.

Layla pulled at the elastic waist and released it with a loud, skin-pinching snap. "I wear it when I go clothes shopping. It holds things in." She hesitated. "And keeps things out."

Sam studied the garment. "Do I cut you out of it? I have a pocket-knife."

"Nothing so drastic." She looked down to hide her mortification. "It kind of . . . rolls."

A choking sound made her lift her head. Sam was leaning against the sink, fingers braced against his forehead, shaking with laughter.

"Do you have any normal underwear?"

"Of course I do," Layla huffed. "And stop laughing. It's not funny. Obviously, I wasn't expecting you to show up and seduce me in a restroom. If I had, I would have worn easy-access pants."

"I can't think of any better way to show you how much I want you than by getting you out of that . . ."

"Shapewear," she offered.

"You don't need shapewear. You have a shape. You're beautiful and all I can think about when I see you is how badly I want my hands on you." He reached for her and she backed away.

"There's no sexy way to get this off me, so if you're imagining some kind of striptease where I slowly peel it off, revealing my body inch by inch, just tuck that image away and replace it with opening a can of Pillsbury Crescent Rolls, or if you're not familiar with that delicious treat, just imagine releasing any product that's under pressure. Everything wants out at once."

Sam put a fist to his mouth like he was either deep in thought or fighting back his laughter. "What if we cut out a strategic access panel?"

"Are you kidding? Do you know how much these things cost? Also, aside from the fact that I don't allow sharp objects near my intimate parts, I can hardly walk around for the rest of the day with my nether regions on display for unsuspecting subway workers who might happen to be working underground when I walk over a grate."

"So what do we do?" Sam asked.

"You're just going to have to turn around, pretend I haven't ruined the moment, and when I tell you it's safe, you can resume where you left off."

Sam obediently turned away.

"Naughty." Layla glared at him in the mirror. "I see you peeking. Face the other wall."

"Your bossiness is turning me on." Sam faced the blank wall.

"I'm glad, because these clearly didn't do the trick." She rolled the shapewear over her tummy, grunting as she inched the elastic material over her hips. Sweat beaded on her forehead with the effort. This was, hands down, the most embarrassing moment of her entire life.

"What's going on over there? It sounds like you've decided to go ahead without me."

"If I tried that, I'd lose a couple of fingers from lack of circulation." Layla leaned against the wall and took a deep breath.

"Is that heavy breathing because you like my ass?" His voice was laced with amusement.

Layla rubbed the sweat off her face with the bottom of her shirt. "You do have a nice ass, as your friend Karen so crassly pointed out, and I'm so desperate to get my hands on it, I am actually reconsidering my rule against sharp objects down below." With another grunt she shoved the elastic over the widest part of her hips.

"Do you need some help?"

"I would honestly rather die." She peeled the underwear down her thighs and pushed it, along with her skirt, down to her ankles. Leaning back against the wall, she patted her shirt against her body, trying to soak up the sweat.

"Now do I get my present?"

"There's an additional complication." Layla stared at her sandals. "This isn't going the way it does in the movies." She bent down to unbuckle the straps. "Next time you decide to surprise seduce me when I'm out, could you let me know in advance? I'll wear a loose dress, a tearable lace thong, and a pair of flip-flops for quick, easy-access sex."

"Does this mean there's going to be a next time?"

She toed off her sandals and stepped out of her clothes. "All I know is that there had better be a *this* time, because I must have burned one thousand calories getting ready for you."

Sam spun around, his gaze raking over her half-naked body as he closed the distance between them. "Now, that's a shape."

"You're just horny and desperate to have some. Lucky for you, I'm ready to go. Getting that shapewear off was its own foreplay." She grabbed the bottom of his shirt and pushed it up, her fingers gliding over the ripples of his abs and the hard planes of his chest. With an annoyed grunt, Sam reached up and ripped the T-shirt over his head, baring his chest for her viewing pleasure.

"Oh God." She pressed her lips to his firm, toned skin. "You look and taste better than my mom's jalebis."

Sam grumbled his displeasure. "Will we always have to talk about your mother when we're having sex?"

"How about we don't talk?" Her breath hitched when he slid a thick finger into her wet heat. Slow. Firm. Agonizingly delicious.

"You're so wet," he murmured. "It really did turn you on."

"You turn me on." She arched against him, pleasure rippling through her core. Sam pushed another finger inside, angling to brush against her sweet spot.

"I thought you needed me, like right now," she panted as he palmed her breast through her clothes.

"I need to give you pleasure first." His heated gaze trapped her, made her insides tighten.

"So you're a gentleman sex beast." She wrapped her arms around his neck, ran her fingers through the softness of his hair. His shoulders were so broad, his neck corded with muscle. But unlike Harman's steroid-enhanced physique, Sam's perfect body was real.

"I don't feel like a gentleman." His voice was deeper than normal, thick and hoarse. He teased her nipple to a peak through her clothes. "The things I want to do to you right now are as far from gentlemanly as you can get."

And yet, he was focused entirely on her body, her pleasure. "I think you could probably make me come with all the dirty things you say."

"Kiss me," he demanded.

"Now you're the bossy one."

His strong fingers stroked their way to her core. "Say my name and kiss me."

"Sam." She cupped his face and pulled him down, kissing him with fevered intent.

A rumble of pleasure vibrated in his chest. "Say it just like that when I make you come."

"There's that big ego again," she said dryly.

"You know what they say about a man with a big ego . . ."

Laughter bubbled up inside her. How could sex be fun and hot at the same time? Were people supposed to laugh when they were making out? Jonas never laughed. Sex was an almost religious experience for him that involved soulful looks, intense gazes, and misquoted lyrics from his favorite songs. Before him, her boyfriends had been unremarkable, noteworthy only for their uniform dullness and rapid disappearance when the deed was done.

"He wears big shoes?"

"He has big hands." He made good use of his big hands, teasing her until she was panting, not from fear, but from arousal, the thrill of being with a man who knew what he wanted, the danger of being discovered, and the sheer exhaustion of shapewear removal.

"I want to taste you." He dropped to his knees, and she saw her raw desire reflected back in his dark eyes. "Yes?"

"Definitely, yes." She threaded her hands through his hair as he kissed his way along her inner thigh, pulling him to where she wanted him to go.

"Slowly, sweetheart. I want this to be good for you."

Most of the men she'd been with wanted it to be good for them. It was about their pleasure, their need. But Sam took his time, his mouth moving to her other thigh, teasing her with the sensual scrape of rough stubble on her sensitive skin, the heat of his breath on her flesh.

"I can't take any more," she groaned.

His mouth closed over the most sensitive part of her and he licked and teased, worshipping her until she was holding his hair so tightly her knuckles had turned white.

Voices filtered through the door. Footsteps. Sam clamped his hands on her hips, holding her in place as his warm, wet tongue did things that turned her knees to jelly.

"Look at me," he whispered.

She met his heated gaze, held it even when the footsteps faded away and his talented tongue sent her over the edge in a storm of sensation. She clapped a hand over her mouth to muffle her cry.

Sam rose and stood in front of her, a slow, lazy smile on his lips. "Sweeter than I imagined."

"That was incredibly hot. Now, it's your turn." She reached for his belt.

Sam gently moved her hand away. "This wasn't about me."

Her forehead creased in confusion. "You said you wanted me. I deshapeweared, if that's even a word."

"And watching you come was the hottest thing I've ever seen." He picked up her clothes. "But I'm not like the guys who hurt you. I can get as much pleasure giving you pleasure as I do taking my own."

"Are you serious?" No way was he denying her. Yes, his oral skills were second to none, but that was just the warm-up. She was ready for the main event.

"Yes."

"You don't want to have sex?" She stared pointedly at the bulge below his belt.

He hesitated, shifted his weight, cleared his throat. "I didn't say that exactly."

"Sam?"

He lifted a curious eyebrow.

"Get naked."

TWENTY minutes later, Layla had to admit that Sam had filled all her wishes, and some she didn't even know she had. Also, who would have thought that restroom mirrors were positioned so perfectly for viewing pleasure while holding on tightly to the sink? Or that running water could hide all sorts of sounds, from moans and groans to a soft scream?

She pulled on her skirt while Sam straightened his clothes. There was no way she was going to go through the effort of putting on the shapewear again. She could survive a few hours going commando.

"I guess this means I should cancel my date with Harman," she said.

"Only if you want him to live." Sam pulled her into his arms and kissed her cheek, her jaw, her neck, and finally her mouth, igniting the fire inside her all over again. What was it about Sam that made her just want to drown in his kisses, the heat of his powerful body, and the strength of his arms?

"We'd better go," she said finally, tearing herself away. "Everyone will be wondering where we are."

"I'll make sure the coast is clear." Sam slipped out, closing the door behind him.

Knees weak, Layla leaned against the wall. She'd rationalized their last encounter as a one-night stand. Sex and nothing more. But this felt different. Intimate. Emotions were involved. And not just hers. Where did they go from here? Did she hold him to the game? Cancel the rest of her blind dates and kick him out of the office? Or was she reading too much into this, just like she always did?

SAM knew something was wrong the moment he stepped out of the restroom. There was a stillness in the air, a curious tension. He looked around for Nisha but couldn't see her.

When Layla joined him, he clasped her hand. It was a small pleasure to take care of someone who looked after everyone around her—whether it was finding jobs for her clients, helping her mother in the kitchen, looking after her nieces, or accommodating Daisy's need to have Max in the office. And now she'd given his sister a little bit of normal.

"Sam." Nisha's tremulous, strangled voice was barely audible above the music and chatter, but it made every hair on the back of his neck stand on end.

"Nisha?" He shouted her name, dragging Layla through the racks of clothes. "Where are you?"

"Sam!"

His pulse kicked up a notch, heart pounding in his chest. He burst through the racks near the cashier only to find Ranjeet standing in front of his sister.

"Well, look who's here." Ranjeet's slick voice unlocked a cesspool of painful memories. "Sam. It's nice to see you again."

Sam's hands curled into fists. He hadn't seen the bastard since the divorce proceedings. Against her lawyer's advice, Nisha had agreed to give up everything she owned—including her wedding jewelry, her interest in the marital home, and her right to maintenance payments—just to be free of Ranjeet. The bastard had even tried to take the insurance payments that paid for her rehab and the house renovations, but the insurance company had resisted.

It had taken three security guards to drag Sam out of the building after the legal papers had been signed. Even then, he'd waited on the sidewalk, ready to make Ranjeet suffer. He should have known the bastard would slither out the back. Nisha had made him promise not to hunt Ranjeet down. She wanted it to be over. But now that he had Ranjeet in his sights, the anger surged again.

"Get the fuck away from her."

If not for his piercing black eyes, the man in front of him would have been wholly unremarkable. His dark hair was short and neatly cut, beard and mustache trimmed. He had a prominent nose, curved like a beak, and a rail-thin frame that made him look deceptively lean beneath his blue button-down shirt, despite the extra inch he had on Sam in height.

"You can't begrudge me a moment with my lovely ex-wife. I was so hoping she had recovered from the brain injury that caused her delusions after the fall."

Sam glanced over at Nisha, his stomach recoiling when he saw the look of sheer horror on her face.

"If you even look at her again, I'll break every one of your fingers and end your goddamn career."

"What's going on?" Layla stepped in front of him, her face creased in consternation. "Who is that?"

"Dr. Ranjeet Bedi."

Layla turned and the surgeon smiled. "Sam and I worked together at St. Vincent's. He was my most promising resident. And Nisha, of course, was once my wife." He tipped his head to the side, studying Layla intently. "And you are . . ."

"None of your fucking business." Sam shoved Layla behind him.

Seemingly unflustered, Ranjeet sighed. "Still so hostile. No wonder poor Nisha hasn't recovered. You're feeding her delusions. It was an accident. Plain and simple. It's nobody's fault. Let her move on, Sam. And you need to move on, too."

Slimy, fork-tongued, slithering snake. If Sam hadn't trusted his sister implicitly, even he might have been fooled by Ranjeet's smooth, friendly manner, his distress when she was brought to the ER, his horror when she was told she might never walk again. The surgeon hadn't cracked once. From the moment he ran into the ER to the day he signed the divorce papers, he'd played everything from the concerned husband to the innocent victim, conning hospital staff, social workers, police, insurers, and lawyers.

Sam's hand curled into a fist. This was his chance to dispense a visceral, immediate form of justice. No more making requests for hospital files or begging security staff to let him see the surveillance tapes. No more fruitless meetings with police and insurance investigators. Ranjeet would suffer the way Nisha had suffered. He would feel her pain.

He moved to strike only to find Layla in his way.

"Don't do it." She placed her hands on his chest, pushing him back. "I don't know him, Sam. And I don't know what happened. But if you hit him, what happens then? This isn't Evan. He's clearly not a friend who you can make up with over a couple of drinks. You might wind up with a criminal record. You could even spend time in jail. Your business could suffer. And what about Nisha? Who's going to look after her then?"

Rage surged through his veins, sweeping away all rational thought. "Get out of my way. You've done enough. This is why Nisha never went out. This is exactly what she was afraid would happen. You should have left her alone. If she'd stayed at home, she would have been safe. If I hadn't been with you, I would have been here to protect her." He regretted the words even as they fell from his lips. At the back of his mind he knew they were wrong. This wasn't Layla's fault. But Nisha deserved justice, and Layla was standing in his way.

Her face paled but her hands stayed pressed against him. "Sam, please. Don't do this."

"What's going on here?" Nira joined them with Deepa trailing behind her.

Ranjeet pulled a card from his jacket pocket and handed it to her. "Dr. Ranjeet Bedi. I called earlier about picking up my sherwani for my wedding. Sam and Nisha are old friends, but it seems they aren't happy to see me."

Unbelievable. He was getting married again. Another woman was going to suffer.

"It's right this way." Nira led Ranjeet away while Deepa hovered in the aisle, blocking Sam's pursuit. Layla dropped her hands and turned to Nisha, who hadn't moved since Sam arrived.

"Are you okay?"

"I just want to go home," she said quietly.

"Of course. I'll take you—"

"I want Sam," she said. "I'm sorry. I just . . . I want Sam to take me home."

Layla's face softened with understanding. "I'll get your bags—"

"No." Nisha wheeled herself toward the door. "I don't want anything. I should never have come. I'm sorry, Layla. You were very kind to take me shopping, but . . ." Her voice cracked, broke. "Bhaiya! Get me out of here."

Caught in a maelstrom of emotion, the world closing in around him, Sam pressed the access button and pushed Nisha out into the cold, rainy evening.

It was only as he was driving away that he realized he hadn't even said good-bye.

· 18 ·

HE'S so much like Jonas ...

Layla studied the bartender who was shaking a martini on the other side of the bar. With his long, shaggy blond hair, wiry frame, and elegant fingers, he could have been Jonas with a bad dye job.

"Can I buy you another drink?"

Already past her limit, Layla shook her head without even looking at the man who had just sat on the stool beside her. She'd turned down several guys in the hour she'd been waiting for Harman to show up for their date, and they just kept coming.

"No, thanks." She'd taken a cab so she could enjoy a few drinks, but it was the last thing she wanted a stranger to know.

"A beautiful girl like you shouldn't have to drink alone." He was a few inches taller than her and solidly built—an athlete of some sort, she figured, definitely someone who stayed in shape. His light brown hair had been shaved close to his head, and he wore a silver medallion over an orange Giants T-shirt.

"I'm meeting someone."

"Hello, Meeting Someone. I'm Matthias. You look like you need cheering up."

He was an attractive man. Fit. And obviously interested in getting her into bed. Exactly the kind of guy she would have hooked up with in New York. But she didn't feel anything when he smiled.

Her heart didn't pound. Her body didn't heat. Her skin didn't tingle. And instead of the rush of adrenaline she'd felt when Sam walked into a room, she felt numb.

She'd felt numb for the last four days, but who was counting?

"Just having a bad day." She didn't want to encourage him, but he supported her team. How bad could he be?

"I think you're suffering from a lack of vitamin me," Matthias said.

She bit back a laugh. "Does that line really work?"

"You're still here." He leaned closer, his hand sliding up her leg.

"Take your hand off me." She braced herself, mentally running through the sequence of moves she was going to use if he didn't take his hand away. She hadn't lied to Sam about learning Krav Maga. It had saved her from more than one bad encounter in a bar.

"Come on, sugar. Loosen up. Your date isn't going to show."

"You heard her. Hands off. Or do you want me to do it for you, broken finger by broken finger?" Sam came up behind them, the low rumble of his voice making her melt inside.

Layla waved him away. "I can handle him, Sam."

"I can handle him better." Sam yanked Matthias off the stool and shoved him aside.

"What the fuck, dude?" Matthias turned on Sam, his hands curling into fists.

Live to the danger, and annoyed by Sam's assumption that she needed saving, she got up and grabbed Matthias by the shirt, turning her furious gaze on Sam. "You handled him like a caveman." She drove her knee between Matthias's legs, and he doubled over in pain. "I use skill."

"Kicking a man in the nuts isn't skill."

"It is when I do it." She released Matthias and he dropped to the floor. "See? I incapacitated him. You just made him angry."

Two burly bouncers pushed their way through the crowd and grabbed Sam by the arms. "Let's go. You're out of here."

"I'm the one who started it." Layla gave an exasperated sigh. "If you're going to throw someone out for fighting, it should be me."

"I helped," Sam offered. "I pulled him off the stool. You'd better throw me out, too."

"Are you with her?" The bouncers released Sam and he smoothed down his shirt.

"I sure am." He wrapped a possessive arm around her shoulders. "I'll be in the doghouse tonight for being late, but I always make it up to her in bed. Don't I, *meri jaan*?"

She was hardly his "dear." More likely she was a thorn in his side. But she doubted the bouncers understood Urdu, so she forced a smile. At the very least she'd gotten rid of Matthias without breaking her nails. Daisy had spent an hour painting tiny orange lotus flowers on the red press-ons for her big date.

"What are you doing here, Sam?"

"What am I doing here?" Sam gave a look of mock horror. "I thought it was date night. Don't tell me the babysitter is at home looking after our six kids for nothing."

"Six kids?" One of the bouncers reached over Layla and shook Sam's hand. "Respect, man. She doesn't look a day over twenty-eight."

"Twenty-eight?" Layla gave an affronted sniff. "I've only just turned twenty-six."

"Married her at seventeen and didn't waste time." Sam patted her tummy. "Good thing I'm not a fan of 'roids. Tonight we're going for seven."

"Guess whose nuts are next if you don't get your hand off me?" Layla muttered under her breath.

The bouncer laughed. "I can't say I envy you going back to a house full of kids, but you're clearly having fun making them."

Layla didn't know whether to be annoyed or amused after the bouncers let them off with a warning. On one hand, she was perfectly capable of handling the unwanted attention. On the other, she'd never had a man swoop in to save her before, and she couldn't help but be touched by the gesture, even after his behavior at her aunt's store.

"Six kids?" She took her seat at the bar and Sam sat beside her.

"Seven after tonight, unless you don't forgive me. I came to apologize." He waved over the bartender and ordered a snakebite, receiving nods of approval from around the bar.

"How did you know I was here?" She nodded when the bartender offered her a refill. The night had suddenly become interesting again.

"Daisy told me about your date. I checked Harman's Instagram to see if he'd posted anything and saw he was doing a photo shoot on Baker Beach. I figured he'd stood you up so I came to make sure you were okay."

"I can look after myself."

"So I see."

Layla put down her glass. "How's Nisha?"

"She's fine." Sam finished his drink in one gulp and motioned for another. "I shouldn't have said the things I said to you. When I saw Ranjeet, I couldn't think straight. He's the reason she uses a wheelchair."

"That's not a bad grovel." She squeezed his hand. "What happened? What did he do?"

Voice thick with emotion, Sam told her about Nisha's arranged marriage and his part in bringing her and Ranjeet together. "No one knew he had a drinking problem or that he was abusive. When Nisha found out, she kept it quiet. She thought she could help him, but he was an angry, violent drunk, and in the last few months of the marriage things took a turn for the worse."

Layla's hand flew to her mouth. "He hit her?"

"No." Sam drained his glass and asked the bartender for a jug of water. "But he scared her and she could see things going that way. One day she came to the hospital to meet him for lunch. She remembers arguing with him in the back stairwell, and then the next thing she knew she was in the ER with a shattered L2 vertebra. She was sure he pushed her, although she has no memory of the accident. Ranjeet says he wasn't there, that he left her in the hallway and only found out when he was called to the ER."

Her heart squeezed in her chest. "Poor Nisha."

"Ranjeet convinced everyone she was delusional because she'd suffered a head injury during the fall, but I know Nisha. I believe her. I had her moved to Redwood Hospital and I did everything I could to get the hospital to investigate. I even contacted the police. But Ranjeet is a highly respected surgeon, and she's a nobody who couldn't even remember the details of the accident. She divorced him and the case was closed, but I heard rumors of a cover-up."

"That's horrible."

"I've been trying to get justice for her ever since." His voice hitched. "Unfortunately, I hit a brick wall at every turn. If there was a cover-up, it was a good one, because no one would talk."

"She was lucky to have you, Sam."

He shook his head. "She wasn't lucky at all. I worked beside him for years and never knew what kind of person he really was. I was the one who brought them together, and he rewarded me for it with privileges the other residents didn't get. He was a mentor, and I thought he was a friend."

She squeezed his hand. "You couldn't have known."

"I should have known."

"Is he the reason you dropped out of your residency?"

Sam sighed. "I couldn't work there and see him every day. He was the antithesis of everything a doctor stands for. Our guiding principle is to cause no harm. I also felt unworthy to be a healer. I was so blinded by ambition and all the things Ranjeet offered to do for my career, I didn't protect Nisha the way I should have."

"You're carrying a heavy burden," she said gently. "One that isn't yours to carry."

His voice hitched. "I failed her as a brother, and I failed my family as a son. I couldn't be part of that culture, or embrace the traditions that had allowed it to happen." He poured a glass of water and drained it dry.

"The only person who failed her is Ranjeet," Layla said firmly. "Culture and tradition have nothing to do with what happened to her. Even if she'd met him in a coffee shop, and they dated before getting married, there's no guarantee he would have shown his true face. She may even have had less information about him than she had when her marriage was arranged. Look at the men we interviewed. My dad screened them, and yet he didn't know that Hassan was a scammer or that Dilip was a dancer, or that Bob wanted a virgin. It took both of us to get that information, and those were just the secrets they wanted to share. The only person who was honest was the CIA agent."

"How's that for ironic?" The tension eased from Sam's shoulders.

Layla laughed. "Maybe I should choose him. He did offer to get me elephants."

He turned his hand so they were palm to palm, and squeezed her fingers. "I think you should consider your alternatives."

"What alternatives?"

"Me."

She tilted her head down to hide her smile. "You aren't on the list."

"I don't care about the damn list, and I don't care about the game. I want you, Layla. And if I have to leave the office—"

"I don't want you to leave the office," she said softly. "I like sharing the space with you. I like being with you. I like that you're caring and protective. I like that you line up your pencils, and color-code your files, and that your shoes are always polished, and your ties are perfectly knotted. I like that you are funny and sarcastic, and some of the best times I've had have been interviewing people with you. I like how loyal you are, even though you support the wrong baseball team. I like that you pretend not to know any movies but you can list almost every horror film ever made. And I like the way you kiss."

His face softened and he gave a satisfied rumble. "You like my kisses."

"Very much."

"What else do you like?"

Layla licked her lips. "Take me to your place and I'll show you."

Sam threw some money on the counter and yanked her off the stool. "Let's go."

"What are you driving?" She half walked, half ran to keep up with him.

"BMW M2. I made the first payment when I became a medical intern and drove it home to show my dad. He was so proud."

"Not too shabby."

Sam snorted. "It can do zero to sixty in less than four freaking seconds. If you have time for a detour, I can show you what it can do on the 101."

"Do I get to drive?"

"Are you crazy?"

A smile spread across her face. "Maybe just a little."

"IT was fun while it lasted." A disheveled Layla climbed into the tow truck and slid across to the middle seat.

Sam settled in beside her, wincing when he put weight on his left wrist. "Car accidents are not fun."

"Well, I wasn't hurt, thanks to your quick thinking."

"There wasn't much thinking going on when you put your hand down my pants." He gritted his teeth against the stir of desire. Even after a car accident, the thought of her naughty touch aroused him.

"I'm sorry about that." She grinned, not looking in the least remorseful. "But it seemed only fair since your hand was under my skirt."

He shook his head. "I shouldn't have taken you on the 101 at night. They don't call it the death ring for nothing."

"Death ring?" She snorted a laugh. "A rogue mule deer jumping onto the road doesn't make it the Bermuda Triangle."

"Did you see the size of that thing?" He glanced over his shoulder at the destroyed front end of his car. "It had to be over two hundred pounds."

"I couldn't help but see it. He was staring right into my eyes. I still can't believe he walked away. Too bad there aren't deer police who could hunt him down and make him pay for his crime."

"It's not funny, Layla."

Her smile faded. "You're right. I'm sorry. I was just trying to cheer you up. I feel like I'm on some kind of high right now." She dropped her hand to his lap. "How about we start where we left off?"

"I'm sure the truck driver would enjoy that."

Her hand trembled slightly when he moved it away, and something niggled at the back of Sam's mind.

"All ready to go." The tow truck driver climbed in beside them. He was a big man, at least six foot four with a barrel chest and thick thighs that stretched across the seat until they were touching Layla's leg.

That wasn't happening.

"Move this way. Give him some room." Sam tugged her sleeve with his right hand, pulling her toward him so he could put an arm around her. She settled close, her warmth soothing his frayed nerves, loosening his lungs so he could breathe again.

Tap. Tap. Tap.

Sam rolled down the window for the police officer who had been the first to arrive on the scene. "Everything okay?"

"I hate to do this because I know you're broken up about your vehicle." The police officer handed him his license and a speeding ticket. "You were doing eighty-five in a seventy zone."

"Ajay Pataudi? Is that you?" Layla leaned over, peering into the semidarkness. "I haven't seen you since Mansoor's wedding."

"Layla." Officer Pataudi reached over Sam to shake her hand. "How's your dad? I heard he was in the hospital."

"Getting better. He still can't talk but he's already bossing people around. How's Ayesha?"

"Pregnant with our third."

Sam cleared his throat and Layla's head jerked up as if she'd forgotten he was there. "Ajay, this is my friend Sam. Can you give him a break with the ticket? He bought that car with his first paycheck when he became a medical intern and drove it straight home to show his dad that all the sacrifices he'd made to give his son a better life were worth it. One minute he was #desiproud and the next, Bambi gets revenge Thumper style."

"I never liked that movie," Officer Pataudi said.

"Of course you didn't, because you have a heart. You feel for the little guy, for all the Bambis who lost their moms and all the immigrants who came here for the American dream only to be crushed by the cruel deer of fate."

"You are so much like your dad." Officer Pataudi laughed as he tore up the ticket. "For Bambi."

"Thanks, Ajay." Layla smiled. "See you at the next wedding. Give Ayesha a kiss for me."

"What the hell just happened?" Sam asked as the police officer walked away.

"Family. He's my father's cousin's sister's husband's nephew."

"Where did you find this little firecracker?" the driver asked as they drove away.

Sam tightened his arm around her. "I didn't find her. She found me."

"STOP being such a baby. I know what I'm doing." Layla wrapped the tensor bandage around Sam's wrist. After dropping the car off at the nearest garage, they'd caught a cab back to the office so Layla could close up and Sam could dig out his insurance paperwork. After the final checks had been done, she had insisted on wrapping his wrist, dragging him into the back office where the first aid kit was kept.

Sam winced when she tightened the bandage, but it wasn't the pain that discomfited as much as the lingering scents from the kitchen—the warmth of cardamom, the spice of cumin, the rich fragrances of incense and tarragon—so painfully familiar that he felt an unexpected pang of regret that he'd turned his back on a culture he had loved. Even in the office, far from the kitchen, there was no escape.

"I'm the doctor. If I say it's too tight, then it's too tight," he grumbled, his irritation not really with her but with the disaster of a night and the pull of longing that was making it difficult to stay still.

Seated across from him on a worn, black desk chair, Layla froze. "I thought you'd given up medicine for the joy of firing people for a living."

"I don't just say *You're fired* and show them out the door. I give them a motivational speech about what a good opportunity redundancy can be."

"You—Sam Mehta—give them a motivational speech?" Her eyes widened, incredulous. "Does it consist of grunts and growls, or actual words?"

"It's a good speech. They appreciate it."

"How do you know they appreciate it?" She moved closer, rolling the chair between his spread legs. His blood rushed to his groin as he imagined wrapping his arms around her, holding her tight, reassuring himself that she was safe and unharmed. He had protected her tonight. When the deer had jumped in front of them, he had reacted with lightning speed, veering off the road and into the bushes, the damage to his car caused not by his lack of skill, but by the unfortunate position of a fallen tree.

Sam shrugged. "They say 'thanks.'"

"Maybe they say 'thanks' because they're in shock." Her voice wavered the tiniest bit. "They don't know what to say or do. Their minds are going a mile a minute thinking about rent and car payments and student loans and helping their parents out. Maybe it's their friend's birthday and they're supposed to be picking up a cake and a bunch of balloons for a surprise party. Suddenly, the thought of spending that much money makes them sick. They almost can't believe what's happening. Maybe the boss made a mistake, and tomorrow she'll be back at the water cooler with a box of donuts and a story about some guy the boss hired to fire her who gave her a pep talk after destroying her life."

Taken aback by her outburst, he frowned. "Are these hypothetical people, or is this about you?"

"Why would it be about me? I got fired but I was fine. I'd just lost my boyfriend, my apartment, my liberty, and my reputation, but I kept it upbeat. I tried to think of it as an opportunity. I went to the party, had a great time, filled my purse with hors d'oeuvres because I didn't know where my next meal was going to come from, drank too much free booze so I couldn't feel the pain, and threw up all over my friend's bathroom floor. There was a guy in that mix, but I don't remember anything about him except that he left before dawn."

The niggle of warning returned. He studied her face, noting the lines of worry on her forehead and the slight dilation of her pupils.

"I think you're in shock. I should have noticed it earlier."

"I'm not in shock." She reached up and brushed his hair away from the cut she'd just tended, her touch feather light on his skin. "You're the one who was driving and got injured. If anyone is in shock, it's you."

Sam cupped her jaw, holding her head still. "Your pupils are dilated."

"It's a design flaw. It happens when sexy men get too close."

A smile tugged at his lips. "You think I'm sexy?"

"You are when you talk in that soft, deep voice and sit so close I can feel the heat of your body, and wear that craze-inducing cologne, and cradle my face like I'm a delicate flower." She licked her lips and his gaze fell to her soft, lush mouth. It was an invitation he couldn't ignore.

"You forgot the part where I tried to kill you by crashing into a deer at high speed," he offered, just in case he was misreading the signs.

"I'm trying not to remember it because you busted out some pretty slick moves to keep us from going over the cliff. Nothing sexier than a man who can stay calm in a crisis and save a girl so she can live to get fired another day. You, Sam Mehta, are a hero."

She thought he was worthy. It was a balm to his soul.

Reassured, he slid one hand beneath her hair to cup her nape. "You're trembling. That's another sign of shock."

"I'm cold. I dressed to test-drive Harman, not pay a late-night visit to the ditch."

"Then I'd better warm you." He edged closer and swept back her hair to nuzzle the soft skin of her neck.

"Most men would offer a sweater or a blanket. Maybe a cup of tea." She tipped her head to the side to give him better access, her hands sliding between them to press against his chest.

"I'm not most men."

"Definitely not. Your warm-by-seduction technique is second to none. I'm hot all over except my lips. They're still cold." She hesitated only an instant. "Maybe you could warm them, too."

"With pleasure." He twisted his hand through her hair and tugged her head back before giving her a soft kiss, his tongue sliding over hers. She tasted sweet and tangy, with a hint of spice.

"Not bad," she whispered. "But I think we need to get back to tending your injuries. Where else are you hurt?"

"I think I bumped my head." He pulled her off her chair and onto his lap, unable to fight the pull of desire any longer.

Laughing, she kissed his temple. "Anywhere else?"

"Here." He tapped his mouth.

"It's not an easy fix," she whispered. "Lips need a lot of attention."

"Then you'd better get started."

His brain short-circuited when she kissed him, and he gave in to the tidal wave of emotion he'd been holding back since the crash. He kissed her hard and fierce, his tongue touching, tasting, owning every inch of her sweet mouth.

She moaned softly, one hand gripping his shoulder as he buried his face in her neck, licking and sucking her skin. He was hard as steel beneath his fly, his body pulsing with need. Everything about her called to his baser instincts—to protect, to claim, to hold, to own. He wanted her with a fierce, urgent need that he didn't fully understand, but if her enthusiastic response to his rough kisses was any indication, she wanted him, too.

"If you were planning on"—he cleared his throat, unable to even form the question as to what she meant by *test-drive Harman*—"a date tonight, does that mean you're wearing easy-access underwear?"

"Maybe you should take off my clothes and find out."

He licked his lips in anticipation and reached for her skirt.

"Beta?" A woman's voice rang out from the hallway. "Are you here?"

· 19 ·

"BETA?"

Layla froze when her mother's voice rang through the restaurant.

"Where are you? I'm here with Mehar."

"Oh God." Layla jumped up and straightened her clothes. "They aren't supposed to be here." Hands shaking, she looked around for a means of escape. "Mehar Auntie can smell men. We have to get you out of here."

Sam buttoned his jeans. "I'm not embarrassed to be with you."

"Are you serious?" She hissed out a breath. "It's not the same for women, and you know it. I'll be grounded for life."

"You're twenty-six years old."

"I'm living at home. I haven't found a new place yet." She pushed him backward. "Get into the closet and stay quiet."

He gave an indignant sniff. "I'm not hiding in a closet. I'm the CEO of a very prominent restructuring comp—"

"You have to." She pushed him again, cutting him off. "I can't be here alone at night with a strange man. She'll think we were up to no good."

Sam smirked. "We were up to no good—at least until we were interrupted."

"Sam. Please. You don't understand. It'll be a big deal. She'll make assumptions . . ." Trying a different tactic, she leaned up and kissed him. "Stay in the closet and I promise to tell you the fantasy that I had about you and me and the Eagerson desk."

Sam ducked behind her father's spare shirts. "Does it involve handcuffs?"

"No handcuffs."

"Rope?"

"No."

"Chains?"

"It wasn't *Fifty Shades of Brown*, so don't get excited." She closed the door, leaving it open just a crack so he could breathe.

Not a second too late. Her mother and Mehar Auntie walked into the office.

"What are you guys doing here?" She straightened the desk chair, surreptitiously checking for evidence of their illicit activities. "I thought I was closing for you tonight."

"Taara couldn't remember if she'd left the gas stove on." Her mother shook her head. "You weren't answering your phone so I came to check after picking Mehar up from her sangeet. I saw your Jeep outside and—"

"I smell a man." Mehar Auntie sniffed the air.

"I'm sure there were lots of men in the restaurant tonight." Layla leaned over the desk and grabbed a stack of envelopes. "I thought I'd go through the mail and sort through the invoices. It's been piling up ever since Dad went into the hospital, and the book-keeper is coming in a few days."

"No." Her mother grabbed the envelopes out of her hand. "That's not for you to worry about. I'll take care of it."

"Are you sure? You've already got so much on your plate . . ." Her eyes widened when she saw Mehar Auntie sniffing her way over to the closet, like a dog who had caught a scent.

"This is a beautiful salwar kameez, Auntie-ji." She interposed herself between her aunt and the closet door. "I love the bright orange and red embroidery. Very Bollywood. Did you get it at Nira Auntie's store?"

"She just got them in." Mehar Auntie smiled. "Look at this beadwork. I thought it was too nice to wear as a guest, but she said it would be good for sales when I hit the dance floor." She danced a few steps of "You Are My Soniya" from *Kabhi Khushi Kabhie Gham*, singing as she made wide circles with her arms and slapped her ample rear.

Layla heard a snort from the cupboard and she moved to block Sam's view. "I'm sure you were a hit."

Mehar Auntie segued into a more vigorous portion of the dance, bending over to shake her breasts. "You should have seen me on the dance floor. The men couldn't tell the difference between me and Kareena Kapoor, even though I'm twenty years older."

"I can imagine." Mehar Auntie was a sangeet hog, taking center stage at every celebration with choreographed dances that she practiced at home complete with outfit changes.

Layla heard a muffled laugh and coughed loudly, trying to hide the sound.

"Come, beta." Mehar Auntie wiped the sweat off her brow. "Dance with me."

"There's not really enough room." She backed up to the closet as her aunt spun around, arms waving in the air. "And my skirt is too tight."

"You should have seen what the young girls were wearing," Mehar Auntie continued. "These young people today. Everything is cut too low or too high and showing too much skin. I told them a good man doesn't want a woman who is trying to get him into her bed before they are married."

"Exactly. You're very wise." Layla's pulse kicked up a notch when her mother fixed her with a stern gaze. She knew that stare.

Layla swallowed hard. "Times are changing, though."

"That's true." Mehar Auntie paused for breath. "Everyone had what they called a *coffee bar name*. Instead of Noopur, the girl is Natalie. Instead of Tarick, the boy is Ricky. And Hardik wants to be called Harry because he says Americans think his name means he is in the dirty movies." She hesitated, frowned. "Do you have a coffee bar name?"

"No, Auntie-ji."

"You're a good girl." Mehar Auntie patted her arm. "But you need a husband." She turned to Layla's mother, who was frowning at the closet door. "We need to find her a husband, Jana. Maybe when Nasir is out of hospital, you can start looking."

Layla's mother lifted an eyebrow. "I don't think she needs our help."

Layla felt the same prickling feeling she'd had as a child when she was caught doing something wrong. "You must be tired, Mom. Don't let me keep you. I'll just finish tidying up here and I'll meet you at home."

Mehar Auntie left to start the car and Layla followed her mother into the restaurant.

"We're having a family dinner on Thursday to celebrate your father coming home," her mother said. "Everyone is invited, including the man in the closet."

Layla's blood drained from her face. She didn't even try to lie. "He was in a car accident. I was fixing him up. I didn't want you to get the wrong idea."

"I already have the wrong idea, but if you think he's a good man, and he cares about you, then he will come to meet the family and declare his intentions."

Layla opened her mouth to tell her mother Sam didn't eat Indian food, and closed it again. Her mother wouldn't understand. In fact, no one she knew would understand. Family was everything. Traditions were important. No matter how bad things got, you didn't cast them aside.

"He'll be there," she said with a conviction she didn't feel in the least.

"I thought you weren't dating anymore," her mother said. "No more immature, selfish boyfriends. No more heartache. Your father and I were going to find a nice man for you—someone stable and serious who would be a good husband and father."

"I know. I found Dad's list."

Her mother frowned. "What list?"

"He posted my marriage résumé online and sorted through all the responses to come up with a list of ten suitable candidates. I've been meeting with them." It felt good to get the secret off her chest, but her mother didn't seem to be happy that she had been trying to find a husband the traditional way.

"And the man in the closet? Is he one of them?"

"No." She swallowed hard. "He shares the office upstairs with me. He's the guy Dad had leased the space to before he decided to give it to me. He runs his own corporate restructuring business."

Her mother patted her hand. "Meet the other men. If your father picked them, then they will all be nice boys."

"Sam is nice," she said feeling defensive. "He's funny, protective, and kind and—"

"He's hiding in the closet."

"That's because I pushed him in there and asked him to stay." She glanced around for Mehar Auntie, uncomfortable with the turn of the conversation.

Her mother sighed. "In all the years I've been with your father, never once have I wanted to hide him away. I was proud to call him my husband. You should feel proud of the man you choose to marry."

"I'm not marrying him." She fiddled with the edge of her shirt. "We're just . . . I don't know what we're doing. There was an issue with the office, and a game we were playing . . ."

"I don't like the sound of him." Her mother pushed open the front door. "And I don't like how you don't know what relationship you have, or that you feel the need to hide it. If he's just a one-night man—"

"One-night stand," Layla corrected, although she didn't know why. "And no, he's not that."

Sam was much more than a hookup, but where did he fall on the dating spectrum? She suddenly realized they'd never had a serious talk about their relationship, or what it meant for her search for a husband, or even how they were going to deal with the office when Royce returned. Now that her mother was asking the difficult questions, she couldn't believe she'd made her search for a husband into a game. There were bigger issues at stake than who got the office. She was looking for someone with whom to share the rest of her life.

"The family will meet him and tell you what they think."

Layla didn't have to bring Sam to dinner to know what they would think. Her mother already had a bad impression of him. And if he didn't eat with them, the family would think he was disrespectful. Not only that, once they found out about her father's list, they would tell her to forget Sam and choose one of the men her father wanted her to meet.

"Don't forget why you came home," her mother said over her shoulder. "Not to go back to jobs that made you unhappy and men who couldn't commit. You came to rebuild your life and put the past behind you. That won't happen if you lose sight of your goals."

"I like him, Mom." She followed her mother into the parking lot. "He's different from anyone I've ever met."

"Then bring him to dinner on Thursday," her mother said. "And let us see if he is worthy of my Layla."

"BREAK out the champagne!"

Seemingly oblivious to the fact that there were other people training in the gym, Royce shouted Sam's name as he wove his way through the punching bags, free weights, and cardio machines to the ring where Sam was sparring with Evan. Out of place in his pin-striped suit, pink shirt, pink and navy polka-dot tie, and a pair of sharply pointed tan leather shoes, Royce had a bottle of champagne in one hand and two glasses in the other, despite the fact that it was seven A.M.

"What are you doing here?" Sam's moment of distraction earned him a solid punch to the jaw, and he staggered back into the ropes.

"What the fuck, man?" He straightened and glared at Evan. "I was talking to Royce."

"When you're in the ring, you are *in* the ring. Fair game. Unless you want to tap out, and then I win."

The last thing Sam wanted was to let Evan win. For the first time ever, he had gained the upper hand in a fight and he could almost taste the victory that he'd been denied for years.

"Gimme a minute, Royce." He shook his head to stop the ringing in his ears.

"We're on the short list for the Alpha Health Care contract!" Royce didn't give minutes. He was all about Royce.

Sam sucked in a sharp breath. What had once seemed to be an

unattainable goal was now within sight. He threw a victory punch that Evan easily avoided.

"That's not all," Royce said, leaning against the ropes. "The rumors were true. The short list is for all five hospitals. Your pitch plus my connections, a couple of faked missed strokes on the golf course, and a little white lie equal one hell of a team."

"What white lie?" Sam heard the whistle of air. Pain exploded in his cheek. He hit the mat, saw stars. Or were they dollar signs?

"You lose again, dude." Evan crouched to help Sam up. "Want to go another round?"

"Are you kidding?" Royce said. "He doesn't have time for fights. We need to make a plan. Everyone on the short list is scrambling to impress the board. We need to stand out from the crowd." He popped the cork and poured the bubbly. "Evan, old friend, grab a couple of glasses for you and . . ." He waved vaguely at John. "This guy, whoever he is."

"This is John Lee," Sam said. "He's an attorney in the law firm on the top floor of our building."

"Hello and good-bye, John Lee." Royce poured champagne into one of the plastic glasses Evan had procured. "We're going to need your office space for our expansion once we have wined and dined Alpha Health Care into our pockets."

John folded his arms across his chest. "We have a ten-year lease with the current landlord. We aren't going anywhere."

"Does the restaurant downstairs have the same lease?" Royce filled the final glass, splashing droplets of champagne on the mat.

"I haven't seen it so I don't know the terms. But I can tell you they are there for the long term. Their son, Dev, was a friend of mine. He bought the building with a few friends as an investment and they leased the top floor to my law firm, and the bottom two floors to his parents so they could move their restaurant from

Sunnyvale into the city. They spent a small fortune on renovations."

"Hmmm." Royce twisted his lips to the side. "A minor hiccup, but not an insurmountable one. I promised Sam I'd do what it took to get that contract, and that's exactly what I'll do." He handed out the glasses. "And now that the sad story is over, let's toast to the success of Bentley Mehta World Corporation. Don't hold back. I've sent another few cases to the office."

Sam's heart sank. "You're back in town?"

"Are you kidding? You're damn good on the business side, but you're no rainmaker. People skills are not your forte. You threw the pitch and I'm going to bring it home." Royce tapped glasses with Sam. "Cheers."

"SAM." Daisy glared at him when he walked into the office after his workout. She'd streaked her hair an angry shade of red that matched her lipstick, and with the death metal shirt and studded bracelets on her arms and neck, she looked every inch the *Hell Demon* her shirt proclaimed her to be.

"Daisy." He nodded a greeting, clueless as to what he'd done to irritate her today but determined not to let her bring down his good mood. Tonight he was going to embrace his desi side again. Now that his company was on the Alpha Health Care short list, he could start looking forward, not back. The Patel family dinner was the perfect opportunity to finally let go of the past and show Layla his true self. He felt something for her that he'd never felt before, and he wanted everyone to know.

The office was the only thing that stood between them. He'd already contacted a real estate agent and made an urgent request to find new space in the same general area. If they won the Alpha

Health Care contract they would just have to move, despite the prime location. And if they didn't, he would just have to sell Royce on the benefits of a new office, because he wasn't going to lose Layla over a game.

"I've left some contracts on your desk," she said tightly. "And I've rescheduled the meetings with Bachelors #7 through #10. It's all in your calendar."

Puzzled, Sam frowned. "I'm pretty sure Layla would have canceled the rest of the blind dates."

"She told me to reschedule them." Daisy's lips curved. "You may want to bring a change of clothes when you meet Bachelor #10. He's a yoga instructor. Your tight pants might tear when you're in firefly pose. Remember not to go commando."

Sam's stomach tightened into a knot. Why was Layla still going ahead with her search for a husband? He'd opened up last night at the bar. Bared his soul. He couldn't remember the last time he'd told anyone he wanted more than a one-night stand. Thinking about the rest of the evening now, he realized she had been uncharacteristically quiet after talking to her mom. She'd turned down his offer to spend the night, telling him she needed to go through the paperwork from her father's office. Maybe it was the truth. Or maybe she'd had second thoughts after he'd exposed his failings and almost crashed the car. Maybe she didn't think he was worthy after all.

Daisy let out an impatient breath. "Anything you need me to do today, or should I just watch you stand there staring into space?"

He finally bit the bullet. "Is something wrong?"

"You coming to a family dinner tonight is all sorts of wrong, but other than that everything is peachy." She pulled a dog treat out of her bag and offered it to Max, who was curled up in his basket beside her desk.

Sam drew in a deep calming breath and took a mental step back to the blissful moment before he'd walked in the door. "We found out this morning we were short-listed for the Alpha Health Care contract. Royce is in town and he wants to wine and dine the clients. Could you find a good restaurant that will take a big group on short notice? Talk to Royce about dates and venues. I'm sure he has some ideas."

"Sure thing, boss man."

Sam couldn't think of anything more entertaining than watching Royce and Daisy butt heads, but he needed to get Layla out of the office in case Royce stopped by. Royce would be less than understanding if he saw her at his desk, and the last thing Sam wanted was for Layla to get hurt. Again.

· 20 ·

"ARE you sure you're ready for tonight?" Layla reached up to rub Sam's shoulders like he was a prizefighter, sliding her hands down his arms to squeeze the muscles bulging under his suit jacket. The scent of his aftershave mingled with the scent of the body wash that they'd used when they'd showered together, and she was tempted to drag him back into his bedroom and have her way with him all over again.

"I'm ready." He straightened his tie, adjusting the perfect knot.

"That was a nice, but naughty, way to celebrate getting short-listed for your big contract. I wish I had more time, but my mother needs help cooking the big family dinner." She leaned up to kiss his cheek. Sam had spirited her out of the office on the pretense of going for coffee, but instead had her drive to his place and they'd spent the afternoon in bed.

"It's about more than the work." He turned and put his arms around her. "One of the hospitals that is restructuring is St. Vincent's where Ranjeet works. If we get the contract, I'll have access to his employment file. I'll be able to find out what really happened in that stairwell, and if there is a cover-up, I'll be able to expose it. Nisha will have her justice."

Warning bells rang at the back of her mind. "Is that ethical? Don't you have to declare a conflict of interest?"

"I'll do what it takes to get Nisha the justice she deserves."

"It may be what she deserves, but is it what she wants?" Layla tried to choose her words carefully. "I can't imagine that she'd be happy if you went to jail or lost your job for something that seems like a long shot at best. She seems to be moving on with her life. Do you think she wants to start digging up the past?"

Sam bristled. "It's my job to protect her. I failed her before; it won't happen again."

"Is this about Nisha or you? It sounds like you still blame yourself for her injuries."

He stiffened and pulled away. "I thought you, of all people, would understand."

Layla winced at his harsh tone. She'd pushed him too far. Maybe that was a truth he wasn't ready to face. All the justice in the world would mean nothing if he couldn't forgive himself.

"I'm sorry. I just want you both to be happy."

After they finished dressing, they climbed into Layla's Jeep. Sam was still waiting for his insurers to decide whether his car was worth saving and she'd volunteered to chauffeur.

"You're really going to do this?" Layla asked as the engine roared to life. "Eat Indian food? Does that mean if I play 'Tattad Tattad,' you might also get up and show us some Bollywood moves?" She loved Ranveer Singh's energetic dance number from *Goliyon Ki Rasleela Ram-Leela*, a Bollywood remake of *Romeo and Juliet*.

"I'm hoping to be too full to move."

"What's your favorite food? I can't believe I never asked you before."

"Masala dosas. Hands down."

Layla winced inwardly as she pulled out of the parking lot. Her mother had a special recipe for masala dosas that involved fermenting the batter for the savory crepes for eight hours. But the real trick was to cook them so they were both thick and had a golden crust. It was a skill she had never mastered. But this was Sam's first Indian meal in years, and his first time meeting the family. The least she could do was try to prepare his favorite dish herself. "I'll make sure you have some."

"I'm looking forward to it."

"Me, too." She forced a smile. All he had to do was win over her family.

How hard could it be?

"TRY again, beta." Layla's father scraped the burned dosa out of the large cast-iron pan. Her mother had brought the pan with her from India, entrusted to her by her own mother when she left home.

"Why is it so hard?" Layla wiped the sweat off her forehead with her sleeve. This was the third dosa she'd ruined, and she felt bad wasting the batter her mother had prepared earlier in the day.

"Everything needs to be perfect." He cleaned out the pan and seasoned it again. "Temperature, seasoning, and you need a light hand when you spread it. You want it to be crunchy on the outside but damp inside." He sat heavily on the stool her mother had brought into the kitchen for him. Only a few days out of the hospital, he tired easily and was thinner than she'd ever seen him in his life.

"Are you okay? Is it the pacemaker? Do we need to go back to the hospital?"

"Stop worrying, beta. It's all good. Probably just the body adjusting to something new, or maybe the heart feeling full to be in my kitchen with my family again." He glanced down at the pan. "Batter now."

Layla poured the batter into the pan, drawing circles with the back of a tumbler to create a large crepe. "I've made coconut chutney, green chutney, and red chutney to go with it, as well as *sambar*." She pointed to the souplike side dish that was one of her favorite accompaniments to masala dosas. The journey through the dips with their hints of salt, heat, sour, and spice were what made masala dosas special.

"I hope Sam appreciates all your hard work." He leaned over to eye the crepe. "I liked him when we first met. He was very well mannered, intelligent, straightforward, and very serious."

Layla laughed. She had told her father about her dates with his list of suitors and how she'd become interested in Sam. He had been surprisingly relaxed about the fact that she hadn't liked any of his choices, despite all the time he'd spent whittling down a list of hundreds to those ten men. "You make him seem dull."

"Not dull, but he kept his emotions inside, unlike us Patels, who let them all out." He looked again at the pan and shouted, "Now! Pour now!"

"Calm down, Nasir." Layla's mother came over to inspect the dosa. "Don't excite yourself."

"Then you'd better get out of the kitchen, because every time I see you, my heart pounds." He pulled Layla's mother into a hug and gave her a kiss. She held herself stiff, even as a smile tugged at her lips.

"This isn't appropriate, Nasir."

"What's not appropriate is having to spend weeks in a hospital bed sleeping alone. There was no one to steal the covers. I was always too hot."

"Nasir!" She pulled away, but not before Layla heard her muffled laughter. "The staff will see."

"Good. Then they will all think *Nasir is back to his strong and virile self and we will have to stop slacking off behind Jana's back*." He looked over at Danny and scowled. "Like this one. I see you always looking at Layla. She has a man, and the family will be meeting him tonight, so turn your attention elsewhere."

"You don't mind that I'm dating someone who wasn't on your list?" Layla poured another scoop of batter.

"I want you to be happy," her father said. "If he makes you happy, then I like him; if he makes you sad, then I will—"

"You will do nothing," Layla's mother said. "You are a sick man. You should be in bed, not in the kitchen making dosas and causing trouble."

Smoke rose from the pan and Layla looked down in dismay. "I burned another one!"

"It's okay, beta." Her father took the pan and gave her a hug. "The only way to get something right is to get many things wrong. Patels don't give up when they burn their dosas. Now, let's start again . . ."

As far as Sam was concerned, a "small" Patel dinner was no different from an Indian wedding.

From his office window, he had counted more than thirty people arriving at the restaurant in everything from brightly colored saris to flowered shirts and feather boas, and one middle-aged man in tight leather pants. He smoothed down his shirt and adjusted his cuffs. What would they think of him?

His stomach rumbled. He hadn't eaten since breakfast, and the aromas drifting up from the kitchen below reminded him of his mother's masala box, filled with all the spices she used to make their meals—zesty cumin, sweet cinnamon, fragrant bay leaves, savory mustard seeds, rich peppercorn, pungent garam masala, and spicy chilies—they were all tied up in a sense of home.

He pulled on his jacket and straightened his tie. Daisy had already gone downstairs. Time for him to meet Layla's family. He'd never been so nervous in his life.

"Hey, partner! Let's get the party started!" Royce burst into the office, slamming open the glass door with a case of champagne in his arms. Five women in barely-there dresses, big hair, and high heels filed in behind him, one of them carrying a long, silver pole. Evan took up the rear with a tall brunette under one arm and a case of beer under the other.

"What's going on?"

"This is how you win the contract." Evan dropped the box on Daisy's reception desk. "Royce and I put our heads together this morning and came up with a plan for an evening the Alpha Health Care board won't forget. These ladies are direct from the Platinum Club, the premier strip club in the city. We even brought Tiffany, their top pole dancer, to keep your clients entertained."

"Evan had the PR and marketing contacts to make it all happen on short notice." Royce shoved Layla's papers aside and placed the box of champagne on her desk. "So I invited him to join us. I told the board it's a very private, very exclusive party. Board members, a few top execs, and the CEO only. Lucky for us they're all men. They're on their way in a limo right now with a couple of very special angels and the best angel dust money can buy."

"You're bringing strippers and drugs to the office?" Sam stared at Royce aghast. "There are children downstairs. It's a family restaurant. And what about John and his partners? They're running a law firm."

"Evan sent them an invitation. He said it's the best way to keep the neighbors from complaining about a party. And don't worry about the restaurant. They've been taken care of. I sent them a little surprise to keep them busy." Royce pulled out a bottle of champagne and popped the cork. Fizzy liquid exploded across the room, spattering on Layla's desk and into the fishbowl, sending the goldfish into a panicked frenzy.

"Jesus Christ, Royce. Stop. People work here."

"Our people. Unless you didn't get rid of the landlord's daughter . . ."

One of the women set up two speakers beside the printer, and Rihanna's "Don't Stop the Music" blasted through the room, making the walls shake and the fishbowl shiver.

"Royce, baby. You're wearing too many clothes." A woman with bright pink hair and a silver sequin minidress tugged on Royce's tie, pulling him back to Sam's desk. With a wink of her extra long lashes, she cleared the surface with a sweep of her hand, scattering pens and pencils onto the floor.

"Uh-oh. Ginger's been a naughty girl." She leaned over Sam's desk and wiggled her bottom.

Royce chuckled and pushed up his sleeves. "Peter said you were a live one."

"Who ordered the booze?" Two deliverymen stood in the doorway with six boxes loaded onto a trolley.

"Toss that basket outside and put them over there," Royce called out. "Someone give these guys a tip. Or a couple of drinks. Or girls . . ."

"That's Max's basket." Too late, Sam lunged. The delivery driver grabbed Max's basket and tossed it in the hall, sending Max's squeaky toys flying.

"Here, dude." Evan handed him a glass of champagne. "You need to chill."

"I can't chill," Sam spat out. "I'm supposed to be meeting Layla's family for dinner downstairs in five minutes."

"You can't leave," Royce said, abandoning his visual appreciation of Ginger's ass. "We're hosting this party. Everyone on the short list will be pulling out the stops to convince AH to choose them. They're all scrambling to book a table at some fancy-ass restaurant, but no one is going to do this. Evan is a fucking genius. If this doesn't get us that contract, I don't know what will. We're going to give them one hell of a good time."

"This isn't my idea of a good time." Meeting Layla's crazy family, eating masala dosas, and going public with his feelings for the woman who had accepted him despite his failings was his idea of a good time. Holding her in his arms while the warm afternoon sunshine slid lazy fingers through the cracks in his curtains was his idea of a good time. Looking up from his desk to see her chewing on the end of her pencil, deep in thought, while a pile of donuts lay untouched beside her, was his idea of a good time.

"Well, it's going to have to be," Royce said tightly. "Or don't you want the contract?"

"Of course I want it. More than anything."

"Then loosen the damn tie. Grab a glass. Kiss a couple of girls and put on your dancing shoes. Our prospective clients are coming to visit the building where all the magic is going to happen."

"Don't you mean the office?"

"Glassware delivery," a delivery driver called out. "I need a signature."

"I mean the building." Royce signed for the glasses. "It's ours. The whole damn thing. I bought it, or to be clear, our company bought it. Hard money deal. One week to close. You said to do what it took to secure the contract, so I did."

Sam let out an unsteady breath. "You bought the building?"

"It's all about location, location, location." Royce grinned. "One of the reasons we got on the short list was because of our proximity to the hospitals and the AH head office. I had a call last week from

Peter Richards, the AH CEO. He was concerned we weren't big enough to handle a five-hospital restructure, so I told a little lie and assured him we owned the building and had the room to expand to accommodate their needs. Then I had to make it a reality. It wasn't easy to get the funding on short notice, but I managed to do it. The deal closed today."

This couldn't be happening. Not now. "How did you make a major capital purchase without my signature?"

Royce pulled out a row of glasses and filled them with champagne. "Aside from the fact I had your consent—*do whatever it takes*—I retained a controlling interest in the partnership when you joined the company. You can't go wrong investing in real estate. It's a win-win for us."

Bile rose in Sam's throat. "What about the tenants?"

Royce popped another cork, spilling champagne over Daisy's desk. "You told me the restaurant owners were having financial difficulties, which was how I came up with the idea of buying the building in the first place. After I talked to your friend John this morning, I called up my lawyer and he said their tenancy wouldn't be a problem. During the due diligence, they discovered the Patels were in breach of their lease for failing to pay rent. It's perfect! We'll be serving them with a three-day notice tonight. If they don't pay up, then we start the eviction proceedings. By the time AH makes the final decision, we'll be in possession of everything except the top floor."

Sam's knees buckled and he grabbed the counter for support. "And what if we don't get the contract? We'll have a building we don't need, no financial reserves, and the Patels will have lost their business."

"Honestly, it would be a small mercy for them," Royce said with a smirk. "I've never seen the restaurant more than half-full. Good food. Bad location. Easy fix. They'll be thanking me in six months. And after this party, the contract will be in the bag and we won't have to worry about finances again." Royce handed him a glass. "I don't understand why you're not happy. This is what you wanted. Now turn that frown upside down. Our guests are here and they're expecting us to show them the time of their lives."

Sam looked up just as Peter Richards and six middle-aged men in dark suits walked in the door, accompanied by three women wearing tiny shorts and cropped T-shirts bearing the *Platinum* logo.

"Oh, honey. Don't look so sad. You'll feel better when you loosen up. Let me help you off with that tie." A woman with heavy makeup and waist-length brown hair unknotted Sam's tie and slid it off his neck, dropping it in the wastebasket beside Daisy's desk. "There, now. Doesn't that feel better?"

"I don't feel anything at all." With a last glance out the window, Sam sent a quick text to Layla, letting her know he had a work emergency, and went to greet his clients.

He was doing this for Nisha. For justice. For the unknown woman who didn't know she was about to marry a monster.

So why did it feel so wrong?

LAYLA flipped her dosa onto the plate. "I did it! This one is perfect. That makes two!"

"Well done." Her father leaned over and pressed a kiss to her forehead. "I knew you could do it."

Layla plated the dosa, adding pots of chutney and sambar to the tray just seconds before her phone buzzed in her pocket. She dropped her head, closing her eyes after she read Sam's message.

"What's wrong, beta?"

"Sam says he has a work emergency and he's not sure when he can make it down. He said to go ahead without him."

Her father pushed himself up. "Then we will go up and give him the dosas while they're still warm to have as a snack. A hardworking man is a good man. I'm sure he is as disappointed he can't come as you are."

"I'll go, Dad." She picked up the plate. "I don't want you to get tired."

"I'm not tired. The doctor said not to lift heavy things. He didn't say to sit around all day like a lump of dough. I want to see what you've done with the office and meet Sam before the family gets to him."

Layla closed her eyes and took a deep breath. "I decided last night that I'm going to move out of the office. Sam has a business partner, and you did offer it to him first." She hesitated, reluctant to hurt her father's pride. "Also, when I was going through the bills on your desk, I realized you need the rent money. I can't afford that office, and if I really want to run my own business, I need to find my own space at a rent I can afford."

Her father's brow creased in a frown. "You don't need to worry about your mom and me. We've been through difficult times before. You're our daughter. If you want that office—"

"Dad, you are operating at a loss." Her voice rose in pitch. "Dev's friends have been more than accommodating, but you owe them almost a year's worth of rent. What are you going to do if they can't carry that debt?"

"This is not your business." Her father's angry shout drew her mother over to the stove. He was a proud man and he took his responsibility as head of the household very seriously. It meant he didn't ask for help; he gave it. When there was a problem, he fixed it. And when something went wrong, he kept it to himself and suffered in silence.

"Nasir." Layla's mother placed a gentle hand on his shoulder. "Calm down. The doctor said no stress."

"I am not stressed," he said furiously. "Why did you let Layla go through my office? Our financial situation is not her concern. She has her own troubles, her own life to sort out. She doesn't need to spend her time worrying about us."

"She's a grown woman. She was just trying to help. But maybe it's time she knew what's going on."

"Go." Her father waved Layla away. "Take the dosas to Sam while they're still hot. Your mother and I have things to discuss."

Layla's mother lifted an eyebrow. "Is he not coming for dinner?"

"He's got a work emergency," Layla explained. "He'll be down as soon as it's done."

"Hmmm." Her mother's lips tightened and she turned back to the stove.

"Don't be like that, Mom. He's running a business with only him and his partner. And how many Indian people show up to something on time? He'll be fashionably late."

"I run my own business with only your father and not once have we ever been late for an engagement—fashionably or not fashionably." Her harsh, clipped tone conveyed the extent of her disapproval, and Layla quickly headed for the door.

"I'll see if I can hurry him up."

"Hey, babe. Let me get that for you." Danny ran ahead when she tried to balance the tray with one hand to open the back door. "You're killing it in that dress, by the way." He gestured to the emerald green sheath dress she'd worn for dinner. "You're looking sweeter than the gulab jamun I just made."

She gave an exasperated sigh. "Are you seriously running game on me in front of my parents?"

"I didn't want the opportunity to go to waste." He grinned. "I thought maybe you'd feel like you owed me."

"For opening the door?"

"People have slept with me for less."

Layla made her way down the alley to the office entrance and up the stairs to the second-floor door. Loud music filled the corridor, and she recognized the heavy beats of Taio Cruz's "Break Your Heart."

"Were you invited to the party, too?" John stepped out of the elevator with a bottle of wine in his hand.

"I didn't know there was a party." Her heart lurched when she saw Max's basket in the middle of the hallway, his blankets and squeeze toys strewn across the carpet.

"Sam?" She pushed open the frosted-glass door to the office and froze at the scene in front of her.

Bottles and cans littered Daisy's desk, along with a half-eaten tray of deli meat, a dish of what looked like caviar, and a tiered platter of hors d'oeuvres. A woman in a red micro dress straddled a man in a blue suit on her purple chaise, and a woman in a sparkly bikini was twirling around a pole that had been set up between the two desks. The office was full to bursting, but except for two lawyers from John's firm, she didn't recognize anyone.

"What's going on?" She stared at the chaos, aghast.

"Evan said it was a party. I didn't expect"—John's gaze flicked from the woman dancing on Layla's desk to the man stuffing money in her G-string—"this."

"Where's Sam?" She thought she'd whispered, but the woman on her chaise looked over and smiled.

"He's in the boardroom with Tiffany." She winked. "I don't think they want to be disturbed."

"Oh my God." Her hands trembled and the sambar sloshed onto the tray.

"Who ordered Indian?" A man in a tight blue-and-pink-striped shirt with a polka-dot tie offered Layla a $20 bill. "Keep the change. I don't have anything smaller."

"She works here, Royce." John knocked his hand away.

"Ah, the girl with the bad designs!" Royce reached for the dosas and Layla took a step back. "You need to focus on what you do well, and it's not branding. Better luck next time."

"What's that supposed to mean?"

Royce looked genuinely puzzled. "I'm wishing you luck in your new venture, wherever it may be. Although I'd recommend you don't set up shop above your parents' restaurant again if they decide to continue their business elsewhere. It projects the wrong image."

Had she fallen down a rabbit hole? Stepped into a different dimension? Maybe an alternate universe? Had Danny put something in her chai? "My parents aren't leaving."

"Sure they are." Denied the dosas, Royce carefully spooned caviar onto a small cracker. "They're being served with the three-day notice this evening. If they can't pay the outstanding rent in three days, we'll start eviction proceedings."

All her breath left her in a rush and she staggered back. If not for John's strong hand on her shoulder, she might have fallen.

"Don't act so surprised," Royce said. "Your dad told Sam they were struggling financially. What did you expect would happen? That the landlords would float them forever? I thought you were a businessperson. This is how it goes. Wake up and smell the balance sheet."

"That's crazy." She curled her fingers around the tray. "The owners of the building are friends of my late brother. They would never evict my parents. Never."

Royce munched on his caviar cracker. "But I would, and I own the building. Well, technically, it belongs to Bentley Mehta World Corporation, but . . ."

"Sam!" This time she shouted his name loud enough to be heard over the music.

Moments later, the door to the boardroom opened and Sam staggered out, a tall, curvy brunette under his arm and a half-empty bottle of whiskey in his hand. His hair was mussed, shirt open at the neck, tie gone, sleeves pushed up to reveal the forearms that had once been the object of her fantasies. She'd never seen him so disheveled or so utterly destroyed.

His gaze flicked from Layla to John and back to Layla. His face smoothed to an expressionless mask.

"What's going on?" Layla asked, her voice wavering. "Who is that woman?"

"This is Amber." He whispered something in Amber's ear and she pressed a kiss to his cheek before making her way over to the pole.

"We're having a party." He held up the bottle, his voice flat. "For Alpha Health Care. We're on the short list and we're showing them a good time."

She drew in a ragged breath, trying to contain her shock and horror. "Royce says your company bought the building and you're evicting my parents."

"I know."

"You know?" Her voice rose in pitch as dismay turned to anger. "That's all you have to say? Why didn't you tell me? Why don't you do something? The restaurant is all they have. It's all we have left of Dev."

Sam took a long pull from the bottle and wiped his mouth with the back of his hand. "I can't."

"You can't or you won't?" Her body vibrated with fury. "This is your company, too. Or were you planning to kick them out all along? And our game? What was that all about? Were you just amusing yourself at my expense while you put your plan in motion? Royce said my dad told you they were struggling financially. Did you use that information to hurt them?"

"You don't understand . . ." He shuddered. "I told Royce to do what it took to get the contract, and what it took was space."

"Where did you think the space would come from?" she snapped. "You know Royce. You work with him every day. Look at what he did to my designs. He's got no empathy, no concern for anyone or anything except the bottom line. You should have seen this coming. But it's clear all you cared about was getting your stupid contract."

Sam's mouth opened as if to speak, but she wasn't interested in what he had to say. With her blood pounding through her veins so hard she could barely think, she raised her voice above the music, drawing the attention of everyone in the room. "Did you tell your clients why you really want the contract? Did you tell them your plan to access the hospital database and read the personnel files to search for evidence of a cover-up and the truth about what happened to your sister? Maybe they should know what kind of person you really are." She regretted the words as soon as they dropped from her lips, but it was too late. Beneath the heavy beat of the music, an uncomfortable silence filled the room.

Shock then alarm flickered across Sam's face. She'd gone too far, but this was so much worse than walking in on Jonas. She hadn't loved Jonas. She hadn't opened herself up for the first time since Dev's death, only to be destroyed all over again. And Jonas hadn't hurt anyone but her.

One of the men in blue suits frowned. "Sam, is that true?"

"Don't listen to her, Peter." Royce handed him a glass of champagne. "She's crazy. She moved into our office and tried to start a company called 'Excellent Recruitment Solutions.' That was the name. *Excellent.* Can you imagine? And her logo looked like a raccoon on drugs. It was a joke."

"I don't know . . ." Peter scratched his head.

"Have you seen Tiffany dance?" Royce dragged him across the room. "Have a seat on that desk and she'll give you a personal show." He waved frantically at a woman in a silver dress as Peter stumbled forward. Unsteady on his feet, Peter tripped over a bottle and fell heavily against Layla's desk. The fishbowl wobbled, then fell to the ground, shattering into tiny pieces.

Layla's hand flew to her mouth. "My fish!"

"Don't worry," Royce shouted. "They were already dead. They had too much champagne."

"I hope you're happy now," Layla said bitterly, her gaze locked on Sam's impassive face. "I hope it was worth it. You got everything you wanted—the contract, the office, the building . . ."

"I want you."

"You never wanted me." She drew in a ragged breath. "You're just like every other guy I've ever been with. I thought I'd managed to turn my life around, but it's just more of the same. I've lost everything again, but this time I didn't hit rock bottom alone. I brought my family down with me."

"It's for the best," Sam said, his voice plaintive. "This isn't a good location for a restaurant. They need to move somewhere smaller, closer to their core customer base . . ."

"Don't throw your stupid motivational speech at me," she shouted. "The restaurant was Dev's dream. He bought this building for them. He planned the whole renovation. They put all their money into fixing it up. And then he died and this is all they had left. They can't just move on. It's not that easy."

"Nisha needs this," he pleaded.

"I don't think Nisha needs it at all." Her voice wavered. "What I saw was a woman who has been so overprotected she's afraid to be independent. She was a different person when you weren't around. She was funny and outgoing and fully capable of looking after herself. She wanted to go shopping and do all the things women her age do, but what she needed was an emotional push, not a physical one. She needed support and encouragement, not protection. Your guilt is stifling her."

She drew in a deep breath, her hands shaking so violently under the tray that two of the little pots of dip had overturned. "This isn't about Nisha. It's about you. You want justice so you don't feel guilty anymore, but it doesn't work that way, Sam. Even if the police lock Ranjeet away for life, nothing will change. Nisha will still need to use a wheelchair, and you will still be the brother who thinks he failed her."

"You don't know anything about my family."

"And you clearly don't understand anything about my family," she retorted. "This is all we have left of Dev. We aren't going to let it go."

"I'm sorry, Layla." He swallowed hard. "It's already gone."

"Let's get out of here." John squeezed her shoulder. "This isn't my kind of party, either."

Layla's hands curled around the tray. The dosas had withered slightly now that they were cold, and only the green chutney had survived intact. "I made masala dosas for you," she said to Sam. "It was my first time. I used almost all my mother's batter to get them right. I made the chutneys, too, and the sambar. It took hours. My dad sat beside me the whole time like he used to do when I was little, because he knew how important it was to me that they be perfect."

"Layla . . ." A pained expression crossed his face, and she trembled. The urge to fling the tray at him was so strong she had to fight it away.

"You weren't worth the effort," she said finally. "You aren't worth the waste if I throw them at you now, and you aren't worth the loss of my self-respect." She fixed him with a glare as John pulled open the office door. "And you certainly aren't worthy of me."

· 22 ·

"I thought you'd be too ashamed to show your face at the gym." John drumrolled the speed bag, his mouth pressed into a tight line. "Are you here to evict my law firm, too, because I'll tell you right now my partners and I have been through that lease and there is no way you're getting us out."

"I came to spar with Evan. I didn't know if you'd be here or not." With a sigh, Sam sat on a nearby weight bench. He had been avoiding the gym for the simple fact that John would be here, but after a weekend with no way to relieve his stress, he'd finally given in.

"I almost wish I hadn't come," John spat out.

Sam ran a hand through his hair. "I didn't know that Royce had bought the building or that he planned to evict the Patels."

John slowed the bag. "But you didn't withdraw the eviction proceedings, did you? Or even put a stop to the whole sorry situation, which, legally, you can do."

"Royce put us in a difficult situation." He twisted his hands between his spread legs. "We got the contract because of our location and because he told them we had the space to hire staff to meet their needs."

"No." John fixed him with a firm stare. "Don't blame Royce. This is all on you."

"Jesus Christ. Chill, dude," Evan said, coming up beside them.

"Give Sam a break. This was a business decision. If the Patels had paid their rent, they wouldn't have been in this position. Sam did what he had to do. We should be congratulating him on landing a big contract and finding a way to take down the bastard who hurt his sister."

"Still no." John turned back to the bag and started the drumroll again. "I don't condone hurting innocent people in the pursuit of a personal goal, and I don't buy that business BS. You could have worked around the location. You just didn't want to."

"It's not personal." Sam said grimly. "It's for Nisha."

"Are you sure about that? Did you ever ask her what she thought?" John lost the beat of his bag and jerked back when it hit his chin. "Did you ask Layla?"

"Layla's not innocent," Evan said. His support meant Sam had definitely crossed the line. He was as morally bankrupt as Royce. Maybe even more. "She almost tanked the deal by spilling Sam's secrets in front of the Alpha Health Care dudes. That wasn't on."

"Do you blame her?" John slammed his fists into the bag again, his gaze focused on Sam. "She spent all afternoon making your favorite dish, her family was waiting downstairs to meet you, her father was just out of the hospital, and not only did she come upstairs to find the frat party of the century going on in her office, her boyfriend drunk and partying with strippers, she also found out you were evicting her and her family. If it had been me, I would have thrown the food in your face, called the cops, and burned the fucking office to the ground. I thought she was remarkably restrained."

Sam had never seen John so angry. His actions hadn't just cost him Layla; he had clearly also lost a friend.

"This is getting boring." Evan climbed into the ring. "Come on. I don't have all day."

"Knock some sense into him," John shouted. "He's destroying

his life and taking down everyone he cares about with him because he can't accept that he's not responsible for all the bad things that happen in the world."

Evan laughed. "I'll be responsible for the bad things that happen to him once he gets his sorry ass in the ring."

Sam grabbed his gloves and pulled one on. "I'm sorry they got hurt, but it's worth it. Ranjeet is getting married again. If I find out he did push Nisha down the stairs and the hospital covered it up, I can save another woman from her fate."

"You're still trying to absolve yourself of a guilt that isn't yours," John said as he helped Sam tighten his gloves. "Instead of dealing with the guilt that is. You need to make things right with Layla and the Patels." He helped Sam on with his other glove and pushed him into the ring.

"She needs to make things right with me," Sam retorted. "We almost lost the contract because of her. And as for Nasir, what would I say? They were in breach of the lease for over a year, and we had a legal right to evict them."

"I can't believe I'm saying this, but just because it's legal doesn't make it right," John spat out. "You've been chasing a monster for so long, you've become one yourself." He held open the ropes so Sam could climb through and then climbed in after him.

"What's going on?" Evan looked from John to Sam and back to John.

"I feel like beating on Sam today so I'm going to ask you to step aside." John held out his hand for Evan's gloves.

Sam tipped his neck from side to side as Evan helped John tie on the gloves. "Don't do this. You've never won a fight against me. I don't want to hurt you."

"You've hurt everyone else." John dropped into a fight stance. "I think it's time you feel what it's like."

Sam had only a second of warning before John's fist hit his nose, and he went down in a shower of stars.

"GET me another one." Layla waved Danny over after he'd locked the restaurant door. With her father still recovering and her business now without an office, she'd been putting all her energy into the restaurant, working from morning to night by her mother's side. They didn't have the money to pay the rent in arrears and stop the eviction, but she would do her best to make sure they went out as successful as they had come in.

"I think you've had enough." He joined her at the bar. "You've spent the last few days eating alone in the restaurant after hours. Don't you think it's time to try a different way of drowning your sorrows?"

"What else am I supposed to do?" Her eyes filled with tears. "I thought I'd hit rock bottom in New York, but I wasn't even close. Now besides having no job, no office, no apartment, no boyfriend, and no husband, I opened myself to love and got hurt all over again, and my parents are being evicted. I'm in an even worse situation than I was when I first came home, except I didn't just get out of jail."

Danny sucked in a sharp breath. "You did time?"

"Two hours of hard time on the police station bench in the local precinct." She shuddered at the memory. "In handcuffs. It was awful. The only reason I didn't go into lockup was because I'd found a job for the building manager's brother, Louie 'the Ax' Moretti, who had decided to get out of the Mafia business. He was married to my father's cousin's wife's sister's husband's niece. He pulled a few strings with his police friends and they let me go. It's a good thing Jonas cheated on me on a Saturday night because Louie was dead by Sunday, and I couldn't come home right away because I had to go to the funeral." She drew a finger across her throat. "Italian necktie."

"That is so fucking hot." He licked his lips. "You're an ex-con."

She handed him her bowl. "Fill it up. And add extra cayenne. I don't want to be able to feel my tongue."

"There is such a thing as eating too much dal." Danny took her bowl away. "Why don't you have a few drinks? I can make you a gin and tonic. That's what most people turn to when they're down."

"Not good desi girls. We want our comfort food. I checked the pot on my way in. There's still lots left."

"You've had four bowls already, and an entire stack of roti . . ."

"Bring more roti, too. Make sure they're hot enough to burn my fingers. I need the pain to remind me that I'm still alive. I think my heart has been broken one too many times."

Danny untied his apron and sat on the seat beside her. "A little melodramatic, don't you think?"

"You should be eating dal, too." She leaned against his shoulder, too distraught to worry about propriety. "The restaurant is closing. You're going to lose your job."

With a sigh, Danny put an arm around her shoulders. "Your mother told me not to worry, so, I'm not worrying. I'm just doing my job, cooking and helping out and supporting people in emotional distress."

Layla looked up, sniffing after her hour-long sobfest. "I am in emotional distress."

"I can see that," he said softly.

"Why do the people I love always betray me? Morgan said he loved me, but it turned out he just wanted someone to share the rent with him and his buddies so they didn't lose their apartment in Greenpoint. And then there was Adam, who hired an actor to play himself, and when I fell for him and asked him to move in with me, this deranged fortysomething bald dude showed up on my doorstep with two suitcases, three cats, and his grandmother's ukulele."

"Have some more dal." Danny handed her the spoon and she scraped the bottom of the bowl.

"And then there was Quentin . . ."

"I don't like him already," Danny said. "What kind of dude is named Quentin?"

"A philosophy professor who broke up with me after three months by writing me a letter. He said in philosophical terms we were fundamentally incompatible. He said he was Sartre, who believed in contingent love affairs, and I was Kierkegaard, who believed in committed relationships."

"He cheated on you."

"Philosophically speaking." She shoved the last spoon of dal into her mouth. Her stomach gurgled in protest. "Then there was Chris." She sighed. "He broke up with me but he couldn't say why because he was crying so much. Then every few months he would show up and ask me to—"

"They don't sound like good dudes," Danny interrupted. "Did you really love them?"

"I thought I did." She hesitated. "I wanted to. But now that I know how real love feels, no, I didn't love them at all."

"I think love is overrated." He put his arm around her and gave her a friendly hug. She hadn't noticed before how good he smelled, like burned roti and mango pickle.

"You know what you need to take your mind off Sam?"

"Gulab jamun? Maybe I need sweets."

"A massage." His hand moved down her back, rubbing small circles over her spine. "Is this okay?"

So relaxing. If her stomach hadn't been so bloated from all the dal, she would have asked him to massage her while she lay on a table. "Yes." She sighed. "Feels nice."

"I can make you feel so good, you won't feel bad anymore." His hand slipped lower to the curve of her rear. Back massages were good. Bottom massages by fuckboys, not so much unless she had sunk so low she wanted to go down this road.

"I don't like feeling bad," she said, considering. "It makes my stomach hurt."

"You won't have to feel bad anymore." Danny pulled her to her feet. "My girlfriend is out of town so I am all about your pleasure, baby. I want to see that beautiful smile."

"Sure. Why not?" If this was her life from now on, she might as well get started and learn to enjoy random hookups with fobby fuckboys in closed restaurants and behind the hedges at weddings where she would always be the bridesmaid and never the bride.

"Sweet." He grinned, flashing a golden tooth. "Why don't we go into the back office and I'll make you forget about Chris and Quentin and Adam and Morgan and Jonas and—"

"Sam." Her voice hitched. "I want to forget about Sam. I want to forget about how he made me laugh, and how good-looking he is, and how he was so protective every time I met a new guy, and how sweet he is with his sister, and how irritating he was in the office when he stole my desk and organized my pencils, and how I never thought I'd love an A's fan, but I do. And yet, he's no better than any of the other guys who broke my heart."

Danny wrapped his arms around her and pulled her against him, his thick erection pressing up against her belly. "I've got all the love you need right here."

Layla's stomach protested the pressure with a loud gurgle. "Oops. I think you were right about the dal."

"That's okay, babe." He squeezed her tighter, his fingers digging like little claws into her rear. "I won't hear anything over your moans of pleasure."

"Maybe don't squeeze so hard." She tried to pull away and relieve the pressure.

"I want you to feel what you do to me, how much I want your sexy ex-con ass." He pulled her tighter, ground his hips against hers.

Bile rose in her throat. Her mouth started to water, and not in a good way. "Actually, I'm feeling something else . . . Maybe you should . . ."

With a huge shove, she pushed him away, just before her stomach heaved the contents of her night of self-indulgence all over the tile floor.

"Oh God." She fell to her knees and vomited again. "Every time I think that's the end, I discover a new level of hell."

"Don't worry," he said. "I've got an extra toothbrush."

She heaved again.

"Maybe not." He checked his watch. "Look at the time. I've got to meet someone . . . somewhere. You good to close up?"

"Sure." She collapsed on the floor, disgusted by how pathetic she had become. If even Danny was running away, she had hit rock bottom. She had to accept that it was all over—the game, the office, the business, and Sam.

"I'M sorry. GenSys Medical has decided to terminate your employment effective today."

Sam couldn't muster more than a sympathetic nod for the dude on the other side of the table. He was a bastard not even his best friend would stand by. Might as well live up to his reputation.

"No." Jordan thudded the table with a meaty fist. "There must be some mistake. Check again." At six feet, four inches tall and weighing at least 280 pounds, Jordan looked more like a professional wrestler than a genetic research scientist with two Ph.D.'s who had spent the last fifteen years in a windowless laboratory.

Claire Watson, GenSys's HR manager, didn't even blink at his outburst. Karen was cold and hard, but Claire took it to a whole new level. She had an app that allowed her to track employee reactions and so far she'd earned nineteen stars for eliciting tears.

"One more for the win," she whispered to Sam before giving Jordan the details of his termination package.

"You've got no fucking heart." Jordan followed Sam to the door where two security guards were waiting to escort him off the premises. Usually, Sam hated same-day terminations for their sheer brutality, but today, he couldn't bring himself to care.

"You've got no soul," Jordan continued. "How can you do this to good, honest, hardworking people? What did I ever do to you? This isn't right."

Sam flinched inwardly, hearing Nasir's voice instead of Jordan's. What had the Patels ever done to him? When had he stopped feeling sympathy for the people whose lives he had to destroy? Was John right? Had he truly become the monster he'd been hunting? Was he no better than Ranjeet?

"It's not personal," he said, more to convince himself than the distraught man beside him. "Sacrifices have to be made for the greater good. If we didn't let some people go, no one would have a job."

"Why me?" Jordan's voice caught, broke. "I never had a bad review in my life."

Why Nasir? Why Layla? Why did they have to suffer for Nisha to be avenged? In his heart Sam knew it wasn't right. When had he lost sight of what was truly important?

"I know this is all a shock . . ." Sam launched into his speech without the usual preamble. ". . . but it could be the best thing that has ever happened to you. Once you put the past behind you, the sky's the limit."

"Don't feed me that BS platitude," Jordan spat out. "You clearly don't believe it. Why should I?"

Did he believe his speech? Was the destruction of someone's life the best thing that could happen to him or her? Nisha's accident had taken him away from his dream of being a doctor and put him on his current path. He felt no joy in his partnership with Royce, but it paid the bills and helped him to shut off his emotions so the burden of guilt didn't weigh so heavy on his heart. But he hadn't put the past behind him. He lived it every day, and it had dragged him farther and farther down into a darkness that had seemed impossible to escape. Until he met Layla.

Before he could answer Jordan's question, the security guards arrived and escorted the scientist away.

"How about dinner at my place tonight?" Claire suggested when he returned to the boardroom. "I'm not much of a cook, but then I'm not really inviting you over to eat." She licked her lips. "Not food, at least."

He was saved from having to turn her down when the next employee knocked on the door. Layla might not want him, but there was no other woman he wanted but her.

"Shari Patel," Claire whispered as she handed him a copy of Shari's file. "She and Jordan worked together in the same lab. If she cries, I'll get a gold crown."

Patel? A cold chill seeped through his body when the next employee walked in. She was shorter than Layla, her face softer and rounder, and her dark hair fell straight to her shoulders. He couldn't see any resemblance, but he needed to be sure.

"Are you related to the Patels who own The Spice Mill?" he blurted out after she sat down.

"Different Patels." She gave him a warm smile. "Although I'm sure if you trace the family tree back, you'll find we are all related in some way. You know Jana and Nasir?"

"I know Nasir and his daughter, Layla." Her name caught in his throat, and the memory of the pain in her face when she walked into the party sliced through his heart like a dagger. It was getting harder and harder to feel the righteous indignation over her attempt to expose him that had sustained him since the party.

"I heard they're closing The Spice Mill," she said. "Such a shame. I remember going to their restaurant in Sunnyvale when I was a girl. They made the best masala dosas . . ."

Sam winced inwardly at the unintended blow. Even the words *masala dosa* made him feel sick inside.

"How about we take that trip down memory lane another time and move things along," Claire said impatiently. "Unfortunately, your employment at GenSys has been terminated effective today . . ."

Sam gave Shari the details: the need to restructure, taking one for the team, her choice of money now or after consulting a lawyer . . .

Shari signed the document and took the check without saying another word.

"Do you have any questions? Any issues you want to raise?" Claire didn't get any points for employees who signed quietly and walked out the door.

"No." Shari stood to go. "I knew it was coming. I've put the word out in the community that I'm looking for work. I'm sure something will turn up." She smiled at Sam. "You know how it is."

Yes, he did know how it was for the Patels. The ties that bound them were so strong they could weather any storm. Lone wolves, however, limped blindly through the snowy wilderness, starving and vulnerable without their pack.

"Thank you for your service to the company," Sam said, thrown off his game by her calm acceptance of the situation.

"You're welcome."

With a puzzled glance for Claire, Sam escorted Shari to the door. "I know this is all a shock, but . . ." He trailed off, suddenly feeling like a fraud. "I had a speech, but it doesn't feel right to give you advice that I'm not following myself. I'm just . . . sorry. I'm really sorry this had to happen to you."

"It's okay." She clasped his hand. "I know you're just doing your job. I forgive you."

I forgive you.

Those three words broke him, even though he didn't know why.

Something inside him crumbled. He hadn't asked for forgiveness, but now he wondered if it was what he'd been looking for all along.

SAM pushed open the door to the office above The Spice Mill and flicked on the light, reeling at the mess. It was clear no one had been in here since the party. Bottles and cans covered every surface. Fruit and canapés rotted on trays. Someone had spilled red wine on Layla's chaise and the angry black stain had spread over the seat.

He put down his cleaning supplies and used his broom to clear a path through reception to the office where the portable dance pole lay discarded on the floor along with Layla's broken goldfish bowl and the two dead fish.

Not so lucky anymore.

"So this is what it looks like when you totally destroy your life." Nisha wheeled herself along the path he'd just cleared for her. After leaving GenSys, he'd driven straight to his parents' house and told her about everything, from the Alpha Health Care contract to the game he'd played with Layla. Far from judging him, she had insisted on coming to the office to help clean up the mess.

"I didn't think things could get any worse, but now I've lost Layla, possibly the contract, and I'm pretty sure I just gave Nasir grounds for terminating the sublease, although he won't be my landlord for long. Royce hasn't answered my texts or calls, so I might even have to leave the partnership, and I haven't spoken to John since he knocked me out at the gym."

"And all because of me."

"No, because of me."

Nisha leaned over to pick up a discarded champagne bottle. "I didn't know you felt so guilty or that you would go to these lengths to bring Ranjeet to justice. I was just so glad to be free; I didn't care what happened to him."

"You don't want justice?" Sam asked the question he should have asked years ago.

"Not at the price you had to pay. My focus is on rebuilding my life. I want to look forward, not back. I love that you tried to make it right, Sam, but sometimes you have to let things go."

His little sister wasn't little anymore. Despite her injuries, she had managed to overcome the anger and bitterness that had been holding Sam back from embracing his life.

Nisha looked over as the door opened. "Who's that?"

Sam followed her gaze, his gut clenching when he saw John in the doorway waving a hand in front of his nose.

"What is that smell?"

"Rotting caviar." Sam's throat tightened when his friend walked toward them. "We came to clean up. What are you doing here?"

"I heard voices and was hoping Layla was back with some snacks from the restaurant, but it's just you." His gaze fell on Nisha and he smiled. "John Lee of Lee, Lee, Lee & Hershkowitz, at your service."

Sam made the introductions. John kept staring at his sister like he'd never seen a woman before. He stuttered through a conversation about the weather with such a lack of language skills it was hard to believe he could even say his own name in court.

"Seriously, dude." Sam stepped in front of Nisha, blocking John's view. "She's my sister."

"Yes, she is." Nisha rolled around him. "And your sister is talking to your friend and doesn't want to be interrupted."

"He interrupted us," Sam protested.

Nisha sniffed. "We were having a conversation about how you need to let people handle things on their own. Weren't you paying attention?"

"If you're worried that her wheelchair is an issue," John said, "I'll just remind you that your *personality* handicap hasn't stopped us from being friends."

Puzzled, Sam frowned. "What personality handicap?"

"Your inability to see things that are staring you in the face."

Nisha laughed out loud, and the look she shared with John suggested an interest in more than just a friendship.

"The only thing that is staring me in the face right now is this mess," Sam said in an attempt to change the uncomfortable conversation.

"Well, let's get busy." John grabbed a garbage bag.

"You're going to help?"

John swept a pile of empty cans into the bag. "I said what I had to say at the gym, and I admit I felt a bit bad knocking you out, although I'm never letting you live that one down. But now it looks like you're starting to pick up the pieces. That's when you need your friends the most."

"It's one hell of a mess."

"Then we'll handle it one piece at a time." John held up a sparkly pink G-string. "Let's get the cleaning party started."

"WHAT have you been doing since you left Glenlyon Morrell in New York?" Miles Fanshaw, executive director of City Staffing Solutions, leaned back in his plush leather chair as he sipped his morning coffee.

Layla had always imagined having an office like this. Huge windows. Incredible view. Giant desk. Thick carpet. Framed artwork on the wall . . . What was that picture, anyway? It wasn't anything, really. Just a scribble of random colors. Messy. Meaningless. Chaotic. Sam would have hated it.

"I thought about starting my own recruitment agency, but it didn't work out," she said honestly. "My parents run their own business, and they made it look easy, but I'm not cut out to go it on my own. I prefer the stability and security of working in an established company where I can learn from people like you who are at the top of their game."

Not only that, she needed the money to help her parents, both with their relocation. She'd hit rock bottom the other night in the restaurant with Danny. After waking up on the cold tile floor beside a pool of her own vomit, she'd decided enough was enough. She'd pulled herself from the brink before and she could do it again. She was a Patel, and Patels didn't give up.

Miles smirked. "Stability is definitely a weakness for you. Or do you just have trouble keeping a handle on your emotions? I know many women do."

Misogynistic bastard. "So do many men," she said tightly. "However, I can assure you, I'm a professional, and I act that way at all times—"

"Maybe not all times." He handed her his tablet with the "Blue Fury" video playing on the screen. "I talked to your previous employer before our interview. She told me why she let you go."

Layla's stomach sank. Would she never be able to leave her past behind? "I'm not that woman anymore."

Miles laughed. "People don't change. Starting a business in a highly competitive field with minimal experience isn't something a conservative person would do." He studied her intently. "We need women like you, Layla. Sexy, pretty, passionate, and willing to think outside the box . . ." He smirked. "We'll just need to keep you away from the balcony."

"I don't think my looks are—"

"You could have a very bright future here," he said, interrupting. "Of course, you'll have to start at the bottom and show us you can keep those emotions under control, but in a few years you could be my assistant . . ."

Layla tuned him out as he explained the long career path to partnership and what she would need to do to work her way up the corporate ladder. Is this what she really wanted? Starting from the bottom again? Sacrificing self-respect for success? Maybe her business hadn't started out strong, but it was *her* business. She'd run it the way *she* had wanted. She'd answered to no one. Even Sam, who had far more experience running his own company, and had never treated her as anything less than an equal.

And Miles was wrong. She had changed. Sam had hurt her deeply, but she hadn't flung her dosas at him. She had held her head high and walked away even though her heart had broken in two.

It was her heart that made her different. She cared about the employees she placed. Everyone had told her to focus on the corporate clients, but if she built a reputation for solid, long-term placements with quality staff, they would come to Layla Patel for their personnel.

Patel Personnel. The name hit her like a thunderbolt. Too perfect. Too late.

Or was it?

"Thank you for your time. I don't think this is the right fit for me." Layla pushed quickly to stand. If she was going to go back to a regular job, at the very least she should work for someone she respected. And if she did decide to be her own boss, she needed to move on, put the past behind her, and figure out exactly who she was and what kind of business she wanted to run.

"You're making a mistake," Miles said. "A big one. No one else is going to hire you."

Layla smiled as she walked out the door. "Maybe that's exactly what I need."

· 24 ·

Sweat trickled down the back of Sam's neck as he hesitated at the door to The Spice Mill. He'd been avoiding this talk with Nasir since the party, but it was long overdue.

"I'm sorry. We're closed until five." A middle-aged woman with short-cropped hair looked up, her smile fading when she saw him. "Oh. It's you from upstairs. Get out or I'll throw my shoe."

Sam had a vague memory of seeing her coming in and out of the restaurant, but he'd never taken the time to ask her name.

"I'm not here to cause trouble, Auntie-ji. I came to see Mr. Patel."

"Don't you think you've done enough damage?" Her eyes narrowed. "Do you know the pain and suffering you've caused? All this. All the hard work. All they have done and you just throw them out on the street."

"Let the boy through, Pari," Nasir called out from the kitchen door. "I want to hear what he has to say."

Sam made his way through the empty restaurant. They hadn't opened yet for the evening and an elderly man was smoothing gold tablecloths over the sturdy wooden tables. The decor was a fusion of Indian and modern, rich with color and over-the-top displays.

Nasir waved him into the kitchen, where a young chef glared at him as he stirred a giant pot of rogan josh. The delicious scent made Sam's mouth water.

"I wasn't sure you would see me."

"We're both businessmen," Nasir said. "This is how business goes. We didn't pay the rent for many months. I knew we were living on borrowed time. My son's friends didn't have the heart to kick us out, but they were struggling to carry us for so long."

"I still want to apologize for what happened." The words tumbled out before he could stop them. "My partner and I were trying to secure a contract and the location was important to our clients. I told him to do what it took to make a deal. I'm not blaming him. The fault is entirely mine. I should have anticipated the outcome."

"Have you ever deboned a fish?"

Sam all but gaped at the sudden turn of the conversation. "No. My mother wouldn't let me do anything in the kitchen."

"Wash your hands. Grab an apron. It's never too late to learn."

Sam wasn't about to say no to Nasir, especially when the chef was holding a knife. He washed up and joined Nasir at the stainless steel counter.

"Do what I do." Nasir slit the belly of the fish in front of him with a flick of his wrist.

Sam copied his steady movements, and they worked together in silence until both fish were deboned and neatly sliced.

"You're good with a knife," Nasir said.

"I used to be a surgeon. It didn't work out." Sam picked up another fish and sliced through the belly.

"You failed?"

"No. I quit."

"Quitting is worse than failing." Nasir's hands flew, deboning another fish in half the time. He'd been holding back, Sam realized, testing him. But now the real competition began.

"Failing means you tried and couldn't do it," Nasir continued. "Quitting means you gave up."

"A surgeon at the hospital where I worked, my mentor, hurt my sister," Sam said. "He was never punished. I couldn't work there anymore. I couldn't be a healer when I should have recognized the kind of man he was and when his continued freedom made a mockery of the oath we had sworn to uphold."

"Selfish," Nasir muttered, half to himself. "Maybe I was wrong about you when we first met . . ."

"Selfish?" Sam's voice rose in pitch and he shot an apologetic glance at the angry chef and the two other cooks who were keeping an eye on them as they worked. "I've spent the last four years trying to bring him to justice. I sacrificed everything to put myself in a position where I could make it happen."

"You deprived the world of a skilled surgeon." Nasir stopped, leaning on the bench as he drew in a breath. "Think of how many lives you could have saved. Instead, you cared only about one—"

"My sister means everything to me. He destroyed her life. The least I could do is give her justice."

"Did she ask to be avenged?"

John had asked him the same question. Nisha had never asked for vengeance. She just wanted to be done with Ranjeet and move on with her life.

Nasir reached blindly for the stool behind him. Alarmed, Sam helped him sit. Without thinking, he placed his fingers on Nasir's wrist and took a quick pulse.

"I'm fine." Nasir waved him away. "I'm just getting used to the new pacemaker."

"Your heart rate is a bit high. You need to rest. I'll finish this while we talk." He washed his hands again and picked up the fillet knife, trying to remember the complications of pacemaker implants. Had Nasir just pushed himself too hard? Infection in the incision? Nasir didn't appear to be feverish. No clammy skin. His eyes weren't dilated. Hands weren't shaking.

"So you did it for you," Nasir said. "To make the guilt go away. To feel like a man again—to feel worthy."

And there it was in a nutshell. Yes, the guilt had been crushing him. He'd wanted to turn back the clock and be the boy who had beat up a gang of bullies for throwing a rock at Nisha in the playground, the teenager who had picked her up from parties, the brother she could count on. Not the narrow-minded ambitious resident who couldn't recognize a monster when he saw one every day.

Nasir moved to stand and Sam shook his head. "You should sit for at least ten minutes. Get that heart rate back down. Take a load off."

"I already took a load off," Nasir grumbled. "Forty pounds. Gone. People will think my cooking isn't good. *Look*, they'll say. *Nasir is so thin. He doesn't eat his own food. Why should we go to his restaurant when Manoj Gawli down the street at Tamarind Restaurant is healthy and round?*"

Sam chuckled. "I don't know anyone who measures the success of a restaurant by the diameter of the owner's belly."

"You aren't in the food business." Nasir settled on his stool. "You're in the quitting business. How would you know how to measure success?"

"I came to see if we could keep you in the food business." Sam slid his knife through the fish, his hands remembering how to cut and slice gently through flesh. "I found office space only a few blocks away that would meet our client's requirements, and I've withdrawn the eviction proceedings. If you would be willing to stay on with us as landlords, then I'm sure I can convince my partner to move to the new location."

"Keep it." Nasir gave a violent shake of his head. "I don't want."

Sam couldn't believe what he was hearing. "You're leaving?"

"It's time we moved on," Nasir said. "Live our own life, our own dreams."

"This wasn't your dream?"

"This was my son's dream." Nasir sighed. "Everything bigger. Everything fancier. He wanted more than just a restaurant. He wanted a Patel family enterprise—packaged meals in the grocery stores, Patel-branded products and spices, cookbooks, television shows . . ." He drew in a weary breath. "It was all going to be run from the office upstairs. He decorated that space. *Bright and modern*, he said. *Leave the pipes and beams exposed, don't cover the brick . . .*" Nasir threw his hand in the air. "The only thing that was mine was the desk. Nice rosewood. Solid and sturdy. A desk like that will last forever."

"It's a great desk."

"I brought it from the old restaurant." Nasir gave him a wistful smile. "We were twenty years there. Small but cozy. Every night it was full. People lined up outside the door, talking and laughing. Jana handed out jalebis to the kids. And it was near the house. No long commutes every day. But for Dev, it wasn't enough. He wanted more customers. A big name. He bought this building with his friends so we could have this space. How could I say no? He was my son."

"He wanted the best for you."

"He wanted it for him. He just didn't know himself well enough to realize it." Nasir pointed to the stack of fish that Sam had just filleted. "Look at that. I couldn't have done better myself and I am a lifetime in the business. This is what your hands wanted to do. I felt ill and you were taking my pulse. You are a healer, and you're throwing your gift away."

"I'm not worthy of that gift." Sam put down his knife. "I failed everyone I cared about."

"You failed yourself by wallowing in your guilt," Nasir said. "You can't be in everyone's head, guessing what they are going to do. The real measure of a man comes not when things go right, but what he does when things go wrong."

"I'm trying to fix everything."

"You can't fix anything until you fix yourself."

"What about you?" Sam asked, trying to steer the conversation away from his failings. "If you leave this place, what will you do?"

"We're going to move back to our old location." Nasir smiled. "We still own the building. I already gave notice to the tenant. We'll freshen it up, bring some of this new equipment, and I can get back to being a chef and not a celebrity. My doctor thinks this is a good idea. Less stress. Less work. And less commuting."

Sam's stomach clenched in a knot. He'd imagined everything staying the way it was. Layla would stay in the office. He and Royce would move down the block. Nasir would be downstairs. He couldn't be with Layla, but he couldn't imagine her anywhere else.

"I drew up a lease for Layla." Sam pulled out the document. "Do you think she'll move back in?"

"That's not up to me. That's up to you."

LAYLA made a perimeter check of the office, taking care to inspect every nook and cranny for any evidence of Royce's crazy party. Whoever had cleaned up had done a good job. Not a trace remained. Her desk had been straightened, photographs in their frames, ornaments in the corner, and there was only a faint ring where her fishbowl had been.

Only Sam's desk wasn't the same. Clean and bare, without the neatly stacked papers or the rows of sharpened pencils, it was as empty as the hole in her chest.

She and Daisy had returned to the office to pack up their stuff, but now that she was back, it was difficult to leave. Not just because of the bittersweet memories, but also because she had finally found her name.

Patel Personnel.

It had everything Royce and Evan suggested—a catchy ring, alliteration, and meaning. But more than that, it was her. Could she have made the business work if she'd thought up the name earlier? Or was there another secret to success?

"There were twenty-seven messages on the phone," Daisy called out. "And they're not just from people looking for jobs. Employers. Lots of them. What do you want me to do?"

Layla's stomach twisted in a knot. "I don't know. I've been interviewing for jobs but—"

"Are you crazy?" Daisy cut her off with an exasperated sigh. "You don't have time for a job. All these people want you, not some big-name agency that doesn't give a damn who they are. What happened to all your dad's sayings? 'Patels like to be their own boss,' 'Patels persevere,' 'Patels and pakoras are made to be together, especially at lunchtime when Daisy's hungry.'"

"Patels are also realistic. I gave this a go and it didn't work out. I thought I could love someone again, and I got hurt. I thought I could make a fresh start and I'm back to where I was before."

"Are you kidding me?" Daisy's voice rose in pitch. "You are nothing like the woman who ran away to New York. That woman was afraid to live. She dated guys she knew she couldn't love and she took a job she knew she wouldn't like so there was no chance she would get hurt again. But look at you now. You didn't like how most agencies were run so you started your own damn business.

You wanted a serious, stable relationship so you went on blind dates with total strangers and you fell for the strangest man of all."

Laughter bubbled up in Layla's chest. "Sam isn't strange."

"Yeah. He's strange. Trust me. The whole pencil thing . . . and the tidy piles of paper . . . and don't get me started on the chai." She sighed. "And then there was the whole avenging his sister thing. Who does that?"

"Pretty much everyone in every revenge movie ever made." Layla ticked them off on her fingers. "*Kill Bill, The Crow, Taken, V for Vendetta, Payback, The Punisher, True Grit, Braveheart, John Wick, Unforgiven . . .*"

"Now you're just showing off."

"It doesn't matter now," Layla said. "I can't love someone who is destroying my parents' business as well as my own. I should never have played that stupid game with him. If I'd kicked him out the day we met, none of this would have happened."

Daisy spun around in her chair. "That game was never about the office. It was about him. If you really wanted him out of here, you would have sent him away."

"That doesn't make sense. If I was interested in him, why would I interview the men on my dad's list?"

"Because of Jonas and all the men before him," Daisy said. "And because of Dev. Because you knew you could get serious about Sam and it scared you. Going on your dad's blind dates was the safe option, and the game meant you could keep Sam around."

Layla's heart squeezed in her chest. "Well, he's not around now, and even if I could stay here, I don't want to."

"So what? You don't need this office to be successful." On a roll now, Daisy stood and gestured wildly. "You can run your business from anywhere—a coffee shop, or a shared office space, or even my parents' garage, if you don't mind sharing with Max."

Max barked at the sound of his name. Whoever had cleaned the office had also fixed his basket and collected his toys, but Max had refused to go near it since they'd come in.

"But it's not going to happen if you give up," Daisy continued. "So you hooked up with a guy you liked and you lost him. So you have to move to another location. When you were in New York, you would never have taken those chances. You were too afraid of getting hurt. But you're stronger now. Your biggest fears came true, and you're still standing."

A smile curved Layla's lips. "Where were you with the motivational speech when I ran away to New York?"

"Right here waiting for you to come to your senses and move back home."

Layla leaned against her desk, toying with the cup of pencils. "I've been to three interviews this week with recruitment agencies and I couldn't see myself at any one of them. The idea of starting from the bottom again, having to answer to someone, pandering to corporate clients, and playing office politics just doesn't appeal after running things on my own. This business was a dream I had that I never thought would come true, and then it did." She pulled out the scrap of paper she had written on after her interview and handed it to Daisy. "And now, I've come up with a name . . . Patel Personnel. I think Lakshmi Auntie would call that a sign."

"That's awesome. I love it!"

The door opened and Layla's father walked into the office. She moved to help him, and he waved her away. "I'm fine, beta. I took the elevator this time. I never got a chance to see your new office so I came for a visit while you are here." His gaze fell on the purple chaise. "Did Deepa Auntie give you that?"

"Yes. And the elephant table and beaded lamp."

"She never did have any taste."

"Are there fresh pakoras in the kitchen, Nasir Uncle?" Daisy already had her bag in her hand.

"I put aside a plate for you, and there's a special treat for Max. You'd better hurry before they're gone."

Max wagged his little tail and followed Daisy out the door. Layla sat beside her father on the chaise as he looked around.

"We didn't really do much with it," Layla said. "We thought one of us was going to leave."

"Dev decorated this office." Her father patted her knee. "It was supposed to be the heart of the Patel family enterprise."

"I remember," she said gently. "He had big dreams, and we could have made them come true if not for what Sam and his partner did."

Her father leaned back, stretching his legs under the elephant table. "Sam withdrew the eviction proceedings and offered us a new lease with better terms."

"That's great, Dad." A wave of relief washed over her. "You don't have to leave."

"I told him no," her father said. "The big restaurant, the Patel enterprise . . . that was never our dream."

"But what will you do?" Her parents had run the restaurant since before Dev was born. She couldn't imagine them doing anything else.

"We're going to relocate the restaurant back to Sunnyvale. That's where we belong. We came here for Dev, and we stayed for his memory. But now it's time for us to go. This illness has made me realize that in the short time we have here, we can't cling to the past. This location isn't good for a family restaurant, and I don't need a big Patel enterprise to be happy. I need my daughter and my wife, my family and my friends, and a small restaurant in the heart of our community where the tables are always full and people drop by for a cup of chai to share their day with us. The eviction was the push we needed to make a new start. I told Sam this so he didn't feel so bad."

"I can't believe you could even talk to him after what he did."

Her father smiled. "When you get to be my age, it's easier to forgive. His motives were good. His methods not so much."

"He lied to me, Dad." Her hands twisted in her lap. "He betrayed me. He destroyed the office. He hurt you, and he hurt me. He had a choice and he made the wrong one." Her blood rushed hot and furious through her veins. "He's no better than Jonas."

"He asked me to give you this." He held out the envelope he'd been holding since he arrived. "Sam offered to lease the office to you on the same terms he offered me."

Layla skimmed the document. "I don't want it. He's trying to buy me off, just like he tried to buy off his clients with the big party. I'm not interested in having him for a landlord. He's arrogant and stubborn and a control freak. He couldn't start work until his pencils were lined up in a neat row, and he never left work without clearing off his desk. The only time I've seen him with a hair out of place was the night of the party. We didn't agree on anything. And he supports the A's. That says it all."

"You are proud, like your mother. She once refused to let a famous critic into the restaurant because he had written that her dal lacked sophistication."

Layla laughed. "Sounds like Mom."

Her father pushed to stand. "Do you know why your mother and I have stayed together for so long?"

"You were friends first?"

"No," he said. "Because we disagreed so often. She liked her dal like a soup, and I like it thick. She wanted to add turmeric to a stew and I wanted to add cumin. She wanted to pack samosas in your lunch and I wanted you to have American food. I never know what the day will hold. Walking into the kitchen every morning is like going into a battlefield. She challenges me. She makes me a better person. I'm a passionate man, and your mother makes my heart race. Maybe that's why I needed a new one. So I could keep arguing with her for the next twenty years."

Layla swallowed past the lump in her throat. "I had hoped there would be someone like that for me on your list. But I didn't meet anyone I could see myself being as happy with as you are with Mom."

"Maybe because you saw yourself being happy with someone else," he suggested.

"Even if I did, it's over now."

"Then why don't you meet the rest of the men I picked for you?" he suggested. "Finish what you started. You told me when you first came home from New York that you wanted to rebuild your life with a fulfilling career and a stable relationship. You have your business. Maybe the man you are looking for is still out there, too. What do you have to lose?"

25

SAM took a seat beside Royce in the boardroom at Alpha Health Care's head office. No wonder Royce had pulled out all the stops at the party. Everything was designed to impress, from the soft leather furnishings to the expensive artwork, and from the spectacular brass-detailed cherrywood boardroom table to the Chihuly glass sculptures on the credenzas along the wall.

"Would you like a drink?" The hostess handed him a leather-bound menu that listed thirty flavors of tea and a wide-ranging selection of coffee and other beverages. "Today's special is chai."

"Nothing for me." He was as unworthy of his traditional food as he was of the relationship he had so utterly destroyed.

"Double espresso and a brioche," Royce said. "Light on the butter." He leaned back in his Eames leather chair and grinned. "I could get used to this, so don't mess it up. If I hadn't convinced Peter your girlfriend was crazy, we would have lost the contract after what happened at the party."

"I think the fact we got it had less to do with your skills of persuasion and more to do with the fact he was already high on angel dust and champagne and couldn't even remember his own name."

Peter Richards joined them a few moments later with the HR managers from the five hospitals that were about to be downsized. Royce and Sam stood to greet them.

"Claire, Julie, Paul, Andrew, and . . ."

"Karen." Sam shook Karen's hand. Of course she'd landed on her feet. Karens always did. "We know each other."

"Sam." A smile spread across her face. "I didn't know you got the AH contract! Congratulations. I'm so glad I bumped into you at the fountain the other night. When you mentioned AH might be looking for extra HR personnel, I sent in my résumé and here I am! I owe you big-time." She squeezed his hand. Hard. Letting him know exactly how she wanted to pay her debt.

While snacks were served, Sam distributed the paperwork he'd prepared. After Nasir had called to let Sam know that Layla had turned down his offer, Sam had moved back into the office, but it wasn't the same. He missed their snarky banter and her teasing smile. He missed the smell of the chai Layla prepared every morning, the boxes of donuts he ate only when she wasn't looking, and the blind dates that had taught him more about her than the men they'd met. He even missed the purple chaise.

"We've been through all the financials," Sam said. "We recommend cutting approximately six hundred jobs as part of the reorganization. That's about five percent of the Bay Area's thirteen thousand five hundred–person staff, spread over five hospitals and one hundred and eighty clinics. Each hospital will be responsible for identifying individual employees for layoff. We'll work with the HR manager of each hospital to make sure there are no legal or PR issues with respect to the termination of individual employees, and assist in the meetings."

Over one hundred of those jobs were going to be cut from St. Vincent's—many of them likely people who had supported Sam's career and helped him during his residency. But Alpha Health Care was running a one-billion-dollar loss, and if they didn't restructure, all the hospitals and clinics would have to shut down, and not only staff, but also patients, would suffer.

"The board of directors has decided the layoffs won't affect any medical professionals," Peter said. "Surgeons, doctors, nurses, and nurse practitioners will all be exempt, so don't include them in your assessments. We don't want to lose our best talent."

A sudden coldness hit at Sam's core. His main goal in securing the contract had been to access Ranjeet's employment file. He'd sacrificed other opportunities for this chance. He'd lost Layla. And now he wouldn't be able to give Nisha the justice she deserved? Could life really be that cruel?

"I wouldn't recommend any exemptions," Royce said quickly. "This is a perfect opportunity to dig up skeletons, identify underperformers or employees with disciplinary issues, as well as those who might be a liability risk."

Sam threw him a grateful look. Royce hadn't judged him when they'd finally talked after the party, although he didn't understand Sam's need for justice. Life was simple for Royce. It was all about the money. And since there was no financial advantage to seeking the truth, he thought it was a waste of time.

"If you feel strongly about it, I can take it back to the board. I'll have an answer for you in a few days."

"Do that," Royce said. "We have a few more restructuring contracts to finish up so the timing works for us. And tell your hospitality people to try Chez Michel for your brioche. This one is exceedingly dry."

"ARE you sure this is the place?"

Layla studied the worn FLAMING TANDOOR sign above the doorway of the rundown building on Geary Street while Daisy tapped her computer on the other end of the phone.

"Yes, that's it," Daisy said. "I don't know why you agreed to meet him in the Tenderloin."

"Sometimes the best food can be found in the roughest neighborhoods." She drew in a ragged breath. This was her first bachelor interview without Sam, but if she was going to run her own business and move on with her life, she needed to know she could handle anything herself, including finishing her father's list, just to assure herself that her soul mate wasn't still out there.

"Okay." Daisy sighed. "Bachelor #7 is Salman Khan. Age thirty-three. He owns the Flaming Tandoor restaurant. It has four reviews. All bad. Comments include: 'Is it possible to give negative stars?' 'Dear police: Guess where the All India Boys street gang is hiding?' 'Five days. Both ends. Broke the toilet.' And 'Bitch. I'm gonna find you.'"

"That doesn't sound so good."

"No." Daisy smacked her lips. "I'm going to go out on a limb here and say I don't think this is your Westley."

"Well, he's seen me through the window, so I can't back out now." She waved to the man who was approaching the door. "Quick. What else do I need to know about him?"

"Ummm. Chemistry degree from USC. If that doesn't ring alarm bells—"

"I've seen *Breaking Bad*."

"Parents deceased. Three brothers. One living in San Rafael, one in Folsom, and one in Crescent City." She sucked in a sharp breath. "You do realize some of the state's worst prisons are coincidentally located in those three cities?"

"He's almost at the door."

"He likes baseball, Bollywood movies, Broadway shows, fast cars, and spending quality time with friends. He does tai chi in his spare time and takes pottery classes. Tell him I need a new coffee mug. Someone broke mine."

Layla reached for the door. "I'm going in. If I don't text in half an hour, send the police."

"Welcome. Welcome. You must be Layla. I'm Salman Khan. Not the actor." Salman shook Layla's hand and gave her a wide smile, dazzling her with two shiny gold incisors.

"That's not the actor I would have confused you with." Layla followed him through the tiny restaurant to a worn wooden table near the kitchen. Faded Bollywood posters, threadbare carpet, and the heavy scent of stale spices gave the restaurant a tired feel.

"Who do you think I look like?" He gestured for her to take a seat.

"Shoaib Khan in *Once Upon a Time in Mumbai*." She jerked her head in the direction of the three men in dark suits sitting at a nearby table. "You even have the bodyguards."

Salman laughed. "Don't mind them. They are like brothers to me."

Except these ones aren't incarcerated. She could almost hear Sam mumbling beside her and she felt curiously comforted by his imaginary presence.

She studied the man across the table as he poured two glasses of water. He was almost as tall as Sam, with a square face, close-set eyes, and slick black hair. His neatly combed mustache extended down to the bottom of his thick lips, and a tiny patch of beard filled the dip in his chin. Beneath a black suit jacket, his white shirt was open at the collar to reveal a thick gold chain.

"The food won't be as good as you're used to," Salman said with an apologetic smile. "We run a simple restaurant here. Just the basics."

"I'm sure it will be lovely."

Five days. Both ends. Broke the toilet, Imaginary Sam whispered.

"Freida!" Salman screamed over his shoulder. "Bring the food. Make sure the roti are hot."

Layla startled. "Is she hard of hearing?"

"Not at all."

"Those are interesting tattoos." She pointed to Salman's fingers, each of which bore a black letter in intricate calligraphy that spelled *ALL INDIA BZ* when he put his hands together. "Were you in a . . . gang?"

Dear police: Guess where the All India Boys street gang is hiding?

She imagined glaring at Sam. He'd probably be out of his seat by now or have an arm around her shoulders. Certainly, he'd be trying to end the date.

Salman's smile faded. "Ah. Folly of youth. But I've moved on to bigger and better things."

Layla glanced over at the three men who had nothing in front of them but glasses of water. "I thought you had to black out your ink when you left a gang. Or maybe that's just motorcycle clubs. I was a big *Sons of Anarchy* fan."

"I wouldn't know," Salman said tightly. "I only watch movies. Mostly Bollywood remakes of Hollywood films. Have you seen *Chachi 420*?"

"The *Mrs. Doubtfire* remake?" Layla brightened. "I've seen it, although I like the original more because it wasn't as raunchy. No lecherous cooks or hot bath scenes."

"Those were the best parts," Salman protested. "What about the dancing CGI bears in *Ta Ra Rum Pum*, the *Talladega Nights* remake?"

"It ends with a murder!" Layla said in mock horror. "It was crazy."

Speaking of murder . . . Imaginary Sam was back, or was it her niggling conscience?

"Not as crazy as *Bichhoo*, the remake of *Léon*." He smiled, almost blinding her with flashes of gold. "That last scene had a kill count of eighteen, and the dude was flying when that explosion hit. Like Superman."

"Except with a lot more gore," Layla added.

Speaking of kill counts . . . Imaginary Sam interrupted again. He clearly wanted her to leave but it wasn't often she got to talk to someone who knew Bollywood films as well as she did.

"That reminds me . . ." Salman pushed his chair away. "I need to check the kitchen to see what happened to our food. It was supposed to be ready for your arrival." He walked briskly to the kitchen, followed by two of the men in suits. The third turned his chair so he was facing her direction.

"Bitch! I'm going to find you!" Salman shouted so loudly the water in Layla's glass rippled in fear. "Where the fuck is the fucking food?"

Pots crashed. Glass broke. A woman screamed. A thud. A loud crack. And then silence.

And we're out of here. Imaginary Sam didn't need to tug her arm because Layla was already out of her seat.

"Gosh. Look at the time. Please give my regrets to Salman. I forgot I have to—"

"You don't disrespect Mr. Khan by leaving without saying good-bye." Moving with a speed that belied his heavy frame, the guard blocked her exit, hands folded over his massive chest. "He likes you. He wants you to stay."

Her heart pounded in her chest. "What if he didn't like me?"

"He would ask you to leave."

Layla swallowed hard. "The way Freida left?"

"Freida's fine. She's big on drama." He gestured her to the table, and she reluctantly took a seat. It's not like they were in a private home. The restaurant was open for business, and the front window overlooked the busy street. If she could see out, people could see in.

Still, she wasn't interested in an ex–gang member who screamed at his staff. Her only chance of extricating herself from the situation without causing offense was to make herself as unappealing as possible. And the best way to do that was to embrace the passion she'd tried to hide away. She'd dyed her hair to cover up the blue streaks before her first interview, but that part of her was still there—raw, emotional, and real.

"Blue Fury," here I come.

"Apologies." Salman joined her at the table, his voice slick and smooth like he just hadn't broken a rib screaming at Frieda before probably murdering her and dumping her body in the back alley. "Just a little trouble in the kitchen."

"Where's my lunch?" Layla thumped the table and raised her voice to a shout. "I'm hungry." She swept a hand over the table-cloth, knocking the stained cutlery and paper napkins to the floor.

Salman and his bodyguards stared at her in stunned silence. And then Salman smiled. "I like a woman with passion." He gestured to the nearest bodyguard. "You. Go to the kitchen. Bring poppadums and samosas. Tell Freida she'll have to cook with one hand, and make sure she doesn't get blood in the food."

Unable to contain her horror, Layla sucked in a sharp breath, her eyes going wide. "Blood?"

"Joking. I'm just joking." Salman patted her hand. "The meal will be out shortly. Can I get you something to drink?"

"I'll have a pint of whatever you've got on tap." Layla put one leg up on the chair beside her, draping her arm over the back of Imaginary Sam's seat. "And you." She pointed at the nearest body-guard. "Turn on the TV. The Padres are playing the Diamondbacks. I want to see the score. They're both leading the Giants right now on wins."

"Do as the lady asks," Salman said to the guard. "Put on the game and get her a drink. It seems Layla and I have something else in common."

No. No. No. She could just imagine Sam smirking in the chair beside her. Bracing herself for the lightning that would undoubtedly strike when she betrayed her beloved team, she took a deep breath and sank to the ultimate low. "Actually, I'm an A's fan." She punched the air. "Go, A's."

Salman stood so quickly his chair toppled over. "I'm sorry. You'll have to go. I can't be with an A's supporter. When I did my time in San Quentin, it was A's fans who . . ." He tugged on his shirt collar, as if he couldn't get enough air. "Let's just say they took rivalry to a whole new level."

"So . . ." Layla struggled to hide her delight. "You don't want me?"

"No." He shook his head, turning away as if she were a bad smell. "Please leave."

Layla made a quick escape and texted Daisy to let her know she was safe.

I'm never going to let you live that down. Imaginary Sam smirked.

"I miss you, Sam," she whispered. "Blind dates aren't much fun without you."

26

"I'M afraid we have to let you go, Diane. On behalf of St. Vincent's Hospital, thank you for your service."

Sam handed the bewildered woman a termination package. St. Vincent's Hospital was the first Alpha Health Care facility to face redundancies. The company had started the layoffs almost immediately after the press release was issued, and Sam was now in the unfortunate position of having to fire some of his former colleagues and friends.

"But I'm the longest-serving employee here," she protested, pushing back her silver hair. "I was the first cook they hired. I know everybody. I even remember you, Sam. I just got my thirty-year pin. Who's going to want someone my age?"

Karen gave her a tight smile. She had been assigned to St. Vincent's Hospital and was delighted to work with Sam again so soon. "You've seen a lot of changes in those thirty years, Diane. Changes that have made the hospital more efficient and better able to serve the needs of our patients. The automation of the restaurant is just another way we can save costs and pass those on to patient care. You do want the best for the sick and injured, don't you?"

"Yes, but—"

"And I know you wouldn't want to stand in the way of progress . . ."

Sam had to hand it to Karen. She had that rare skill of appearing sympathetic while being utterly brutal underneath. Royce would have loved her technique.

"Well, no . . . But . . ."

Sam tried to tune out her story, but his usual tricks didn't work. The walls he'd built to protect himself had come down. He felt deeply for this woman who had tried to cheer him up on the hardest days of his residency, and he couldn't hide his compassion behind platitudes and lies.

Karen segued into the paperwork, handing over Diane's final check and the termination contract. She explained the details and then looked at Sam expectantly.

Sam opened his mouth, but nothing came out. How could he tell her how to fix her life when he hadn't figured out how to fix his own?

"Sam has a little speech," Karen prompted.

"Actually, I don't."

Karen snickered. "You're supposed to tell her to think of it as an opportunity, try something new, put the past behind her, blah blah blah."

Blah. Blah. Blah. Karen had hit the nail on the head. His speech was nothing but air.

Sam handed Diane one of Layla's EXCELLENT RECRUITMENT SOLUTIONS cards. She'd left them in the trash after clearing her stuff out of the office. He wasn't sure if that meant she'd decided to close up her business or if she was starting something new, but he'd kept them and tucked some into his wallet for no reason other than that he liked seeing her name. "If you are looking for work, try Layla Patel. She's the best. Very caring and supportive. She has a good roster of corporate employers and she'll make sure you find something worthy of your talents. She might not be at that address, but her social media and phone details will be the same."

"You've lost your edge," Karen said when he returned from seeing Diane out.

"I have a lot on my mind."

"Well, you'd better get focused because the board agreed to include medical professionals in the layoffs. Dealing with surgeons who think they're gods is a totally different ball game."

"I think I can handle it."

"I almost forgot to give you this." She handed him a computer access token. "Royce told Peter you would need access to the employee database to flag any high-profile employees who might prove difficult if they're targeted for redundancy. No one wants a lawsuit or a PR nightmare."

Sam's hand shook when he took the token. Either Royce felt guilty for what he had done to the Patels or he finally understood Sam's need to avenge his sister. In any event, he was finally holding the key to his redemption.

"Are you okay?" Karen asked. "You kinda look like Charlie when he found the Golden Ticket in *Charlie and the Chocolate Factory*."

When Sam gave her a puzzled stare, she shook her head. "Never mind. You don't have kids."

"When is our next meeting?"

"After lunch." She licked her lips. "You want to christen the boardroom in our special way?"

Even if he hadn't had the Golden Ticket in his hand, he would have turned her down. There was only one woman he wanted, and being with anyone else felt like a betrayal. "You go ahead and grab a sandwich. I think I'll catch up on some work. I'll see you back here in an hour."

Just in case she didn't get the message, he flipped open his laptop and started to type.

With a disappointed sigh, Karen left the room, leaving him finally and blissfully alone.

It took only a few minutes to log in and find Ranjeet's file. And then he was lost in a sea of complaints related to Ranjeet's alcohol problem, including sexual and verbal abuse of staff, inappropriate behavior, and the performance of his duties—including surgeries—while intoxicated. For the most part, hospital administrators appeared to have swept the complaints under the carpet. There was nothing about Nisha or the accident in the file.

"Is that the kind of guy you and Royce are worried might pose a risk to the company?" Karen asked from behind him.

Sam froze, his hands on the keyboard. He'd been so engrossed in the file he hadn't even heard Karen come in. Now that she'd read the screen, lying wasn't an option.

"Yes."

"That's pretty standard," she said, taking a seat beside him. "Surgeons have a lot of power in the hospital, especially the ones who bring in a lot of money. The hospital will bend over backward to protect them so they don't lose them to the competition. I'll bet there isn't even a disciplinary note on the file."

"What if it were something more serious?" He scrolled down the page. "What if a physician committed a crime and the hospital covered it up? Would there be any records?"

Karen twisted her lips to the side. "If there is a serious liability issue for the hospital, the legal team gets involved. They'll often have the file scrubbed and the details restricted to people at the highest level." She looked over at him, considering. "Legal files can only be accessed by the legal team."

"What about old security footage?" He was beyond caring if Karen knew what he was after. He'd already crossed a line by accessing the file.

"It's stored off-site and not easily accessible." She frowned. "Your computer access will likely have been limited to HR and employment files, finance, and corporate administration."

"So that's it. He wins." Hope withered and died. Sam had dreamed of this moment for so long, he almost couldn't believe that all his efforts and sacrifice had come to nothing. There were no answers, no justice, and there would be no redemption.

"What did he do?" Karen asked softly.

"He pushed my sister down a flight of stairs at this hospital and broke her back. She's partially paralyzed and uses a wheelchair now."

"Oh God, Sam." Her hand flew to her mouth. "And the hospital covered it up?"

"My sister thinks so, and I believe her. I wanted to find the truth so she could have justice."

Karen tapped the screen. "And it's somewhere in there."

"Or on a security tape or a witness statement . . . Someone knows what happened and may have been afraid to come forward, like you said. Or maybe there was no one else in that stairwell and only the two of them know what really happened."

"This is outrageous." Her lips pursed together. "We need to talk to someone."

"No." Sam shook his head. "I can't do this anymore. I spent four years and lost everything trying to find the truth. I blamed myself for the longest time. I thought I should have seen what kind of man he was. I thought my family should have looked deeper into his background. But it's clear he was very good at hiding his addiction, and what he couldn't hide, the hospital covered up."

And it would always be the same unless someone stepped up. He couldn't turn back time for Nisha, and he couldn't give her the justice or even the answers he had hoped for, but he could help to improve the system by returning to medicine and becoming a voice for change.

"If you feel you need to go to your manager and tell her I have a conflict of interest, or that I was looking at this file—"

"I don't," Karen said firmly. "Do you know why I got the kids in my divorce? It's because my ex was just like this guy. He was a mean drunk, and I knew if I didn't get out of there, he would turn his anger on the kids. You were only trying to help your sister, and I'm just sorry you didn't find what you were looking for."

"I did find something," he said. "A way to forgive myself and move on with my life."

Karen pulled out her keys. "We still have a bit of time before the next employee arrives . . ."

"Another time I would have said yes." Sam gave her a warm smile. "But one of the things I lost was the woman I loved, and now I need to make things right."

"Sunil Singh. Hedge fund manager. Age thirty-five. Founder of Sunkey Capital. They employ eighty professionals in four countries and manage capital for foundations and high-net-worth individuals."

Layla could hear Max barking at Daisy on the other end of the phone. Patel Personnel was now working out of a dog-friendly shared office space in Bernal Heights while they looked for a new place to set up shop.

"What's wrong with Max?"

"He's hungry for your mom's pakoras. I don't know what I'll do when your parents move the restaurant to Sunnyvale. He's developed Michelin-starred tastes."

"The elevator just reached reception," Layla told her. "I'm going in."

"Maybe he's the one."

"I doubt it." Layla took in the white backless leather sofas, glass-tiled floor, and the mural of a snow-covered mountain made of cotton balls. "His office looks like Elsa's ice palace in *Frozen*."

Layla announced herself at reception and poked at the cotton balls until Sunil's personal assistant, dressed in an ice-blue suit, her long blond hair braided down her back, arrived to escort her to Sunil's office.

Layla threw up a hand to shield her eyes from the sun shining through two floor-to-ceiling windows when the assistant opened the door. By squinting, she could make out the vague shape of a man behind a desk.

"Sunil Singh. It's a pleasure to meet you."

"Could you lower the blinds?" Layla felt around for the chair and guided herself into the seat as the door closed behind her. "I need a visual of the man I'm considering for marriage."

"Ah. I think your father may have misunderstood my inquiry." Sunil pressed a button and the blinds snapped closed, shrouding the room in semidarkness.

Layla blinked as her eyes adjusted to the light and Sunil came into focus. He was thin and wiry, with an oversize lollipop head topped with a glossy thatch of hair. His long, slim fingers were almost skeletal in appearance, and although he was definitely brown, he looked like he bathed in saffron paste or one of the many skin-lightening creams elderly aunties always recommended to attract a better husband.

"Here's the deal." Sunil leaned forward. "I can't marry you because you're not a Singh."

Layla slumped back in her chair and feigned disappointment. "I'm sorry to hear that. I would have thought that personal flaw would have been evident from the fact that my last name is clearly stated on my desilovematch.com profile."

"I invited you here because you looked hot in your picture," Sunil continued as if she hadn't spoken. "I'm attracted to you so I'm willing to bang you."

"I beg your pardon?"

"Bang." He made a lewd gesture with his hands. "You and me. I'll do it."

She stared at him, appalled. "My dad didn't post my profile because he thought I was desperate to get laid."

Sunil was exactly the kind of man she'd hooked up with after Dev died. Shallow, narcissistic, and interested in only one thing. She could sleep with Sunil without any fear of an emotional connection. She could drown the pain of losing Sam in a few mindless moments of pleasure, the way she'd done after Dev.

Except she didn't want to forget. She wanted to keep her memories of Sam from the day she threw office supplies at his head to the last afternoon they'd spent together. He'd shown her that it was okay to love again and that she could survive another heartbreak.

"But you are desperate," he said. "I can tell from the way you looked at me when you walked in. You want me. Bad."

"Am I supposed to be grateful that you're willing to sleep with me?"

Impatience vibrated around him. "Yes."

Unwanted and unexpected, she had a fleeting thought about texting Sam. She'd enjoyed meeting new people with him, not just for the sake of finding a husband, but because those were the moments when she'd found out that he loved horror movies and donuts, supported the wrong team, and was fiercely protective of the people he cared about.

"I don't think so." In her imagination, she heard a growl, the thunder of feet. The door flew open and Sam stalked into the room, grabbed Sunil by the neck, and slammed him up against the glass.

Except it wasn't Sam grabbing Sunil. It was her. Flinging open the door and walking away. And, damn, it felt good.

She called Daisy from the elevator. "That was a total bust. Who's next?"

"Akhil Jones. He's waiting across the road in a coffee shop. He's in the middle of an engineering degree at USC. He likes long walks on the beach, picnics in the park, and lazy Sundays in bed at his home where he still lives with his parents. Musical influences include R5, Paramore, Panic! at the Disco, and Sleeping with Sirens." She sighed into the phone. "Sounds dreamy. If you don't want him, I don't mind robbing the cradle for a man who isn't afraid to send a picture of himself screaming on Splash Mountain at Disneyland."

Layla was across the road and in the coffee shop by the time Daisy finished extolling the virtues of younger men. She knew Akhil right away from his solar-powered Transformers backpack and the fact he was the only person in the café drinking juice.

"Akhil? I'm Layla." She held out her hand and smiled at the skinny kid with the five-finger forehead.

"It's nice to meet you, ma'am."

"Ha ha. Nope." She gave him a tight smile. "I'm going to cut it short right here, Akhil. I'm looking for someone a bit more . . . mature."

Someone with a deep voice and broad shoulders and a sarcastic sense of humor. A friend and companion who could make her smile at the worst times and laugh at the best times. Someone who treated her like an equal and made her feel like a princess. Someone who wanted her whether she was wearing pima cotton briefs or shapewear or nothing at all.

"I'm sorry, ma'am."

"That's okay, Akhil." She turned away. "Your Buttercup is out there. You just have to know how to find her."

27

SAM realized where he'd been going only when he pulled up in front of his parents' house. He'd been driving for hours since receiving Nisha's text telling him she didn't need a ride home from rehab. Sam didn't know if she'd found out about Layla and didn't want to see him, or if she really was going out with a friend, but since he'd never had a Monday evening free since the accident, he didn't know how to spend the time.

Through the window, he could see the flicker of the television. Although his mother had quickly adapted to streaming services—likely because they offered her an endless supply of horror films—his father refused to watch anything that wasn't on cable.

His heart ached when he saw movement behind the curtains. He couldn't remember the last time he'd had a real conversation with his parents. Save for the most basic greetings, and discussions about Nisha's welfare, he'd shared nothing of his life, and what he knew of theirs came through his sister.

A knock on the window brought him back to the moment. He lowered the window and nodded a greeting at his father.

"What are you doing sitting out here alone in the dark?"

Sam shrugged. "Nisha canceled on me. I didn't know what to do."

His father smiled. "She has a new friend from rehab and they went out together for dinner. She's taking the disabled transport bus home. I said I would pick her up, but she said no. She wants to do it herself. All this since you introduced her to your friend Layla. I don't know this girl, but I like her already."

She needed an emotional push, not a physical one.

"Layla said I was smothering her."

"You were protecting her," his father said. "We all were. But maybe we forgot to let her fly." He handed Sam a paper bag. "Your mother saw you sitting here so she made you something to eat. Don't worry. It's Western food. Some kind of sandwich."

"Thanks, Dad."

"Why don't you come inside where it's warm? We don't have to talk. You can watch a scary movie with your mother like you used to do. I don't like all that blood and screaming, and the people have no sense. Why go alone into a basement without a flashlight? Why do the girls all fall down when they run?"

"I had a chance to get justice for Nisha and I blew it." The words tumbled out before he could stop them. "And not in a small way. I lost everything."

"I thought I lost everything, too." His father's voice thickened. "But today my son came home."

Sam was out of the car before his brain even processed he had moved. He wrapped his father in a hug. "I'm sorry, Dad. When Ranjeet wasn't punished, I needed someone to share the blame."

"I forgive you." His dad clapped him on the back and they held each other for a moment longer. "For the first few months, I was like you. What if I'd made more inquiries? What if I'd gone to India to see his family there? What if I made them spend more time together? You can torture yourself forever but it doesn't change anything, and in some ways it gives him more power. Do we let him destroy all our lives or do we show him we can't be defeated? The best revenge is to move on and live your best life and give Nisha all the love and support she needs to live hers."

"It's hard to accept he'll never pay for what he did."

"I believe in karma. One day he will pay." Sam's father squeezed his shoulder. "You've let Ranjeet define your life for too long—you left medicine because of him, you took a job you don't enjoy because of him, and now you tell me you've lost everything because of him. You have a chance to make a change. Let go of the past and decide what you really want out of your life. Be the man I raised you to be."

"What kind of man is that?"

"A good one."

"Okay. Hit me." Holding her phone to her ear, Layla ran down the main hallway at St. Vincent's Hospital, looking for the yoga studio as Daisy read out the details of the last bachelor on the list. Sweat trickled down her back under her blouse, and her face glistened despite a quick stop in the restroom to pat it down. Although she'd been to the hospital once or twice over the years to visit friends and family, she wasn't familiar with the new wing and she'd lost time trying to navigate the identical white corridors.

"Sunny Kapoor. He's the yoga program manager at St. Vincent's. He designs and manages yoga and stress-management classes for employees and patients. Previous jobs include flight attendant and marketing consultant. His dad passed away when he was ten. Mom works in a bank. Vegan. Loves the outdoors and spends a few months each year in India learning new yoga skills. Try to let him down gently if he's not the one. You don't want any bad karma."

Layla laughed. "I'll do my best, but I might not be able to control myself if he wants me to squeeze my ass into a pair of yoga pants and bust out a downward dog."

"That could be his way of checking out the merchandise." Daisy snickered. "Just don't do a happy baby pose or he might get the wrong idea."

Layla turned a corner and pulled up short when she saw Sam standing in the hallway, so solid and handsome it took her breath away. Too bad about the woman with the short blond bob wrapped around him.

"Layla?" A man in loose athletic pants and a tight black tank top walked past Sam toward her. He was totally ripped, all lean sinewy strength, his abs rippling beneath his tight top. With a chiseled jaw, arresting features, and warm, expressive brown eyes, he could have put any Bollywood heartthrob to shame.

Sam's head jerked up and their eyes locked, the world going unnaturally still. She was acutely aware of the harsh rasp of her breath, the cool breeze from the open door, his heated gaze on her body. An electric tingle raced through her, only to fizzle away when the blond woman leaned up and kissed his cheek.

"Hi, Sunny!" Layla wrenched her gaze away from Sam and tried to feign a familiarity that would hide the fact she was meeting Sunny for the first time. Sam had clearly moved on and she desperately wanted him to think she had, too.

"Give me a hug," she whispered when Sunny got near.

"No problem." Sunny wrapped his arms around her and gave her a squeeze while she glared at Sam over Sunny's shoulder.

"I'm looking forward to next week," the woman said, seemingly oblivious to the electric current arcing across the hallway. "It's going to be so much fun."

"You enjoy these things a lot more than I do, Karen."

Karen. Layla's upper lip curled. She remembered her now. This was the woman who had interrupted their almost-kiss at the fountain. Had he been with her all this time? No wonder he hadn't called after the party. Layla was just another hookup to him after all.

"I've got a little surprise for you." A smile spread across Karen's face, revealing unnaturally pointed incisors. "I'll give it to you tonight."

Layla's lips pressed tight together when Karen wrapped her octopus tentacles around Sam's arm. Did he realize she was at least ten years older than him? Or was he blinded by her bleached and streaked blond hair?

"Do you need more hugging?" Sunny whispered.

Her entire body strained to move toward Sam. If not for Sunny's arms around her, she would already be across the hallway, despite his new appendage.

"Yes, and a kiss."

"Lips or cheek?" an accommodating Sunny asked.

"We'd better get back." Karen clasped Sam's hand and pulled him gently in the opposite direction.

Only Sam didn't move. His gaze fixed on Layla. His body utterly rigid as if he were frozen in place.

"Cheek," Layla whispered.

Sunny dutifully pressed his cool, dry lips to her sweaty skin. "Can I let go?"

"Yes."

"You ready for lunch?" Sunny asked. "There's a great vegan café just around the corner. I promise you won't be able to tell their mac 'n' cheese from the real thing, and their gluten-free donuts are divine."

"*Gluten-free* and *donuts* aren't really words that should be spoken in the same sentence." She put an arm around his waist and looked back over her shoulder as they walked away. Sam's jaw was clenched, his lips pressed in a tight line, the familiar expression making her ache inside.

"You're so affectionate." Sunny pressed another kiss to her cheek. "The other women I met on desilovematch.com have usually had family with them, or expected me to keep a few feet away."

"If you want, you can squeeze my ass," Layla offered.

"I'm not sure that would really be appropr—"

"Squeeze it."

"Okay." He dropped his hand down and squeezed her rear cheek.

Layla held her breath, waiting for Sam's response. Was it really over or did he still care?

"Layla!" Sam's angry shout echoed down the hallway, sending a thrill of excitement up her spine.

"I'll meet you outside in a just a minute." She gently detached herself from Sunny. "I think I know that guy. I just want to say hello."

They met halfway. This close, she could smell the familiar scent of his body wash, see every line and shadow in his handsome face. Her blood heated and her glisten became a glow.

"You bellowed?" She clenched her teeth as she tried to contain the emotion welling up inside her.

"Who is he?" His smooth, deep voice made Layla melt inside.

"Hi, Layla." She mocked his deep voice. "Nice to see you again after all this time. How are you? How's the business? How are your parents doing? What are Daisy and Max up to?"

He shut his eyes for a beat. "Are you with him?"

She looked over at Karen with her perfectly smooth hair, trim figure, glisten-free skin, and the arms that had been wrapped around her Sam.

My Sam. Layla's chest tightened. For a brief time he had been hers. She wanted to tell him how much she'd missed him. How it wasn't the same working without him or going on blind dates alone. She wanted to tell him how many times she'd seen something that would have made him laugh and felt an ache in her heart that he wasn't there to share it. She wanted to tell him she loved him, but when she heard Karen's heels clicking on the tile floor toward them, all that came out was:

"Yes."

It wasn't a lie. She was with him today.

"Are you . . ." His voice caught, broke. ". . . marrying him?"

"Why do you care?"

"We didn't finish the game."

Her mouth opened and closed again. "You own the building, Sam. The game doesn't matter. The office is yours."

His corded throat tightened when he swallowed. "It was never about the office."

"What was it about, then? Was it just about the win?"

"Sam." Karen touched him lightly on the arm. "We need to go."

Layla had to fight the urge to slap her hand away. Could her nails be any longer? She'd seen tigers at the San Diego Zoo with shorter claws.

Still, Sam didn't move. "It was about—"

"Sam, the CEO just arrived," Karen said loudly. "We can't keep her waiting. This is the only time she has free before you leave for New York."

New York? Layla didn't want to ask, but she did. "Are you . . . moving away?"

"I've decided to go back into medicine." His face lit with hopeful anticipation. "I'm trying to get back into the residency program here, and if that doesn't work out, I'll go with whoever wants me. New York is a possibility because I have some contacts there. I've been away for so long, I'm not sure I'll have many options."

Layla's mouth went dry. "That's great. I mean, going back to medicine is great. But . . . moving away? What about Nisha and your parents?"

"They're doing fine. We're all moving on. I couldn't help Nisha the way I had wanted, but hopefully, as a surgeon, I'll be able to help people like your dad and advocate for changes to a system that failed to hold Ranjeet accountable for his actions."

How irritating. Why couldn't he be his usual arrogant, obnoxious self? Why, when he had found someone else, did he have to be so nice?

"What about your downsizing business?"

"Royce and I are looking for someone to take my place," he said. "I have to brush up on my skills before I apply for my residency, so we have some time."

"Layla?" Sunny opened the door. "Are you coming? I only get forty-five minutes for lunch."

"Can we talk?" Sam asked. "Later?"

Her gaze flicked to Karen, and she shook her head. It had been one thing to tell herself she could survive loving and losing again. It was something else to have Sam standing right in front of her and know he could never be hers.

"No." She swallowed past the lump in her throat. "We can't."

If her refusal affected him in any way, he gave no sign. Instead, he just nodded. "We're remodeling the office. You left some papers behind. They look important, so you might want to collect them before the contractor starts work tomorrow. I'll be in New York, but Royce will be around if you have any problems." His cold, impersonal tone hurt more than the speed with which he'd moved on.

"I'll do that." Her hand fisted by her side, nails digging into her palm as she struggled to maintain her composure.

Sam hesitated, and for the briefest of seconds she thought she caught a glimpse of pain in his eyes. Or was it regret? "If you change your mind about talking . . ."

This had to end. The torture was unbearable. "I won't."

And with one last, lingering look at the man she loved, she turned and walked away.

LAYLA pushed open the door to the office above her parents' restaurant. With the movers coming tomorrow to take the furniture to the new Sunnyvale Spice Mill, she wanted to see it one more time and pick up the papers Sam said she'd left behind.

"Can I help you?"

Layla startled when she saw the unfamiliar woman sitting at the reception desk. She'd gotten so used to seeing Daisy when she walked in the door that the neat, tidy desk and the perfectly ordinary-looking woman behind it just seemed wrong.

"I came to drop off my keys and pick up some stuff. I used to work here."

"You can give them to Royce. He's at his desk. Go on in."

Layla walked past the gray leather couch that now took up the space where her purple chaise had been. Her new shared office space was fully furnished so she'd brought the chaise to her cozy new apartment in the Marina District, only one block from San Francisco Bay near Fort Mason.

"Look who's here. It's Excellent Recruitment Solutions." Royce leaned back in his chair as she took a quick look around. Other than the Eagerson desk that her father had happily parted with, the rest of the furniture had been replaced with glass and steel—cold, corporate, and ultramodern.

"Actually, I changed the name to Patel Personnel," she said stiffly, dropping the keys on his desk.

"Good name. The other was ironic."

She'd never had a proper conversation with Royce before. Clearly she hadn't missed anything. He certainly didn't pull his punches. "I'm glad you approve."

"So that's it, then." He studied her so intently her skin prickled. "You and Sam. It's over."

"I guess so." She looked around. "He said I left some papers behind."

"In the boardroom." He jerked his thumb in that direction. "It's a tragedy."

"What do you mean?"

"He didn't get justice or the girl . . . I'm sure you've seen a Shakespearean play or two."

"*Romeo and Juliet.*"

"My favorite." He followed her to the boardroom. "Boy meets girl. Boy loses girl. Boy regains girl. Boy dies for girl. Girl dies for boy. Audience is spared a saccharine happy ending."

Layla turned and frowned. "Are we talking about the same boy? I just saw Sam at St. Vincent's. With his girlfriend."

"What girlfriend?"

"Karen."

"The HR chick?" Royce chuckled. "Sam and I had lunch with her the other day. Those two together would be a tragedy."

"But . . . they looked . . . friendly. They were going out after work . . ."

"With me." He perched on the edge of the table. "I'm thinking of hiring her to take Sam's place when he moves to New York."

Layla's heart squeezed in her chest. "He said he's trying to get into a local program."

Royce shrugged. "There's nothing to keep him here. He reconciled with his parents, and his sister hooked up with John 'I'm so nice it's a character flaw' Lee, who convinced her to live her dream of becoming a lawyer because we need more lawyers in the world." He shuddered and loosened his tie. "That's my idea of a nightmare. Rooms of books filled with laws and rules, being lectured by people who couldn't make it in the business world . . . I can barely breathe thinking about it."

Can we talk?

No.

Oh God. Had she just made the biggest mistake of her life?

"Where are the papers?" She clenched her fist around the strap of her handbag. "I need to go. Fast."

Royce pointed to the box. "There wasn't much. You should just go through them here and we can shred what you don't need."

Layla sifted through the documents—mostly old logo designs and lists of companies she had cold-called when she didn't even have a name. "Sam said he thought the documents were important, but there's nothing here."

Royce gave an exasperated huff. "Keep looking."

She checked every document in the box until, finally, at the very bottom, she found a copy of the lease agreement between her father and Bentley Mehta World Corporation.

"This isn't mine." She offered it to Royce, who raised a dismissive hand.

"You might find the legal opinion stapled to the back interesting, so I'm waiving my attorney-client privilege."

Layla skimmed the legal opinion. The one-page document stated in no uncertain terms that Sam had the full legal right of occupancy to the office and that her claims had no merit. John had signed and dated it at the bottom. Instantly, she understood why Royce had let her read it.

"This is dated the day after Sam and I met."

"Fancy that."

Her heart skipped a beat. "He always knew I had no right to be here. He could have kicked me out at any time."

"If it had been me, you and your purple couch would have been out on the street on day one, but then I'm coldhearted that way."

Layla sat heavily on the nearest chair. "Then why did he play the game?"

Royce shrugged. "Maybe he didn't want you to marry a douche."

"Or someone like Ranjeet," she said, considering. "He was trying to protect me. But if I didn't find someone, would he have honored the rules and walked away?"

"He does have that character flaw." Royce leaned back in his chair, folding his arms behind his head. "That's why we made a good team. I have no scruples and he has too many."

"Would you give him a message from me?" An idea started to form in her mind. "I deleted his contact details from my phone."

"Do I look like a receptionist?"

"You look like a guy who pretends not to care, but whose colorful clothes hide a warm heart."

His lips curved. "What does that make me in this tragedy? The comic relief?"

"It's not a tragedy." Layla wrote a quick note on the back of the legal opinion. "It's a romance. Except in this version, Buttercup saves herself."

· 28 ·

THE game is over. You win. Enjoy your prize.

Sam stared at the words on the document Royce had given him. "What does it mean?"

"How should I know?" Royce put his feet on his desk as he nibbled his brioche. "I have no magical insight into the inner workings of the female mind."

"It sounds like she's getting married." Sam slammed the note on Royce's desk. "Did she read the legal opinion? You were supposed to make sure she read it."

"Jesus Christ." Royce dropped his head back. "I'm a businessman, not a matchmaker. Yes, she read it. I sat in the boardroom and made sure she got to the bottom of the box. She noticed the date right away."

"And then what?" This wasn't how the scenario was supposed to play out. After getting the message that the game had really been all about her, she was supposed to connect with him, and then they would apologize to each other and he would pull every string to secure a residency in San Francisco, and she would move back into the office to run her business, and they would live happily ever after.

"Then she wrote the note, told me this was a romance, and walked out the door."

"A romance? Fuck." He slammed his fist into the wall. "A romance means marriage. She's marrying one of the dudes on her father's list. It's probably the yoga guy. You know how flexible they are."

"Wasn't that what she wanted?"

Sam paced the room. "She was supposed to want *me*. I waited too damn long. I wanted to fix everything first. I wanted to show her I was worthy."

"Worthy of what?" Royce dabbed at the corner of his mouth with a napkin.

"Worthy of her. I wanted to be her Westley."

Royce froze, the last piece of brioche half in and half out of his mouth. "I thought your name was Sam, but sure, if you want to be Westley, go for it. I don't know many brown Westleys but it's a new world out there."

"He's a character in *The Princess Bride*." Sam folded the paper and shoved it in his pocket. "It's Layla's favorite film. I watched it three times with Nisha and my mom. Westley storms the castle with his friends, defeats the bad guys, stops the wedding, and rescues Princess Buttercup."

"I thought you liked horror films, although a movie with a male lead named Westley and a princess named after a flower sounds horrible to me." He sipped his espresso, long fingers curled around the china cup.

"I'm glad you called. We have to find her." Sam pulled open the door. "We have to stop the wedding. Let's go."

"Do I look like a sidekick?" Royce waved a vague hand over his dove gray suit, pink shirt, and cartoon-graphic tie. "I think you might find what you're looking for downstairs. They're planning some kind of party. Maybe you can pick up a few expendable crew members to assist you on your quest. At the very least, they might know where to find her."

Sam raced down the stairs and pulled open the back door to The Spice Mill. Although the restaurant wasn't open for business, the air was fragrant with spices, and he could hear the rattle of pots and pans.

"What do you want?" Daisy stood in front of him, blocking his path. Her bright green leggings matched the bow in her Kool-Aid red hair. She had thrown a leather jacket over a high-necked lace dress that looked to be at least one hundred years old.

"It's vintage." Daisy smoothed down the full skirt as she followed his gaze.

"I'm looking for Layla."

"She's not here. Good-bye."

"Daisy. Wait." He took a step forward. "She left me a note. Is she getting married? Is it someone from the list?"

"You'll have to ask Nasir Uncle." She gave him an evil smile. "He's in the kitchen. That means you'll have to run the gauntlet of aunties, and only if you survive will you get an answer to your question."

"That's ridiculous," he spluttered. "You obviously know. Just tell me."

"You didn't earn it."

Sam tipped his head from side to side, making his neck crack. "Okay. I'll do it. Point me in the right direction."

"You need to be loose and relaxed."

Sam jumped up and down a few times and shook out his hands. "I'm loose."

"There are four aunties in there plus Jana Auntie. You are a young, handsome, single man, albeit everyone hates you for evicting the family. It's going to get nasty."

"I have aunties. I know how they work." He smoothed the collar of his shirt and wiped his brow with the back of his hand.

"Don't let them smell your fear. Once that happens . . ."

Sam bent forward and took a deep breath. "I know. I know. They'll never leave me alone."

"Never," Daisy said. "They'll be showing up at your office with boxes of Indian sweets, bumping into your mother in the grocery store so they can invite you all over for tea, walking up and down in front of your house with their daughters and nieces in tow on a pretend Sunday stroll. You have to be strong."

"I'm strong," Sam said.

"You have to be determined. This is for Layla. Don't agree to look at pictures of nieces or granddaughters or cousins. And don't tell them where you work or how to contact you. And whatever you do, don't smile. You're too handsome for your own good."

"I can do this." He wiped his hands on his black dress pants and scowled.

"Max and I will run interference."

"Wait." He paused on the threshold. "Why are you helping me?"

Daisy grinned. "It's part of my charm."

They walked quickly through the kitchen. A woman in a blue salwar kameez skewered bright orange pieces of chicken to go into the tandoor. An older woman was peeling and slicing a bag of onions. Two cooks in white aprons stirred pots full of spicy potatoes, braised lamb, and chunks of paneer swimming in creamy spinach. At the back of the kitchen, the cook who had glared at him when he had come to talk to Nasir used a giant paddle to stir a vat of what appeared to be goat curry.

Sam breathed in the sweet mixed aroma of cardamom, turmeric, garam masala, and fresh chilies as Daisy led him past the stainless steel counters. It was the smell of his mother's kitchen last night when they'd had dinner together. The scent of home.

"That smells divine. Are you using fenugreek in the *murgh makhani*?" Daisy blocked one auntie's inquisitive stare.

"Better check the oven, Lakshmi Auntie," she called out. "I think that naan is overcooked. You don't want three days' bad luck."

"I love that color on you, Charu Auntie. So bright!" She spun the woman in the blue salwar suit around to face the door so Sam could slip past.

Too late. Sam sensed a change in atmosphere. The low chatter and laughter died down. Tension thickened the air.

"Daisy! You've brought someone to visit." A woman in a pink sari pushed her way past the cooks toward him. "Who is this?"

"This is Sam, Salena Auntie. He has business with Nasir Uncle."

"He looks like an engineer." Salena waved over another auntie. "Pari. Come see. Daisy has brought a boy who looks like an engineer."

"An engineer!" Pari wiped her hands on her apron and ran over to greet them.

"Actually, I ran a downsizing business," Sam said. "But now I'm—"

A tall, thin man with a receding hairline joined them. "Who's an engineer?"

"This boy, Hari Uncle."

"I'm not really a boy . . ."

"He doesn't look like an engineer. Now, Nira's son . . . he looks like an engineer."

"Actually, I'm a doctor," Sam said.

Daisy groaned. "I'm not going to be able to help you now."

"Doctor?" someone shrieked. "He's a doctor!"

Daisy tugged on Sam's arm, but it was too late. The aunties rolled toward them like a tidal wave, spilling out of doors and alcoves, crashing around counters, and thundering across the floor.

"Is he single?" Salena asked.

"Who's single?"

"This man. He's an engineer."

"No, he's a doctor."

"A doctor engineer? Does he have a Ph.D.?"

"Does he know Dagesh Gupta? He's an engineer in Florida."

The conversation flew thick and fast around him. With so many people talking, Sam couldn't keep up.

"My boys are going to be doctors. Their teacher says they are rascals, but it's because they are so intelligent they are bored at school."

"Someone get him a plate of food. He's too thin."

"Who is his family?"

"Stay strong," Daisy whispered. "Here comes Jana Auntie, Layla's mom."

Layla's relatives parted like a tidal wave to reveal a woman in a worn red apron, her long, dark hair braided and pulled through the back of a bright orange Giants cap. He could see Layla in the shape of her face, but her eyes, when he met her gaze, were cold and hard.

"So, you're the one," she sniffed.

Sam didn't know if she meant he was the one who had evicted the family, or the one who had steered Layla away from an arranged marriage, or the one who had distracted everyone in the kitchen, but in any event, it clearly wasn't meant kindly.

"It's nice to finally meet you, Mrs. Patel." He swallowed hard. "I'm looking for Layla."

"She's at Oracle Park for the game." She tapped the Giants hat. "First game I ever missed."

Hope swelled in his chest. "So she's not getting married?"

"Sam!" Nasir's voice boomed through the kitchen. "Nice to see you again. Everyone, leave him alone. Get back to work. He's not on the market. Put your photos of nieces and daughters away. Stop taking pictures. Who tied that rope around his ankle?" He made a dismissive gesture with his hand and instantly the crowd melted away, the rope sliding off his foot as someone pulled it into the crowd.

"Layla . . ." Sam made a helpless gesture with his hands. "I messed up, Mr. Patel. I love her. She can't marry someone else."

He heard a collective sigh, but when he looked over his shoulder, everyone was busy with their cooking.

"Sam." Nasir sighed and shook his head. "It's too late. She picked someone from my list. The family has already met him"—he looked around the busy kitchen, one eyebrow slightly quirked—"and they approve. We're expecting a big proposal at the ball park—something spectacular, maybe on the big screen or that kissing camera."

Sam's eyes widened in dismay. "I have to stop him. Tell me where they're sitting and I'll go—"

"I don't know . . ." Nasir drummed his fingers against his lips. "I think she really loves this boy."

"She doesn't know him!"

"I think she knows him very well." He patted Sam's shoulder. "Well, it was nice seeing you. I believe your sister is out in the restaurant with John. We're having a little going-away party this afternoon and invited our friends from the law firm upstairs. You and your partner are welcome to join us. Maybe Layla and her new fiancé will be back to celebrate, too."

Sweat trickled down Sam's back. Why did nothing go the way he planned? He scrambled for something that would change Nasir's mind. "Wait! The kiss cam. He can't propose to her like that.

She would hate it. She wouldn't want her personal life splashed all over a big screen for a stadium full of people to see. She had a terrible experience being filmed in New York, and then there was an incident here at a sports bar . . . If he doesn't know that about her, he shouldn't be marrying her."

"Hmmm." Nasir turned to Jana. "What do you think? Should we tell him where they're sitting? I don't want to ruin her big day."

Jana shrugged. "He's right that she wouldn't want it to be so public. But the game already started. He would have to drive very fast."

God. It was just one obstacle after another. "I ran into a deer and my car is still being assessed by the insurers." He pulled out his phone. "I'll call an Uber."

"An Uber?" Nasir stared at him in horror. "You would leave something so important to a stranger? This is my daughter's future. Arun can drive the big van we use for picking up supplies. We can all fit in."

"All?" Sam frowned. "You don't all need to come."

"We're family," Nasir said. "Of course we do."

"CAN he drive any slower?" Sam muttered as old chef Arun inched the van along the I-80.

"It's the traffic. Calm down." Daisy patted Sam's arm. "Do you want to hold Max? He can give you some emotional support."

"Thanks, but I want to get there with all my fingers intact."

"Don't throw shade on Max. He's gotten me through some hard times." She patted the dog's fluffy head. "Like now. It's emotionally trying to sit beside you listening to you mutter and grumble like an old man. We'll get there when we get there."

"What if we're too late?" Sam's hands clenched into fists. "What if it's kiss cam time, and he proposes, and she's humiliated but she's forced to say yes because tens of thousands of people are watching her, but she really doesn't love him, and she can't back down because it was so public, and she marries him and lives an unhappy life . . ." He paused for breath, and Daisy gently placed Max in his lap.

"Work your magic, Maxy."

Max looked up at Sam and curled up in his lap, his razor-sharp teeth nowhere in sight. With a sigh, Sam patted Max's head, his tension easing despite the fact that they were almost at a standstill.

"Do you want to eat something?" Taara Auntie handed him a Tupperware container. He'd been given a quick introduction to the relatives who had joined them in the van, and thanks to Layla's briefing the afternoon before he was supposed to have met them, he'd been able to remember them all.

"Thank you, but I'm not hungry right now."

"Layla told me never to eat anything in a Tupperware container," he whispered to Daisy.

"Very wise. Taara Auntie made candy crab trout cream surprise. Anything that ends in *surprise* will send you to the restroom for at least three days. Not what you want when you're trying to rescue the woman you love from marrying the wrong guy."

"Do you have his marriage résumé? I need to know what I'm dealing with before we get there. None of the guys on Nasir's list were worthy of her. What makes this one different?"

Daisy shot him a sideways look. "I'll see if I can find it. Meantime, you'll need to download the ballpark app so I can transfer your ticket."

"I can buy my own ticket."

She gave an exasperated groan. "Clearly you haven't thought this through. I happen to have an extra ticket right beside her."

"Why?"

The van lurched forward and he put his hand around Max to keep him secure. So far, so good. Max seemed content to lie on his lap and stare at him, but he was careful to keep his fingers away from the Westie's mouth.

"Arun!" Layla's mother's bellow belied her slight frame. "You drive like an old man. The game will be over before we get there. Pull over at the next gas station and let me drive."

A few minutes later, her Giants hat pulled low over her eyes, seat jacked up as high as it could go, Layla's mother pulled onto the road and wove in and out of traffic like a race car driver. "I'm getting off the I-80," she shouted. "We'll take the back roads. Hang on."

She yanked the wheel to the side and the van screeched as they barreled off the freeway.

"That's my wife." Nasir looked over, pride etched across his face. "She taught Layla to drive."

Teeth clenched, one hand braced on the seat in front of him, the other holding Max, Sam gritted out, "Why am I not surprised?"

By the time they neared the stadium, Sam's back was covered in sweat, his heart was racing, and he had turned his wrist so many times to check his watch that his forearm ached. Even Max's soothing presence on his lap couldn't calm him down. How had he let things go this far? What had he been thinking? If he lost her now . . .

"Next stop sign, you jump out," Layla's mother called as they turned down Third Street. "You can go in through O'Doul Gate. We have friends nearby where we can park. We'll see you inside."

"Inside? You're all coming? Do you have tickets?"

"Of course," Nasir said. "We would never miss the end of the game."

· 29 ·

"Layla!"

She heard him before she saw him, and even when she saw him, she almost didn't recognize him in the orange Giants jersey he had pulled over his suit jacket, and the navy and orange ball cap shoved on his head.

Sam thundered down the stairs, skirting past a woman with a toddler and two teenagers carrying loaded hot dogs. With the sun setting and a soft breeze blowing from the bay, it was a beautiful evening for a game. She'd already seen Kevin Pillar catch some fly balls right near her, finished her Dungeness crab sandwich, sung and cheered with the enthusiastic crowd. It was her favorite place in the city and she wanted to share it with the person she loved.

"Where is he?" Sam glared at the empty aisle seat beside her. "Did he do it? Are you engaged?"

It was hard not to laugh at his fierce expression. If she had brought someone to the game, she doubted he'd be long in his seat. "No." She patted the seat beside her. "Why don't you sit down? You're blocking people's view."

"Is it Hassan? You can't marry him. He's a scammer."

"It's not Hassan." She held out a bag. "Nuts?"

Sam waved them away. "Dilip? Did you choose him because he can dance? I can dance." He put his fingers together the way she'd shown him at the fountain and twisted his hands. "Wolves. Flowers. See. I remember."

Layla pulled him down to sit beside her. "I don't think dancing right now is a good idea. People are trying to watch the game. And no, it's not Dilip."

"The firefighter? You said he was too much of a jock."

"Daisy would kill me if I married him. She's meeting him for drinks next week."

Sam clenched and unclenched his fists. She had never seen him so agitated. Even when she'd walked into Royce's party, he'd still held it together.

"It better not be Faroz. He's delusional."

Layla laughed. "I was tempted to be a spy wife, and I don't think many people could get me elephants for my wedding, but it's not Faroz." She heard the crack of the bat and the crowd cheered. She hoped Sam realized how much she cared. There were very few things that could pull her away from a game.

"Not . . ." His voice caught. "Harman?" He flexed an arm. "I've been working out four times a week."

"Are you kidding me? Not after he stood me up, although he did inspire me to think of my own brand."

"Baboo?" He clearly wasn't going to let it go.

"You kind of ruined me for Baboo—multiple times."

Sam gave a growl of satisfaction, puffing out his chest with masculine pride like he was solely responsible for the fact that she wasn't a virgin.

"And it's not Salman, the restaurant owner," she said quickly. "You never met him, but you were there with me in spirit. He had gang tattoos, bodyguards, and . . ." She cleared her throat. "One day, I'll tell you how I escaped." She picked up a tray from between her feet. "Garlic fry?"

Sam stared at the boxes and containers on the ground. "How much food did you buy?"

"Let's just say that the empty seat beside me wasn't really meant for a person."

Sam glanced around, like he still believed there was another man in her life. "Were there others?"

"Just three. Sunil, a hedge fund manager, who wasn't interested in marrying me, but just wanted to bang me. I thought about you before I walked out the door—"

A smile ghosted his lips. "I wish I'd seen that."

"And then there was Bachelor #9, Akhil. He was twenty. Need I say more?"

Sam held up a hand. "Please don't."

"And finally Bachelor #10 was Sunny, the yoga instructor. But he's vegan." She held up her Super Duper Burger. "And you know how I like my meat."

"That's it?" Sam frowned. "You said in your note that I won. According to the rules of our game, that means you have to marry someone from your father's list."

"My dad added one more name." She pulled out her phone and flipped to the marriage résumé that Nisha had helped her write. "I'll tell you about him. Bachelor #11 . . ."

Sam's jaw tightened. "I don't care who he is. You can't marry him. You hardly know this guy. Does he make you laugh? Can he save you from a rogue deer? Would he make your elevator fantasies come true? Or save you from unwanted advances in a bar?" He grabbed his Giants jersey. "Would he betray his own team and wear this for you?"

"Sam Mehta." She read off the screen. "Age thirty-two. Arrogant. Stubborn. Controlling. Obsessed with lining up his pencils."

"Layla . . ." His voice was raw and rough. "What are you—?"

"I don't do the briefing as well as Daisy, but let me get through it. You need to know what you're up against." Emotion welled in her throat. Hopefully this was the last marriage résumé she would ever have to read.

"Mother is a teacher," she continued. "Father is a computer programmer. Sister, Nisha, who is one of the nicest people I've ever met, is planning to become a lawyer. He has lots of degrees and credentials that mean he saves lives. He stays in shape doing MMA at the gym and beating up dudes who hurt the people he cares about. Very practical. No imagination. Couldn't recognize a spy when the dude was sitting right in front of him. Jealousy issues. Amazing in bed. Stellar driving reflexes. Enjoys long walks in empty fountains, sex in dress shop restrooms, and women with healthy appetites who order their own dessert. Sometimes he makes mistakes, but his motivations are always pure. His is fiercely loyal, supportive, protective, deeply moral, intelligent, kind, funny and . . ." She drew in a ragged breath. "I love him."

"You love me?" He stared at her, his face a mask of disbelief. "There is no other guy?"

Layla put down her phone and turned in her seat. "I pick Bachelor #11. Sam Mehta, will you marry me?"

STUNNED, Sam couldn't move.

She wasn't marrying someone else. No other man was coming to sit in this seat. She wouldn't suffer the humiliation of being proposed to in front of a stadium full of fans. And she hadn't come here just for the game.

It was about him.

Even after he had hurt her. Even after he had failed to get justice for Nisha. Even though there were ten other men her father thought worthy.

She wanted him. Sam Mehta. Friend. Partner. Brother. Son.

Not just for today, or tonight. Not for a short time or a good time. But forever.

He didn't deserve her. Didn't deserve her forgiveness. But he wasn't going to let her go again. He would have a lifetime to prove himself worthy of her love, of being her husband.

He had come to save her, but instead she had saved him.

"Sam?" Her brow creased with consternation. "If you don't . . . I mean . . . it's okay. There's no kiss cam or anything. It's just us." She looked over her shoulder. "And my family."

Sam followed her gaze to the crowd behind their seat. Everyone was there—Jana, Nasir, Daisy, Max, Arun, the aunties and uncles from the van, others he hadn't met, two cute little girls, John and Nisha in a wheelchair-accessible area. Even Royce. Standing in someone's way in his $2,000 suit.

"Did he say yes?" Arun shouted. "I couldn't hear. There's too much noise."

"They all knew?" Sam asked.

"I had to tell them. Marriage is a family affair, and everyone had to approve."

Sam huffed. "The man is supposed to make the proposal."

"Are you seriously going to start with that *man* thing again?" Layla's smile faded. "I told you; when I decide to get married, I'm going to ask the man myself."

"But I have a ring." He pulled out the Giants fan ring he'd bought along with the shirt and hat, and dropped down to one knee. "Layla Patel. You are passionate, sweet, funny, generous, and kind. You made me believe in myself again. You gave me back my faith in the goodness of people. Every day I spend with you is an adventure, whether it's dodging office supplies, meeting desi spies, careening through the streets in your Jeep, or hiding in a restaurant closet. I think I fell in love with you the minute you walked through the door, and every moment I've spent with you since then has just made me love you more."

"That's a pretty good impromptu speech for a guy who's used to being in control."

"I learned from the best." Sam slid the ring on her finger. "I would be honored to marry you, Layla. But please don't ask me to support your team. After those last two strikeouts, I think the Giants are on the verge of the worst home season in Oracle Park history."

"It's a deal." Her smile became a grin. "Now give me a kiss. Everyone is waiting."

Cradling her face in his palms, Sam pressed his lips against hers and kissed her.

Long and deep. Soft and sweet. Forever.

"He said yes," Nasir shouted.

A cheer rose up from the section behind them.

"I brought your sherwani!" Nira Auntie held up a suit bag. "It's ready for the wedding. Just like I said."

"Stand up," Layla said. "Dad wants to take a picture."

"I can't." Sam looked down. "I think I kneeled in your fries."

· 30 ·

LAYLA walked into The Spice Mill Restaurant for a final good-bye. Sam and Royce had allowed her parents to stay until the Sunnyvale renovations were completed, but now that everything was ready, it was time to move on.

"The tablecloths go in the box in the corner." Her mother handed her a stack of freshly laundered linen. "And don't forget the napkins. Lakshmi Auntie embroidered elephants on every one. For luck."

"You won't need luck. I think everyone in Sunnyvale knows you're coming back. Dad says you're booked solid for the next three months."

Her mother smiled. She'd been smiling since the engagement, and now that the new restaurant was ready, she was positively joyful.

Layla couldn't imagine a more different moment than the night she'd walked into the restaurant six months ago at the lowest point of her life. It hadn't been easy, but she had done what she set out to do, reinventing herself and building something even more wonderful than she had ever imagined.

She walked past the empty tables, the saffron walls, colorful frescoes, and paintings of her parents' hometowns. They'd sold the water feature to Manoj Gawli down the street at the Tamarind

Restaurant and had kept only enough furniture to fit their new cozy space.

Dev would have been disappointed, but she knew in her heart he would have understood. Her parents were happy again, and that's all that really mattered.

She chatted with the aunties who had come to help pack for the move. Pari Auntie was putting the finishing touches on a new apron for her mother while her kids played hide-and-seek under the chairs. Vij Uncle was asleep in the corner, his new glasses dangling from his fingers while his wife, Nira Auntie, smoothed out the garment bag she had brought this morning. Over in the bare space where the waterfall had been, Mehar Auntie was teaching Anika and Zaina the dance "Kajra Re" from *Bunty Aur Babli* and Salena Auntie and Taara Auntie were arguing about something in a plastic container.

Rhea, her sister-in-law, had taken time off to help, and was chatting with Charu Auntie and Deepa Auntie over by the bar where Hari Uncle was pouring himself yet another drink.

The air was still fragrant with spices and she followed the scent to the kitchen, where her father was pouring batter into a pan.

"Dad, what are you doing? The movers will be here any minute."

"I promised Sam some masala dosas before he goes for his big interview. He needs a full stomach if he's going to impress the Redwood Hospital residency board."

"He's applied other places . . ."

Her father frowned. "No. No other places. He needs to stay in the Bay Area. This is where the family is—his family, your family. This is where you are. You have your business to manage upstairs. There is no going away. We lost you once. We won't lose you again."

"You'll never lose me, Dad." She put her arms around him and gave him a hug. "Sam and I will be down in Sunnyvale so much, you'll be sick of us."

"Make sure he sees Lakshmi before he goes. She has lucky things for him to take to the interview." He flipped the dosa so effortlessly, she made a mental note to work on her dosa-making skills. After reconciling with his parents, Sam had made up for years of denial by eating his way through The Spice Mill menu and then shamelessly visiting her relatives and asking to stay for dinner.

"Not more elephants. She's given him so many elephant things he had to buy a special shelf to keep them all." For the sake of propriety, they both had to keep their separate apartments until the wedding, although Layla secretly spent most of her nights at his place in the Mission.

"We can't take any chances." He flipped the cooked dosa onto a plate. "How can he plan a wedding if he is far away? No. I've decided. He will get the residency here, and we will have a big celebration party in the new restaurant."

Layla kissed her father on the cheek. "I'll let him know. He's coming up to the office before he goes."

Although Sam had technically won their game, he hadn't accepted her father's hasty addition of his name to the list. As a result, since she hadn't chosen any of the original ten bachelors, he'd declared her the winner of the marriage game and somehow convinced Royce that the restructuring business could operate successfully from the building across the street.

Daisy was tidying up her desk when Layla walked into the office. Max was playing with a new squeaky toy in the corner, a present from his new best friend, Sam.

"I've typed out a handover note for your new receptionist. It's got all the details she needs to run things almost as well as me, including the recipe for your mother's chai."

"You didn't have to do that." Layla sat on the purple chaise—the first thing she'd brought back to the office after Royce had moved out.

"I want everything to go smoothly for you," she said. "You'll be busy with your two new hires. You need at least one person who knows what's going on while I'm busy revolutionizing the world one line of code at a time."

Daisy had decided to go back to work as a software engineer and had found an exciting opportunity with a new start-up. Although Max couldn't go to work with her, he would be spending his days being pampered by elderly aunties and uncles, and his nights eating pakoras at home with her and her dad.

"Where's your man?" Daisy asked.

"He was at the gym this morning. He finally beat his friend Evan in a fight and Evan is determined to even the score. After that, he had some termination meetings to get through—he'll be working with Royce at their new office until his residency is sorted out. And when those are done, he's coming here to help with the move and go over some final wedding plans."

"So he's a nice guy after all," Daisy said dryly.

"He was always a nice guy; it just took me a while to see it."

"MEGAN, we've called you here today because the hospital is going through a restructuring. I'm sorry to say that we have to let you go. Today will be your last day."

Karen immediately launched into a speech about the necessity of downsizing to allow the hospital to stay operational. Sam waited patiently until she was done and gave Layla's business card to Megan. He'd cleared the referral with the AH board, who were happy to give their ex-employees a little hope for the future.

"I miss the old speech," Karen said after Megan left the room. "It was inspiring."

"It wasn't the right time for them to hear it. When people are in shock, they need time to process before they're ready to move on."

It had taken him years to work through his guilt after Nisha's accident, but now that he had laid that burden to rest, he could help others work through their pain.

"You inspired me in another way." Karen opened her laptop. "After I read the file of that surgeon who hurt your sister, I took matters into my own hands."

"You talked to your manager?" He could only hope that Ranjeet would be flagged for redundancy. He'd handed over the St. Vincent's terminations to Royce because of his conflict of interest, but with so many people being let go, it wasn't unfathomable that Ranjeet might be named.

"No," Karen said. "Paul, the head of HR at Alpha Health Care handed in his notice a few weeks ago, and I got the job. It meant I had access to the entire database. And guess what I found?"

"HAVE you seen Nisha?" Sam dodged two movers carrying a heavy table as he ran into the restaurant. He'd texted and called everyone who might know where Nisha was, but so far he'd come up blank. His residency interview was in two hours, but all he could think about were the minutes ticking by that Nisha didn't finally know the truth.

"I haven't seen her." Arun lifted a giant potted palm. "Nasir is in the kitchen. Maybe you should ask him."

Sam ran through the restaurant and slammed open the kitchen door.

"Just the man I want to see." Nasir waved him over to the stove.

"I've made your favorite masala dosas to give you energy for the interview."

"That's very kind, but I need to find Nisha." His hands shook with excitement. "I have some news."

"She's with John upstairs in Layla's office." Nasir put the plate in Sam's hands and carefully added a small bowl of sambar and some coconut chutney. "There's enough to share. Don't spill the dip."

Sam took the stairs two at a time, slowing when he heard voices on the second floor.

"Sam!" Nisha's eyes sparkled when he walked into the office. "Guess what?"

"I've been looking all over for you." He put the dosas on the reception desk. "I called everyone I knew. I drove around . . ." He drew in a ragged breath. "It's over, Nisha. Karen in HR—"

"You wouldn't believe what happened—"

"We saw the surveillance tape," he said, cutting her off. "And there was a witness. It was exactly as you said. You were arguing with him because he was drunk and about to go into surgery. You threatened to tell me if he didn't cancel it."

"The whole elevator was filled with flowers." Nisha's face lit up. "And when I got to the top—"

"He was angry," Sam continued. "So angry. He pushed you. I don't know if he meant for you to get harmed, because he seemed genuinely shocked when you fell. But then he walked away and left you there. Karen took it straight to the CEO, and she made a copy for us so we can go to the police if they try to bury it again—"

"John proposed!"

AFTER the shock of the engagement announcement had faded and John and Nisha had gone, Sam sat on the purple chaise and ate his masala dosas while Layla finished her work. He couldn't get enough of his favorite treat, and Nasir had been more than accommodating. He already felt like part of the family, although Layla couldn't convince him to change his last name.

"Ready for the interview?" She joined him on the chaise, and he pulled her onto his lap.

"I've had my daily dosas, and I've got two pockets filled with lucky charms. Your dad also contacted the secret 'Patel network' to pull in some favors, your aunts and uncles are on the case, and someone went around to my neighbors and asked them to keep their black cats inside. With your family behind me, skill seems irrelevant."

Layla laughed. "If you remember, that's how I got my business off the ground."

"I thought it started with flying office supplies." He pulled her down for a kiss, and she melted against him.

"Actually, I think it started with a game . . ."

THE

Marriage Game

· SARA DESAI ·

Questions for Discussion

1. What is the difference between a comedy, a romance, and a romantic comedy? How would you classify *The Marriage Game*, and why?

2. If you were making a movie of this book, who would you cast?

3. Although he loves her deeply, Layla's father adheres to traditional cultural views that put higher expectations and more responsibility on sons. How do those views affect how Layla sees herself, if at all? Do those cultural attitudes impact the decisions she makes in life? How do those same attitudes come into play with respect to Sam, and what role do they play in his decision to abandon his family after his sister is hurt?

4. Sam and Layla are physically attracted to each other when they first meet. When do you think they first feel an interest that goes beyond physical attraction? How does it change their behavior, if at all?

5. Let's talk about the big fight in the parking lot outside the sports center. What triggered it? Why did they become intimate after stripping each other emotionally bare, when the obvious thing to do was run away?

6. Sam becomes emotionally invested in the relationship before Layla. How does he discover that Layla does not feel the same way, and how does he react? What is holding Layla back at this point?

7. Sam is faced with an impossible choice when Royce shows up at the office with the board of directors. Why does he make the choice he does? Do you agree with his decision?

8. When does Layla realize that she still wants to be with Sam despite his betrayal? When does she forgive him? How does he show her he is finally worthy of her love?

Photo copyright Linda Mackie Photography

Sara Desai has been a lawyer, radio DJ, marathon runner, historian, bouncer, and librarian. She lives on Vancouver Island with her husband, kids, and an assortment of forest creatures who think they are pets. Sara writes sexy romantic comedies and contemporary romance with a multicultural twist. When not laughing at her own jokes, Sara can be found eating nachos.

CONNECT ONLINE

SaraDesai.com

Ready to find
your next great read?

Let us help.

Visit prh.com/nextread

Penguin
Random
House